Books by
Elaine Stienon

Lightning in the Fog

Utah Spring

The Light of the Morning

In Clouds of Fire

The Way to the Shining City

a story of the early Mormons in Missouri and Nauvoo, Illinois

Elaine Stienon

AuthorHouse™
1663 Liberty Drive
Bloomington, IN 47403
www.authorhouse.com
Phone: 1-800-839-8640

This book is a work of fiction. Places, events and situations in this story are purely fictional. Any resemblance to actual persons, living or dead, is coincidental.

First published by AuthorHouse 6/9/2011

ISBN: 978-1-4567-5415-0 (e)
ISBN: 978-1-4567-5416-7 (sc)

Library of Congress Control Number: 2011907405

Printed in the United States of America

This book is printed on acid-free paper.

...Yet there shall be a river, the streams whereof shall make glad the city of God, the holy place of the tabernacle of the Most High.

For Zion shall come, and God shall be in the midst of her; she shall not be moved; God shall help her right early.

...The Lord of hosts shall be with us, the God of Jacob our refuge.

—From Psalm 46

In a dream, I found myself in a dark, pleasant place with shadows, the outskirts of a city. I could see the dim outlines of trees and buildings, of houses and porches. It was the hour just before the dawn, and everywhere there seemed to be order and beauty. A feeling of peace and rightness pervaded everything.

As it began to get lighter, I sensed someone next to me, and he spoke these words:

"It is well that you are here in the early morning, for if you could see this place in the full light of day, you would grieve all your life that you could not live here. Many people have sought this city, and seek it still. And there are those who have given their lives, that the foundations of it might be established. But the time has not yet come for this city to be upon the earth."

—E.S.

1

Nauvoo, Illinois
November, 1845

How shall I begin? How can I write the story of my people, and this city which meant so much to them? If ever my heart was broken for them all, it is now.

The things which have happened here are beyond belief. Even if I were to describe them one by one in detail, anyone reading it would only shake his head in wonder.

My friend Nathaniel said he had a strange feeling about it from the beginning. He settled across the river on the Iowa side, about four miles from Montrose. He was going to move his family closer to Nauvoo a few years ago, but thought better of it. A careful man, Nat. He said we must wait and be patient, but he says that about everything. I have run out of patience.

If I were to describe my feelings at this time, I would say that the sense of loss is overwhelming. The loss of what? My family is intact, my little group of close friends still surviving, albeit confused. But the city that we knew—the larger community—is in disarray.

Joseph Smith, our beloved prophet and leader, is dead, assassinated by a mob at Carthage jail. Our charter has been revoked, and even now, marauding groups of men are organizing 'wolf hunts' and attacking our citizens who live in outlying areas. The city is ruled by the Council of Twelve—the quorum of twelve apostles—under the direction of Brigham Young, the president of the Twelve. While I like Brother

Young personally, I question some of the steps he has taken to assume this position of authority.

What is worse—-and this last makes me feel physically ill—we seem to have lost the Church as I first knew it. I came from another faith to join what I perceived to be the restored Church of Christ, a gathering of people like the New Testament church—simple, beautiful, truly a 'marvelous work and a wonder.' In just a short time, a matter of months, I find the ones who now lead it urging rebaptism. Celestial marriage, a man taking more than one wife, is being practiced, but with great discretion. They advocate other things too, such as sealing for eternity and ceremonies to be performed in the temple—'endowments,' they call them—which were never had in the church at Kirtland. They say these things were taught by Joseph, but I never heard him expound upon any of these, much less urge people to do them. They have an answer for that too—they say he did it secretly.

As if things were not bad enough, anyone who does not subscribe to these beliefs is being called 'weak in the faith.' I have heard these words applied to Sister Emma Smith, of all people, because she has not wavered in her stand against plural marriage. Brother William Marks, stalwart in his insistence that such things should not be taught, has been stripped of his position as Nauvoo Stake President. I understand they brought him before the Council two times, but have not yet excommunicated him. William Smith, the prophet's youngest brother, goes about saying that the oldest son of Joseph should be the rightful leader, and that he, William, should hold the Church in trust until young Joseph is of age. I don't think he will remain un-excommunicated for long.

Brother James Strang, a new convert, claims to have not only spiritual authority, but a letter from Joseph proclaiming him as the new leader. Strang has more followers than you might believe, but they are keeping quiet lest they be denounced as apostates.

Those who support the Twelve and the new doctrines—'Brighamites,' as they are being called—are planning to leave the City of Joseph, as it is now named, and travel in a body to a place west of the Rocky Mountains, where they can live unmolested. I have many friends among them, and I watch their preparations for departure with anguish and misgiving. I have wondered repeatedly—what is best to do in all this turmoil?

For myself, I can no longer sit by and wait as Nathaniel suggests.

I have chosen a course, and I will go and tell him tomorrow morning. I have not had that much to do since the Twelve announced through the *Times & Seasons* that good Christians should depend upon the priesthood rather than doctors when they are ill.

As a mental exercise, partly to keep from losing all sense of reason, I have tried to look back and determine how these strange notions crept into our religion. I have talked about it some with Nat, and he thinks things started going awry as early as the Far West days. He claims that the more militant portion of the church began influencing the actions of the body.

"They were a persecuted, desperate people," he said. "Who can blame them for what happened?"

Nat seems very quiet these days, but I sense he feels torn apart—still grief-stricken at the death of Joseph.

Far West, Missouri...I am trying to think. What made it so different from Kirtland? It was settled by a persecuted people, to be sure—refugees from the disastrous attempt to 'build Zion' in Independence, and others fleeing from troubles in Ohio. Our little group, which Nat led out of Kirtland, was one of the latter, and we didn't reach that part of Missouri till April of 1838.

Enough musings. They are calling me to supper, and I find that, even in the midst of trouble, I can always partake.

—From the journal of Gabriel Romain, physician and elder in the Church of Jesus Christ of Latter Day Saints.

Drizzling when they reached the outskirts of the little settlement. A sorry lot they were by this time. Her husband Nat clicked to the oxen.

Hannah, huddled under the blankets with three-year-old Jody, tried not to think how wet and tired they looked. Eleven persons—three married couples, one child, two young single men, one freedman with a wife still in slavery, and a young woman. All riding or walking beside a team of oxen and a wagon, a carriage pulled by two bays, and another, smaller wagon pulled by an old piebald horse. Oh, yes, and one small dog, who trotted at Nat's heels in the muddy road.

"Keep covered." Nat's voice came at her above the rising wind. He looked at her, half-frowning in the misty light, his eyes narrowed, the lines around his mouth and eyes etched deeper than she'd ever seen them. A scar over his mouth gave him a rugged, weather-beaten look. Worried about her, she knew. She'd seen the glances exchanged by Nat and Gabriel, their young physician-friend, who'd lately studied and worked with a doctor in Mentor, Ohio.

Unbelievable. Tears stung her eyes. Always so strong, the picture of health. Doing things most women wouldn't consider—traveling, leaving her father's house in Pennsylvania to seek out a new religion, following her betrothed across four states only to lose him in the Missouri persecutions. Finally returning to Ohio and having the good fortune to marry Nathaniel. Now, when she needed to be strong, she felt weakness in every part of her body.

The miscarriage. She remembered how she'd asked for Gabriel when the pains began, and how they'd sent word to fetch him from his medical apprenticeship, a partnership by this time. Wiry, short of stature, with unruly black hair and temperament to match, he nonetheless had a gentle, reassuring manner with those who sought his help. With firmness and good sense, he'd tried to shepherd her back to health.

She was in the process of recovery when they had to leave Kirtland. An unfortunate time to depart, before the winter had even ended. She had her choice of jouncing in the wagon or walking beside it. Each day she walked a bit less before the weakness hit her. In these last days she walked very little.

"Give her a few weeks rest, with warmth and good food," Gabe had told Nathaniel. "I reckon she'll pull through good as ever."

But where was rest and warmth, and food other than dry johnnycake? She looked at the collection of cabins and clapboard shacks, some in the process of construction, and wondered what help she could possibly find here. She saw a dry goods store and a grocery, and what looked like a school building. The caravan came to a stop in the middle of a grassy square.

"I told you to keep covered up," Nat said. Didn't he see the blankets getting soaked? Jody stirred in her arms and gave a little cough. Poor baby. Any more traveling, and he'd be as sick as she was.

Voices behind her. Sarah, her father's new wife: "If this ain't the place, I vote we stay here anyway. I reckon I've gone far enough."

Then her father: "It has to be Far West, less'n that map's completely cockeyed."

People hurried from the houses and stores and gathered in a little crowd around the wagons. She thought she recognized faces from her first trip to Missouri; others she knew from Kirtland. More voices echoed around her.

"Hello, Brother Ephraim."

"Well, if it ain't Nat Givens. And Sister Hannah. You look soaked clean through. Come set by the fire till we have a place to put you."

"There's wagons from Kirtland comin' in every few days now. The question is, where to put 'em all."

Nat's voice: "Give me a hand. My wife is poorly."

"Brother Gabriel, we're right glad to see you. Got some sick folks down in one of them cabins."

Hannah remembered someone lifting her out of the wagon—she thought it was Nat but she couldn't be sure. Someone else carried Jody, and the next she knew, she was sitting in a rocker by the hearth, a cup of warm broth in her hands. She sipped the broth as the comforting smell of fresh-baked bread drifted to her. A cheerful, well-padded woman, round-faced, sat on the settle with Jody in her lap.

"Now, then. You've come a far piece. Brother Joseph and his family got in here just a few weeks ago, with Brother Brigham Young. The people went out and met them eight miles from town with a brass band."

Nat came into the room, rubbing his hands together. "The animals are all warm and fed. And we have a place to stay, big enough for six of us—a little cabin just down the way. Gabriel and Eb and Rusty be stayin' here, with these good folks. And the Crawfords found some friends t'other side of the blacksmith shop."

"Have some warm soup, Brother Givens," their hostess said. When she smiled, her eyes became little slits.

"I sure do thank you, Sister Peck. But we should get to our resting place. Are you about ready to move, Hannah?"

Hannah, half-asleep, tried to raise her head.

"Land's sakes, brother," Sister Peck said. "Look at her. Exhausted. Let her rest a spell. At least wait till the rain stops—give 'er a chance to dry out some."

Hannah was thinking she would miss the boys. Wrong to call them boys. Gabriel after all was twenty-one already, and Eb the freedman even older, although he didn't know his exact age. And Rusty, her own young brother—all of nineteen. Growing up at last.

Her mind doing strange things. Sister Peck's voice fuzzy and far away. "She be right pretty, now that I look at her, with that red hair and all. A bit thin, though."

"She's not been well. This journey hasn't helped."

Closing her eyes. Feeling the warmth all around her. The last sound the crackling of the fire.

When she first woke up in the strange place, she tried to think where she was. Not her house in Kirtland—that was weeks in the past. No longer in a wagon. The scent of fresh-cut lumber drifted to her, mingled with wood smoke and bacon frying. Then she remembered about Far West, and how they were all crowded together in a tiny cabin.

She stirred under the mound of blankets, warm at last. Must get up. She felt a hand on her shoulder, heard the gentle voice in her ear.

"Stay sleeping as long as you like. I'll take care of Jody."

Sweet-voiced Bethia. Sarah's niece, a part of their extended household even before her widowed father had taken Sarah as his wife. A godsend.

Hannah sighed, thinking of the times she'd given up her bed to strangers and slept with her family on the floor. At the dedication of the House of the Lord, their Kirtland home had been packed with people. And she, with the help of Sarah and Bethia, had been able to provide meals for them all.

Now she was the one needing help. Thanks to Nat's habit of offering hospitality and even living quarters to those in need, she had a communal family willing to take care of her. Nevertheless, she wished she felt well enough to be on the giving end. Hard to lie still and hear Bethia answering Jody's questions.

"Yes, your Papa's helping build cabins. Places for folks to live. And Grandpa too—he's helping."

Nat and her father Calvin. Already at work. Her brother Rusty and Eb the freedman most likely with them. As for Gabriel, they probably had him tending the sick by this time.

"No—your mother has to rest, so she'll get strong again. Did you finish your cornbread? Let's go out and see where your father's working."

The cabin door opened and closed. Drifting in and out of sleep. Tendrils of mist hung at the edges of her consciousness. Worried about Gabriel—more sensitive than the others. Time he found himself a wife. Bethia would make a good match for him—both of age, by this time. He'd always seemed partial to her, but things had changed. Since he'd received his medical training, he'd acted aloof, no longer interested. Perhaps he considered Rusty a rival for her affections, and didn't want any conflict with him.

Poor Bethia. No wonder she acted confused and distracted. For it was clear she preferred Gabe to any of the others. Hannah sighed and stretched her feet out under the covers. Strange...despite their situation—refugees fleeing from trouble and persecution—the little human dramas kept playing themselves out.

Sarah's fault. If only she'd allowed them to remain friends. But in the brief time of prosperity in Kirtland, she'd taken Bethia away from the others and tried to introduce her into the higher social circles of the community, in hopes of making an advantageous marriage for her. The bank failure and financial ruin had toppled that scheme as well as countless others.

Hannah threw back the covers and got to her feet. No wave of weakness this time. Alone for a while. Sarah gone too—probably out at one of the neighboring cabins. Soon she'd come back full of local gossip.

Hannah found the cornbread and broke off a hunk. The room had a piece of wood on sawhorses for a table, a rough bench of pine boards, and an upended log big enough to sit on. She sat on the log and nibbled at the cornbread. Sunlight streamed through a tiny window and made a bright pool of light on the floor. Charming little place, though primitive. She wondered how long they would stay there—most likely till Nat had a larger cabin ready.

Then would they be safe at last? She heard sounds outside, a wind rising, and little bits of dust hitting the outside of the cabin. She thought of all the places her people had lived since the founding of the church in 1830. First New York, then Kirtland, Ohio, seeking peace and a safe place to build a community. A group of them had tried to settle in Independence, Missouri, which they believed had been designated as the land of promise, where the temple of the Lord would stand in the last days. But the first pioneers had other ideas, and the Mormons had been forced to leave. They'd moved north, finally settling in a county created just for them—Caldwell, with Far West as the gathering place. The church leaders, no longer safe in Ohio, had fled to Far West. Many of the Kirtland people, her own group included, had followed.

She finished the bit of bread and pushed her long hair back over her shoulders. If all the Kirtland folks came in at once, there'd be a scramble to relocate everybody. Lucky to be among the first. Time to concentrate on other things—regaining her health, and taking over the care of her child. Her family group needed her. Obvious that Dr. Gabriel, for all his new knowledge and his care of her, didn't have the common sense to manage his personal life. Must speak to him about Bethia—not like Gabe to hold a grudge because of what Sarah had done.

As she stood up, she heard the wind again, and this time she felt it coming through the chinks in the logs.

2

THE FIRST TROUBLE HAD to do with the dissenters. Gabriel heard about it at the home of one of his patients.

"Oliver Cowdery's been excommunicated,"the old man said.

"Good heavens! Are you sure?"

"I just heard. They had a church court. You know about them Whitmer brothers—David and John, and Brother Phelps? Same thing, 'cept they was all excommunicated in March."

"But why?"

The old man gave a cough. "They sold their property in Jackson County is what folks are sayin'."

"But they were driven out. What else were they supposed to do?"

"Blamed if I know. There's the matter of some money that disappeared."

Gabriel tried not to show how disturbed he felt. "Money does that, I've noticed. But why pick on Brother Cowdery? He's not been well, I understand."

"They said he brought vexatious law suits, made false insinuations, and I don't know what all. Turned to the practice of law, left his calling. There was something about 'filthy lucre,' but I forgot."

Gabriel finished the instructions for his patient and left the house. Being of a skeptical turn of mind, he tried not to jump to conclusions. Had he heard a-right? Oliver Cowdery, the faithful 'second elder,' who had helped with the work since the beginning? The one who had served as scribe, writing down the words as Joseph translated them from the ancient engravings, later to comprise the Book of Mormon? Bad enough about the others—-the Whitmers, instrumental in the founding of the church. What was happening to them all?

His next stop—the Givens cabin to see Hannah, his friend and now his patient. Since she and Nathaniel had given him a home in his late teens and made possible his medical education, he thought of her more like a mother or older sister. He'd looked forward to the visit all day. But now, as he walked across the square, he felt dismay rather than joy.

What was wrong with a little dissent? As far as he was concerned, the church could well harbor a range of beliefs and opinions. He thought of Hannah's family, her father Calvin Manning and her brother Rusty, and the French heritage they held in common—with one major difference. The Mannings were of Huguenot descent, while his own family was Roman Catholic. Enemies for centuries, all during the religious wars of France, now united in the Church of Christ. Surely, if such barriers as these could be overcome, there was room enough in the church for everyone.

He passed the large log home being readied for Sidney Rigdon, the prophet's counselor, and headed for a tiny cabin to the west of it. Just as he knocked at the door, he remembered about Bethia. Of course she'd be there; what else was he thinking? The door opened, and sure enough, she stood before him, a slight figure, even shorter than he was, with large brown eyes and dun-colored hair. She looked more startled than he would've imagined.

"Oh—hello," he managed to say. "I came to check on my patient. Hannah, I mean. How's she doing? Behaving herself, I hope."

Since his return to his communal family and the flight to Far West, he'd treated Bethia with polite coolness. She inclined her head and stepped aside so he could enter. "I do think she's better."

"That's good to hear." Difficult enough to be in the same room with her—he couldn't let her know how deeply she'd hurt him. She must have known how he felt about her. Yet she'd left their Kirtland house with her aunt and dressed in fancy clothes in hopes of attracting some rich suitor. He'd been a common laborer then, and she'd passed him by without a word.

She spoke in a soft voice. "Hannah—it's Gabriel."

Hannah looked up from poking at the fire. "Why, so it is. Come in, Gabe, and sit down. I hope you won't mind if I don't call you Dr. Romain."

"Not in the least." He pulled out the wooden bench by the table and sat down. "You're looking a lot perkier than the last time I saw you. I hope you're feeling better."

She moved over to sit across from him. Her blue eyes crinkled at the corners as she smiled. "I surely am, thanks to you. With all the good food and such, I almost feel strong enough for another walk across the prairie."

He laughed. "Let's hope you won't have to. At least, not too soon. Nat still fixin' to settle up by the creek?"

"Yes—he says with all of them working, he can get a cabin raised in no time. Then he can start the planting." As she spoke, he observed that her eyes looked bright, her face had its normal, high color, the cheeks no longer pale and sunken. Her alert, intent expression had returned, as if she were once more open to all the possibilities life had to offer. A voice spoke in the back of his mind: *she's healed.* He hunched forward, his elbows on the table, feeling a gratitude too deep for words. *Grâce à Dieu.*

"Pardon?" Too preoccupied to catch her last remark.

"I said I wanted to speak to you privately, Gabriel. I asked Bethia to leave us for a few moments."

"Well—" He looked around; Bethia had Jody by the hand. Wondering. "Of course. What is it?"

Hannah waited until Bethia and Jody had stepped outside. The heavy oak door closed behind them. Hannah leaned forward, her eyebrows drawing together. "It's about—that is, I wanted to speak to you about Bethia."

"What about her? Is she ill? She looks well enough to me."

She paused, as if trying to choose the right words. "No—of course she's not ill. Gabe—forgive me if I be mistaken. But it seemed like you once took a fancy to her."

Instantly alert, he felt the muscles in his jaw tighten. "I might have."

"I think you did. Why are you so changed, just because you have standing in the community?"

"If you recall, it wasn't me who changed."

Hannah looked at him, then went on. "I should think you'd forgive her for one little mistake. Especially when it was Sarah made her do it."

He shrugged. "At the time, it didn't seem so little."

"I realize that. But everything's changed now. You're both older, more mature. We've all had to leave our homes and make the best of things."

He gave a little laugh. "You think we should let bygones be bygones?"

"Truthfully, Gabe, I worry about both of you. Time was, when I thought you were too young. But now I reckon you need someone—and she needs you. You're of an age to marry, and you can provide for her."

Not knowing what to say, he laughed again. She gave him a hurt look, and he tried to explain. "Dear Hannah—it's good of you to be concerned about me. But I—I'm not sure what to do. There're all sorts of reasons—What about Rusty? He liked her well enough."

"She's not interested in Rusty."

He sat silent while this bit of information worked in him. Then he shook his head, embarrassed at having to deal with feelings he'd tried to suppress. "I—I can only say—"

Footsteps sounded outside. He looked up. The door opened, and Nathaniel entered, his dark hair tousled by the wind. Behind him walked Calvin Manning, a stocky man in his late fifties, rugged-looking, with a broad nose and thick, gray eyebrows. Calvin ran his hand through his shock of graying hair. "Well, look who's here."

Gabriel pushed the bench back and started to his feet. He felt Nat's hand on his shoulder.

"Don't get up, son. I just be sayin' to Calvin how obliged we all are, now that Hannah's herself again."

Calvin sat down heavily on the bench beside him. "I reckon that doctor feller you studied with taught you right well."

"A miracle, what nourishment and rest will do." Out of the corner of his eye, Gabriel saw Bethia in the doorway with Jody. Hannah held out her arms, and the boy rushed over to her. As she picked him up, someone's foot collided with the dog under the table. The animal gave a yelp and shot out into the room.

"There, Nell," Nathaniel said. "It's all right."

The dog, a small black-and-white mongrel, shook herself and waved her tail. Gabriel, watching, had one of those tricks of mind where he imagined himself back in their Kirtland house, with the household all gathered together. As if sensing his thoughts, Hannah said, "Stay and eat with us, Gabriel. We have more than enough."

Bethia began to set the table with the plates they'd brought from Ohio. She set out cornbread, and brought a pot of soup which had simmered over the fire all afternoon. Nathaniel went to sit beside Hannah, and the dog scurried under the table again.

"Sarah be coming in soon," Hannah said. "She went to visit a lady she knew in Kirtland."

Gabriel looked at Nathaniel. "I just heard about Brother Cowdery. You know he's been excommunicated?"

"We heard." Nathaniel broke off a piece of cornbread and moved the bread board over in front of Calvin.

"But doesn't it seem surprising? I mean—him, of all people. Not to mention the others."

Nathaniel put the bread on the plate before him and glanced at Gabriel. "Let's pause for a word of blessing."

Gabriel bent his head for the prayer. Even with his eyes closed, he sensed the nearness of Bethia as she sat on the end of the bench.

"Amen," Nathaniel said. "Pass the butter."

Gabriel cut a piece of cornbread. "I can't get over it—Brother Oliver, the one who ordained me."

Nathaniel swallowed and laid down his knife. Then he gave Gabriel a stern look. "It's hard being a leader—I reckon it's the hardest job there is. Did it ever occur to you that there might be some circumstance we don't know about? Some good reason why it happened?"

Bethia ladled soup into a bowl and set it before Gabriel. He met her eyes and smiled, then turned back to Nat. "Well, other than selling their land in Jackson County—"

"A tremendous breach of faith." Nat picked up the knife and pointed it at him. "Don't you see? If everyone does that, how will we ever go back in there?"

"I'll admit, it don't seem likely anyway soon," Calvin said. "Folks is still mighty riled."

"But they're dismissing some of our best men." Gabriel looked around at the others. The women were watching Nat with troubled expressions, Bethia's pale eyebrows drawing together. Jody was mashing bread on his plate with his fist.

"I know," Nat said. "But we'd best accept it. Don't do that, Jody.

We've gone through a terrible lot of persecution, and now they're tryin' to set things right—make us stronger, somehow, so it won't happen again."

Bethia served soup to Calvin and Nathaniel. Gabriel tasted the soup. "This is right good. But eliminating dissent isn't going to strengthen anything."

"Warn't dissent as much as drinking tea and coffee," Calvin said.

Gabriel began to laugh. "Don't tell me it's come to that! A cause for excommunication? Lord knows, they drank plenty of it all during Zion's Camp."

"I guess it depends on who it is," Calvin said. "And how publicly they do it. But there's the matter of some missing money too."

Gabriel gestured with his soup spoon. "Money, property—it all comes down to insubordination. Acting on their own instead of taking orders from the prophet."

"Now, there'll be no talk of that in this house," Nat said.

Calvin nodded. "He means it, too."

Gabriel sighed. "So we should just overlook this blatant form of control—"

Nat picked up his spoon. "I didn't say that. I said, 'accept.' We don't rightly know why, but we have to trust it was done for a mighty good reason. To keep peace in the community—that's good enough for me."

They ate in silence. Darkness had invaded the cabin as they sat. Firelight flickered on the rough logs. Bethia brought their only lamp to the table, then fetched a burning stick to light it.

"You did that well," Gabriel said to her in a teasing voice. She blushed and said nothing.

Calvin said, "I wonder what's keeping Sarah?"

Hannah smiled. "She'll be along. Reckon she's gettin' more gossip than she needs."

Gabriel sat talking with Calvin and Nat as the women got Jody ready for bed. Nat spoke of the place by the creek where he wanted to build. "Everything's there. Water, fertile ground, timber. And Brigham Young's puttin' up his homestead just three miles to the east."

"Build it big enough, we can all live there," Calvin said. "The Crawfords too, if they've a mind to."

"I'll drink to that," Gabriel said.

"That way, with all of us working, we won't be as poor as if we was each by ourselves." Nat looked up as the door opened. "Here's Sister Sarah now."

"Where've you been?" Calvin asked.

Sarah, stout and middle-aged, looked at them as she removed her cloak. She was of medium height, round-faced, with gray hair and eyebrows. "Old Sister Winter was poorly, and I helped care for her. She has a misery in her chest." She moved into the circle of light. "Why, I declare—Gabriel's here. Dr. Romain. Sister Winter sure would like to see you—they're aimin' to send for you tomorrow morning."

He stood up. "I'll be over there soon as it's first light."

She looked alarmed. "You leavin' already? Don't let me send you runnin' off."

"You're not. I should get back, or Eb will worry. He frets when he doesn't know where I am."

He said goodbye, and nodded to Bethia as she stood helping Jody with his nightshirt. The color came into her cheeks, but she gave no other sign that she noticed.

Hard to figure women out. If only she were more forthright, like Hannah. Or steady like his sister Marie-Françoise, who had loved him unreservedly. He opened the door and stepped outside. The door closed behind him, the solid 'thunk' of log hitting log. In the dimness he could see the darker shapes of buildings, the outline of a fence. Feeble light streamed from the house windows.

Thinking of his sister. Her face rose before him—fine-featured, her gray eyes set far apart under beautiful dark eyebrows. He remembered how her hair, black like his own, cascaded to her shoulders. He sighed, feeling a sudden homesickness for Gallipolis, Ohio, where they'd grown up. Meaning to write to Marie when he got to Kirtland. He'd put it off for a time when he'd be more settled. Now he realized that such a time might not come.

He felt the wind on his face. Familiar—how often had he set out in Gallipolis on nights like this? His mission—to find escaped slaves trying to make their way north. Nimble, able to find his way through any wilderness, he'd led them singly and in groups to the local safe house. There they would be fed and sent on to the next place of safety.

Leading people to freedom. He might still be doing that, if he hadn't been forced to seek freedom of his own. He remembered leaving the Gallipolis home for the last time, anxious to escape the trip to the seminary in the morning. For it was his family's intention that he enter the priesthood of his ancestral faith. And that he could not do, having found new conversion in the pages of the Book of Mormon.

He walked past the row of houses to the large cabin where he shared a room with Eb and Rusty. Light shone from an open casement window. He stopped to look inside. Eb sat at the long table with a book open before him. Rusty leaned on the table, his elbow beside the book, serious for once as he followed what Eb was reading. Rusty's reddish hair, the same shade as Hannah's, looked bright in the candlelight.

"That's 'cockatrice.' 'The weaned child shall put his hand on the cockatrice' den.'"

"'They shall not hurt nor destroy in all my holy mountain; for the earth shall be full of the knowledge of God...'"

Isaiah. Rusty helping Eb with his reading, a task they'd neglected lately. Gabriel stepped away from the window. If he entered now, he'd only disturb them. Treading softly, Indian-fashion, he made his way around to the back of the house. He passed the last row of dwellings and set out across the field. By the light of stars he found the path that led down to the water. Shoal Creek, they called it, though it seemed bigger than a mere creek. Strong enough to turn a mill.

The wind blew against him, ruffling his hair. Cold for April. A memory stirred...a chill November on the outskirts of Gallipolis. *Like this the night...* The wind made his eyes water as he reached the shore. *The night he found Eb in the river.*

The years fall away; he is back in southern Ohio on that night, following the bank of the river to the trail that will lead him north. Leaving his childhood home, seeking his own way to freedom—little chance of any escaped slave needing help on such a night.

Then he hears it. A rustle in the underbrush, a moaning above the wind and the creaking of branches. Following the sound. Finding the man half-submerged in the water. Wading out, dragging him shivering from a log just offshore. Helping the man to the safety of the bank, seeing one arm dangling useless. Urging, persuading the man to stand and walk. Leading him back through town toward the only safe place he knows. Tree branches waving wildly in the moonlight, casting strange shadows on the path. Gabriel struggling with the weight of the fugitive. Knocking at last at the door of his friend, Dr. Beauchamps—

A twig snapping. Alert in an instant, his memories dissolving into the darkness. He stared at the shadows on the other side of the stream. Nothing more. Deer, most likely, or some other wild creature. What enemies, after all, would they have in such a remote spot as Far West? Safe, now—all of them. Eb rescued from slavery, his arm long since healed. Hannah recovering, the others resting from their journey. Ready to build and plant again. More important—far enough from their persecutors so that they could practice their religion in peace.

He began to relax, in spite of the cold. A long journey he'd weathered, full of surprises. Not everyone finds his best friend and traveling companion in a river. He remembered how Dr. Beauchamps had judged the broken arm to be in a good position, not in need of the bone-setter. The doctor splinted the arm, and gave both Gabriel and Eb shelter for the night. The next day, after food and rest, the two set off for the nearest safe house. They made their way north, from one place of safety to the next, finding at last the restored gospel and the community of Kirtland near the shores of Lake Erie.

It was more than a community—he'd found friends who were kinder to him than his own family had been. Because of the generosity of Nathaniel, he'd had a home when he most needed one, and people his own age who made up for the loss of his brother and sisters. Except for Marie. No one could replace her.

His dilemma lay in the fact that he was now expected to reciprocate, according to Hannah—to approach Bethia as his intended wife. He liked her well enough, in spite of what had happened. If he could clear up the obstacles between them, he would have no objection to courting her. Another reason held him back—the promise he'd made to Eb soon after the rescue. They were going to find work, scrape together enough money, and buy Eb's wife her freedom.

They managed to work, although not in a blacksmith shop—-the one thing Gabriel had been trained to do. They labored at odd jobs in Kirtland, bringing home payment in kind when they weren't helping to build the House of the Lord. They helped to feed the communal family. But they never collected enough money to buy anyone out of slavery.

Now, with his medical training, he might have a chance at it. But not if he got married first. He let out his breath in a sigh loud enough to frighten any wild creature. Any courtship of Bethia would have to wait. He turned and followed the stream east, toward the spot where their new home would be.

3

In one month's time they'd done it. Under Nathaniel's supervision, Calvin, Rusty and Eb had managed to raise the major portion of a good log house. Some of the other settlers had assisted, and Gabriel too, when he wasn't wanted by some sick person. But the first four had done most of the labor.

"Family all moved in? Crops in the ground? Now, that's right good work." Owen Crawford had ridden over on his piebald horse to see if he could help.

"They're steady workers." Gabriel stood beside the carriage, holding the reins of the team he'd just harnessed. "Nat knew just what he was about."

"I'm not surprised." Owen shook his head, and his forelock of gray hair fell over his deeply-lined forehead. "When he worked for me, he could always do as much as three ordinary fellers."

Gabriel had to admit, it looked to be a fine cabin. It had a main room with a stone fireplace, three small rooms and a loft. A shed already stood on the property, left by some Gentile family. Nat lost no time in converting it to a shelter for the animals.

"Nat plans to have another room for storage, just a small one in the main house," Gabriel said. "And he talks of putting up other cabins—one for you and Sister Crawford, if you aim to settle here."

Owen scratched at his sparse beard. "I reckon us Kirtland folks should try to stay together."

"That's what Nat keeps saying. You goin' to meeting?"

"Yes. I hear Brother Sidney's gonna speak."

Nat tramped around the side of the house. His best clothes, newly unpacked, had seen too much time in the back of a wagon. He brushed his hands over his jacket, as if trying to smooth away wrinkles. "Morning, Brother Owen. Remember how you once gave me a place to live? Well, now I can offer you one."

Gabriel knew he was speaking of the time he'd left the Shakers and found employment on the Crawford farm. Brother Owen, who'd lost everything in Ohio, stood blinking furiously before he replied. "You're a true Christian man, Nat. And a brother."

"Let me show you the place before we leave for town. The ladies are ready, Gabriel—you take them on ahead."

No matter how he steeled himself, the sight of Bethia always caught him off guard. She looked especially fetching as she stepped toward the carriage in her best dress, a soft gray with blue trimmings. She saw him, and an expression of uncertainty crossed her face. Don't look so unsure, he begged silently. Love should be a joy, not fraught with misery. Perhaps he should begin the courting of her, despite his resolution. He smiled and reached out to help her into the carriage. Trying to sound casual.

"You look mighty nice, Sister Bethia."

Her eyes met his. "Thank you. So do you."

Embarrassed then. "Well, and where's Jody?"

"Hannah's bringing him."

"Why don't you sit up in front with me? The scenery's better."

She made no protest, and he handed her up. Soon Hannah and Sarah joined them with Jody, all dressed in the best they had. Gabriel took his place beside Bethia and clicked to the horses.

"Not too fast," Bethia said. "Eb and Rusty are coming."

Gabriel pulled back on the reins. Eb and Rusty caught up and slowed to a walk on either side of the carriage.

"It's right pretty by the creek this morning," Gabriel said.

Bethia looked at him, then glanced away. "It's a nice spot."

"If I were to build my own place, I'd do it where the creek bends, just up by that stand of trees."

"Would you?" She turned her eyes on him.

He returned the look. "I reckon so. Maybe someday I will."

On the left side, Rusty stumbled and put a hand against the carriage. "Gabe, yesterday when you were gone, a man came by to look at what we were building. He said there was a bunch of folks meeting secretly, tryin' to get rid of the trouble-makers."

"Trouble-makers?" Gabriel spoke sharply, annoyed that his moment with Bethia had been interrupted.

"You know—David Whitmer and them others. He said some of them actually wanted to kill 'em, but Thomas Marsh put a stop to it. These sound like pretty mean characters. He said they call themselves 'Daughters of Zion.' Ain't no daughters among them, sure as I can figure."

Eb spoke from the other side of the carriage. "I wouldn't put no truck in what that man said. Just shootin' off his mouth, tryin' to sound big."

"*Eh bien.*" Gabriel shrugged and turned back to Bethia. "Sounds like a bunch of nonsense to me."

"I reckon we sure don't need any more trouble then we already got," Eb muttered.

Then Sarah's voice filled the air. "Can't we go a little faster? Land's sakes—the preaching'll be done before we even get there."

"I wouldn't worry," Rusty said. "Once they wind Brother Rigdon up, he's good for at least three hours."

They drove the remaining three miles and made their way to the town square. Gabriel secured the team on the outskirts of the crowd. Hannah and Sarah took Jody and went to join some of the other women. Gabriel watched them go, thinking they hadn't had much chance to socialize since the move to the new home. To his surprise, Bethia stayed at his side. Touched, he took her arm and they followed Rusty and Eb to a place in front of the speaker's stand. Nathaniel, Calvin and the Crawfords moved in just behind them.

The preacher began with a text from Matthew—if the salt has lost its savor, it must be cast out and trodden under the feet of men. Well enough, Gabriel thought. Brother Rigdon expounded on it in his characteristic, forceful way. Then suddenly he was comparing the salt that should be cast out to certain apostates living among them. Without mentioning names, he accused dissenters in Far West of committing crimes and seeking to overthrow the church. *Oliver Cowdery?* Gabriel felt his face getting warm; perspiration broke out on his forehead.

He tried to control his agitation—aware of Bethia gazing at him in an anxious, puzzled way. Eb and Rusty exchanged glances, and Nathaniel's eyebrows rushed together in a frown.

On the way home, Eb said, "I'm sure glad I'm not one of them dissenters."

"It's a warning, is all," Nat said. "We've all got to work together, and not make any more trouble."

"You think that's all it was?" Gabriel walked beside the carriage now, while Nat sat in the driver's seat. Calvin rode beside him, and Bethia sat in the back with the other women. Gabriel shook his head. "That part about seeking out trouble-makers and reporting them for punishment? The duty of the Saints is to trample them underfoot? Is he serious?"

Nat flashed him a look. "That will do, Gabriel."

"But—" He stopped, aware of Bethia looking at him in concern. Just before they reached the stable, Nat jumped down and stood holding the reins. He spoke deliberately, his eyes on Gabriel.

"I think it's best not to make too much of it. Elder Rigdon sometimes overstates things—he gets worked up over something, and emotion gets the best of him. I reckon that's what happened."

"Sure makes you listen," Rusty remarked. "I bet that's one sermon no one slept through."

Nat let out his breath in a sigh. He handed Rusty the reins and began helping the women out of the carriage.

The next afternoon a lone horseman came galloping up. When Gabriel hurried into the yard, he found a boy in his early teens, freckle-faced, just dismounting from a gray speckled horse.

Panting. "Please, sir. You the doctor? They said in the town there was one here."

Gabriel took the reins. "I'm Dr. Romain. What's the matter?"

"Oh, sir, it's my sister—she's like to die. My father sent me for help. See, he's laid up—had a fall—he couldn't come himself."

"Where's your home?"

"Six miles south of Gallatin."

"That's clear up in Daveiss County. Good heavens! You must've had a good long ride."

Eb had joined them by this time. "Want me to go with you?"

Gabriel thought of what he should carry with him. "No—I'll be all right. You'd best stay here." He looked at the boy. "I'll just gather up what I need."

He fetched his knapsack and told Nathaniel where he was going.

"That's Gentile territory," Nat said.

"I reckon so. A physician goes where he's needed."

"Just be careful," Eb muttered. Gabriel mounted the gray horse. The boy swung up behind him.

"What be your name?" Gabriel asked him.

"Sam. Sam Peterson."

"Well, Sam Peterson. I think we can let your horse rest a little. We'll still be there before evening. A good thing I'm not too heavy."

The boy grunted and put his arms around Gabriel's waist. Gabriel said, "Now—tell me about your sister."

By the time they reached the homestead in Daveiss County, Gabriel had an idea of what was wrong—some severe intestinal disorder, possibly cholera. He thought of the men he'd treated in Zion's Camp and hoped that, one more time, he might help someone through it.

Dismounting, he gave the reins to Sam and hurried toward the house. A thin, mousey-faced woman, her hair tied back in a bun, opened the door.

"Good evening, ma'am," Gabriel said. "I'm Dr. Romain."

A man rose with difficulty from a straight-backed chair. He ran a hand through his reddish beard. "About time you got here."

Sam appeared in the doorway. "I had to go all the way to Far West."

The man spoke again. "There's nothin' down there but Mormons. If you're a doctor, son, you look about as young as they come. And scrawny as a chicken that's been wintered-over."

Gabriel tried to make his voice strong. "It's true, sir, about my being young. I don't weigh a lot, and yes, I be Mormon. But I studied with one of the best doctors in Ohio. Now—where's the sick one?"

The man gave a laugh. "Well, I'll be diddled. You've got spunk, I see. Come on, then. Elise is in here."

He moved with an effort, bent over, one hand on his side. Gabriel followed him into a small hallway. "How did you fall, sir?"

"Cleanin' leaves off the roof."

"Soon's I examine her, I'll see what I can do for you."

The man grunted and stooped to enter the small bedroom. On the bed lay a beautiful child around eight years old, her yellow hair spread out on the pillow. The father stood by, watching as Gabriel did his examination. Just as he feared, she had all the symptoms of cholera.

"You gonna bleed her?" the father asked.

"No—I don't hold with that. Now, I want you—or Sam—to get me all the water you can. Buckets—at least two buckets of it, to start. Cool, fresh water—keep bringing it."

He began making her drink, sponging her with cloths dipped in water. He urged them all to help. "Mother, you can do this, too. Just lay it on her head, like this."

After looking at Sven Peterson's back, he recommended applications of heat. "Nothing's broken. You've sprained a muscle—it'll just take time."

He went back to the child's bedside and took over the job of sponging her with the cloths. He spoke to her in his most soothing voice. "Drink this, Elise. It will heal you."

The hours went by. Sam and Sven both retired to rest; the girl's mother stayed to help. Gabriel looked at the dark hollows under her eyes. "Why don't you get some sleep while you can? I'll be with her—I won't leave. And I'll not drowse either."

Finally she sank down in a rocker by the foot of the bed. In minutes she was asleep. Gabriel perched on a stool by the bed, alone with the lovely, golden child. He looked at the beautiful arch of her eyebrows, the pearly skin, and thought of what his childhood mentor Dr. Beauchamps had told him. 'If you're going to do this kind of work, you can't let sympathy get in the way. It clouds your judgment—and that's no good to anybody.'

Dr. B. had never mentioned not praying. Gabriel didn't think of himself as particularly religious, even though he held the office of Aaronic priest—a family minister—among the Saints. Too much of a skeptic to be termed 'righteous.' A rebel from the start. Nevertheless, he laid his hands on her head, the way Hannah did for ailing household pets, and breathed a prayer for God's protection over her.

He continued his watch, applying cloths to her head and chest, making her drink. Shadows grew close around him. He remembered the end of Zion's Camp and how he'd submerged his body in an icy stream to throw off his own fever.

Her fever broke with the first light; she fell into a deep sleep. Gabriel hunched over the bed, laid his head on his folded arms and dozed. He woke to find Sven Peterson gazing down at him. He sat up, blinking.

"She's sleeping peacefully, sir. I think she's come through all right."

Sven's reddish eyebrows drew together. "Looks like you can use some sleep yourself. We have a cot in the spare room."

Through his grogginess, he saw that Sven moved with a quicker step.

"I feel right spry," Sven said later as they sat in the keeping room.

Gabriel looked at the eggs and toast Sven's wife had placed before him. "Well, rest up before you start working again. And stay off the roof for awhile. I thank you," he said to the wife as she poured coffee in an earthenware mug.

"No need to thank us," Sven said. "We're as beholden to you as we've ever been to anyone. Oh—I forgot. Mormons don't drink coffee."

Gabriel smiled. "This one'll drink anything."

That last remark seemed to breach any barrier that was left. Sven talked and laughed, even joked about the distrust between Mormons and Gentiles.

"I tell you, when we heard they was flocking into these parts, folks got all hot and bothered. But then they calmed down when they got to know those leaders. Them Whitmer brothers, and what's his name—Cowdery—now, they're right good men. Keep their word. And Lyman Wight—feller with a place up north of here, on the Grand River. Feisty cuss. But an honest man if I ever saw one."

Gabriel stayed with the Petersons another day, making periodic checks on his patient. By the end of the second day, she was able to sit up and sip chicken broth. Gabriel prepared to depart the next morning.

"I reckon I've done all I can."

"You done more than I figured anyone could," Sven said. "I just about give her up. Wait here."

Gabriel stood beside the front stoop while Elise and her mother smiled at him from the doorway. The boy Sam walked from the stable with the gray speckled horse saddled and ready. Just as Gabriel was mounting, Sven appeared leading a speckled colt.

"This here's a two-year-old—ain't been broke yet. Halter-trained is all."

"Nice looking horse," Gabriel said.

"He's yours. I know you'll treat him good."

Gabriel drew in his breath, amazed. "Sir, I—"

"You deserve more than we can ever give you. Next time you come up this way, it'll be on your own horse."

Sam mounted behind Gabriel, and they set off with the colt trotting behind them on a short lead.

Gabriel kept turning to look at his new property. He marveled at what it meant—mobility for himself if he kept it. Then he realized—if they trained the animal and sold it, they could buy Eb's wife out of slavery.

"*Grâce à Dieu*," he murmured to the boy and the horses.

"What's that mean?" Sam clutched Gabriel's waist.

"Don't let go of that colt. I was giving thanks for my good fortune."

"What you gonna name him?"

"He doesn't have a name? I think—why, I reckon I'll call him 'Freedom.'"

"That's a right fine name."

In mid-afternoon they splashed across the creek and trotted west past the little settlement by the mill. In the far distance he spotted two familiar figures walking side by side along the road. Squinting in the light, he recognized Eb and Rusty.

"I'll be blamed! That's my family, come out to find me. Let's stop right here."

He dismounted and retrieved his knapsack. Sam slid into the saddle and handed over the colt's lead.

"Thanks, lad. If you need me again, you know where to look. On your way now—you'll be home in time for supper."

"Goodbye, Freedom," the boy said in a choked voice. He turned and rode away. As Gabriel watched, Sam brushed his sleeve across his eyes. *Weeping?* Freedom gave a little whinny and pawed the ground. Had Sven given him Sam's own colt? He stood silent for a moment, not moving, then stepped close to the colt.

"I'll be as good a friend as you ever had," he said to the animal. "*Un bon ami.*" The colt moved his ears, listening. Gabriel patted him on the neck and began to lead him along the road.

Rusty kicked a stone out of the road. Dust rose from their feet; he felt it in his nose, on his skin. Eb let out his breath in a sigh.

"That sun sure gettin' hot."

Rusty looked at him. "We can walk in the shade if you want. Over there by the creek."

Eb shook his head. "We can see more out here."

Rusty wiped the perspiration from his forehead. "How we gonna tell him?"

"Have to find him first."

"He's gonna be fit to be tied. Not like Nat, just hiding in his study all day."

Eb brushed his sleeve across his face. "Don't fool yourself. Nat's more upset then he let on."

"Well, Gabe's gonna tear the place apart, once he hears. He's not one to keep his feelings to himself."

"News travels fast in these parts," Eb said. "Like as not, someone's already told him."

They hiked up a little rise and caught sight of Gabriel in the next valley.

"Isn't he supposed to be riding the horse?" Rusty asked. "Why's he leading it?"

Eb squinted. "Not the same horse."

"How do you know?"

"I was there when he rode away." Eb broke into a run, and Rusty tried to keep up. From the look of joy on Gabe's face, Rusty knew he'd had no word of events in Far West.

"You look plumb wore out." Eb took the knapsack and slung it over his own shoulder.

"The colt," Gabe said. "They just up and gave it to me—can you beat that?"

Eb said, "Sounds like you did what they wanted."

"Oh, they're both gettin' well—the father and daughter. But the horse—we still have to train it."

Eb walked around the animal. "Looks gentle enough. Won't be too much work."

Gabe was gesturing, talking with his hands in his excitable way.

"Do you know what this means? *Tiens*—that's your wife's freedom, there on the hoof. We'll teach him well, and when he's all grown and it's time to sell him, I reckon we can get at least a hundred dollars. More, if he's a good horse. We'll have almost enough."

Eb stood speechless. Gabe clapped him on the back. "I told you we could do it. I even gave him a special name. Freedom."

Eb swallowed as he looked at Gabriel. "If he's that good, maybe you won't want to sell him at all."

"Now, what's the matter with you?" Gabe sounded annoyed. "You know our agreement."

Eb shook his head. "We'd better take special good care of him, then." He reached for the halter. "Let's get him in the shade and cool him down some."

A fine thing, Rusty thought—they'll walk in the shade for a horse, but not for me. They moved under the willows and followed the stream to the west. The horse's hooves made a steady clopping behind them. Eb said, "I expect the first thing is to see what Nat thinks of him."

Home lay just ahead; they didn't have much time. Rusty started to speak, but the dust made him cough. He tried again. "Have you heard about what happened in town?"

"No. What's going on now?"

Rusty glanced over at Eb. Eb looked down at the ground. Gabriel slowed to a halt. "Well, speak up. What is it?"

"You see," Eb mumbled. "That talk stirred things up real bad."

"What talk? Rigdon's sermon? What do you mean?"

Eb shot a pleading look at Rusty. "You tell 'em. You're the one started it."

Rusty felt a dryness in his mouth; uneasiness gripped him. "You go ahead."

Gabriel frowned. "Well, someone better tell me, or I'll stir things up right here."

Rusty swallowed. Even though he stood at least six inches taller than Gabe, he felt a twinge of fear. "Well—-that is—there was this letter, see—"

"I hear about eighty-three men signed it," Eb said.

"They sent it to Cowdery and them, telling 'em if they knew what was good for them, they'd leave the county."

"*Mon Dieu*," Gabriel said. "What'd they do?"

Rusty tried to think of the best way to say it. "Wait'll you hear. Cowdry and the others, they took the letter and went off—some say to seek legal advice. And on their way back, they—"

"They met their families," Eb said. "All turned out of their homes. The women and children cryin', their belongings all thrown out on the prairie."

"Did you see it?" Gabriel demanded.

"I saw the stuff scattered all over," Eb said. "Like as not, it's still there."

"Where'd they go?"

Rusty shrugged. "No one knows. But they're no longer anywhere around here."

"Dissenters. Driven out," Gabriel said in a tone of disbelief. *Here it comes*, Rusty thought. He drew in his breath, glancing at Eb. To his surprise, there was no explosion of angry words, no quick gestures. Gabriel stood motionless, his dark brows drawing together as if he were trying to get his thoughts in order. He rolled his eyes and muttered "*Mon Dieu*" at least twice. Then he began walking again. He stumbled once, as if dazed. "Where's the colt?"

"I got 'em," Eb said. "You can be sure of that."

Gabriel looked at Rusty. "How—what did Nat say when he heard?"

"He went and sat a long time in that room—you now, where his books are."

"I 'spect he's still there," Eb said. "He didn't say much to us."

"We figured you'd want to know right off." Rusty could see the house ahead through the clump of willows.

"And the women. Bethia and the others. Did it upset them?"

"Didn't seem to," Rusty said. "'Course with women, they never let on."

Gabe gave a sigh. "*Eh bien.* Let's go tell Nat about the colt."

They left the shade and tramped across the field toward the house. Gabriel walked with his head bent, tight-lipped, his brow wrinkled. Eb moved up beside him and put a hand on his shoulder.

4

The Fourth of July. Still early. Bethia, feeding chickens, stands barefoot in the yard between the stable and the house. Even though the sun has not even cleared the trees by the creek, she feels the warmth on her arms and the back of her neck. A warning of the heat to come.

"Chick, chick!" She scatters the last of the scraps on the ground. The hens peck at the greens and apple cores with jerky motions. Three of them come close—Red Lady, Buffy and Pom-Pom. Her aunt's words echo in her mind: "Don't you be naming them chickens. You'll just feel bad when we have to eat 'em."

But she can't help it. Each is an individual, unique, with its own particular beauty. She thinks of the other creatures stirring in the stable, the two oxen munching hay, the horses—a pair of bays belonging to Calvin, and the colt Freedom. Soon Eb would come out and lead Freedom through his daily exercises, out through the yard and around the stable, over to the main house, around the smaller log house being built for Owen Crawford and his wife. Then the final leg of the journey, down to the creek and back.

"Gets him used to folks," Eb explained. "Another month, he'll be ready for a saddle."

At first she wondered why Eb did most of the work of training, since the colt belonged to Gabriel. Obvious answer—Gabriel had less and less time. Requests for the doctor came at all hours of the day, even into the night. That might explain why he pays so little attention to her—often he appears at the breakfast table looking exhausted.

A reasonable answer. But it does little to sooth the pain that throbs like a festering wound inside her. For she knows now—she loves him, despite his strange moods and his neglect, his apparent reluctance to court her. The hurt, once a faint bewilderment, has increased—she feels it just before she falls asleep, senses it upon awakening.

What to do? She cannot move away, and as far as she can tell, Gabriel has no intention of leaving. Hannah has counseled her to be patient. Easier said than done, when each day brings fresh hope, fresh disappointment. At least today they would have the Fourth of July celebration, with band, parade and speakers. She hears hoof beats, someone galloping along the creek from the east. She hurries to empty the rest of the scraps. The hoof beats grow louder, then slow to a trot. She looks up. Startled to see Gabriel mounted on the Crawfords' piebald gelding.

He pulls back on the reins. He slides to the ground, more like a fall than an orderly dismount. Then he looks at her. He shakes his head. "Oh, good morning. It is morning, isn't it?"

Trying to hide her surprise. "Where—where have you been? I thought everyone was still asleep."

He walks toward her, leading the horse. "Oh—they fetched me sometime after midnight. Trouble with a birth, over east of Haun's Mill. A breech—feet first." He runs a hand through his black hair. "But it was fine. The child was born with the first light."

She sees then how tired he looks, his face pale, his eyes red-rimmed. A day's growth of beard covers his chin. "You've not slept at all," she says. "And this the Fourth."

"I don't reckon folks look at the calendar before they need help. But you're right. I wouldn't miss the Fourth for anything." His chest rises and falls. "Tell you what. When it's time to leave, you come and scratch on my door. I'll be up like a shot—you'll see."

Suddenly shy. "I—I will. But you look plumb tuckered out."

He smiles, a thin, quick smile. To her surprise, he puts a hand on her shoulder. "Dear sister, it's good of you to be concerned for me. But I'll be fine—all I need is a few hours rest. I'll just put our friend here in his stall."

"No, you won't." Eb has come up beside them. He takes the reins from Gabriel. "You go along to bed."

Gabriel turns without a word and walks toward the house. He stumbles a little as he reaches the door. Eb shakes his head. "If he won't look after himself, we'll have to."

"Will he be all right?" Her shoulder still tingles from the touch of his hand.

"He be fine if he'd say no to a few folks. Let's hope they all stay healthy for awhile." Eb leads the horse into the stable and emerges with the colt Freedom. Bethia watches, thinking of the first time she saw Freedom—Eb leading him, walking with Gabriel and Rusty after Gabe's return from the sick family in Daveiss County.

"Look what they gave me," Gabriel said as she opened the door. "I have to tell Nat."

Eb and Rusty waited with the colt while Gabriel went inside. He stayed with Nat a long time; sounds of their voices, low undertones, drifted from the window.

"What's keeping them?" Bethia asked.

"They sure ain't talkin' about no colt," Eb muttered.

"'Course not," Rusty said. "It's the dissenters—Gabe's not takin' it too well."

"I didn't figure he would." Eb patted the colt's neck.

At last Gabriel and Nathaniel walked outside. In spite of Gabe's eagerness over the colt and Nat's approval, she sensed less joy than she would've expected, as if some sort of cloud hung over them all.

Since that time, Nat, Calvin and the younger men have visited Daveiss County at least twice, riding up to a new Mormon settlement north of Gallatin—Adam-Ondi-Ahman on the Grand River.

"It's about the prettiest place you'd ever want to see," Gabriel told her. "All these lovely trees, lots of them in bloom."

"Good forest land," Calvin said. "I hear they're sending a lot of the Kirtland people up there. And Saints from Canada."

"Someday we'll take you there," Gabriel said. "You have to see it. I'm almost tempted to go up there and settle."

Her heart pounding. "Will you?"

He raised his eyebrows. "I reckon not. Most of the folks I care for are down here."

Was that a significant look he gave her? In her confusion, she couldn't be sure.

Smoke rising from the chimney. Time for breakfast. She picks up the empty dish and walks toward the house.

By mid-morning she'd concocted a plan. Gabriel obviously had no idea how she felt about him. If he knew, he would behave differently. She would begin by apologizing for her behavior in Kirtland—she hadn't done that. Once he'd accepted the apology, things would take a different turn. If—she added—he cared for her at all.

And surely he did care. She remembered how he'd held her hand at the dedication of the House of the Lord in Kirtland. He even remarked that if he were an angel, he'd dance around her instead of on the roof of the building. Was he jesting? Time to put it to the test.

She went over all these things in her mind as she rode to town with the others. Squeezed in between Hannah and Sarah, she held Jody on her lap. Hannah, expecting another child in the fall, took up a good half of the seat. Up front, Nathaniel guided the team of oxen. Gabriel, looking as if he'd slept soundly all night, sat beside him, with Calvin on the outside. Eb and Rusty walked alongside the wagon, one on each side.

"Horses," Jody said. Men on horseback, other wagons from neighboring settlements, plodded toward the rutted road that led to the southwest. They converged and streamed into town, a bright caravan of wagons, buggies, riders, people on foot, everyone dressed up and ready for a holiday celebration.

As she thought of that day later, through the mists of memory, she recalled how at first everything had gone well. Gabriel had even stood beside her as they watched the parade of horsemen and the marching of the military band. He flashed her a brief smile as the music filled the air. The band stopped in front of the improvised speakers' stand, where Joseph and Hyrum Smith sat with some other men whom she didn't recognize.

"Gentiles," someone said. "Important people."

A vertical object caught her eye. "What's that?"

"Too late for a May pole," Gabriel said.

"It's the Liberty Pole," Eb said. "Didn't you just hear them say?"

Gabriel shrugged. "Looks like a tree to me." From its top, the flag hung limply. The music stopped. Nathaniel, with Jody on his shoulders, motioned the little group to be quiet. It was time for the cornerstones to be laid on the temple site.

As Bethia watched the men moving around the designated area. she thought of the House of the Lord they had left in Kirtland. This would be a much bigger building, with plenty of space for worship, and two floors for educational purposes. She wondered if they all would have to sacrifice as much in the building of it. She hoped not. She glanced at Gabriel—it was hard to hear the words which were being said. Prayers, most likely. He met her eyes and smiled.

"Enough of this," Rusty said. Nat gave him a warning look. The crowd was beginning to murmur—people talking among themselves.

At last Sidney Rigdon rose to begin the Fourth of July speech. His words, delivered in his usual commanding style, were not so loud that one couldn't talk over them. She listened to the extolling of liberty's blessings, which turned into a recital of the persecutions the Saints had suffered. All things they'd heard before. A good time to put her plan into action.

"Gabriel?"

He turned, and his dark eyebrows drew together. Brother Rigdon had paused. Gabriel leaned his head closer to her. Her voice sunk to a whisper.

"I'm mighty sorry about—about the doings in Kirtland. You know, when Aunt Sarah and them found another house and made me move there too."

Gabriel straightened up, a faint smile on his lips. His eyes gleamed, as if he were ready to burst into laughter. "You mean, when they made you get all gussied up and go to all those parties with the rich folks?"

She blinked, not knowing what to say next. The scene she had imagined did not include such a reply. He said, "Sure, you're sorry. You're sorry that none of them asked to marry you."

Rigdon was speaking again. She felt close to tears. "Oh, Gabriel, no. That's not what I—"

"Hush." Nathaniel gave her a fierce look. At the same time, Gabriel put a hand on her arm, a warning gesture. She tried to center her thoughts on what Rigdon was saying.

"We take God and all the holy angels to witness this day, that we warn all men in the name of Jesus Christ, to come on us no more forever, for from this hour, we will bear it no more, our rights shall no more be trampled on with impunity...And that mob that comes on us to disturb us; it shall be between us and them a war of extermination, for we will follow them, till the last drop of their blood is spilled or else they will have to exterminate us, for we will carry the seat of war to their own houses, and their own families, and one party or the other shall be utterly destroyed—remember it then, all men."

She gasped—this was something far beyond the usual patriotic homily. She looked at Gabriel. He was frowning, his face pale, his mouth open a little. She felt his hand trembling as it rested on her arm. Nathaniel shifted his feet and glanced around at the members of his household with a troubled expression.

Rigdon raised his hand above his head as he finished. "We this day then proclaim ourselves free, with a purpose and a determination that can never be broken—no, never! no, never!" His voice rose to a shout. "NO, NEVER!"

People burst into cheers all around them and waved their hats in the air. Joseph Smith stepped forward. The crowd began the Hosanna Shout: "Hosanna! Hosanna! Hosanna to God and the Lamb!" The sound had a frenzy about it, an edge which made her uneasy. She turned to Gabriel.

"It's like they've all gone crazy," he said. "We'd better get you and Hannah out of here. Jody, too." He started to move toward Nathaniel.

"Stay where you are," Nat said. "I reckon they'll get tired and quit in a minute."

Still the cheering went on. Men were flinging their hats in the air. Then the band struck up a lively, spirited march. The cheers and shouting diminished. The crowd began milling around, moving closer to the speakers' stand.

Suddenly Sarah cried out, "Hannah! Oh, my God!"

Hannah had sunk to the ground. Bethia, on the point of renewing her conversation with Gabriel, had to abandon it and take Jody instead. Nat gathered up Hannah in his arms and motioned with his head for Gabriel to follow him. "Excuse me," he said to the people around him. "Excuse us, please."

Finally they reached the shade of a building. Nat got to his knees with Hannah still in his arms. She lifted her head and tried to push him away. "It's all right, dear. Don't look at me so worried-like. It just got too hot, was all."

Gabriel knelt beside them. "It's right warm out there in the sun. No pains of any kind?"

"No. Just a powerful thirst. I reckon I should've stayed home."

Gabriel said, "Well, we'll take you home to rest. Rusty, see if you can get some water from the hotel."

Nat's mouth relaxed in a half-smile; he wiped his forehead with his sleeve. "A good thing we have a doctor in our house."

Gabriel raised his eyebrows. "All thanks to you."

Nat went to get their team and wagon, and they helped Hannah into it. Eb and Rusty decided to stay in town a while longer, "just to see what they do next," as Rusty put it. The others were silent as they pulled out and headed across the prairie. This time Bethia sat beside Nat with Jody on her lap, to give Hannah more room. Hannah sat leaning over, her head in Sarah's lap. Calvin and Gabriel walked beside the wagon.

"Just keep her covered from the sun," Gabriel said. "That water should help."

"I declare," Sarah said. "And her time's not till November, if the reckoning be right."

"She'll be just fine." Gabriel's voice sounded firm and weary at the same time. Bethia remembered about his sleepless night. Should've thought of it earlier. Between that and Mr. Rigdon's fiery oratory, she couldn't have chosen a worse time to implement any plan.

"Like as not, there'll be time later," she told herself.

But even after they got Hannah settled in her chair at home, and the oxen and Jody fed, there was no opportunity to approach the subject. As she and Sarah prepared dinner, she could hear the men talking.

"A more inflammatory statement I've never heard," Gabriel said. "All those visitors up there—what was he thinking?"

Calvin spoke from his usual place at the table. "More to the point, what were *they* thinking?" He shrugged and let his hand fall on the wood, palm down.

"That's the worry." Gabriel made a quick, little gesture, as if he were about to say something else.

Sarah moved over to the table with plates and utensils. "I didn't pay him no mind. It sounded like the usual harangue to me."

Nathaniel left the settle, where he had been sitting beside Hannah. He walked toward them. "We all know Mr. Rigdon tends to exaggerate. He gets carried away, is all. I reckon that's how we better look at it."

Sarah sniffed. "Then what are we all riled up about?"

Gabriel looked at Nathaniel. "You better hope those Gentiles see it that way. That 'war of extermination' business isn't likely to make us any new friends. Or calm the fears of those we have."

"Now, why should they be afraid of us?" Nathaniel asked. "We've done nothing against them."

They gathered around the meal of bread, cheese, and leftover ham. Eb and Rusty returned just before candlelight.

"Folks sure be talkin' 'bout that speech," Eb said. "All over town, that's all we heard."

"Did they agree with it?" Gabriel asked.

"Mainly. But some thought he could've said things softer, like."

Rusty sat down on one end of the settle, next to Hannah's chair. "I hear those Gentiles didn't know what to do. They started to join in the cheering, but they thought it was 'Hurrah!' The hosannas really confused them. They just stood there looking dazed."

Gabriel shook his head and gave a short laugh. "Let's hope that's all they do."

Bethia, listening, felt disappointment rush over her like a wave. Clearly Gabriel was too upset to hear any apology. Another day or two, and she'd try again.

But the next morning Gabriel saddled one of the bay horses and prepared to head north. When she hurried out to inquire, he gave her a brief smile. "I have to check on my patients in Gallatin. And there's one up near Diahman."

Eb brought out the other bay horse. "We better start before it gets any hotter. I reckon there be one heck of a storm before long."

Gabriel glanced toward the west. "Not for a while." He mounted and looked down at her. "Take care of Hannah for me. Keep her out of the sun. Tell her to drink lots of water."

She nodded, unable to speak. She had the sudden feeling that all aspects of her life were moving beyond her control. Nathaniel and Calvin carried on their duties as usual, moving slowly in the heat, their faces glistening with perspiration. They worked grim-faced, not speaking, as if their thoughts were elsewhere. Bethia tried to tend to Hannah and keep Jody occupied, but she kept thinking of Gabriel on the road to Adam-Ondi-Ahman. Silly of her. Perhaps he didn't care for her one bit.

When the storm hit, Gabriel had not returned home. Bethia looked at the dooryard filling up with water and wondered where he was now, how he would seek shelter. Nathaniel came in from seeing to the animals and stamped his feet. Droplets of water flew from his hair. He glanced at her, then winced as the thunder crashed. Nell went into a frenzy of barking.

"Oh, hush," Nat said. "We're safe enough, if the creek don't rise. This puts me in mind of the storm we had during Zion's Camp. I never did hear such thunder."

Gabriel had told her about Zion's Camp, the expedition organized to help the Saints after their expulsion from Jackson County. According to him, he'd almost died of cholera at the end of the march. A chill went through her as she thought about it.

That evening, Rusty came in with the news that lightning had struck the liberty pole in the town square. "Just shivered it. Nothing left but splinters."

That unnerved them all. Two days later, Eb and Gabriel returned. They looked weary—tight-lipped and grim. Something else wrong. She had to wait until they'd taken care of the horses before they tramped into the house.

"Land's sakes!" Sarah said. "I never saw such ones for tracking in the mud. Can't you wipe those boots afore you come in?"

Gabriel looked at Eb, and a slight smile played on his lips. "Shall we go out and try again?"

Bethia couldn't help herself. She rushed forward. "No! It's all right. I'll clean it up."

"Too late now anyway," Sarah muttered.

"Here." Bethia pulled out a chair. "Sit down, and—and tell us what happened."

By this time, Nathaniel and Calvin had entered. Calvin took a seat, but Nathaniel remained standing at the head of the table. "What is it, Gabriel?"

"Well—" Gabriel glanced around, then sank down in the chair Bethia had offered. "I don't rightly know how to begin."

"Start with the newspaper," Eb said.

"Oh, yes." He gestured, his long fingers shaping the air. "They went and printed that speech over in Liberty, and now just about everyone's read it."

"Printed it?" Nat asked.

"Yes—in that weekly newspaper. *The Far West*."

Nat put his hands on the back of a chair. "Well, I reckon you can't keep it hid forever."

"And every Gentile I've talked to is fit to be tied." More excited gestures. "You know the Petersons, the family that gave me the colt? We bided with them two days."

"They're all well now," Eb said. "Don't forget that part."

"Well, old man Peterson, he sets me down, and I swear, these are his exact words. 'What's gotten into you folks? First you get rid of all the leaders that we trusted—the Whitmers and Cowdery. Chased 'em out—is that a way to treat anybody? Then you go and start settling Daviess County—crowdin' in there like flies. Everywhere you look, there's another Mormon. And now, this talk of extermination, and carrying destruction to our homes and families—what's this all about?'"

"Gabe really worked to pacify 'em," Eb said. "Took all night, and at least two jugs of whiskey."

Bethia let out a little gasp. "Thanks," Gabriel said to Eb in an undertone.

Eb shrugged. "Just givin' you credit for tryin'."

Nathaniel paused before he spoke. "It's true they've been sending folks up north. Most of the Kirtland families be gathering there. But there's not enough room for everyone in these parts. And if we live peaceful-like, what does it matter?"

"Tell about the liberty pole," Calvin said.

Rusty related the incident, his voice eager. "I hear tell that Joseph Smith went out and walked over the splinters—said that's the way we'll trample our enemies under our feet."

"If that don't beat everything," Eb said.

Gabriel shrugged and threw up his hands. "All they need to hear is more words like that. Talk about sitting on a powder keg."

Before the evening meal, Bethia saw Nathaniel draw Gabriel aside. Her acute hearing picked up the words.

"Do you reckon it's as bad as you say?"

"I can only tell you what I heard. I don't know—there's a lot of hotheads around, on both sides."

She had her chance with Gabriel two days later, and this time it caught her unprepared. It was early dusk; she'd just herded the chickens into their coop for the night. Now she sat on the back stoop to rest. She loved looking over the fields and outbuildings just at this time, when candles were beginning to glow inside the houses.

Suddenly a figure moved away from the side of the house. She gave a little gasp. Then she saw Gabriel standing with one hand on the logs. Her voice quivered. "You startled me."

He gave a little chuckle. "My apologies. I wouldn't want to do that for anything."

"Oh—well, I—" Everything she wanted to say had fled from her mind.

He spoke again, his voice gentle. "It's right peaceful out here, isn't it?"

"Yes, it is."

"Makes you think nothing could go wrong. When I first came here, I thought we'd be safe—no one could possibly harm us in this remote spot."

"You don't think so anymore?"

He sighed and looked out into the distance. "A lot's happened since then."

Now was the time. "Gabriel, I feel I must apologize for—for—well, about Kirtland."

"Oh, you want to talk about that again?"

"I think we should."

He moved closer to her and leaned his back against the side of the building. A teasing note crept into his voice. "Well, if you think so, then I reckon we will."

"I said I was sorry."

He gave a little cough. "If I were you, I wouldn't waste my time feeling too sorry."

"What do you mean?"

"*Tiens*—if things hadn't happened the way they did, I might not've gone off to Mentor, to study and work with my physician friend. He really did become my friend, always handy with advice. It was my dream, you see, to study medicine. And if I hadn't taken that chance, I might not've had another."

She drew a quick breath, not knowing what to say. He went on. "And now, here we are. I've learned a little bit more about helping sick folks, and it seems I'm one of the few people around who can. Although sometimes I'm struck by how much I don't know."

She wondered how to get the conversation back to the subject of *them*. He gestured and spoke again.

"I can't tell you how much it means, to learn the things I did. It helped me get beyond the—well, any hurt I might've felt about us. And I discovered a strength in me that I didn't know I had."

"You—you got beyond it?"

"Oh, yes—*grâce à Dieu*. It was like fording one of those fast rivers. You try to keep your footing and avoid the rocks. Finally you reach the other shore, and it's all green and beautiful. Full of hope. No more adolescent folly."

She blinked. "That's all I am—an adolescent folly?"

He laughed. "Now, I didn't say that. I was trying to describe what I felt at the time, and how my studies helped restore me to a saner state."

The trouble was, she hadn't got beyond it yet. How to tell him? "Gabriel, I was forced to do those things. I was younger, and Aunt Sarah—you know how determined she can be."

He said nothing for a moment. He ran a hand through his hair and stroked his chin. When he spoke, he sounded amused. "Tell me, Bethia. If one of those rich Kirtland fellers had asked for your hand, would you have hesitated?"

"I—I reckon so."

"Sarah would've been all the more determined, from what I know of her. That was her aim, as I see it—to get you well provided for. Not that it was a bad idea—it's natural she would want it."

She felt close to tears. "Well, I didn't, and—and nothing came of it. I didn't accept anyone." She paused for breath. "Can't you see that? It's Sarah you should be angry with, not me."

"Who said I was angry at anyone?"

She began to weep then, dabbing at her cheeks as she felt the hot tears on them. She turned so he wouldn't see, and in spite of herself she burst out, "Oh, Gabriel, I suppose you don't care at all anymore."

The instant the words were out, she wished she could have unsaid them. What could he possibly say? Maybe he would just turn and go back into the house. She wouldn't blame him if he did. His voice cut through the stillness.

"Now, why would you suppose such a thing? Not care?" He gave a little laugh. "The trouble is, I care too much. I care about my patients, my family—my sister that I'll not see again. That is, it seems most unlikely. I care about you, and the whole group of us. Hannah, and her unborn child. I promised to take care of that child, and see that it has a good birth. Will I be able to do that?"

"I know, Gabriel," she said. "I'm sorry."

He gestured. "I lie awake at night worrying about what's going to happen to all of us, 'specially now that our leaders don't know how to speak prudently. I care about my life, and how I'd do some serious courtin' if the time was right. But then I think about Eb, and wonder how I could be happy when the one he loves is still in slavery."

"I shouldn't have said anything." She sniffed and wiped her eyes with the hem of her apron.

"You should say anything you want to. But let's understand one another, Bethia. Never think that I don't care."

In the silence, she felt that they were approaching each other on two different levels, hers being the immature, selfish one. He had indeed gone beyond her, and she wondered, grieving, how she could catch up with him. From that moment she determined not to speak of any feeling for him, and to concentrate instead on the greater good of the community.

In the deepening twilight, he spoke again. "Don't fret about the Kirtland days. If there's anything to forgive, I've done it."

She murmured her thanks. The last light left the fields; the shed and other outbuildings stood dark against the sky. She wished that the moment could go on and on, be preserved in time, just the two of them looking out into the semi-darkness. Suddenly gunfire echoed in the distance, three shots, then a fourth. Gabriel straightened up. "Wonder what *that* was."

"Someone shooting at a varmint, most like."

"The four-legged kind? Let's hope so."

She stood up, and he held the door as they went into the house.

5

NATHANIEL SAT AT THE small table that served as his desk, facing the window. He ran his eye over his meager library which sat between two blocks of wood—the Bible, the Book of Mormon, and an English grammar. He also had two copies of *The Elders' Journal* which he'd managed to save.

Warm today. With his sleeve he wiped the dampness from his forehead. Behind him on the bed, Hannah slept. He turned so he could watch the rise and fall of her chest, the light blanket lifting with each breath. Her face was beautiful in repose, her bright hair spread over the pillow. Even after four years, he still felt a quickening of the pulse as he looked at her. He marveled at the good fortune that she was his, the one he had sought and longed for without much hope of her returning his affection. But return it she had, and now, knowing that her time was not far off, he didn't think he could ever bear to lose her.

"Don't worry. She's doing fine. Just let her rest all she can." Gabriel's words echoed in his mind. He wished he could be as certain as the doctor.

He put his elbows on the table and gazed at the gnarled wood surface. The corners of his mouth twitched as he sighed. Worries crowded around him like gnats on a warm afternoon.

First, Hannah. Many a young wife had died in childbirth—one heard it all the time. Even though she'd given birth to one healthy child, he remembered the miscarriage, and what Gabriel had said. "Sometimes these things happen without warning, and we don't know why." He tried to put his faith in Gabriel's more recent words. "She's strong and healthy. And her body knows just what to do."

Despite Gabriel's assurances that he would attend her, he spent most days away from home caring for sick folks. What if she went into labor and the doctor was nowhere around? Beads of perspiration stood out on Nathaniel's forehead.

Second, the rumors of happenings outside their immediate household. Were his people really safe? And safe from what? The belief that nothing would befall them if they purged themselves of all iniquity had reached alarming proportions. No one was supposed to deviate from the Word of Wisdom, now considered a commandment. This meant that liquor of any kind was prohibited, along with hot drinks such as tea and coffee. Any dissent was discouraged. In fact, Nathaniel had heard of a certain loyalty oath being required of all the brethren, binding them to support the heads of the church in everything they should teach. While he had no objections to such an oath, he disliked the way it was being enforced—by a bunch of extremists known as the Sons of Dan.

Sons of Dan, indeed. Also called the 'Daughters of Zion.' Sons or daughters, who were they to judge if a person were a dissenter or not? He worried about Gabriel and his fiery temperament, outspoken to the point of rashness. Gabriel didn't hesitate to provide whiskey to his patients if the medical procedure demanded it. How else could he diminish their suffering?

Then there was the business about all the new folks coming in. In July, a large group of people—some said as many as five hundred—had left Kirtland for Far West. When they all arrived, they would have to live somewhere. Already Caldwell County was crowded. He thought of DeWitt, where families had been gathering since the beginning of July. A group of Carroll County citizens had already met to oppose the small Mormon settlement. According to Gabriel, the Saints there lived in a constant state of alarm because of the threats against them.

A horse neighing. Hooves striking the ground. Nathaniel sprang up and peered out the window, but all he could see was Eb leading the colt toward the edge of the creek. From the bed, Hannah gave a little sigh. "What is it?"

He went to sit on the edge of the bed and took her hand. "Nothing to fret about. I reckon it's just Gabriel, come back from Diahman."

"Oh." Her features relaxed as she smiled.

He brushed his fingers against her cheek. "Best you stay resting."

"Oh, I'll be all right." She threw back the cover and got to her feet. "It's nigh time for Jody to wake up."

"Bethia has him in her room."

They went out into the main room, Hannah moving slowly with Nat just behind her. Gabriel opened the back door and rushed in. His face was red, his breath coming fast, as if he'd been running.

Nat pushed past Hannah. "What is it, lad?"

Gabe grasped the back of a chair and leaned on it. "Are Rusty and Calvin about?"

Nat shrugged. "They went into town. Something about a saddle for your Freedom horse."

"What's the matter?" Hannah asked. She sank down heavily in the rocking chair.

Gabe began gesturing in his characteristic way. "There's big trouble in Gallatin. A humdinger of a fight, is what they're saying."

Bethia appeared in the doorway of her room, with Jody beside her rubbing his eyes. "Go on," Nat said.

"It seems a bunch of our people went in to try and vote, it being election day up there and all. They were surrounded by this crowd of folks itching for a brawl. One of the candidates—William Peniston, it was—got up on a barrel and started denouncing the Mormons—called us horse thieves and worse. He said we shouldn't be allowed to vote any more than slaves. While they was passing around the whiskey, someone took a swipe at old Brother Brown. Soon everybody was going at it with anything they could find—whips, clubs, rocks, knives. One feller—Brother Olmstead—even had a sack of crockery he'd just bought. Well, he started swingin' that around, and it was the biggest knockdown fight you can imagine. Lucky nobody got killed."

"Did any of 'em actually vote?" Nat asked.

Gabe gave a harsh laugh. "Hard to say. One feller called on the Danites for help. I think he got plenty of it. Dozens of gentiles got knocked to the ground, so they say, and several of 'em had to be carried off. One of our boys got a knife between his shoulders."

Bethia and Hannah looked at each other, Bethia's dark eyebrows drawing together. Gabe shifted his feet. "Nat, I need to speak with you in your study."

"Of course. Excuse us." Nat led the way back into the bedroom.

He closed the door and took the chair by his desk. Gabe remained standing.

"I didn't want to alarm the women. I don't like what I'm hearing. It's like all of Daveiss County's organizing against us."

"But—we haven't done anything. We're innocent."

Gabe shook his mop of black hair out of his eyes. "I wish we could say that. From what I've heard, those Sons of Dan are doing more than enforcing the Law of Consecration."

Nat blinked as he looked at Gabriel. "You don't mean—"

"I mean they've been making mischief of their own. Harassing settlers, threatening them. Hard to blame them, after what we've been through. But they're not above torching a cabin here and there."

"No." Nathaniel felt as if he'd just been punched in the stomach. "You—you're certain—"

"I'm sure of my sources. Some of them think I've saved their lives. They wouldn't lie to me."

Nat let out his breath in a sigh. "How can God protect us if we do such things?"

"A lot of us think we have to protect ourselves. But what I wanted to say—I'm not even sure we're going to be safe here much longer."

"You may be right." Nat tried to think, but he felt caught off-balance, his mind reeling from the news. He gripped the edge of the table. "We'd best be prepared."

"I reckon that's wise. Let's hope we're wrong. But it's like there're spots of trouble everywhere—Daviess County, DeWitt. They'd like to see us all out of here."

"And Hannah..." Nat gave Gabe a long look.

Gabe drew in his breath, then raised his eyebrows. "*Tiens*—we'll worry about that when the time comes. Worse comes to worse, it won't be the first child born in the wilderness."

The next day Rusty hurried in with the news. "They say two Mormons got killed in Gallatin and the Missourians won't allow their burial. The settlers around Gallatin are organizing a mob."

"How can they?" Calvin asked. "There ain't that many of them."

"The whole county's up in arms," Rusty said. "A bunch of the Danites are riding up to Diahman to protect the people there. Joseph Smith said he'd lead them. I was figuring on going along, if I can take one of the horses."

"Hold on, now," Gabriel said. "If you're talking about that fight yesterday, I heard things weren't that bad."

"Best you stay here," Nat said. "They got enough men for another brawl; they don't need you."

"He's right," Gabe said. "The way things are going, we may need both you and the horse here."

Rusty sighed, but Nat thought he detected a look of relief. For Rusty, such an expedition would have meant a major effort. This way, he could spend his time over at the public house and listen for any other news.

Nat had other reasons to keep Rusty home. Raised by pacifist Shakers, he could not lose the belief that most violence was unnecessary and wrong. To the best of his ability, he wanted to protect those under his roof from participating in bloodshed. Or delay it as long as possible.

They learned later that the Danite band, one hundred and fifty strong, found the people at Diahman in a state of fear. They prepared for a siege, but the settlers around Gallatin did not come upon them. Then they attempted to obtain the promises of certain prominent settlers, among them Judge Adam Black, that no attacks would be made.

"Derned if they didn't think they were being forced to sign," Calvin said later.

"Well," Gabriel said. "Maybe they were."

These citizens spread word of a Mormon 'invasion,' which led Daviess County judges to issue writs for the arrest of Joseph Smith and Lyman Wight.

Mid-August. Terrible heat. Bethia felt faint as she stood in the shadow of the stable. Must get water. She saw the unfamiliar figure on horseback as she crossed to the back steps. In a matter of minutes he was in the yard, a young man, his straw-colored hair wind-blown, riding bareback on an old sorrel horse.

"Dr. Romain here?"

"I believe so. I'll get him."

She roused Gabriel from a nap and he walked out into the yard shaking his head. She could hear them talking, but she couldn't make out the words. She was drinking a cup of water when Gabriel came back into the house.

"Bethia, I need an assistant. There's a woman ill, one of our people, about six miles east of here. Will you come with me?"

"Well—I reckon." She tried to hide her surprise; usually he took Eb, if he needed someone.

"Fine. I'll get my things. We'll take the carriage."

She splashed some of the water on her face and hoped she wouldn't disgrace herself as an assistant. She heard him telling Nathaniel and then rummaging in his room for whatever he needed. He hurried out to harness the horses.

She was waiting when he drove the carriage to the back step. She tried not to think how they'd never ridden out alone before. In fact, she'd been trying to avoid him since their last encounter, convinced that her feelings for him were not returned.

He helped her up, then clicked to the team. "Now, according to that feller, his elderly aunt has a misery on her neck and shoulder. She's in a lot of pain. It sounds like an abscess to me. That's why I want you along."

She got up the courage to ask, "Why me?"

He looked at her, one eyebrow raised. "You have a gentle way, and I'm hoping it'll soothe her."

"I—I do?"

"Well, you're gentle with chickens and Jody, and I think it might work for elderly aunts too. No matter what you see or hear, just be patient and kind. I know you can do that."

She couldn't think of a reply. They rode in silence. She looked at the rolling hills planted with corn, and the stretch of forest that ran alongside the creek. They passed two little settlements, clusters of cabins by the water's edge.

"Looks peaceful now," he murmured, as if talking to himself.

"And why shouldn't it? Don't you reckon we're safe here?"

"Well, Bethia—I'm hoping so. I'm not sure anywhere's safe, unless it's the grave."

She smiled. "I didn't realize you were such a pessimist."

He laughed then. "That's what doctorin' does for you. I keep learning more every day. Mainly learning that I need to know more."

Silence again. When he spoke, all mirth had left his voice. "About being safe—I figure it's the ones off by themselves who are having the troubles. If we stay together, close to Far West, we should be all right."

"Why do they hate us so? We're not that different."

He chuckled. "Oh, we're different, all right. How many of us own slaves? None that I ever heard of. As far as hating—I'm running into folks who don't seem happy less'n they're mad at someone. I didn't understand it at first. But it's true—it gives their lives impetus, a reason to get up in the morning. Look—we're almost there."

He guided the horses down a narrow trace and pulled them to a halt. He jumped down, secured the reins to a tree, and helped her to the ground. Then he reached in the back of the carriage for his knapsack. By this time the young man Bethia had seen earlier was at his side. "That was fast driving, Doctor. We didn't look to see you before noon."

"This is my assistant," Gabriel said. "Miss Bethia."

"Morning, ma'am."

They followed the man into the house. Half a dozen people, relatives and neighbors, sat in the main room. Gabriel looked around at them. "And which one of you needs my help?"

"She's lying down," someone said. "In there."

"Well, I reckon I'm going to need some hot water. Better set some to boil."

Two of the women got up and hurried to the fireplace. Gabriel knocked at the door, then walked into the sickroom. Bethia followed.

As Gabriel began his work, she wondered at the change in him. He seemed to be completely in control, no longer uncertain or questioning. He examined the woman, reassured her and explained what they were going to do. Bethia tried to play her part with as much gentleness and patience as she could muster. Obeying instructions, she held the woman close to her while Gabriel lanced and drained the abscess.

"What relief!" the woman gasped. "I can't believe it."

Gabriel cleaned and dressed the wound, all the while commenting on how well she'd come through, and how she was going to be just fine.

Afterwards, they stayed for the midday meal with the family. "We can't pay you nothin', Doctor, but we'd take it right well if you'd stay and eat with us."

As they served the food, Bethia saw another side of Gabriel. No longer in control, he relaxed and grew expansive, full of helpful comments and encouragement for each one of them. He explained how to care for their Aunt Margaret, then went on to tell anecdotes about his medical apprenticeship.

"...I swear, this feller got up from his deathbed, grabbed a razor, and lit out after the doctor. And derned if that doctor didn't run like wildcats was after him."

He had them all laughing, as if one could believe that the life of a physician contained one hilarious incident after another. Bethia, listening, felt the familiar ache in her chest. Despite his indifference to her, and her resolve to distance herself from him, she did not think she could love him more. The others began bantering with him.

"So, when you gittin' married, Doc? High time you settled down."

"You need someone to keep you outa trouble. Besides, you can't have that much fun all yer life."

Gabriel gave Bethia a broad wink. "I don't reckon you know what a doctor's wife has to put up with. Not only the jokes—the poor soul. But an old man sleeping most all the time, 'cause he's out tendin' sick folks all night."

"That'd be a blessing," someone said. "At least you'd know right where he was."

The laughter died away. The young man said, "D'you know Brother Parley Pratt stopped in here t'other day? Said he was powerful tired, riding in from DeWitt. Had a nap in the guest room while his horse rested."

"A sensible thing to do," Gabriel remarked.

The young man went on. "He said about a hundred armed men rode into DeWitt and threatened the Mormons. That was after this committee of Carroll County citizens ordered us to leave the county."

"We be livin' in strange times," Gabriel said.

"He said there was groups and—what do you call 'em? Vigilantes—meeting in the upper counties to help bring Mormon 'criminals' to justice. Don't that beat all? They're talkin' of riding to join up with the others in Daveiss and Carroll Counties."

"Sounds like a good idea to stay put for awhile." Gabriel collected his surgical instruments, checked on his patient once more, and prepared to leave. "I'll look in on her before the week's out. Meanwhile, you know where to find me."

On the way home, Bethia leaned close to Gabriel. "Do you reckon Brother Parley's right?"

Gabriel looked off into space and tightened his lips before he spoke.

"Well, I figure a lot of what I hear is exaggerated. You aren't sure how much is true. But Parley gets around, and I think he knows what's happening. Best we all be on our guard." He sighed and ran his hand through his hair. "And, I might add, our best behavior."

Bethia felt the sun beating down on her bare head. "What do you mean by that?"

He looked at her. "Well, for instance, no more 'war of extermination' speeches by Brother Rigdon. Here—you're looking red as a roasted skunk."

The light stabbed her eyes. "It's powerful warm." She felt faintness lapping at the edges of her mind.

"And you without a shawl, or even a bonnet."

She tried to fight back the weakness. "I—I reckon I'll be all right."

"Speakin' of behavior, I wanted to commend you on yours. You were a right fine assistant."

She opened her mouth to thank him, but the faintness rushed up over her. *Please,* her mind begged—*not in front of him*. She felt herself pitching forward.

When she came to, she was lying on the ground in the shade of the carriage. Gabriel leaned over her, and she felt water on her face. Tears of frustration? No; he was sponging her with a cloth.

"Too hot for you. Good thing you had a doctor along."

"Oh." She tried to get up.

"Stay right there. We're almost home. There's no hurry." His voice was gentle, the same soothing tone he'd used with old Aunt Margaret. "Drink some of this."

He put an arm around her shoulders and lifted her up. With his other hand he offered the jug. Whiskey? She took a drink. wondering. It was water; she felt it running down her chin.

He laughed when he saw her expression. "You thought it was something else? Well, not today. Leastways, not for you."

Why did he have to be so charming? Didn't he know the effect it had on her? She got to her feet. This time he didn't stop her. "I reckon if you get in the back seat, you'll find some shade."

"I can ride in front."

He squinted in the sunlight. "You're gettin' in back if I have to carry you there myself. Take the water jug with you."

Too weak to argue, she climbed into the back seat.

"Now," he said. "Keep drinking water, and cover your head with this." He handed her his jacket, a bundle of gray flannel. Then he swung himself into the front seat.

Feeling foolish, she tried to obey his instructions. When the horses finally entered the stable, she told herself she felt better. But the walls of the building kept spinning around her.

Gabriel unhitched the team and put the horses in their stalls. Then he stopped to look at her. "My poor girl. I plumb wore you out."

She tried to protest. "Oh, no. It wasn't you."

"Come on." He held out his hand. She took it, and he helped her down. He retrieved his jacket and knapsack while she stood leaning against the side of the carriage. To her surprise, he put an arm around her as they started for the house.

She managed to say, "I feel I should apologize."

"For what? For being sensitive to the sun on a very hot day?"

"Well, no—"

"Dear Bethia. You must take better care of yourself, is all. I don't want to see you in the sun without a shawl or a sunbonnet. Or a parasol."

"I'll remember."

He fixed his dark eyes on her and raised his eyebrows. "I have a special reason for asking. You see, you mean a great deal to me. More than I'm willing to say right now. In fact, I'd even kiss you, but I'd be taking advantage."

She looked at him, unable to speak, afraid she would faint again. If he had kissed her, she couldn't have been more astonished. He gave a quick smile and opened the back door. "Well, now I've said it. You go on and rest now. Keep drinking water. That's important. I'm going to finish my nap before someone else comes for me."

He disappeared into the room he shared with Eb and Rusty. She put a hand against the wall and stood breathing fast. She wanted to treasure up all the things he'd said and how he'd said them. He'd done everything except come right out and say he loved her. She wondered if any of it would've happened if she hadn't been ill from the heat.

Then, walking with surer steps, she made her way to her own room.

6

"At least they're still servin' cider." Eb looked at the mug in front of him.

Rusty set a second mug down on the table and took the chair next to Eb. "It looks mighty weak to me. They might as well call it apple juice and forget it."

Eb lifted the mug and drank. "Not bad. Kind of tart. Wakes you right up."

Rusty looked around at the empty tables. The part of the hotel that served as a public house was deserted except for the proprietor, who sat reading a folded newspaper. Too early for most folks. Nat had sent them to town for rope and an ax handle. That errand done, they'd stopped for a spell. "Hard to get news when there's no one about."

Eb shrugged. "Maybe there's no news to get."

Rusty took a drink of cider. It was stronger than he'd expected; tears stung his eyes. "Could be it's gettin' too cold to persecute us. Maybe the mobbers all headed home for the winter."

"Not likely." Eb set the mug down. "Gabriel said Governor Boggs had ordered twenty-eight hundred troops to get ready to march. That oughta calm things down a little."

Rusty felt a twinge of jealousy. "He can't know everything, even if he is a doctor."

"He knows more than you think. Folks tell him what's happening."

Rusty sensed he had to be careful; he was sitting next to Gabe's best friend. But his envy got the better of him. "Looks like he's got Sister Bethia right where he wants her."

"What d'you mean?" Eb's eyebrows rushed together as he frowned. "He's had his eye on her for a long time."

"Seems all he has to do is look at her, and she'll do anything he says."

"I reckon she returns his feelings." Eb took a deep drink of the cider.

Rusty set the mug down hard. It made a heavy clunk on the table. "So why doesn't he up and marry her? It's fixin' to be the longest courtship on record."

Eb didn't smile. "I reckon he'd like things to be more settled. Soon as he figures out it's not gonna happen, most likely he'll ask her. But I 'spect he wants them to have a place by themselves, away from the others. Like the Crawfords' cabin."

Rusty was silent, his eyes tracing the lines on the worn table top. Finally he said, "Time was, when I fancied her myself."

Eb nodded. "She be a pretty little thing. But there's lots of others about. Jest look around you at the meetings."

Rusty looked at him. "But none like her."

Eb laughed then. "How d'you know? You won't give yourself a chance to find out."

Rusty took another swallow of cider and considered the advice. It meant some concentrated work, to pay court to an unfamiliar young woman. And he wasn't much for work.

A shadow fell over them. Rusty raised his head. Parley Pratt stood looking down at them. Square-jawed, stocky of build, he regarded them with a serious look. "Mornin', boys."

Rusty got to his feet. "Mornin', Brother Parley. Care for a spot of cider?"

"Don't mind if I do." Pratt took a chair beside Eb as Rusty went to fetch another mug. "Cold out this morning. November weather already."

Rusty returned with the cider. Brother Parley grasped the mug and lifted it to his mouth. "That's right good. So what brings you out so early?"

Rusty told him about the rope and the ax handle. Brother Parley wiped his mouth. "Trust ol' Nat Givens. As if a rope and an ax is gonna help him through the worst."

"What's been happenin'?" Eb asked.

Brother Pratt hunched forward with both hands around the cider mug. "Well, I reckon you know about Brother Joseph and Lyman Wight having to stand trial for that business up in Daveiss County."

Rusty nodded. "When they got that judge Adam Black to swear that he wouldn't join in any attack against us? Yeah—we heard that."

"Well, Brother Joseph went and hired lawyers—Atchison and Doniphan. He also figured he'd study a little law himself. He and Brother Lyman were tried at a preliminary hearing up there in Daveiss County—the seventh of September, it was. They appeared before Austin King, and that judge ordered 'em to post bail and appear at the next hearing of the grand jury. A few days later, derned if we didn't capture three men trying to transport guns to the Daveiss County mobbers. Well, both sides petitioned this same Judge King to do something about the disturbances."

"So what'd he do?" Eb asked.

"So he orders General Atchison—the lawyer fellow—to raise four hundred troops and disperse everybody—both the Mormons and the gentiles. At the same time, the ones in Carroll County are making new threats against our people in DeWitt."

Eb frowned. "It do sound confusing."

"Well, what's happening is, they put down one disturbance, and derned if two more don't pop up somewhere's else. And the government troops are never where they're needed. For instance, Governor Boggs and his two thousand men prepared to march. They received word that the mobbers had dispersed. So he dismissed his men, headed back to Jefferson City, and the troubles started up again."

Eb shook his head. "It don't sound good."

Pratt looked at him. "It isn't. I'm not sure we can depend on the governor for anything. And yet we're not supposed to defend ourselves. What are we expected to do?"

"Blamed if I know," Rusty said.

"Well, they're not going to pick us off like sitting ducks." Pratt drank the rest of his cider and set the mug on the table.

"So what do we do?" Eb said.

Pratt stood up. "If I were you, I'd keep a close watch. Stay near home—don't go wandering too far. And if you sense danger at all—if you don't feel safe—bring your families into town. 'Specially women and children, and sick folks. And any livestock—if you can save them." He turned to leave. "Thanks for the cider."

His footsteps sounded on the wooden floor boards, loud in the empty room. Rusty and Eb stared at each other across the table.

"I reckon Gabriel was right," Rusty said as he set down his cider mug. "About the governor and all the troops."

"Except they went home." Eb drained the last of his drink.

"Which is maybe what we'd better do."

Rusty paid for the cider and they picked up the rope and the ax. Were they all in some gigantic trap, with the forces of evil closing around them? Eb had a sober, troubled expression. Rusty wondered if they would ever laugh together again.

As they went out the door, he felt his jealousy about Gabe and Bethia evaporating with the morning mist.

For once Gabriel had enjoyed a full night's sleep. He walked outside with the first light and stretched his arms toward the sky. Then he bent to touch his toes. He needed more physical exercise. If his luck held, he'd be able to eat breakfast without anyone interrupting him. Then maybe he could take a walk by the creek, possibly with Bethia.

He looked at the fields stretching to the horizon, broken only by the trees near the creek. Everything still; nothing stirring except one of the chickens. It came pecking at his boot.

"Go along," he said. "I'm not the one who feeds you."

A slight breeze fanned his face; he felt it lifting the ends of his hair. The air had a chill to it. Maybe snow before long.

Voices inside the house. Nat and Calvin both up. A woman's voice—Bethia. He felt warmed by the thought of her and turned to go back inside.

"Gabe," Nat said. "You be eating with us this morning?"

"A rare treat," he replied. "For me at least."

Sarah turned from the fireplace. "I declare, this calls for a celebration."

Gabriel shrugged. "Celebrate if you want. But I wouldn't wait too long." He caught Bethia's eye and smiled. She flushed and bent over the loaf she had just set to cool.

Calvin took his place at the table. "Sit here, lad."

Gabriel pulled out the chair beside him. The others gathered around—Bethia holding Jody, and Eb and Rusty at the far end. Nat sat at the head of the table.

"Hannah still sleeping?" Gabriel asked.

Nat looked at him. "Yes—she's a mite tired this morning."

"That's all?"

Nat shook his head. "Otherwise she's fine. Shall we pause for the blessing?"

They waited while Bethia made Jody fold his hands.Then Nat prayed over the food, and they ate. Gabriel was just sipping a cup of weak tea when the knock came at the door.

Gabriel started up to answer it. Calvin said to him, "Stay where you are and finish. They can wait."

When Sarah opened the door, a middle-aged man stood there, hat in hand. "The doctor in?"

"He's right here." On his feet by this time, Gabriel hurried toward the door. "Brother Portman, isn't it? What can I do for you?"

"It's my daughter-in-law. Been in labor most of the night. We think something's not right. We'd be most obliged if you'd come."

"Of course. We'll start right away." Gabriel looked at Bethia. "Bethia, will ye come with me?"

Sarah agreed to care for Jody that morning, and Nathaniel let them take the carriage. Gabriel fetched his knapsack, and in a short time they were in the carriage heading to the southwest.

"They just live a little ways from us," Gabriel said. "I recollect going there when we first moved to our place—it can't be more than five miles."

She fixed her gray eyes on him. "What if something's not right, like he said? What will you do?"

He thought how to answer her. "Well, my dear, I'll do the best I can. Times like this, it seems like folks always wait too long to call the doctor. They hope he can work a miracle."

Bethia frowned. Gabriel said, "Let's hope that this one can. But I want you to be just as kind and soothing as ever. Even if something should go terribly wrong." He paused. "There's another reason why I wanted you along."

She gave him a questioning look. He went on. "Hannah's time's almost here. Oh, it won't be tomorrow, and it probably won't be next week. She's carrying it high, you see, which means it'll be some time yet. I wanted you to know what to do, in case I'm late getting back to her. Like as not, what you'll see today isn't a normal birth. But hers will be. And it's important that you understand some things."

She nodded, then gave a faint smile. "All right, I reckon."

"You reckon? By the time I'm through with you, you'll be a first-rate midwife. Here—this is the turning we take."

Inside the small cabin, they found Brother and Sister Portman, and their son Ben, a thin young man who looked in the throes of labor himself.

"Bessie's in there." Sister Portman, a plump woman who made nervous, fluttery motions with her hands, followed them into the bedroom.

Bessie lay propped on a stack of pillows, a girl in her mid-teens, her eyes wide with anguish. He spoke to her as he did the examination. Yes, it was her first labor; the pains had begun early yesterday. Finally he straightened up.

"It looks to me like you're just not ready yet. Sometimes a first labor can be slow. So what we're going to do—we're going to get you up and walking around. That should bring on some good contractions." He turned to the older Sister Portman. "If you've got some weak tea or broth, let's get some nourishment into her. Up you get, now."

Bethia began to walk with Bessie, holding her arm and talking to her. Gabriel said to Sister Portman, "Tell me, do twins run in the family?"

"Twins!" The mother-in-law's eyes widened. "Are you saying—"

"Don't be surprised," he told her. "I'm thinking I felt two heads."

Most of the day they walked Bessie up and down in front of the cabin and gave her broth and tea. In the late afternoon they put her on the bed to rest. Sister Portman sat with her while Gabriel and Bethia gathered around the table for a bit of bread and cheese. Brother Portman sliced bread and handed it around.

"They say the mobbers bark like dogs," Ben Portman said. "Just before they strike, there's all this barking. Signaling each other, I reckon."

Gabriel nodded, his mouth full of bread. He took a drink of water. Ben's father said, "And the way they take down cabins, is they get one or two lariats looped around a ridgepole. They just get the horses to lean into the ropes a little, and that roof swings open with a crack. Some folks, that's the first warning they hear."

Gabriel said, "I'm told a lot of them wear the same get-up—a coat made of a white blanket, and a leather belt with a scabbard attached to it. Then they stick a bowie knife in that. If they blacken their faces real good, they can do all the mischief they want, and no one can identify 'em."

Bethia looked distressed. He hastened to say, "But all that's a long way from here, I'm sure."

The father and son were talking again, but Gabriel wasn't listening. His mind was racing. With luck, the child—or children—would make an appearance well before candlelight, so he would have a clear view of what was happening. Good to have Bethia here, with her gentle, soothing presence. What's more, he knew her manner was genuine; she had one of the most compassionate natures he'd ever known. A truly loving heart. He could no longer hold back. Time he asked her to be his wife. Only, how did one do it? He could say, "Bethia, you and I make a right fine team." Too obvious. But maybe direct was better. He should just tell her he loved her and ask her to marry him. But what if she said no?

He decided to ask on the very last leg of their journey home. That way, if she refused him outright, they wouldn't have far to go before they went their separate ways. As he planned it out in his mind, she looked at him from across the table and smiled. Startled, he almost dropped the last of his bread. Suddenly a cry came from the next room. "Brother Gabriel!"

He sprang to his feet and hurried into the room with the others behind him. Sister Portman's lip quivered as she wrung her hands. "She's—she's starting to really push."

In an instant Gabriel's mind made the leap from friend to skilled physician. To Sister Portman he said, "We're going to need hot water. You'd best set some to boil."

She left, making little whimpering noises. Gabriel glanced at the two male Portmans. Ben looked pale as death. Did he require medical help as well? "Brother Portman," Gabriel said. "Get your son out of here—take him for a long walk. Somewhere out of earshot. If you've got any whiskey, give him a good snort."

Brother Portman nodded. "Come on, Ben. You heard the man."

The first child, a boy, was born just before candlelight. Sister Portman lit the candles, then took the child from Bethia. The twin, a girl, followed some moments later. Gabriel left the women to attend to the babies while he stayed with the mother. He felt tired, dead on his feet, relieved that his training had brought him through one more time.

"Come on, Bessie. You've done wonderfully. Push just once more. We want to make sure there's nothing left."

By this time the male portion of the family had returned. Gabriel drew a deep breath. "Well, Ben—meet your family."

Ben looked with amazement at the tiny bundles. "Derned if there ain't two of 'em."

Well past candlelight. In the excitement of bathing the babies and putting them to nurse for the first time, it seemed half the night had gone. Gabriel, drained of energy, knew he had to rest before they started home.

"Sister Portman, if you have a spare place to lie down, we'd be much obliged. In fact, I think it best if we stay the night."

She looked troubled as she fluttered her hands. "We've only the one spare room, doctor. But you're more than welcome to it."

"We'll take it." He looked at Bethia. "Time for us to get some rest."

Bethia looked exhausted in the half-light, with dark hollows under her eyes. "But—"

"Come on. It's all right." He carried one of the candles into the room. The flickering light revealed a small bed and a wooden chair with a cushion. "This will do. You take the bed, and I'll take the cushion and a blanket."

"Gabriel, we can't."

"What is it?" He looked into her startled eyes. "You're safe here—you've nothing to fear from me. I'll not come near you. And—and I do this all the time. They give me a place to sleep, and believe me, I sleep."

"Even with—with strange women in the same room?"

He managed to laugh. "Well—no women that I can recall. You're the first. But it's better this way than trying to go home in the dark. Brother Portman saw to the horses—everything's taken care of."

A determined look swept over her face. "You're forgetting about my reputation. We're not married—we're not even betrothed. And you expect us—"

"Do you want to sew me into a sack? Would that ease your mind?"

"No. I only think—"

It wasn't supposed to happen this way. What should he say? Something like, "Bethia, I'm very tired, and I don't need any of this nonsense."

No. Think, he begged himself. The words formed before he could stop them. "Bethia—I've not been much for courting you. Not enough time, for one thing. But I've loved you—I reckon, since I first saw you. And just lately, I've been convinced that we belong together. What I'm trying to say is—if you'd consent to be my wife, I'd be the happiest man in three counties. I'll make it up to you, I promise—all this neglect."

She blinked, then swallowed. I sprang it on her too sudden-like, he thought. She should think about it and take her time. He opened his mouth to tell her. She looked at him with a dazed expression, then said, "I will, Gabriel."

"You will?"

"Be your wife."

"Thank you." Not knowing what else to do, he hugged her and kissed her on the ear. They held each other wordlessly while the candle sputtered. After a moment he said, "Well, that's settled. You'd best get some sleep now. They may want us later, if the babies have trouble."

She climbed into the bed. He felt her eyes on him as he took the cushion from the chair. He stretched out on the floor and pulled the blanket over him. "All right, my dear. I'm blowing out the candle."

"But won't you get cold?"

He gave a little laugh. "Not with you in the room. *Bon nuit.*" Within minutes he fell asleep.

Bethia lay trembling under the covers. How could he sleep so easily, after what he'd just said? Then she thought about what he'd done—helped Bessie deliver twins after she'd labored for two days. He'd earned his rest.

Joy flooded her mind; the pain of loving him had fled. She felt tiredness creeping over her like a dark mist. As she sank into slumber, she thought she heard little sounds—the rise and fall of his breathing, one of the twins crying. Hoof beats on the ground outside, a horse neighing, footsteps and men's voices. She even imagined that the door opened and a voice said, "Gabriel?" More footsteps.

A door closing. She sat upright. Had she dreamed it? She could no longer hear any sounds from Gabriel. She waited, then reached down to feel where he was lying. She felt the cushion, the length of blanket. He wasn't there.

She wondered what to do. Should she get up too? The rest of the house lay silent, still as death. Perhaps Gabriel was still there, and she'd only imagined he was gone. She fell into a trancelike sleep in which she thought she was awake but she couldn't move. Time passing. How much? Suddenly outside, more hoof beats, men's voices. A light by the window. Mobbers? Footsteps inside, then the door to the room opening.

"Gabriel?" she asked.

"Yes—I'm back."

"Where—where did you go?"

"I was called to a farmhouse just up the road—two young lads got in trouble up north of the creek. The youngest looked about fourteen. The mobbers tied 'em to trees and whipped them till their backs were raw. Then they just left 'em tied there. They might've died if someone hadn't found 'em. I never saw anyone beaten so bad. It's like the ones that did it aren't even human."

"Will they be all right?" she asked.

"Hope so. I did the best I could for 'em."

"How'd they know you were here?"

"Brother Portman took Ben over there in the afternoon. They were hopin' I hadn't left yet." He gave a deep sigh. "How could they do this to young boys—hardly more than children? Punished for the crime of being Mormon. Bethia, I never thought to see such times."

She made a sympathetic little noise in her throat, not knowing what to say. He sighed again. "Best we get some rest."

She closed her eyes and prepared to sink into sleep. Gabriel here; both of them safe now. As the darkness closed around her, she thought she heard a faint barking.

Dogs barking. Nathaniel, lying with his hand across Hannah's belly, stirs awake. Something not right. He strains to hear. Wind rushing, trees rustling by the creek. Rain. A cascade of droplets hitting the roof. Suddenly Nell leaps to her feet and barks—once, twice. "Hush, girl," he says.

"What is it?" Hannah asks.

"I don't know. Some wild creature, I reckon." He stands. Then he hears it. The cracking sound of the roof tearing apart.

"Hannah. Get up and get dressed." He fumbles in the dark, pulls on his trousers, reaches for his boots. Outside, more noises. A horse neighing, men shouting. A light flickering. Sounds around the stable. *The animals.* His heart sinks. Smoke. Hard to breathe. He rushes out into the main room. Looks at the fireplace. Logs smoldering. A reddish glow outside.

"Fire!" He begins screaming names. "Rusty! Eb! Get out here! Calvin!" He races to Jody's crib, in Bethia's room. He lifts the boy out, covers him with a blanket. "Hannah! Leave everything! Get outside!"

Holding Jody with one hand, he throws open the front door. The Crawford cabin is in flames. Dark figures race across the yard. He prays that two of them are Owen and Polly Crawford.

Hannah, swathed in blankets, moves at his side. Calvin rushes to join them with Sarah close behind.

"Eb went out the back way!" Rusty yells. "The dad-blamed stable's on fire!"

Keep your head. Nat leads the women away from the houses, toward the creek. The ground is wet; a cold drizzle is falling. Polly and Owen are there with soot-smeared faces.

"Owen, stay with the women. Here." He hands Jody to Sarah. "Take 'em down by the creek. Wait in the trees till we come for you. You can bet those mobbers aren't far away. Come on, Rusty. Calvin."

Grabbing blankets. Rushing for the stable. They flail at the flames and scoop water from the horse trough. All the chickens have gone.

"I'd git, too," Eb says. He has led out Freedom and the Crawfords' piebald horse.

"Where's Gabriel?" Calvin's breath rasps in his throat.

"Still away." Eb is breathing hard. "Sometimes he stays, when folks is really sick."

"And Bethia's with him." Calvin's face is damp, glistening in the red glow.

"Don't worry about them—they be safer than us right now," Nat says. "The fire's all on this side. I'll get the oxen. Rusty, you take those horses and get 'em away from the fire. Eb, I need you to bring out the wagon, and all the gear you can find. Calvin, get the small wagon."

"Owen's cabin's done for," Calvin says.

"Forget about that!" Nat is shouting now. A shower of sparks as the rain hits the flames. "There's not much time! Hurry!"

Mid-morning. As Gabriel harnessed the team, his thoughts tumbled over each other like young puppies. Safe to leave the twins? One of them, the girl, so very small. But both vigorous; with good care, they might have a chance. They'd lasted the night. He tried to remember—had he told the parents all they needed to know? Common-sense things like keeping the babies warm, the mother well-rested. At any rate, if they needed him, he was just down the road.

The boys, now. He'd look in on them before he left. A few days rest, and they should be all right. Physically. What scars remain in the mind when children are beaten for their religious beliefs?

A presence at his side. Bethia. He smiled and put his hand on her shoulder. "Are you ready, *ma chèrie*?"

"Yes."

"Then so are we. Up you go." He helped her up into the front seat. Then he climbed up beside her. With the reins in his left hand, he put his right arm around her. She turned toward him, and he kissed her on the lips.

"Gabriel, they'll see."

"No, they won't." Breathing fast. His heart rate increasing. He kissed her again. "They're all busy with the twins. Besides, what do you care?"

"They don't know we're betrothed."

He chuckled. "I should tell them? It'd only confuse them. Besides, we'll be married soon—I reckon Brother Nat'll perform the ceremony tonight, if we ask him."

"Tonight?" She looked at him wide-eyed.

"Or tomorrow. Next week. Whenever you say the word."

She smiled, but her lip quivered as if she were uncertain. "I'd like to have a nice wedding, with a—a pretty dress, and Hannah for a matron of honor."

"Then you shall, and a celebration as well, with cake and cider." Warmed by the sun, Gabriel felt affable, in an expansive mood. He began to speak of the spot by the creek where they would build a cabin. "Nat will help—in fact, he'll supervise. With Calvin and Eb and Owen all working, we can git it raised before the snow starts flying."

She listened as if hypnotized, then said, "By the way, where are we going?"

He laughed. "I want to look in on those youngsters I saw last night. Did you think I was abducting you?" Still laughing, he turned the horse toward a stand of trees and a cluster of small log houses.

After the brief visit, they trotted to the northwest over the road made soft by the night's rain. She looked at him, her lovely brows drawing together, and he sensed the sobering effect of what they'd just seen. He kissed her on the forehead. "Don't fret. The boys'll heal up just fine."

"I was thinking of the twins too. So tiny. Do you reckon they'll make it?"

He looked off into the distance. "I don't know. We did the best we could for 'em. But not everything works out the way we'd like."

Her sensitivity. He hadn't figured on that. He felt touched, yet troubled too. "I think it's time to tell you about my friend Dr. Beauchamps. You might say he gave me the first medical training I ever had."

He began to describe the doctor, his house full of books, the wise way he had of acquiring and dispensing knowledge without offending the superstitious people he tried to serve. As Gabriel spoke, the road and carriage seemed to melt away, and he saw Gallipolis on the night he decided to leave. The sights and sounds came back to him, the wind rising, the waves of the great river lapping the shore. His way lighted by the Hunter's Moon, he came to the place where he'd found Eb in the water.

"You've told me that before," Bethia said.

"But I haven't told you about the doctor. After I brought Eb to him, he cautioned me. If I wanted to do this kind of work, he said, it was best not to get too emotionally involved. That way, I could keep a clear head, and could help them better."

Bethia thought a moment. "I don't see how that's possible. How can you not care? In fact, you told me you did."

The logic of women. "Yes; I do care. Perhaps more than I should. But I try to remain detached—I feel I'm doing folks a disservice if I don't."

"But—"

"I'm just telling you that all we can do is our best. Sometimes our best isn't good enough. But if we know we gave the best we had, then we're not left feeling as if we've failed entirely. The next time, we might make all the difference in the world—the difference between life and death."

Slowly Bethia nodded. How lovely she is, he thought. Not strikingly beautiful, like Hannah, but shining with a quiet gentleness. Joy flooded his mind at the realization that he had her to himself at last. Accepting him, after he'd agonized about how to ask her. He leaned over and gave her a long, lingering kiss. His heart was racing; he felt lightheaded, as if he were seeing distant objects through a mist. She nestled against him. Over the next rise was home. He wanted to prolong their journey, to kiss her again and again. He drew the horses to a stop and removed the comb from her hair. She shook her head, and the hair cascaded down over her shoulders. She made no protest as he buried his face in it. He kissed her neck, marveling that Gabriel the skeptic had come under the power of another person at last.

He found himself wondering what else she would let him do. He tried to dismiss the thought. Best they be married as soon as possible. He clicked to the horses and bent to give her one more kiss.

Something not right. A scorched smell. He straightened up. Had Sarah burned the stew again? He listened. No sounds—no horses neighing, no chickens. No human voices. He tightened his arm around her shoulders and looked at her. She returned his look. "What is it?"

"Hush. Don't make a sound." He guided the team to the crest of the hill and stopped. She followed his glance, then drew in her breath.

The main house stood roofless, like a grotesque caricature of itself. The remains of the roof lay in a heap beside it. Debris littered the ground, bits of planks and splintered wood. Gabriel felt a sick flutter in his stomach; he urged the horses forward, then reined them in as he saw the stable.

Half of the stable had collapsed, the wood blackened and shapeless. Beyond the main house to the east, the Crawford cabin lay in ruins. The smell of damp, charred wood was everywhere. Bethia cried out and began to sob.

"Stop that," he told her. The side of his nature that dealt with medical emergencies took charge. In a whisper: "We must be as brave now as we've ever been. I know you can do it. Don't make a sound."

She looked at him, her face tear-stained, then nodded. His mind was racing. What if they were the only ones left? What to do? How to protect her, to shield her from what they might find? He spoke firmly, his voice low. "Bethia, I want you to take the carriage down to the creek. Tie up the horses and hide in that little copse of trees. You know the place. Stay there till I come for you."

She nodded again, her breath coming in short bursts. He kissed her. "If anything should happen to me, you wait till things are safe. Then you head for town. If you have to walk, do it."

"I'll wait for you," she said.

"You'll do as I say. If the ones that did this are still around and they attack me, you stay hidden. When they're gone, you get into town. I'll meet you there." He put the reins in her hand and gestured toward the creek. Then he jumped to the ground.

He waited until she'd driven the horses past the main house. Then he entered, stepping over the fallen back door. He hurried from room to room, checking beds, glancing everywhere. Jody gone. No sign of Eb or Hannah. No bodies anywhere. Nothing but damp blankets and clothes. He opened the front door, convinced that none of his household was still here.

The stable. He rushed around to the back and stumbled across the yard. He slowed his pace when he reached the stable. Freedom gone, both oxen and Owen's horse gone. Then he realized the wagons were gone too. Somehow the family had made it out with the livestock and wagons. Unless the mobbers had beaten them to it.

He moved among bales of hay, stepping over dead chickens. Just off to the side lay Bethia's favorite barn cat, a gray tabby. He turned it over with his foot. Already stiff. One side of its body caked with blood.

She didn't need to know. Good thinking, not to keep her with him.

He walked close to the smoldering ruin where the Crawford's cabin had been. No sign of life. He hurried down to the bower where Bethia was waiting.

"There's no one left here," he said. "All the people and the large animals got away."

"What about the chickens?"

"They're all gone somewhere. There's nothing left alive in there."

She nodded then. "Gabriel, I've been hearing something. There, in the bushes. Like some animal."

He paused; were they still in danger? Then he took her hand and led her toward the carriage. "Best we go into town. Most like, we'll find the others there."

He handed her up into the front seat. As he started around to the other side, he heard a noise. He stiffened. A series of short whines.

"Stay here." He handed her the reins. Then he moved toward the clump of bushes. A trap? Someone in ambush, waiting? He parted the bushes and saw a small, dark shape. The dog Nell. No longer black and white, but mud-colored.

"Here, girl." He snapped his fingers.

She whined and started toward him on three legs. She held up her right front paw and made little squeaks.

"Another patient. Bethia, there's a towel behind the front seat. Throw it to me, if you will."

He took the towel and started to wipe the mud from the dog's fur. When he reached to examine the paw, she growled and bared her teeth. He tore a piece from the towel and tied it around her jaws. Then he explored the paw with deft fingers.

"It's crushed. Like a wagon ran over it. Or maybe a horse stepped on her." He handed the dog to Bethia. "Just keep her warm in the towel. And leave the muzzle on her till we get to town."

"Will she be all right?"

"We're gonna hope she heals up just fine." He urged the horses out of the woods and toward town. As they reached the buildings around the square, a cloud covered the sun. More clouds massing to the west. Rain before long. Time to find the others, wherever they were.

"Dr. Gabriel!" The proprietor of the hotel waved from the side of the road.

Gabriel slowed the horses. "Lookin' for Nat Givens, or any of his family. You seen 'em?"

"The whole bunch of 'em's down in one of them old cabins, jest south of the Rigdon place. Came in early this morning."

"Thank God," Gabriel said. "I was hopin' for the best. I found one cabin burned, the other without a roof."

"So they said. They all look mighty sick, coughin' and a'sneezin'. Like they could use a doctor."

Drops of rain were falling when Gabriel and Bethia finally found the cabin. He tied up the horses and took the dog in his arms. The door flew open, and the family rushed out. They stood embracing each other in the rain, weeping.

"Here." Gabriel handed the dog to Nathaniel. "You forgot this."

Later, when they all crowded inside, Gabriel took Bethia's hand and announced their betrothal. No one seemed too surprised. Nat made some remark about his excellent sense of timing. Gabriel, looking around, wondered where they were all going to sleep.

"I was aimin' to go back and see if we could find some bedding," Nat said.

"I should've grabbed what I could," Gabriel said. "My main thought was to find you."

"I reckon everyone out there's in danger, after what happened to us," Eb said.

Gabriel told them about the newborn twins. "They can't survive a trip like that in the middle of the night, when it's cold and dark and all."

"Don't seem like they could." Nat thought a moment. "The rain's letting up some. We'd best go bring 'em in now. On the way, we'll stop and salvage what we can."

Soon Eb and Nat had the oxen hitched to the wagon, and Gabriel followed behind them in the carriage as they plodded eastward.

7

WHAT WOULDN'T HE GIVE? Half of next year's harvest if he didn't have to be out here in the town square with the others. Nathaniel glanced skyward, at the clouds gathering in the west. A bite in the wind. Snow before long. He bent to tighten the saddle on the bay horse Jeb and wondered how in the world he had got himself into this present mess. An avowed pacifist, riding with an armed force to defend a city.

His fault. He should've seen it coming. He shook his head and sighed. First, the insistence on following the Law of Consecration, where all surplus property was to be consecrated—or given—to the Church. After that, the people were expected to give one-tenth of their yearly increase as a tithe, each one deciding for himself how much was surplus. Then, the dietary restrictions—no tea, coffee, or anything with alcohol in it. In addition, the talk of a loyalty oath, with threat of punishment if it were not signed. And now, after losing his home, with his wife expecting a child at any moment and his family members all crowded into one tiny cabin, this final blow. The news that any man who did not ride to the defense of Diahman was to be treated like a dissenter, and cast out.

What to do now? He recalled the stories of men willing to die for their beliefs rather than engage in warfare. He'd always imagined he was such a one. Then he thought of Hannah and Jody, and the unborn child. He could not risk their lives for his principles. That a Christian religion should lead him to such an impasse.

"Ready, Nat?" Calvin, astride Jenny the bay mare, reined up beside him.

"I reckon." He hoped the despair didn't show in his voice. Close by were Eb on Freedom and Rusty riding the piebald horse Spot. Poor Spot. Too old for such an undertaking. And Rusty much too young. Nat put his foot in the stirrup and mounted. Jeb snorted and stamped his foot.

"You'd rather pull the carriage, wouldn't you?" Nat patted the horse's neck.

"We're movin' out," Calvin said.

Nat and Calvin rode together through the northern part of town. Everywhere, between the tiny makeshift cabins, huddled tents and covered wagons. Along with the influx of Kirtland Saints, the families from the DeWitt settlement had all come in. Calvin looked at Nat and shook his head. They'd heard stories of the siege at DeWitt, where the Mormons were not even allowed to venture outside for food or other supplies. Some had butchered the Missourians' stock, to keep from starving. After the surrender, Joseph Smith himself had led the refugees from DeWitt to Far West.

"Sure is a heap of folks here," Calvin said. They reined in their horses. An old man trudged by with an armful of kindling. His face had a vacant, bewildered look. Nat had seen the same expression on Owen Crawford, whom they'd left in the cabin with the women. Worried about Owen. Not the same since the fire. Calvin spoke again. "Lucky we're in a cabin."

"I reckon. Better for Hannah and Jody."

Calvin paused, then gave a little cough. "I know you don't hanker to see any fightin'. I'm right sorry to be ridin' myself."

"Don't look like there's anything we coulda done. Maybe gone off by ourselves while there was a chance."

Calvin grunted. "I don't figure there was much chance to speak of. We just be hated everywhere."

"That's not so," Nat said. "Gabriel, now—he gets along with most everybody. Gentiles, soldiers—even the worst folks you care to think about."

"And drinks liquor with 'em too, from what I hear."

Nat sighed. "I wonder where he is now."

"Better not to ask. Just trust him. He's one of the smartest fellers I ever knew."

They rode in silence. The horses' hooves made a steady pounding on the gravel. Nat remembered the same noise of hooves as Alexander

Doniphan and his sixty armed men rode through Far West two days earlier. That was the day Gabriel had come to him and said, "Nat, I won't be riding with you to Diahman. Not enough horses, for one thing."

"But, how will you—"

"I aim to disappear for a while. No one will know I'm gone, or where I am. But I'll be keeping a close eye on that cabin. I'll be there in a flash if Hannah needs me, and I reckon Owen could use some help too. And I have other patients to look out for. I can't just desert them."

Nat had no inclination to argue. "Take care of yourself, son."

"You, too."

What was he up to? Simply avoiding trouble with the authorities? No call to feel uneasy. Gabe had come through escapades before without a scratch. But now he had the remainder of their little group in his charge. Hannah's time not far off. What if he didn't get there when she needed him? What help could she expect from a bunch of women, a child, and Owen, who sat huddled in a corner looking dazed?

Calvin spoke again. "Don't fret about the family. We left 'em in God's care, and that's how we have to look at it. We ride up there, join Doniphan and make a show of force. Then we come back and rebuild."

Nat sighed. "I'm not so sure."

"Don't you remember what Eb told us? He caught them burning the stable, and they yelled, 'These ain't Mormons! They own slaves!' Then they all ran off. That's why the stable was still standing."

Nat turned to look at him. "So? We're supposed to pretend he's a slave, and then they'll let us alone? I can't live such a lie."

Calvin rolled his eyes and gave a little shrug, then reined in and dropped back to ride beside Eb and Rusty. Nat rode ahead. As he shifted his weight in the saddle, he saw the tiny white flakes on the horse's neck. Snow.

It became a swirling blizzard. They learned later that eighteen inches of snow had fallen in thirty-six hours, and that people on both sides of the conflict had hoped it would put a halt to any hostilities and send everyone back home. But the Mormon force waited out the storm.

"Come on, boys!" their leader said. "Let's have a snowball fight!"

They pelted each other with snow until Nathaniel almost forgot what their true mission was. Then, as they rode out from Diahman to pacify the outlying area, Rusty's horse went lame. The others clustered around.

Rusty shook his head. "It ain't packed snow. I checked that, first thing."

"Well, don't get back on 'em," Nat said. "He's old, for one thing. Here." He swung down from the saddle and handed Jeb's reins to Rusty. "You ride this'n. I'll take Spot back to town."

He held the reins of the injured horse and waited as the others filed past. He could hear the hooves crunching in the snow. A good horse, Jeb. He could even take care of Rusty, if Rusty treated him right. Nat tried to breathe a prayer for the safety of them all, but his mind was in such a turmoil he could hardly form the words. Things so muddled. Would he ever see Hannah and Jody again?

He led Spot to a place where he could examine the left front hoof. A loose shoe. He found the blacksmith shop, but the blacksmith was out. Nat led the horse to the livery stable. "No battles for us today." Then he sat waiting in the local store. Just before it got dark, he found a place to stay the night.

The blacksmith returned the next afternoon, a small, heavy-set man. From him, Nat heard the first rumors from outside town.

"I hear tell our troops marched on Gallatin, and them Missourians was so scared they just cut their horses' reins and left 'em hangin' on the fence posts. There warn't no one left, 'cept three that didn't ride fast enough."

"So what happened then?" Nat asked.

"The word is, they looted the place. They piled the clothes and bedding and such on the street and loaded it on their horses. Then they set fire to the town. My brother says he could see the smoke rising when he stood on Tower Hill."

"And the Mormon force?"

"Our boys? None of them injured, so I hear. No one to oppose them. Far as I kin tell, they pillaged that whole town."

Feeling sick to his stomach, Nat paid the blacksmith. He reached for the reins and led the horse out into the frosty air. What to do now? Unwise to ride out alone. He decided to wait around the store for more news.

He didn't have to wait long. Everyone who came in had a new incident to report. Raids on Millport. Reports of a vigilante army massing at Grindstone Forks. The Mormon force that rode to Clinton County found no army gathering, but they plundered and burned all the way, driving Daveiss citizens out of their homes. They carried plunder from the raids back to the bishop's storehouse at Diahman.

"That's consecrated goods," someone said.

Nat sighed. "It sure sounds like out-and-out stealing to me."

"What's the matter with you, brother? You know what they done to us. They brung it on themselves."

"You hear 'bout Sister Smith?" an older man said.

"Which one?" a second one asked.

"Why, Sister Agnes Smith. The prophet's brother's wife. There she was, alone in her cabin with her two little children, and derned if the raiders didn't ride up and make her get out. Then they burned her home. She had to carry a child in each arm and walk three miles in the night, and I have to tell you it warn't the warmest day we ever seen. If that warn't enough, she had to wade across the river to reach where our soldiers was camped. When they finally found her, I reckon she was almost froze."

"If that don't beat all," the second man said.

The old one raised his cider glass. "She says the raiders wuz burning their own homes, to make it look like we done it."

Nat sat in silence. Had he made the right move? Not obligated to fight this particular battle. But what about Rusty? Should he have ordered Rusty back to town with Spot, and ridden with the others? Like as not, Rusty wouldn't have taken the time to care for Owen's horse. Most likely would've just found another horse and joined them.

The old man spoke again. "Them leaders, I hear tell they're really somethin'. Old Lyman Wight, ridin' up and down through the ranks, telling 'em it'd be only a breakfast spell to whip them Missourians."

"And David Patten. Now there's a real fire-eater. If Gallatin's a ghost town, it's thanks to him."

When Nat finally rejoined his companions, he sensed a strangeness between himself and them. Rusty fidgeted in the saddle, looking uncomfortable. Eb didn't raise his eyes. Calvin had a grim, matter-of-fact expression. Nat rode up beside him. "I reckon we can ride for home now."

Calvin didn't look at him. "That's what they said."

"Where'd they send you?"

"We rode into Gallatin," Rusty said.

Nat tried to choose his words carefully. "I take it you saw everything."

Calvin finally met his eyes. "Don't ask. You don't want to know. We did what we had to do and got out."

A light snow was falling, tiny, white flakes out of a leaden sky. Voices echoed behind them. "I figure them fellers won't be botherin' anyone for a spell."

"Let's hope they leave us in peace now."

Nat felt a growing uneasiness as they crossed the river. An ambush in the timbers? No one there—no sound but the crunch of hooves in the snow. He glanced at Calvin, but Calvin did not return the look. What indeed had they been forced to do? Nat drew a deep breath. Grief for Calvin. Grief for them all. Was he the only one who felt sorrow descending upon them with the snow?

They reached Far West late in the day. Puddles of melting snow lay everywhere. The road a sea of mud. Nat left the others and urged Spot toward the cabin where he'd left his family. What to expect? A new son or daughter? Hannah in good health? His eyes brimming, he knocked at the door.

No sound. Not even footsteps. He threw open the door. Hannah pushed herself to a sitting position from the pile of blankets. Jody stirred beside her. Bethia and Sarah got up from the makeshift table.

"Brother Nat!" Owen's voice cracked; he sat in a corner of the room. The others rushed to embrace him—Hannah bigger than ever, Jody hugging his knees. Nat gave Bethia a brief hug. "But where's Gabriel?"

Sarah sniffed. "He be sleepin' in the wagon. Says there's too many women in here."

"He stops by every day," Bethia said. "He stays around the hotel. That's where the sick folks go to find him."

"Like as not, that's where he is," Sarah said.

Nathaniel looked around. "It's mighty quiet. I didn't reckon anyone was home."

Sarah looked at him. "You'd be quiet too, if'n you was a bunch of women and the mobbers be everywhere."

Mobbers here? He was about to say how they'd driven the Gentiles out of Daveiss County. Heavy footsteps sounded behind him, horses neighing. Calvin pushed into the room. He hurried to embrace Sarah. "Eb and Rusty be seeing to the horses. I reckon both those boys'll sleep in the wagon with Gabe."

Later that night, Rusty pounded on the door. "You heard the latest?"

Nat blinked in the flickering light of the lantern. "What? And stop swinging that thing."

"There's been a lot of mob activity down south of here. Word is, they captured three of our men—accused 'em of being spies. They be planning to execute 'em, come morning."

Calvin shook his head. "Things sure is stirred up."

Rusty went on. "A bunch of our soldiers are ridin' out to rescue 'em. Gabe took one of our horses and went to join 'em."

"What horse? Not old Spot?" Nat heard Jody and Hannah stirring behind him.

"Freedom. Eb said that one had plenty of spunk left."

Rusty hurried away. They could hear the bugle sounding, the beating of the signal drum. Through the haze of weariness, Nat wondered—should he be out there? He'd done his share. Besides, with Gabriel gone, his family needed him here. He sighed. *Sick of war.* He crept close to Hannah and put an arm around Jody. As he sank into sleep, he felt the dog Nell licking his foot.

Just past noon. Gabriel felt numb, chilled to the bone. Shivering, he rode Freedom into the stable and pulled him to a halt. Shadowy figures rushed to meet him. Eb took the horse's reins. Rusty reached to help him dismount.

"I'm all right." The sound of his own voice. Hollow, without inflection—as if the ability to express emotions had long since fled.

"You don't have to say nothin'." Eb led the horse to an empty stall.

"The scouts came in with the news," Rusty said. "About Patten being wounded and all. And the others."

Eb's voice. "I reckon you be wantin' to eat."

"Not hungry."

Eb again. "Nat's back. Doncha want to see him? He's at the cabin with Bethia and Hannah."

"I don't want to see anybody." Gabriel sat down heavily on a bench at the stable's entrance. He leaned forward, his elbows on his knees, and put his head in his hands. Out of the corner of his eye he saw Eb and Rusty exchange glances. Eb nodded to Rusty. Rusty hurried off, presumably to report the news to Nathaniel.

When had he slept last? He thought of the soft mound of hay in the corner of Freedom's stall. But he didn't dare lie down, even for a moment. Knowing if his eyes closed, he would see the battle scene play itself out again. Fifty soldiers, at the latest estimate. Fifty Mormons against a larger band of armed Missourians.

It went on in his head anyway...crossing into Ray County, dismounting, proceeding on foot to the Gentile encampment. A sentry ordering them to stop, then firing into their ranks. Alerted, the enemy taking up their positions along the river, well-hidden, the Mormons left out in the open. Daybreak, and their captain Apostle Patten leading the charge. Swords drawn. Cries of "God and Liberty!" The confusion, horses neighing, men fleeing. Missourians shouting "We are brethren!" as they tried to escape.

Then the regrouping, reloading. Gathering up the wounded, the dying. Nine of their company wounded, David Patten among them. Begging to be left on the road, the agony of the return journey too much for him. Bearing the fallen captain to the Winchester house, four miles south of Far West.

A sound in the doorway; someone there. Gabriel raised his head. Nathaniel stood looking at him. Gabriel had the feeling that the depth of compassion in Nat's expression was more than he deserved or was worth. He blinked, wondering if he was seeing clearly.

Nat glanced at Rusty and Eb. Eb nudged Rusty, and the two retreated into the shadows of the stable. Nat sat down beside him. Gabriel stirred the bits of straw with his foot. For a moment no one spoke. He began to fear that Nat would leave if he didn't say something. What to say? The words seemed to stick in his throat.

"It's a fearsome thing, combat."

"I reckon it is."

"Not just the actual fighting. It's seeing them fall. I didn't know it would be—*tiens*—so sudden, like."

"What made you join 'em?"

Gabriel raised his head and met Nathaniel's eyes. "I figured I owed 'em something, after you'd done all that ridin' up north."

"I see."

He gave a quick little gesture with his hands. "I thought it was just a matter of rescuing those prisoners. I could've done it—I could've crept through those woods without makin' a sound."

"But you don't know."

Gabriel searched his mind for a reply. After a while Nat gave a little cough. "The thing is, the simplest act leads to something else. Before you know it, there's a battle."

Gabriel gestured again. "And—and we couldn't do anything for the wounded. Captain Fearnought is dying. They had a surgeon waiting for him, but he..." His voice trailed off.

"A very brave man. Impulsive, they say. Impetuous. But brave."

Gabriel shrugged. "Once they started firing on us, there wasn't much else he could've done."

"You rescued the captives?"

"Yes. But one of 'em's wounded. I don't think he's gonna make it. I—I hope I never have to see the like again."

Nat sighed. "Well, now you know how I feel. And I don't have to witness it to know I want no part of it." He sat staring into space for a moment. "I'm going to tell you something, and then I'll not mention it again. There's an ancient teaching, something the Hebrew prophets tried to express. It's in our religion, too. We just haven't paid much heed to it."

Gabriel began to relax; trust old Nat to throw in some scripture. "What is it? About not killing, I suppose."

"It's so simple. It's the idea that it's better to have evil done to you than to actually do it."

Gabriel leaned back against the rough boards. He looked at Nat. "That's a right powerful statement. Does it mean we're supposed to let ourselves be slaughtered, like cattle?"

"No. It means maybe we should've rethought some of the choices we made. 'Cause sometimes you can't turn back. And you have to face the consequences."

Gabriel felt his tiredness ebbing away. "Talk about consequences—not everybody agrees with what's happening. In fact, they had this one meeting while you were gone, and the subject of all the dissenters came up. Too many people packing up and leaving. Now, I know you like Brother Rigdon, and I don't aim to rile you up. But derned if he didn't declare that the last man had run away from Far West that was a going to. These were his words: 'The next man who started, he should be pursued and brought back, dead or alive.'"

Nat gave a short laugh. "Don't fret yourself about riling me. I've been upset ever since the roof came off our house."

"And Hinkle too—he even told the prophet that the course of burning houses and plundering would ruin us. He said it couldn't be hid, and would bring the force of the state upon us."

"I reckon it already has."

"I got to tell you, Nat—there's a bunch of dissenters planning to pull out as soon as they get the chance. It'll be done secretly, in the night—as quickly as possible."

Nat's face lit up. "I be thinkin' we should've done that to begin with."

"Don't get any ideas. You don't want to take Hannah anywhere right now. But from what I'm hearing, the whole state's arming against us. This trouble in Ray County's just a beginning."

Nat took a deep breath. "The thing is—most folks didn't do anything really bad. They're innocent—like Jody and Hannah."

"Tell that to the pukes, and the governor. Nat—what in tarnation do we do?"

Nat paused before he spoke. "If we can't flee, then we wait. I figure we get ready to travel—make sure the animals and wagons are in good shape. Make a place for Hannah in the wagon. One of us will have to take care of Owen's rig—I don't think he's up to it."

Gabriel's mind was racing. "You're right—it's not just us we have to help. If they invade our town, we have to figure out how to take care of a whole bunch of folks. People who can't look after themselves. Like the family with the little twins. One of the babies has already died."

"Sorry to hear that."

"She was too little. Born too soon. *Eh bien*. I guess we can go back to the cabin now. It's time I checked on Hannah."

Nat said, "There's fresh bread. I baked it myself early this morning, like I did in the Shaker days."

Gabriel got to his feet and brushed straw from his trousers. "I reckon I'm a healer, and not much else. I'll leave soldierin' to the others."

Parley Pratt frowned as he looked at the youthful interviewer.

"Now, son. Don't ask me to explain why. To begin with, it was a long time ago. I can only tell what I remember. So, what really happened? The truth is, we only killed one Missourian and wounded six others in that Crooked River skirmish, when we lost David Patten. But word got around that we'd killed thirty or forty of Bogart's men. People believed we'd destroyed that whole company. When the news reached Governor Boggs, he issued his extermination order—October 27, I believe it was. To my dying day I'll never forget those words:

'The Mormons must be treated as enemies, and must be exterminated or driven from the State if necessary for the public peace—their outrages are beyond all description.'

"Now, you notice there was nothing about criminals, or punishing crime and protecting innocence; sufficient to be called a "Mormon." I mean, a peaceable family just emigrating, or a missionary, an aged soldier of the American revolution—a widow or young wife—it didn't matter. They included all of us in this—this order of banishment or wholesale extermination.

"It's hard to believe, but our people didn't know anything about the governor's orders and the military movements which followed. Even the mail was withheld from Far West. Well, of course it was—you couldn't get anything in there. By the end of October, we were besieged. And we knew it was no longer mobbers, but Missouri militia.

"What did we do? We prepared for battle. We built up a breastwork of fence rails, planks, wagons—anything we could find. While the men worked to fortify the town, the women packed up their belongings.

"What's that? Well, of course we called for help. We sent to Diahman for reinforcements. The next day, Lyman Wight came in with a hundred and fifty soldiers.

"Now, our best hope was to negotiate some sort of compromise with the militia. We selected a group of men to send out to the militia camp. Three of them—Reed Peck, John Corrill, and W. W. Phelps, had opposed any of our military activities. The others, Arthur Morrison and Colonel George Hinkle, had led some of our forces.

"Oh, Lord help me. Dreadful news that day. Word came in—the village of Haun's Mill attacked and destroyed. Some twenty of our people killed. If that weren't bad enough, we learned that General Lucas, one of our worst persecutors in Jackson County, had assumed control of the militia.

"That's when Joseph finally realized it. Too much was against us. The men in the negotiating party went out with orders to 'beg like a dog for peace.' Lucas read them the extermination order. I have to say, they were in utter shock. They agreed to the four demands—to give up their leaders to be tried and punished, give up their property for the payment of debts incurred in the course of the hostilities, to agree to leave the state, and to surrender all arms. Those who participated in the Crooked River attack on Bogart's company were to be tried and punished, as well as those who took part in the activities in Daveiss County.

"Oh, yes, the hostages. We're coming to that. Let's see, there was Joseph Smith, Sidney Rigdon, George W. Robinson and myself. All to be delivered an hour before sundown, or the city would be destroyed.

"The negotiating party came back with the news and rushed to round up the hostages. Meanwhile, the army was marching toward the city. The bulk of the people knew nothing of the negotiations and assumed that they were being attacked. They prepared for battle, and that's when they stationed themselves along the fortifications. Brother Peck and Brother Corrill had to rush out to inform the officers that the hostages were on their way.

"Well, we approached the camp, and the general rode up and ordered his guard to surround us. They marched us into camp, and derned if the soldiers didn't set up a constant yell, like so many bloodhounds. We were placed under a strong guard. Would you believe they kept us out there in the open for hours, exposed to the cold and rain? I swear, their yelling and oaths went on all night.

"In the morning, a few other hostages joined us, among them Amasa Lyman. We learned that the officers had held a secret council during the night. They'd sentenced us to be shot at eight o'clock in the public square. Brigadier-General Doniphan came to us with the news, and said he would revolt and withdraw his whole brigade if they persisted. His words were, 'It is cold-blooded murder, and I wash my hands of it.'

"That's right—that's how it happened. His stand, and that of others, so alarmed our enemies that they dared not execute the decree. Our lives were spared—call it a miracle if you want.

"What happened then? Son, it's hard to tell it. General Lucas demanded that the Caldwell militia give up their arms. As soon as the troops who had defended the city were disarmed, they were all detained as prisoners. This left the enemy soldiers free to ravage, steal, plunder and murder without restraint. Houses were rifled, women ravished, goods taken—you name it. Cattle were shot down for sport, and I fear that some of our people fared no better.

"They marched us into Far West. The army halted in the public square. They permitted us to go with a guard to take final leave of our families before we left as prisoners for Jackson County.

"I'm sorry, child. You'll have to wait a moment. This part—it was the most trying time of all. The cold rain was pouring down. I entered our little cottage and found my wife. Picture this—she had a fever, and she was lying in bed with our three-month-old son Nathan at her breast. Our little girl, five, lay at her side. A woman in travail lay on the foot of the same bed; she'd been driven from her house in the night.

"I stepped to the bed. My wife burst into tears. What to say? I spoke a few words of comfort, telling her to try to live, for my sake and the children's. I expressed my hope that we should meet again, though years might separate us. I kissed the little ones.

"That was it. What more could I have done? I went to General Moses Wilson in tears. I stated the circumstances of my family in terms which would have moved any heart that had a spark of humanity remaining. But he only laughed.

"Similar scenes were being played out all over town. As the guard escorted me toward the troops in the square, we halted at the door of Hyrum Smith. You could hear the sobs and groans of his wife as he tried to tell her good-bye. She was then near confinement, and needed more than ever the comfort and consolation of a husband. As we returned to the wagon, we saw Sidney Rigdon taking leave of his wife and daughters. They stood at a little distance, in tears of anguish.

"Joseph Smith sat in the wagon, while his father and mother came up, overwhelmed with tears. Bless their hearts, they took each of the prisoners by the hand with a silence of grief too great for utterance.

"I can still see it in my mind. Hundreds of the brethren crowding around us as we moved away. Grabbing our hands and pressing them without speaking.

"Twelve miles brought us to Crooked River, where we camped for the night. Would you believe that General Wilson now began to treat us more kindly? He became downright sociable, and told us he knew perfectly well that from the beginning the Mormons had not been the aggressors at all. He said he knew how we had been compelled to self-defense, and how it had been construed as treason, murder and plunder.

"We arose to continue our march. Then Joseph Smith spoke to me and the other prisoners in a low, confident tone.

"'Be of good cheer, brethren; the word of the Lord came to me last night that our lives should be given us, and that whatever we may suffer during this captivity, not one of our lives should be taken.'"

8

IT WAS EARLY MORNING when Gabriel, mounted on Freedom, crossed over into Caldwell County. He guided the horse with care, watching for any activity on the road. When the sun began to flood the fields with light, he left the road and entered the woods. At last they stood on the crest of the hill overlooking the east-west route across northern Missouri. Far to the east lay Illinois; to the west sprawled the Indian lands and uncharted wilderness.

Another road, hardly more than a wagon trace, ran south, and some five miles down this road lay Far West. So near. Did he dare go any closer?

He'd been told to flee. "They're after anyone who attacked Bogart's men. Our best advice—get out of town and stay there."

Seventy-five men had left that night, he heard later. Anyone connected with the Bogart skirmish. Some dissenters. Mostly soldiers afraid of what the next day would bring. He'd ridden north, to the home of one of his patients. There he'd learned about the Mormon surrender, the order to leave or be exterminated. When he heard about the looting, he became frantic.

"I've got to get back there."

"Are ye completely daft?" Sven Peterson said. "You'll go to your death."

"But my—my betrothed is there, and my family. My brother Eb—the only brother I have now. And Rusty."

"Renounce your faith—tell 'em yer no Mormon. Others are doing it. It's the only way to stay alive."

Gabriel looked at his friend. "I—I reckon I might as well be dead if anything happened to them. Thank you for all you've done—putting me up and such. But I just can't—I can't—"

Sven's eyes watered; he turned away. "God go with you, son."

Gabriel felt the bite of the wind as he waited on the hilltop. He pulled his jacket up around his ears. More snow before long. He kept his eyes on the rutted road that led south. If his people were leaving, they would most certainly come up that way. Although it was still early for a wagon to be loaded up and moving.

Sounds in the distance. The clatter of hooves. Two men on horseback riding up from the south. He could tell by the guns slung over their shoulders that they were not his people. He dismounted and led the horse behind a thicket of trees.

Had they seen him? He reached to touch his only weapon, a knife at his belt. They turned onto the main road and kept going. He let out his breath in a sigh. This was no good. He'd never get into town at this rate. Better he should pretend to be an enemy soldier and swagger into town than wait any longer. No; that would get him killed for sure.

What was that? A dark object on the road. He strained to make it out. A small wagon, hardly more than a cart, pulled by two mismatched horses, a large work horse and a smaller sorrel. He watched as they drew closer. He could see the driver of the team, an older man about the age of Calvin. The man sat hunched up, thinner than Calvin; he wore an old grayish jacket and his body shook with coughing. Better he'd stayed in bed, Gabriel thought. Then he saw the two women.

One looked young and thin, a girl not yet in her teens. The other—ah, of an age to be interesting. He wondered if she were the man's wife and the young one their child. At any rate, there was nothing to fear from them.

He stood, watching idly. Just as they made the turn onto the east-west road, the man clutched his chest. He stood up in the wagon, then pitched back in the seat. He fell to the ground. Gabriel heard the young woman cry out, "Father!"

Gabriel tied Freedom's reins to the nearest sturdy branch. Then he ran down the hill on foot, jumping over boulders. He crashed through the brush at the bottom of the hill. Loose stones clattered down after him. When he reached the wagon, the young woman was bending over her father. The girl in the back of the wagon was sobbing like a little child.

Gabriel got down on one knee. The young woman looked up, her eyes wide with surprise and fright. He spoke quickly.

"Don't be afraid. I'm from Far West, like you. And I'm a doctor."

She caught her breath. Gabriel blinked, transfixed by her eyes; they were blue, the color of the sky on a cloudless day. *Strange.* He could not remember ever meeting her before, yet her face looked familiar. It was a strong face, with full lips and arching eyebrows. The kind of face that, once seen, one never forgets.

"I know who you are," she said. "You're Dr. Gabriel. My father—he hasn't been well. He's had a—a misery in his chest, a bad cold."

Gabriel checked the man for a heartbeat, listened to the labored breathing. He glanced up briefly and met her eyes. "You may know me, but you must tell me your name."

"Corey."

"Corey? And your father here?"

"Jubal. Jubal Langdon."

Gabriel felt for any injuries from the fall. "Well, now, Corey. I think he's coming out of it. But he's too sick to be traveling."

"I know, sir. If it weren't for my sister, we would've tried to stay. But the mobbers are running everywhere—stealing food, livestock, taking anything they see. Abusing women. We were so afraid for her—see, she sometimes runs outside and I have to hunt for her. If the wrong person found her...We—we thought it was best to leave as quick as we could."

Gabriel shook his hair out of his eyes. "I see. Then you did right."

Mr. Langdon stirred; he made an effort to get up. Gabriel helped to lift him. A wail sounded from the wagon.

"I'd better see to her." Corey stood up and climbed into the wagon.

Brother Langdon struggled to his feet. His bushy white eyebrows had flecks of moisture in them, like dew. His eyes, blue like Corey's, squinted in the light. "I musta plumb passed out."

"A fierce cold can do that," Gabriel said. "What you need most is rest."

"I'll drink to that."

"How far do you plan to go today?"

Brother Langdon fished a tattered handkerchief from his pocket and blew his nose. "We have relatives t'other side of Livingston County." His voice broke into a series of coughs.

"Don't talk any more," Gabriel said.

Corey spoke from the wagon. "It's my aunt, doctor. My mother's sister. My mother's dead now, but my aunt married a man named Sidwell. They have a farm a day's journey from here."

Jubal Langdon climbed into the front seat. He brushed a hand over his white mustache. "I reckon I can still drive."

Corey was holding her sister, rocking her back and forth and murmuring soft words to her. Gabriel looked at them. "What's your sister's name?"

Corey brushed the hair back from the girl's forehead. "Casey. It's really Katie Cassandra. K. C."

"Can she speak?"

"No," Corey said. "She never could. Sometimes she makes a noise—it sounds like singing. And she cries."

He looked away, touched. "I—I see." He straightened up. "Things must be very bad in Far West. Do you know anything about my people—Nat Givens and his family?"

Corey looked at him with her straightforward expression. "Nat and Calvin Manning are both in jail."

"Jail?"

"They arrested a bunch of the men and took them away."

"By thunder!" Gabriel shook his head. "They hadn't done anything."

"It doesn't matter. They was Mormons, some of the leading men."

Gabriel's mind was racing. "How about the women? Hannah and them."

"The women are all afeard to go outside."

"Hannah's expecting a child. Do you know if it's born yet?"

"Not when we left. I think we woulda heard, somehow. But—I think I should tell you—" She flashing him a knowing glance. "Bethia is just fine."

She knew then—he was an engaged man. He smiled. "I thank you for that piece of news. I should get over to them as soon as possible."

"We won't keep you, then, doctor," Jubal said. "Thanks for your help."

"One thing—" Gabriel put a hand on the side of the wagon. "Can you drive a team, Corey?"

"I reckon I can if I have to."

"I was going to suggest that your father rest in the back of the wagon, with Casey here. Make him a place to lie down, with blankets. Then you can drive if he should feel faint again."

"That's right smart advice." Jubal coughed again. "We'll do it if we need to." He clicked to the horses.

Gabriel stood watching as the wagon moved past. Corey, one arm around her sister, was spreading out a blanket on the wagon floor. Gabriel wondered how long the father could manage to guide the horses before he gave the reins up to her.

He crossed the road and climbed the little hill. He kept glancing at the wagon until it was out of sight. *Corey.* Her face lingered in his mind—the firm chin and full lips, the high cheekbones. Not a conventional beauty. But lovely all the same.

Then it hit him—Corey had complete care and responsibility for the other two. A double burden for her. Could she take them through? Perhaps he should've gone with them—fetched Freedom and driven the team. But from what he was hearing, his own family needed him now.

He reached the top of the hill and tramped through the underbrush to where he'd tethered Freedom. He untied the reins, mounted, and rode back down the hill. Once on the road, he turned to the east on the other side of the creek. He followed the creek, keeping in the shadows of the trees, until he reached what was left of the Givens' homestead.

Most of the fallen boards had been taken—most likely to help fortify the town. Part of the stable still stood. Inside, he found an intact, protected stall, and put the horse in it. He pulled hay from the loft and filled the feed bin. Then he unsaddled Freedom. He stood stroking the horse's nose. "I'll be back soon. *Sois sage.*"

The horse stamped his foot and took a mouthful of hay. *Stealing livestock, were they?* A risk, to leave the horse here, but to take him into town was riskier. Gabriel shouldered his leather knapsack and prepared to walk the four miles into town. He pulled his jacket up around his ears.

He reached the outskirts of the town. He saw men on horseback in the spaces between the cabins. Moving slowly, he kept to the sides of the buildings. A loaded wagon lumbered past, pulled by two oxen. Folks heading out. They weren't anyone he knew, so he paid them no mind. Once he sensed someone watching him. He began to affect a limp, the way a very old man would move.

At last he reached the cabin where he'd last seen his family. He knocked at the door.

Noises inside. His heart pounding. He didn't recognize the hoarse voice that answered. "Who is it?"

Puzzled. "It's me. Gabriel."

He heard the wooden bar sliding over the door. It opened. He pushed inside.

"I'll be hornswoggled!" Rusty gripped the wooden door.

In the dim light, Gabriel could see that the young man's eyes were watery, his nose red. Another bad cold. That explained the hoarseness. "Land's sakes, I hardly knew you! Your voice—"

"What in tarnation are you doing here?" Eb rushed out of the shadows and gripped him by the shoulders. "They said to clear out—it don't matter none what's goin' on here."

"Of course it matters." Gabriel reached up to loosen Eb's grip and clasped both his hands. He looked earnestly into Eb's face. "I couldn't stay away any longer."

Eb snorted. "They gonna git you fer sure. They're rounding up anyone they can find."

Gabriel looked around at the circle of faces. Hannah and Bethia were staring at him, as if the power of speech had fled. Sarah opened her mouth, but no words came. Gabriel shrugged, smiling. "It's all right—I'm not a ghost. Or an angel either. How're you feeling, Hannah?"

"I'm right pert." Her voice sounded weak. "But without Nathaniel—"

"I know he's gone, and Calvin too. Now, where's my Bethia?"

She ran to him then, and he planted a kiss on her cheek. Sarah rolled her eyes. "Well, they can pretend like everything's fine. But we haven't enough food to get us through the week."

Gabriel kept one arm around Bethia. "Close that door, Rusty. Now, listen. From what I'm hearing, I think the best thing is to pack up and leave. We still have the oxen?"

Eb nodded.

"What about the horses and our wagons and carriage?"

Eb said, "Derned if they didn't take old Spot first thing."

"Spot—" Jody began to whimper.

Polly Crawford spoke from the corner. "Don't start that again. That horse was old. Old."

"What about the others?" Gabriel asked.

Eb gave a shrug. "They was back further in the stables. The mobbers haven't took 'em yet."

Gabriel nodded. "Then we got a good chance."

Rusty said, "The Crawford's wagon is broke. The wheel's plumb busted."

Gabriel gestured with his free hand. "Then we got two oxen, two horses, and one wagon and carriage. That's more than a lot of folks have."

Hannah dabbed at her eyes. "But—Nathaniel. And Calvin. We can't just up and leave."

"'Course we can. We have to. They'd want us to."

"Folks is beginning to clear out," Eb said. "The Johnson family left two days ago."

"But—" Sarah's voice rose. "How will they find us? They'll come back here and—and—"

"And one of the neighbors'll tell them where we've gone." Gabriel looked at her. "There's not many roads out of here, and they all go east."

Her mouth worked; she frowned. Gabriel said, "You said yourself we're running out of food. And look at this place. Hardly room enough for four, let alone all of us. Better to take our chances out on the road. We're sure not safe here."

"And they want us to go," Bethia said. "I reckon they'll stop bothering us if we do."

Gabriel said, "We'll find food. And shelter, too. We've done it before. We'll do it now."

"I 'spect you're right." Hannah's eyebrows drew together. "How long will it take to pack up?"

Sarah sniffed. "Well, there sure ain't much to pack."

"Mostly bedding and clothes," Bethia said. "We'll see if the neighbor folks'll give us some flour and such. Corn meal for johnnycakes."

"All right." Gabriel turned to Eb and Rusty. "Here's what you do. Pack up what you can and harness the teams. Make sure there's a place for Hannah in the back of the wagon. Start in the morning, early as you can."

"Where you goin'?" Rusty asked.

"Like you said, I have to get out of here. I'll meet you on the northern road, across the creek from where our homestead used to be."

Rusty frowned. "You'll meet us—"

Gabriel said, "If I'm not there, you keep going. Don't wait for me. I'll catch up. Understand?"

Rusty blinked. "I think so."

"Even if you don't see me, you keep going."

As he reached for the door handle, Bethia stepped in front of him. She gave him a long look; in an instant he sensed the bond between them. She knew the full implication of what he'd said. He might not make it to the rendez-vous point.

"Don't worry." He kissed her again. "All will be well." As he said the conventional little phrase, she gave a slight intake of breath and nodded. Seeming acceptance. If Rusty understood as well, he gave no sign.

"If'n Nat was here, he'd make us all pray," Eb said.

"Then that's what we'll do." Gabriel clapped Eb on the shoulder. "You go first."

"I reckon we c'n still pray." Owen shuffled over to join the little circle.

Sarah sniffed. "It's about all we can do."

They gave brief prayers for the safety of Nathaniel, Calvin and the others who'd been taken prisoner. Special prayers for the brothers Joseph and Hyrum. Prayers for the protection of himself and guidance for all of them as they prepared to leave.

Feeling abashed and humbled, Gabriel embraced each one in turn. He held Bethia a long time in a final hug. "Now, don't cry. I'll see you tomorrow." He pulled the door open and closed it behind him.

He started out across the frost-covered fields, hoping it wasn't a falsehood he'd told her. How could he be sure he wouldn't be waylaid and never see them again? So far, so good. He reached the little trace that ran beside the creek and followed it to the east.

Snow began to fall, a flurry of tiny flakes out of the gray sky. It swirled around him as he tramped toward the shed. A neigh rang out—Freedom still there. He began to think they might escape intact.

An apple orchard lay just north of the creek. He saddled the horse, forded the creek, and spent part of the afternoon harvesting apples. He filled his saddlebags and part of his knapsack. He didn't question whose apples they were; they belonged to him now.

Toward evening he went to what was left of their cabin and investigated the root cellar. Five seed potatoes, three turnips, seven carrots, two sacks of grain, and a hunk of bacon. He looked in the grain sacks—one wheat, one corn. He filled his knapsack. He found a burlap sack and packed it full. On the way out, he picked up the little mill they used for grinding.

"I reckon we'll eat something." He carried everything out to the stable. Freedom stamped his foot and gave a little whinny.

"You're gonna have a load to tote." Gabriel put the sacks against the wall near the entrance. Time to make up his own supper.

Freedom neighed again. What was that? A noise from outside. An answering neigh. Gabriel froze. His heart pounding. Fingers reaching for his knife. He was a healer; he had no desire to kill. But if this was a Missouri mobber come to kill him, he had no choice. Thoughts of Bethia, Hannah, Jody, flooded his mind. He heard the dismount, listened as the footsteps crunched in the layer of leaves. Closer. A shadow in the doorway. *Now!*

He grabbed the man from behind and held the knife to his throat. "Don't make a move, or you're a dead man."

To his surprise the intruder began to sob. "Please, sir—don't kill me. I'm not armed. And I seed enough killing."

Gabriel sheathed his knife and backed the man up against the door. A young man, about the age of Rusty. Large eyes, brown as a collie dog's, darting all around. Soft, wispy hair, in need of a barber. A beard just beginning on his chin.

Gabriel relaxed his grip. "Don't be afraid. I don't aim to harm you."

The stranger was breathing fast. "I just—I saw the shed, and I thought—well, I thought there might be someone in there."

"And there was." Gabriel gave a harsh laugh. "Me."

"Someone needing help, I mean. You see—I was over there, at the mill. Haun's Mill."

Gabriel remembered hearing something about a skirmish at a mill. "You were there?"

"I seen it. The whole thing. And seen what it was like when they left."

"When who left?"

He was sniffing now, tears running down his cheeks. "Why, the soldiers. The ones that done it. Some two hundred of 'em, they said. Men with blackened faces and—and red cloths on their hats and shirts. Just marching in and killing folks."

"Relax, now. You're safe here." Gabriel's mind felt numb; he tried to think how to reassure the man, as he would a patient. "First, tell me your name."

"Palmer. Zeke Palmer. See, I was—"

"And you didn't get hurt?"

"We wuz in tents. My mother and my little sisters. Camped for the night, waitin' to go into Far West. We was at the end of a bunch of tents—right up near the river."

"Oh—you mean the creek."

"Whatever you call it. It makes a turn there—that's all I know. I heard the shooting. I managed to get my wimmin-folks out and across it. We hid up there in the bushes and waited."

"You say there was shooting?"

"Folks was jest goin' about their business, gathering crops and such. The sun was shining—I remember that. And they attacked for no reason. None that we could see."

"I understand." Gabriel tried to conceal his own horror; he felt his chin shaking. "And what happened then?"

"Well, that was it. Folks ran around yelling. There was terrible confusion. Some of the women and children rushed across the creek and hid wherever they could. The men tried to get in the blacksmith shop. But it was unchinked, and—and—"

"Rest, now. Take a deep breath."

"No. You gotta hear the rest. The soldiers surrounded that shop, stuck their weapons in the chinks, and—" He was trembling. Gabriel put a hand on his shoulder. Zeke swallowed. "It was over quicker'n you could tell about it."

Gabriel took a breath. "The blacksmith shop—"

"Nobody in there got away. One man was shot with his own gun tryin' to escape. At least eighteen died. Fourteen wounded. I know because I saw what was left. But that ain't the worst part."

"What could be worse?"

"They was killing children. Three young boys were in there with the men. Two of 'em got shot. The one that was left, the brother of one of them, told how the man put the gun to his ten-year-old brother's head. And you know what the man said? He said, 'Nits make lice, and if he lived he would have become a Mormon.' Then he shot him dead."

"*Mon Dieu*." Shaken beyond words, Gabriel searched for something to say to the young man. Were they both still in danger? "Let's bring your horse in here. And I reckon you can use something to eat. I have a few apples and a bit of bread and cheese."

"I ain't eaten since that—since yesterday morning. I haven't been hungry."

With the horse hidden inside and Zeke seated on a bale of hay, Gabriel gave him some of the food which Sven Peterson had provided. "So—you came back across the creek and found all this mayhem—"

"All night," Zeke said. "I can't forget it. The wounded groaning and the women and children weeping. Warn't nothing we could do. We knew we had to get out of there. So we finally dragged all the bodies to the new well they'd been digging—most of 'em was froze by that time. We put 'em in the well."

"What about the wounded? Anyone still there?"

"No. I went to make sure. All of them was carried into town."

Gabriel nodded. Wondering what to do. What to say to someone who'd seen too much at too young an age. "Your family is all right?"

"Yes. Scared to death. But they're together, back in the wagon."

"In Far West?"

"The only place we could go."

There was a pause. In the last light, Gabriel could see Zeke wiping his face with his sleeve. Gabriel gave a little cough. "Well, son. If'n your family's unharmed, I'd count my blessings. Now, you need to get them out of here. Come with us, if you like. My folks are pulling out tomorrow, with a wagon and a carriage."

Zeke looked at him. "Where you goin'?"

"Why, Illinois, I reckon. We all got to get out. That's the word. You can stay longer if you want. But we're heading to somewhere safer."

Zeke nodded. "I best be getting back."

"Be of good cheer, son. Somehow we'll make it to a better place. I'm ordained, although you wouldn't know it to look at me. I'll pray with you before you go."

It was dark when they had finished. Gabriel wondered what more he could give his young brother. "Take care for yourself. Don't come out alone anymore—stay close to your family."

"I will."

When Zeke had left, Gabriel gathered enough straw for a bed. He covered himself with straw and two of the burlap sacks. With his jacket over him, and the warmth of Freedom close by, he lay waiting for sleep. But what he'd heard about Haun's Mill went on in his mind, as vivid as if he'd been there himself. The murder of children. The supreme event in a series of outrages. Grief and anger rushed over him. All he had seen and experienced, all he had heard, seemed to culminate in one great surge of rage. Rage not so much at the soldiers, but at God for allowing such evil to be played out to its bitter end.

Where was God anyway, that such things should happen to innocent people? If this was God's idea of protecting persons who were supposed to be following and obeying Him, better they should all scatter and forget about any idea of living together in peace. Zion, indeed. A cruel joke.

In the morning Gabriel fed himself and Freedom, then loaded the sacks of food across the horse's back. He led the horse across the creek and up toward the road. A light snow was falling. In addition to his anger, he felt a nagging anxiety. Somehow he had to survive. What lay ahead? He might still be accosted, unable to meet his family at the chosen place. Try to think rationally. Concentrate on the journey ahead. Now, in the absence of Nathaniel, he had to assume the lead and take responsibility for the safety of at least eight other people, one of them about to give birth.

Something hopeful. Something pleasant to think about. Corey. Her face intent with determination and hope, her dream of taking her sister to a place where she could run outside without danger. Maybe that was the most they could expect—a place where a child could run out and not be hurt. His memory of how she looked was fading, but he thought of certain details—her blue eyes, her open, alert expression. The way her hair poked out from beneath her hood. He'd seen enough to notice that it was the color of dried pine needles.

Hope stirred in his own mind as he thought of her. Beautiful that she should exist and be part of his experience. The same world where innocents were massacred also had people like her. He felt less cold as he trudged through the snow with the horse behind him. He could do it—lead his own household to a place of safety. Finally the road stretched before him, the traces dark with fallen leaves between the banks of snow.

Bethia knew something was wrong the moment she saw him. He stood holding the horse's reins, his face drawn and pale, as if he'd spent the night sitting up with a patient. But there was something more—as if he'd had some earth-shaking experience. What had happened? Who had interacted with him, to trouble and distract him so deeply?

Gabriel on his part paid little attention to her. He looked over the wagon, checked the harnessing of the oxen. Hannah lay on the bed of blankets in the back of the wagon. Gabriel spoke briefly as he loaded the sacks beside her. "Everything all right this morning?"

"I—I think so."

Bethia sat holding Jody in the front seat beside Eb. Gabriel's eyes flicked over them; he nodded, then went to inspect the carriage. Rusty sat in the driver's seat with Owen beside him. In the back seat, Sarah and Polly huddled close to each other. At their feet crouched Nell, her paw still bandaged.

"We couldn't leave her behind," Polly said.

Gabriel's mouth twitched in a fleeting smile. "Of course not. Rusty, did you bring the cover for the wagon?"

"It's in the back."

"We'd best put it up. We may need it, if'n this snow keeps up."

They rigged up the canvas cover, Gabriel still looking drained and distracted. Bethia tried to get his attention. "Where did you spend the night?"

He gave her a quick look. "With Freedom, in the burned-out stable. What was left of it." He pulled at one of the ropes. "There. That oughta hold it."

He mounted Freedom and urged him forward. "Let's get moving. We've a ways to go."

Rusty climbed into the carriage. "Just once," he said fervently. "Just one time, I wish they'd make us leave in good weather, when the sun was shining. Like maybe in spring, when it warn't so cold."

"Oh, hush up," Owen said. "If it was hotter than the hinges of the hot place, you'd still be complainin'."

They started to move. Human voices were lost in the scrunch of hooves in the snow, the creaking of wheels and wood. Bethia tried to amuse Jody by urging him to watch for deer. She kept glancing back at Gabriel, hoping that he would look like his old self. But the troubled expression never left his face.

They stopped for a bit of lunch. Soon after they resumed the journey, she became aware of another sound. Soft at first, then increasing. She listened for some minutes before she realized Hannah was moaning.

Bethia looked back. "What is it? Are the pains beginning?"

"Somethin' not right." Eb pulled to a stop. "I reckon Gabe better know."

Bethia called him. He rode up and looked at her. She faltered under his gaze. "I—I think Hannah's in trouble."

Gabriel dismounted and lifted a corner of the canvas. Bethia heard him speaking softly; she couldn't catch the words. Hannah answered, her voice faint. Gabriel walked to the front of the wagon.

"Bethia, I want you to get back there with her. Just talk to her quiet-like. Comfort her. The birth's still a ways off. Eb, you can ride Freedom. I'm going to drive. And, here—I'll take Jody."

The boy held out his arms and Gabriel carried him back to the carriage. "Here's Aunt Sarah—she'll take care of you."

Bethia moved into the back of the wagon, to a place between the front seat and the sacks of provisions. She made a seat for herself among the sacks. Eb climbed down from the front seat and handed the reins to Gabriel. The wagon began to move.

Gabriel spoke from the front seat. "How's she doing?"

"Everything's quiet," Bethia replied. "What—what should I do?"

"Rub her back. Keep her warm and comfortable. If she wants to stop, we'll stop. Meanwhile, we'll go as far as we can."

After a while Hannah began moaning again. She turned her head as Bethia tried to stroke her forehead.

"She's getting restless," Bethia said to Gabriel.

"Hold on. We're going to try and find a place for her."

"A place?"

The wagon stopped abruptly. Bethia heard the boards creak as Gabriel jumped down. He shouted something to Eb about seeking shelter. Bethia lifted the canvas flap. "Where's he gone?"

"He thinks he knows some people here. He's asking at that farmhouse."

Bethia tried to see the farmhouse, but the wind blew snow in her eyes. Blinking, she lowered the flap.

"Where's Gabriel?" Hannah asked.

Within moments he returned. The wagon shook as he climbed into the front seat. He clicked to the oxen. "We're gonna take the first road to the north. If I've guessed right, we'll find people—our people. And Hannah will have a roof over her head. Hang on."

The wagon turned. They started over a rough road. To Bethia, it seemed an eternity, with the wagon creaking and shaking, Hannah moaning, tears running down her cheeks. Bethia wiped away the tears, wanting to cry with her. Finally the wagon stopped.

"Everybody stay here," Gabriel said. "I'll be back."

Bethia lifted the flap. The snow had stopped; everything looked crisp and clear in the light of late afternoon. She saw a fence and a sign which read 'H. Sidwell.' Behind her, Hannah began to sob.

"Oh, why did he leave us now?"

Bethia was about to reply when she saw the two figures approaching from the house. One was Gabriel. The second, a young woman, drew her hood up around her head. Her face looked vaguely familiar—someone from Far West. Bethia, watching, felt puzzled at first, strangely disturbed. When she saw the animated look on Gabriel's face, his eyes lighting up as he talked with the young woman, she knew she had more trouble than she'd ever imagined.

9

The child, a girl, uttered her first cries long after candlelight. Gabriel wondered if it weren't closer to midnight. He bent over to ease the little one into the world. "Isn't she a beauty?"

Bethia didn't reply. Gabriel shrugged. *Bethia acting strange all during the birth, as if she were in some sort of trance.* Exhausted, like everyone else, he figured. He cut the cord, then placed the child in the towel which Bethia was holding. "You know what to do. I'll stay with Hannah."

He could hear the women in the next room as they bathed the child by the fire. He stroked Hannah's arm. She made a slight sound and opened her eyes.

"You're going to be fine. Push once more for me." He tried to keep his voice alive and eager. Just a little while longer, and they could all rest. Lucky he'd remembered—*Sidwell.* Lucky that Corey had said the name, back there on the road.

Most fortunate of all, the Sidwells had taken them in without question, had given them shelter and the best of what they had. *Maybe this is Zion,* he thought, wondering. And them not even Mormons.

As he went through the procedure of checking the afterbirth, he recalled a conversation with Bethia some hours before the birth. She'd asked, almost in a demanding way, "Where'd you meet these people?"

"Uh—on the road, when I was coming back to town."

"You never saw them before?"

"Not that I recall. The father was ill, and I stopped to help. He seems better, now."

Bethia sniffed. "Corey's not even her real name, you know. It's Coralee."

"It is, eh?" He shrugged. "So—a nickname."

"You should call her by her real name."

"She told me her name was Corey. So I reckon that's what I'd better say."

A shadow in the doorway...his tired mind jumping back to the present. The candle flickering. He looked up. Corey tiptoed into the room.

"Good morning," he said.

"It's a good morning, indeed." She moved closer; their eyes met. "That child is just beautiful. I—I'm struck with admiration, that you could—that you knew just what to do."

He smiled. "That's why I'm a doctor. I'd better know, by this time."

"I—I just came in to tell you—if you need anything, we'll get it for you. There's warm soup on the hearth."

"That sounds good. We're beholden to your kinfolks—it's best for the mother and child to be indoors, in a warm place. I'm hoping it'll make all the difference for them."

Bethia appeared in the doorway. Corey moved away. "Don't forget about the soup."

"*Merci.* Hannah should have some, too." He bent to wash his hands in the basin of hot water. "I reckon what everybody needs most is rest." He looked at the two women as he dried his hands. Bethia did not smile. Not knowing why, he felt uncomfortable. He gave a little cough.

"I'll just have a look at the baby. Time to see if she'll nurse a bit. Then I'll bed down out there by the fire, where I can get to both of them easily. You two should go on off and get some rest."

"Doctor, we've plenty of rooms," Corey said. "You don't have to sleep on the floor."

"This is fine. All I need is a pillow and some blankets. Believe me, it's a lot better than the back of a wagon."

All the women gathered around as he held the baby. She looked at them with bright eyes and made motions with her mouth. Gabriel drew a deep breath. "What a sight. I reckon Nat'll be right pleased."

"How do you know?" Bethia asked.

"Well, *I* sure would be. Here—" He took a step toward Bethia. "Carry her in to momma and see if she'll take her first meal. I'm going to have some of that soup."

Bethia looked at him coldly. "I'm tired, too."

Gabriel stopped, at a loss. Corey moved forward. "Oh, let me. I've done this before." She took the baby.

Sarah got up from beside the hearth. "I reckon I'll go in there with them."

Corey held the child close to her. "I've never seen such a pretty baby. Most of 'em look all smooshed up at first."

Gabriel nodded. "This one came quickly."

"All I can say, doctor, is if I ever give birth, I want you to be there."

"Fine." Gabriel ladled soup into a brown earthenware bowl with a handle. "As long as it's not tonight."

Everyone laughed except Bethia. Gabriel offered the soup to her, but she shook her head. He sat down at the table and held the bowl, blowing on the soup to cool it. Eb stood up and moved over to sit beside him. "I reckon you're plumb wore out."

Gabriel didn't reply. He lifted the bowl to his lips and drank. Eb said, "The animals is all bedded down. The wagon's in the shed. Rusty and I figured we'd sleep out there."

"Jody and Owen went to sleep long ago," Polly said. "Reckon I'll go join 'em."

Gabriel smiled. "See you in the morning. Not too early."

Bethia spoke from across the table. "Don't we have to be up and on our way?"

Gabriel looked at his half-empty bowl. "Let's give Hannah and the little one at least one day to rest. Should be more. We'll clean up the house, help wash all the towels and such. Maybe chop them some wood."

Bethia set her lips together in an expression Gabriel had never seen before. Without another word, she left the room.

Gabriel looked at Eb. "I reckon we all better sleep while we can."

Eb laid a hand on Gabriel's shoulder and stood up to leave.

When Bethia woke the next morning, it was already late. She'd shared a bed with Sarah, while Jody slept beside them in the trundle bed. The boy, usually an early riser, did not stir.

She got up and dressed without making a sound. Outside, someone was chopping wood. She lifted the edge of the curtain and saw Eb busy with the ax while Rusty threw the split logs on the wood pile. As she watched, the troubles of the past day crowded around her. Was Gabriel deliberately taunting her? Or did he in fact have some sort of relationship with this Corey or Coralee?

She closed the door to the room and tiptoed down the hall. The house smelled of bacon and fresh rolls. She crossed the keeping room where their hostess, a short plump woman with reddish hair, was putting bread dough into pans. "Morning, Mrs. Sidwell."

"Mornin'. The doctor's up and at work again."

She saw that Gabriel's bedding had been folded and set against the wall. "Nothing wrong, I hope."

Mrs. Sidwell held out her hand to test the fire. "I don't see how things could be better."

Wondering, Bethia walked toward Hannah's room. The door was open. Hannah was sitting up in bed, propped on pillows. The child nursed, looking at her mother with intent, dark eyes. Gabriel sat in a rocker by the bed, one foot resting on the other knee. He had a cup of something in his hand.

"Tea," he said, in answer to her look. "As for momma, she's having soup."

"Isn't Jody up?" Hannah asked.

"Not yet," Bethia replied.

Hannah put the baby up on her shoulder and rubbed the tiny back. "Time for him to meet his sister."

"Let's not rush into it," Gabriel said. "Let him get up like it was an ordinary morning."

Bethia went in to help prepare breakfast. They ate in shifts, little groups sitting down together. Most of the men had already eaten. Gabriel ate with the women, after carrying a hearty breakfast to Hannah.

"Well, they both made it through the night," he remarked as he sat down at the table.

"I hope you didn't fret none," Mrs. Sidwell said. "That's one of the hardiest young'uns I ever seen."

"I was anxious." Gabriel reached for a piece of bacon. "She lost the last one, you see. And I promised her a healthy baby this time."

"I reckon you made good your word."

"We didn't figure on having to leave so sudden-like. If she can make it through the first week, I think she'll be fine."

Hannah and the child rested while the other women spent the day washing towels and linens. Eb and Rusty worked chopping wood. Gabriel took Jody for a walk and apparently told him about the joys of having a younger sister. Bethia heard him describing it to Eb. "I said that mine was named Marie, and I surely missed her. She was my best friend, growing up."

Toward evening, Eb knocked at the front door. "There's a heap of folks out in the yard. And horses pulling a little cart."

Some of the women hurried out to see, and Gabriel followed. "Why, land's sakes," he exclaimed. "If it isn't Zeke Palmer."

"Who?" Bethia asked.

"And these are my sisters," the one named Zeke was saying. "There's Theresa and Larissa, and Jane's the little one—"

"I have a sister too," Jody said.

Bethia watched as Gabriel embraced Zeke and clapped him on the back. "How come you to find us?"

"We just followed the tracks. They all led up here."

Bethia waited to be introduced, but Gabriel didn't bother. He turned to welcome two other people—Sam and Jean Willis. Bethia did know them, an older couple who'd lived on Shoal Creek. Sam Willis had good news.

"They let most of the prisoners go free. Couldn't find nothin' to charge 'em with, 'cept civil disturbance. Nathaniel and Calvin be on their way, 'cept they're comin' on foot. Take 'em at least two days to git here."

"They're all right?" Sarah asked.

Sam scratched at his white beard. "They're fine. Mad about losing all their property."

Sarah gasped. "It's all lost?"

"Gone to pay for the war. That was one of the stipulations. The other was to leave the state as soon as possible."

"I reckon they're doing that now," Eb said. Gabriel hurried to give the news to Hannah.

While the supper of bread and porridge was being prepared, Bethia said to Gabriel, "So where'd you meet Zeke and them? On the road too, I suppose?"

"No—in the stable."

She raised her eyebrows. "The stable!"

"Yes—I was inside, and he came in to see who was there."

She shook her head. "Well, you do get around."

Gabriel looked puzzled, then shrugged. Now that she had his attention, she said, "There be too many people here now. We can't stay forever."

He frowned before he spoke. "Now, Bethia. I wouldn't be in such a hurry if I was you. We don't know where we're going, and we've a newborn to take care of. And we're welcome here—I know it. We're safe and warm. We'd best wait till Nat and Calvin get here. Another two days at the most."

She sighed. "We're gonna wear out any welcome we have if'n we stay much longer."

"I reckon that's true. But it won't be long now. Hannah and the baby'll have a little more rest. And I promised Brother Jubal I'd help tighten the wheels on his wagon. They be aimin' to come with us, him and his daughters."

The news hit her like a blow; she gave a sudden intake of breath. She thought for a moment she was going to faint. Gabriel gave her an anxious look.

"Bethia, sit down a spell. You're pale as a sheet. I reckon yer workin' too hard."

She gathered up her skirts and pushed past him. Before he could say another word, she left the room.

Time to eat. Rusty had a lot to think about besides eating, but he always knew when it was time. He'd tried to pretend it didn't matter—as if he didn't care whether he ate or not. But he wasn't a very good actor.

For one thing, provisions were scarce. The bits of cornbread and dried apples were hardly enough. If he held back, he might not get anything. But tonight was different. Eb had taken the shotgun Mr. Sidwell had given them, and shot two squirrels. Rusty had helped Eb skin and dress them, and now they were simmering in the iron pot. Knowing that the stew had to feed a large number of people, Rusty took a position within easy reach of the fire.

He'd already found food for the oxen—dried grass under the snow.

They didn't have all that much to eat either. And the horses were looking thin.

"Can't be much longer," Nat had said over breakfast. "Two, maybe three days at the most."

Rusty could only hope that was true. Other troubles crowded around him. Hannah and the baby not doing well. Too cold; not enough to eat. He felt physical pain, like a wound in his chest, at the thought of anything happening to Hannah. What hadn't they endured together? The trek from the farm in Pennsylvania to Kirtland, then out to Missouri, where she'd stayed and he'd come back to Ohio. Then her return to Ohio and her marriage to Nathaniel. The flight from Kirtland to Far West. Now, here they were, leaving Missouri again, this time for good.

She had to hang on. He could not imagine life without her. He went over to the wagon and lifted the flap. He could hear the faint cries of the child.

"How you makin' it, Hannah?"

"I'm tryin'. But I'm so cold."

Rusty got his own blanket from the carriage and brought it to her. He tucked it around her and the baby.

She looked at him, her eyes large in her pale face. "But what will you do?"

"Don't worry about me none. Take care of you."

Polly sick too. He could hear her coughing from where she lay in the back of the carriage. And no doctor. Gabe off somewhere, in the wilderness of northern Missouri. His mind went back to when they were waiting for Nat and Calvin, and Gabe had sent him to watch for them on the main road. He and Eb took turns, riding Freedom back and forth, to spell each other.

"The others is pullin' out this noon," Eb said on their second day of watching. "The Willises and them. Jubal and his girls, too. They want to get going before winter sets in."

Rusty rubbed his hands together. "It's already settin' in. I reckon we shouldn't wait much longer."

"Gabe says one more day. Then we'll figure they've taken another road."

On the third day, Rusty spotted two figures moving on the road. He waited, unsure. They walked slowly, the shorter one limping. As he squinted against the light, he recognized his father. He ran toward them, waving his arms and hallooing.

"Hush, lad," Nat said as Rusty embraced Calvin. "You'll tell the whole flippin' army where we are."

"What army?" Rusty turned to hug Nat. Nat had a growth of beard as dark as the hair under his hat.

"The Missourians. There's soldiers all up and down the road."

"We hain't seen any."

They tramped the two miles up to the Sidwell's farmhouse. Rusty told them about the birth. "And she wants to name it after Gabriel."

Nat shook his head. "The poor little soul. I hope she lives, for Hannah's sake."

Rusty's father had been injured in a fall on the courthouse steps. Rusty took his arm. "Gabe'll have you fixed up right soon."

"Tarnation!" Nat's eyes widened. "Is he still here?"

"I reckon so. He's been leadin' us."

Nat looked at Calvin. "I'm gonna run ahead. Rusty, you stay with your father." Nat bounded over the fence and raced for the house.

Rusty shook his head. "What's he in such a hurry fer?"

His father leaned against him, breathing hard. "There's soldiers on horseback, comin' up behind us. We saw 'em stopped back there. They're lookin' fer anyone who had anything to do with Crooked River. Better for Gabe if he hadn't come back."

"But—but he came to help Hannah, and to get us out of there. If it weren't for him, we'd still be waitin'."

"Well, now we gotta hope those fellers don't follow us. Like as not, they'll stay on the main road."

Even as he spoke, they heard the thudding of hooves. "Jest keep walkin'," Calvin said. "We don't know a thing."

Three men on horseback, guns slung over the shoulders, halted their mounts in a whirl of snow. A tall, whiskered man spoke first. "Lookin' fer Gabe Roman. Know him?"

"Never heard of 'em," Rusty said.

"Heard he was in these parts. A funny little Frenchman, a doctor."

Calvin stared straight ahead. "What was the name again?"

"Let's try the house," one of the others said. They dismounted and threw the reins over the fence rail. Two of them ran up to the front door. The third hurried around in back.

"He's done for," Rusty said.

Calvin squeezed his arm. "Don't say nothin'. No matter what happens. You hear?" Calvin was panting as he climbed the two front steps. He nodded, and Rusty pushed open the door. They went inside, Calvin still holding Rusty's arm.

Bedding and pillows lay scattered on the floor. Rusty glanced around. No sign of Gabe or Eb. Hannah teetered in the bedroom doorway, the baby in her arms. Nat stood by her side. Over by the hearth, Sarah stood, tears rolling down her cheeks. Beside her, Bethia knelt holding Jody's hand.

Mrs. Sidwell sat at the table, her mouth open and eyes wide with astonishment. Her husband stood behind her. He shrugged, his palms up. "I tell you, this is my place. And we're not Mormons."

"Shut up," the whiskered man said. "I reckon I know a pack of you when I see 'em. Now, where's the doctor?"

"I'll check t'other rooms." The second soldier strode toward the hallway. "They can't hide 'em fer long."

Suddenly the back door flew open. The third soldier rushed in. "Stop what yer doing! These folks can't be Mormons. Derned if they don't have a slave!"

"A slave?" the whiskered one asked.

"Out by the stable. Says he's been out there all day and hain't seen no one."

The whiskered one drew a breath. Then he smiled. "I'll be dad-burned. I sure am sorry. Here you are, good Missourians and slave-holders, like proper folks."

"Sorry to disturb you," one of the others said. "We got so rattled-like, chasin' that Frenchman, we could hardly see straight. The sneaky little varmint."

"We'd better go look for 'em somewhere's else," Whiskers said. "We know he's around here."

The three left as abruptly as they had entered. Rusty heard the hooves crunching in the snow. Even after the drone of hoof beats had subsided, they waited, looking at each other in disbelief. The baby started to whimper.

Nat embraced Hannah, then held out his arms to Jody. The boy rushed over to him. The others gathered close around.

"I'm sorry to put you to so much trouble," Nat said to Mr. Sidwell. "But I thank you for taking care of my family."

Calvin hugged Sarah. "Someone better go tell the sneaky varmint it's safe to come back in."

Soon Eb and Gabe both hurried inside. Gabe began gathering up clothes and items for his knapsack.

"Take Freedom," Nat said. "Head north, fast as you can. Two days of hard riding should get you into Iowa Territory, or close to it."

""I'm fillin' yer saddlebags with food," Eb said. "Some for the horse, too. Take care of that horse."

"There's an old Indian trail," Mr. Sidwell said. "Crosses the stream 'bout half a mile east and goes up toward a place called Honey Creek. It's wild; no one uses it 'cept the Chippewas and Sacs and Fox. The only white men up there is maybe a French trapper or two. There's burial mounds up near the bank of the Grand River. If you c'n get that far, like as not those soldiers won't find you. Just keep north and don't stop moving."

In a moment, it seemed, Gabe had left. Rusty remembered how Gabe had embraced them all, even Bethia who'd been acting annoyed with him. As he turned from her, she just stood there and sobbed.

"Don't cry," he'd said. "I'll see you again."

"Not in Missouri, you won't," Nat had said. "Now, get going."

The clank of iron. Bethia lifting the lid of the cooking pot. The aroma of stew filling the air. Rusty's mind leaping back to the wooded campsite, the wagon and carriage, the hobbled horses and oxen, and the fire.

"I reckon it's ready." Bethia began ladling stew into pottery bowls and mugs lined up on a plank between two stumps. Rusty picked up the first one.

"Take it to Hannah," Nat ordered.

Rusty did so, wondering if he would get any. Seeing his face, Hannah said, "Taste it for me, Rusty. I have to get sitting up first."

Rusty took the first swallows of it. He felt new strength flowing into him. He handed it to her and she held it to her mouth. She took a sip. "Go get you some."

Soon most of them sat or stood around the fire with bowls of the stew. Bethia shared hers with Jody.

"A bit watery," Calvin remarked. "But it's better than nothing."

They finished the meal with cornbread, dipping it in the remains of the stew. Owen walked over to stand beside Nat. "Polly doesn't feel like eating."

The corners of Nat's mouth worked as he thought. "We'll save some for her. Bring her close to the fire. We'll try to keep 'er warm."

All that night Owen sat up beside Polly, who lay by the fire. Rusty slept under the wagon, on a bed of pine boughs beside Eb. They took turns getting up to tend the fire. As Rusty gathered wood, he could hear Polly coughing feebly. Toward morning, the coughing stopped.

The next thing he knew, Nat was gripping him by the shoulder. "Get up, lad. We've a sorry duty to perform."

"What?" He struggled to his feet. "Hannah. Not Hannah. The baby—"

"They're fine. It's Polly. Take the shovel, you and Eb. Dig us a grave under that big pine."

In the gray light of dawn, Rusty saw Calvin sitting with Owen, one arm across his shoulders. Rusty nudged Eb and the two of them got the shovel from the back of the wagon. As they walked to the pine, Rusty heard Nat talking to Hannah. "You women stay in the wagon till we're ready. No sense in everybody gittin' cold."

He and Eb cleared away the brush from the foot of the tree. They took turns digging. Eb went first. "Lucky the ground ain't froze yet."

As Rusty started to dig, it began to drizzle. "I wondered what else we needed."

"Don't talk. Just dig. It's gotta be deeper than that. So the varmints don't get her."

When it was ready, Nat and Calvin brought the body of Polly, wrapped in a sheet. They laid her in the grave, and everyone gathered for the brief service. Rusty, looking around, thought how ill-clad they appeared for such an occasion. Even their shoes looked worn-out. Eb's had given out completely; he had pieces of toweling wrapped around his feet. Owen stood in ragged clothing, the hem of his jacket tattered, while Calvin waited beside him with a hand on his shoulder.

Bethia held Jody by the hand, her eyes and nose red. Her face had a strained, pinched look, as if she'd been weeping for days. Her beauty seemed to have faded overnight. Rusty wondered if Gabe would even want her if he could see her now. She could still cook; maybe he, Rusty, had a chance after all. He shot her a look, but she did not meet his eyes.

Hannah walked over with the baby and stood beside Sarah. They were wrapped in blankets, Indian-fashion. Rusty moved to Hannah's side, wishing he could protect her and the littlest one from whatever they faced next. Then he began to marvel that they'd come this far, most of the time in weather not fit for a dog, with only the loss of one of them.

Nat stepped forward for the committal prayer. Rusty watched his face. The lines around the eyes looked deeper than he'd ever seen them. Rusty wondered if Nat, too, worried that Hannah or her child would be next.

10

A NIGHT OF HARD RIDING. Following a faint trail by moonlight. A day of hazy sun and snow flurries. Another night. Keeping to the woods, crossing the tracks of deer. Once he saw the paw prints of some large carnivore, possibly a catamount. No sign of anything human.

Someone after him? Sounds of horses behind him? Not possible, he told himself. By this time, the snow had wiped out any trace of hoof prints.

He needed rest. Even a horse like Freedom couldn't go on forever. He reached what he thought were the mounds near the river bank. A place to cross the river. A few more miles. Forcing himself a bit further. A stand of trees ahead. Evergreens...pine and cedar. Dismounting, he led the horse deep into the woods. Satisfied that they were completely hidden, he fed the horse and ate some of the bread and apples Eb had packed for him.

Too bad Eb couldn't come with him. They could've made it an adventure. Sitting around a campfire, joking and bantering. But the others needed Eb more than he did. Gabriel wondered if he should build a fire. Too risky. Then he remembered the catamount. Soon he had a small fire going. He lay with his back against a tree, Freedom close beside him. If he had to, he could jump on the horse in a minute and be off.

Too tired to think. Here he was, a fugitive again. His friends and affianced bride far behind. That was a joke. The way she was acting, it didn't seem like she wanted to marry him at all. Maybe she was trying to find a way to end it. *Tant pis.* She would've made a good wife. Just before he fell asleep, he thought of Corey. Her face came close to him, the blue eyes large in the strong, serious face. Corey, who spent her time caring for a sister whose voice sounded like singing.

Trotting north the next morning. Reining the horse in, not driving him as hard. Muttering words, talking loud enough for the horse to hear.

"I reckon, from what I've seen, that life's meant to be hard. Not just hard—miserable. Folks is supposed to suffer. I mean, it's set up that way. Why else would a whole bunch of people have to leave their homes, when they haven't done anything wrong? Babies dying, 'cause they don't have proper care. Old folks not makin' it. Children being murdered."

Freedom put his ears back. A soft, deep whinny burbled up from his chest. Gabriel reached forward and patted the horse's neck.

The terrain flattened; the stands of trees grew scarce. He stopped beside a small stream. He climbed down the embankment and knelt, cupping his hands to drink. Ice-cold. He decided to let the horse rest a bit, then lead him down to the water.

As he started back up the embankment, his left foot went into a hole. He fell. Pain like a knife wound shot through his ankle. He lay still, panic-stricken. Would he damage himself more if he moved? The palms of his hands were black from the mud. Most likely bruised as well. He pulled himself up. Waves of pain rushed over him as he tried to draw his foot out of the hole. He reached to feel the ankle. Nothing broken. A severe sprain, most likely. An injury he didn't need. The sound of his own breathing filled his ears. At any rate, he couldn't stay there. Already he felt the cold creeping over him.

Freedom whinnied on the bank above him. With a supreme effort he pulled himself up to stand beside the horse. Holding the reins, he led the horse down and let him drink. When the horse lifted his head, the water dripped from his muzzle, silver in the light.

Gabriel knew that without the horse, he was as good as dead. He managed to mount Freedom again and urged him up the embankment. They followed the stream for a while. His foot throbbed with each movement. If he didn't find help soon, he wasn't going to be good for much of anything. Think, he begged himself.

He wasn't sure just when he made the decision to turn eastward. The way he figured, it was better to fall into the hands of the Missourians than to die in the wilderness. That way, he might have a chance of seeing his family again. Another thing—he'd heard there were Indians who didn't like the French all that much. Something about a war up in Wisconsin Territory. If they found him, he might as well have stayed in Far West.

Daylight fading. Time to make an early camp. Foot swelling, aching. No longer able to bear any weight. Hopping on one foot, dropping to his knees in the snow. Finding bits of dry brush close to the ground. His fire started, he looked at the food that was left. Hardly enough for another day. And him with no weapon, no way of killing anything.

He tied the horse's reins to a branch. Then he made a place for himself against a tree. Maple, from the looks of the bark. He put snow on his foot. After a while he wrapped it with his spare pair of socks. He leaned back against the tree and closed his eyes.

Toward morning he heard a distant neigh. He opened his eyes. He could see the shapes of trees, the embers from the fire. He looked again. Freedom was gone. He stared for a moment at the broken branch where the horse had been secured. Then he gave a deep sigh. This was it. Just as well. He couldn't have gone much further. Not sure if he could even get to his feet, let alone chase down a horse. The cold was creeping up over him. He would simply go to sleep, and hope that the others got through to Illinois.

Before he gave it up for good, he prayed for them all—for Bethia, that she would have a good life and meet someone who would care for her. For Eb, that he would find his wife and not miss the one who'd pulled him out of the river. For Hannah and her children, that they would be healthy and strong. Finally, for himself, that he would be in God's hands, and that death would come quickly. He fell asleep before he was finished.

A horse neighing close at hand. A creature leaning over him. Freedom back? His eyes flew open. A large brown dog of the shepherd variety stood over him. He felt the animal's breath on his face. It's going to devour me, he thought. Then a voice spoke from the other side of the campfire.

"Ho. *Qu'est-ce que c'est?*"

Gabriel shook his head. Was it possible? His voice sounded weak. *"Vous êtes français? Quelle chance!"*

The man clapped his hands. "*Holà!* Whisky!" The dog bounded away. The man stepped closer to Gabriel and leaned over him. Gabriel saw a swarthy, powerfully-built person, black-haired, much taller than himself. The man wore buckskin trousers and jacket, with a long vest of the same material. *"Mon père est français. Ma mère est Peau-Rouge.* Chippewa. *Et vous?"*

Gabriel managed to say his name and indicate that he was injured. He didn't mention anything about being Mormon and fleeing the state of Missouri. The man was speaking again.

"Je m'appelle Dulac. Pierre Dulac." He was out checking traps when he'd seen a horse all saddled, without a rider.

"Freedom," Gabriel said. "My horse."

Dulac had caught Freedom and followed the tracks back to the campfire. After a few more exchanges in French, Dulac asked if they could speak English. "I try to learn."

Gabriel gave a laugh. *"Eh bien,* I'll teach you. It's about all I'm good for, right now."

Together they packed up his few belongings. He needed help mounting his horse. Dulac finally took the reins and led Freedom over to where he'd left his own horse, a black gelding. The dog trotted alongside.

"That's some dog," Gabriel remarked. *"Un bon chien."*

"He knew you were there. He led me to you."

They rode out of the woods and headed east across a stretch of prairie. Dulac kept giving Gabriel sideways looks out of eyes fringed with long dark lashes. Gabriel began to wonder if he were completely safe. He was certainly at the mercy of this stranger, injured, with only a knife to protect him. Maybe anything was better than freezing in the wilderness.

"Any idea where we are?"

"Pardon?"

"Où sommes nous?"

"This is all Iowa Territory. I take you to my home. I have Indian wife, name of Pentoga. Chippewa name. We live near a place called Mount of Roses."

"Is that anywhere near the Father of Waters?"

"Yes. Big river. It's right there."

Good enough. Gabriel began to relax. His foot aching again. Shivering with the cold.

"Your coat's no good," Dulac said.

"I reckon not." Gabriel drew the jacket up around his neck.

Dulac pulled a blanket from his bedroll and draped it over Gabriel's shoulders. Ashamed to show such weakness, Gabriel turned away. "*Merci beaucoup.*"

The other nodded. Finally Gabriel said, "I reckon it's the hurt foot, makes me feel the cold."

At dusk they stopped. Dulac helped Gabriel dismount. Then, leaving Gabriel with the horses, Dulac took an ax and cut branches from the evergreens. He set the stems in the ground to make a windbreak of pine boughs. Gabriel watched with admiration. "Clever."

Dulac made a fire, then fashioned a resting place with more pine branches. "This how we camp in the north country."

He hung a kettle of snow over the fire. After securing the horses, he helped Gabriel to a seat on the pine branches. "Best bed in all the world. A few blankets, and we'll be warm all night."

They drank tea out of a single cup, and shared cornbread and apples. Dulac said, "In these parts, it's better not to ask a man where he's from, or what he's runnin' from."

"I'll remember."

"But there's one group of people we're all feelin' bad for. And them's Mormons. If ever folks was treated wrong, it's them."

Gabriel looked at him in surprise. Dulac went on. "To make a whole bunch of folks just up and leave, in the middle of winter. Even old people and little children. Why, that's what they do to Indians. Them Missouri pukes is a sorry lot."

Gabriel opened his mouth to speak. Dulac touched his arm. "You don't have to say nothing. I knowed you was Mormon when I see'd you. Why else would you have no coat and no gun, no blanket? No proper food. Travelin' fast as you can, I reckon. Well, yore safe enough here."

Gabriel managed to smile. He threw up his hands in a gesture of amazement and resignation. Dulac said, "And whatever you did, I hope you did it to 'em good."

"Well, as a matter of fact, I didn't do anything. I was in the wrong place at the wrong time."

"*Eh bien.* Like the rest of your people."

"It sure seems so."

Gabriel slept on pine branches that night, swathed in blankets. In the morning they pushed on to Mount of Roses and the Mississippi.

Mount of Roses
March, 1839

I have brought babies into the world, and sat at the bedsides of dying patients. But I'm more and more convinced I know nothing. Who would have thought a simple injury would take so long to heal? And I should have known that days of exposure, a starvation diet and no rest would bring on a case of grippe that would almost carry me off. A little less than three months of being too ill to travel. Fortunate that I was in good hands.

A bit about my circumstances. Pierre Dulac proved to be as kind as any caregiver I'd ever met. He brought me to his cabin by the shores of the Mississippi, gave me the warm spare room by the chimney, then watched over me till the grippe had run its course. He and Pentoga by turns brought me food—soup, roasted acorns, cornbread, and sometimes venison.

After two weeks or so, I was able to be up and about. But the ankle injury prevented me from doing too much. A weakness in the leg, and in fact, the whole body, kept me from any inclination to travel. This in spite of my desire to reunite with my family—to see Eb and Bethia and the rest of them. Sometimes I lay awake at night thinking...all I had to do was follow the river south, join the Ohio, and I would find my way to my childhood home in Gallipolis. Was my mother still alive? What about my older sisters and brother—and my favorite sister, Marie?

I started to help with the chores here, splitting wood and stacking it. One day Pierre took me to his parents' home, a log cabin a few miles south. I met his father, Jean-Jacques, an elderly man who had lived as a trapper and a *voyageur*. His mother, a middle-aged Ojibwë woman—or Chippewa, as the white men say—lay sick with the same kind of illness I'd had. I bade them give her as much soup and water as she could take, and keep her warm.

When they discovered I was a doctor, their excitement knew no bounds. Pierre and Jean-Jacques gave me a seat by the fire and described the great need of the people for any kind of medical help. They told me their own predicament—how Jean-Jacques, strong as an ox all his life, had developed a weakness in his hands and arms which made it increasingly difficult to work his farm. What was he to do?

Then I had my idea. Suppose I went and found my communal family and brought them here? "You'd have plenty of help, to work and repair and plant. They've lost everything, you see, in the Missouri troubles."

We discussed it into the night. "They could even put up other cabins, places for them to live. And they could rent land from you, or even buy it, once they got on their feet again."

At last it was agreed. As soon as I felt well enough, I would saddle up Freedom and ferry across to Quincy, where the Mormons were said to be gathering. I would look until I found my family; then I would do my utmost to bring them here. From what I knew of them, I figured they'd be chomping at the bit to get to a place where they could begin again, and help someone else out at the same time.

When I returned home with Pierre, I found the news had spread. Now, not a day goes by that someone does not come for the doctor. I go willingly, and after seeing the extreme poverty of these people who live in the so-called Half Breed Tract, I seldom accept payment. It has become apparent to me that my mission is to the very poor. The rich have enough doctors.

Somehow I must tell Eb of this conviction, and hope that Freedom and the little money I've saved will be enough to buy his wife out of slavery. Or, as Rusty suggested, we could "just go steal her."

—From the journal of Gabriel Romain

Bethia had no call to be tired. After all the things they'd endured, this was only a short journey. A few steps from the farmhouse where they had found shelter, the climb into the wagon, the short haul to the water's edge, and then the wait while they loaded horses and oxen onto the raft. The trip across the river with the sun sparkling on the water in little points of light. The sound of the waves lapping at the logs, Jody crying, "Look! Look at the boats!" Then the unloading, the sound of the animals' hooves on solid ground.

Now she sat in this primitive cabin while Gabriel unloaded bedding and clothes. They had decided that Gabriel would remain with Pierre Dulac, and she, being Gabriel's betrothed, would sleep in a little loft in the cabin. Nathaniel, Hannah, and their children would live with the senior Dulacs, so Nat could begin work on the farm. Calvin and Sarah would stay in the wagon until cabins could be built, and Eb and Rusty would bed down in the stable.

All this without even consulting her. Or Hannah and Sarah, for that matter.

"Now, child," Sarah had said. "We couldn't stay much longer where we were. A new start is just what we need."

One good thing—they'd left Corey far behind. All that winter and spring, while Nat and Rusty had driven the oxen into Missouri three times to fetch more people, she'd had to stay in close quarters with Corey. Just her luck—wouldn't you know it? When Gabriel finally found them, Corey had been out front to greet him. Hannah glanced out the window and exclaimed, "My stars! I do believe it's Gabriel! Yes—there he is, and the horse too!"

They rushed out, Hannah with her baby over her shoulder, just in time to see Gabriel pick up Corey's hand and press it. The exchange was interrupted as Gabriel hurried to embrace each member of his family. They brought him inside and made him sit down as he told them about his injury and illness. He related his idea for their resettlement.

"Mount of Roses?" Calvin asked. "I think they be calling it 'Montrose' now."

"We'd better wait for Nat and Rusty," Hannah said. "They'll be getting back any day now. Nat'll have to decide. It does sound like the thing to do."

So Gabriel prepared to wait for Nat's return. At the first opportunity, Bethia asked him, "When are we going to be married?"

He drew in his breath as he looked at her. Then he smiled. "Why—*eh bien*—any time you say. I'm afraid it can't be a big wedding, with all the things you wanted. I—I don't even have a cabin for us to live in. But we will—right soon, I reckon."

So it was settled. They would be married as soon as possible. Everyone seemed to accept it without any fuss. Whatever Corey's feelings were, she didn't express them. Bethia felt a bit puzzled by the lack of excitement. As if everyone were still too tired for any kind of celebration.

Hannah in particular seemed listless. When Nat heard of Gabriel's relocation idea, he frowned. "I hope it's as promising as you say. I don't figure on moving much any more. With Hannah the way she is, I reckon we'd better settle and stay put for a good long spell."

"I'll drink to that," Calvin said.

Bethia sighed. And here they were. After days of anticipating the move, they'd ended up in something a little better than an Indian village. Gabriel seemed to sense her dismay as they unloaded.

"See how beautiful it is here," he exclaimed. "Look at those tall trees. All hardwoods. And the river's right here—you'll see the sun rise over those hills."

She didn't reply. Gabriel introduced her to the couple with the strange names—Pierre and Pentoga. Pierre looked like something out of the Old Testament—long black hair and beard. And he was dressed in skins, not even proper cloth. Pentoga had a lined, patient face, dark eyes, and black hair worn in tight braids. She wore a long skirt of some material that looked like denim. Possibly an animal skin.

"Welcome," she said in a low-pitched voice. "We are glad you are here. We are so sorry for your people."

Not expecting such sympathy, Bethia could only nod. Later, Gabriel drove her and the others over to meet Jean-Jacques and his wife, whom they called 'May' or *Maman*. After a meal of acorns and squash soup, which Bethia found tasteless, they left all the others with Jean-Jacques. Rusty drove Gabriel and Bethia back to Pierre's cabin in the carriage.

"We'd leave the horses with you, but there's no proper shelter for them. Jean-Jacques has a stable."

"Fine," Gabriel replied. "Get along, now. It's getting late."

So they were essentially stranded, without even transportation. As they stood outside in the twilight, she mentioned this fact to Gabriel. He nodded, looking out at the river.

"Well, there's always the water. Pierre has a little skiff tied up down there. And we still have Freedom—there's an old shed just big enough for him. We'll have to go to work and build what we need."

She sniffed. He put his arm around her. "And most of my patients mainly come to me. Or their families fetch me, and I walk to where I'm needed."

"Oh." She hadn't thought he would find patients so soon. "You must be making some money."

"I'm afraid not. We aren't going to get rich here." He patted her shoulder. "But it's useful work, and I've helped a number of folks."

"You mean we're going to stay here?"

He looked at her. "For the moment—yes. We're safe here. We're not being chased or shot at. Where else could we go?"

"It's just that—well, everything's so strange. Even the names. Jean-Jacques. Pentoga."

He laughed. "Wait'll you meet Adriel. And Crazy Charley."

She felt a stab of uneasiness. "Who are they?"

"They live down by the waterfront, closer to town. Adriel—he's a scout. Knows this country inside out. As for Charley—he's not a bad fellow, really. But if you want anything stolen, he's the man to do it."

A shiver ran through her. "How do you manage to meet such people?"

"I take them as I find them. Bethia—trust me. It's going to be all right. Pierre saved my life, out there in the wilderness. That should tell you something. These are good folks."

The river rippled, pink with the afterglow of sunset, and the trees stood out dark against it. The scent of fresh water, mingled with wood smoke and a faint fishy odor, lay everywhere. There was a dampness about things, as if they were standing in river-mist. So different from Far West. She sighed, trying to hide her annoyance. "I wonder you didn't ask Corey to come too."

A startled look went over his face. "Corey? It never entered my head. I reckon she's safer where she is."

"What do you mean by that? Here you were telling me this was a good place—-that we're all safe here."

"I only meant—well, we needed people here who could work—maybe build some kind of settlement. And Corey—she has her hands full already. You notice Owen Crawford didn't come with us either. He needs to rest a bit."

She could not define what caused her to say the next words. "If I didn't know, I'd say you were sweet on Corey."

He stepped into the shadows; she could no longer see his face. He gave a little laugh. "Sweet? Oh, that's not how I think of her."

She pressed on, determined. "What is it, then?"

"*Eh bien*—I feel she's a lovely, strong person with burdens I can only guess at. Her sister, for one thing. The child will never be normal. And her father's not really well."

"So?"

"So she manages to be cheerful and helpful, in spite of these things. And I admire her for it." He turned. "Shall we go inside?"

She followed, abashed anew by his compassion. At that moment she decided to be cheerful and helpful too, no matter what it cost her. She would have to manage here, whether she liked it or not.

11

Gabriel heard the news from Crazy Charley one week before the wedding.

"You're certain? Joseph and Hyrum escaped?"

"That's what they be sayin'." Charley spat a stream of tobacco juice in the direction of the corner spittoon. It splattered on the floor.

"Need to repent," Gabriel remarked. "Improve your aim."

Charley glared at Gabriel, his eyes blazing out of his wrinkled face. "I'll repent when hell freezes over. Anyway, the prisoners was loaded into a wagon and sent off for another county, is what I heard. They bought the guards enough whiskey, got 'em drunk, and took off into the woods. Yer prophet's in Quincy now, and the word is, he's lookin' fer a place where you kin all resettle. He's even buyin' up land."

"Can you beat that?" Gabriel drained his glass and set it on the table.

"And that ain't all. There's talk of some kind of conference next weekend, over in Quincy."

"A church conference? I guess it's about time."

Charley spat again. This time he hit the mark. Gabriel started to express his admiration, but he stopped under Charley's intense gaze. Charley chewed slowly. "So, you fixin' to up and follow them?"

Gabriel shook his head. "I figure we're settled here. We may go over to the conference, I reckon. But Nat and Calvin are puttin' crops in and buildin' cabins. They be just finishing one for me."

Charley grunted. "I like the way he built them cabins—small, like the Dulac's place. Nothin' fancy about them."

True. Unlike the house at Far West, Nat's latest cabins were compact, like a settlement of native American dwellings. He had taken care to build each one in a separate grove of trees, so that it was not visible from the road.

"I reckon he's tired of having his home destroyed. This way, if they torch one cabin, there're still others."

"You still aimin' to git married?"

"Next Saturday, if she'll have me. We may have to do it earlier, on account of that conference."

Charley waited before he spoke. "You're a good man, Gabe. I hate to see any feller give up his freedom so willing-like."

Gabriel laughed. "I'm gaining more than I'm givin' up. She's a right good cook."

"So are they all." Charley squinted, then gave him a broad wink. "Tell you what. The night before that wedding, you come down here and we'll drink one last toast. Maybe a bunch of 'em."

Gabriel stood up. "See you, Charley. Thanks for the news."

He strode out into the bright sunlight. The door of the public house swung shut behind him. He found the road that led south to his new home. Mud left by the rains lay everywhere. He picked his way from one high spot of ground to the next, wanting to hurry, to be the first with the news. Their leaders free at last. And by this time, everyone out of Far West except the few that had chosen to renounce their religion and stay.

The scent of damp earth and growing things hung in the air. New life, stirred into being by the warm wind and rains. In spite of what had happened in Missouri, the unspeakable sufferings of his people, life went on, the ceaseless round of growth and rebirth. A marvel, what Nat and his helpers had managed to do. Three cabins built, his own even now being furnished with a bed and table. Crops in the ground, just the way Jean-Jacques had wanted. Nat, with the help of Calvin, Eb, and Rusty, had planted wheat, squash, and beans. According to Ojibwe tradition, the women took care of the corn. And together May and Pentoga had done it.

"That's a good idea," he'd said to Bethia. "If we could get all our women to go plant the corn, the men could just take it easy."

Joking, of course. But she set her lips primly. "What a thing to say. You should be ashamed."

He tried to tell her he didn't mean it. But she turned away, shaking her head.

He just didn't understand her. When he'd said the same thing later to Hannah, she'd laughed.

Jean-Jacques' cabin just ahead. Scattered off in the woods, expertly hidden, stood the new cabins. One for Nat and his family, one for Calvin and Sarah, and the third for Bethia and himself. In addition, they'd enlarged the stable and made a room for Eb and Rusty. There was even a place for Owen Crawford, who had just joined them.

The trouble with so many cabins was trying to guess which one had the people in it. He tried Jean-Jacques' house first.

"They're all over at your place," May said. "Getting everything ready for you and your bride."

He thanked her and ran up the path to his cabin. A place of their own! It was more than he'd ever hoped for. His home stood further up the slight hill than the others, and was the farthest from the river and the road. Privacy for the doctor.

Voices inside. First, Jody. "Why are you putting it there?"

"That's where I want it," Bethia said.

Sarah's voice. "Good thing Gabriel's not too big. He'd never even get in the door."

He opened the door. For a brief second he marveled that so many people could fit in the one room—Sarah and Bethia over by the wooden bed-frame, Nat and Calvin checking the table legs, Jody under the table. Hannah stood by the only window, holding the baby on her hip in a leather sling Nathaniel had fashioned. Eb straightened up from the hearth, where he'd laid the first fire. Rusty and Owen were stuffing corn husks into a huge sack of burlap.

Calvin glanced up. "Well, if it ain't the bridegroom."

"Stop, everybody!" Gabriel came to a halt himself, since he couldn't get any farther into the room. "I've got news!"

They all looked up as he repeated what he'd heard. The work stopped.

"If that don't beat all," Eb said.

Nat's brows drew together. "A conference in Quincy?"

"Where in Quincy?" Calvin asked.

"I dunno. I figure if we just go over there, we'll find it."

It took Gabriel a few moments to realize that Bethia was sobbing. Hannah put an arm around her.

"Whatever is wrong?" he asked.

Bethia's voice shook. "The weh-weh-wedding. We're supposed to be getting married. And you're all ready to go off to some—some conference."

"Oh, hang it all," Calvin exclaimed. "That's right. Maybe just one of us should go."

Gabriel blinked. "Well, I—"

"I reckon we'd all like to be there," Nat said. "See the prophet again. Learn what's happening. We could have the wedding when we get back—"

"Or before we leave," Hannah said.

Gabriel shrugged. "What about getting married over there? We'd probably have a lot more folks than just us."

Nat smiled, stroking his beard. "There's an idea. Maybe we could get somebody like Sidney Rigdon to perform the ceremony."

"No." Bethia spoke through her tears. "We want you."

Rusty waved a corn husk. "Like as not, there'd be lots more to eat if we did it over there. We could sort of get the word out first, and folks would bring cakes and such."

Eb shook his head. "I reckon you'd like that."

Nat said, "As long as we have the ceremony, does it really matter where we do it?"

Hannah stroked Bethia's hair. "All our friends will be there—folks from Far West."

At last she appeared convinced. They began making plans for the trip across the water. "Gabe," Hannah said. "Do you remember how we made those little cakes—petits fours—for when I married Nathaniel?"

He nodded. "I'll get us some extra flour and eggs. We'll start baking tomorrow."

As the others left, Bethia crossed over to him. She looked weepy and unsure. He put his arms around her. "Now, Beth. Everything will be fine."

"But why did it have to be *this* weekend?"

"Things will work out. You'll see." He felt her cheek close to his. Then she sniffed.

"You've been drinking."

"Me? I had a drink with Crazy Charley. I—I thought it was cider."

She drew away from him. "You did. You went down and had a drink with that scoundrel."

Puzzled, he kept smiling. "Come on, now. Only one drink. It didn't hurt none. Besides, that's how I got the news."

She gave him an accusing look. He decided to change the subject. Gesturing: "How do you like our new home?"

"It seems rather dark."

"We can whitewash the walls. That's what a lot of folks do—it gives more light."

She didn't say anything. He shrugged. "Well—I'd best go see if Eb's fed Freedom. Chances are, he hasn't yet. Then we'll see about those wedding refreshments."

She didn't respond as he kissed her. He went off to find Eb.

"I don't know, Eb. Some folks aren't cut out for marriage. And I think I'm one of them."

"Nonsense. Folks get nervous before a wedding—'specially their own. Once it's done, you be fine." Eb slapped Freedom on the rump to make him move over. He set to work currying the other side. Gabriel folded his arms and leaned against the side of the stall.

"It's just that—well, she's acting strange. After me because I had a drink with old Charley."

"So? She's antsy too. She'll settle down right fine after the wedding. Be her old self."

"I sure hope so. Otherwise, I reckon I'm in for a peck of trouble."

"It's late in the game to be wantin' out. Is there someone else you fancy?"

Corey's image filled his mind. Ridiculous. He hardly knew her. "Well, no. I always figured Bethia'd make a good wife."

Eb grunted. "She will. A right good choice. Don't fret none about it—just do it. Once it's done..." He lapsed into silence. Gabriel wondered if he were thinking about his own wife, Jess, whom he'd left in Virginia. High time they went to fetch her. Gabriel straightened up.

"I'd better get into town before someone comes needing a doctor. Have to find some flour and other things."

"You want the horse?"

"No. Let him rest. I'll walk."

"I'll come with you. We're about done here." Eb pulled the loose hair out of the currycomb and put the tool up on the shelf. "Let's go."

Rusty didn't think he would shed any tears over the loss of Bethia. He tried to assist the other group members as they prepared for the wedding, even offering to take all the food across in Pierre's skiff. He didn't protest when Bethia insisted that Eb accompany him so he wouldn't eat any of the little cakes. But when it came time for the actual ceremony, when Bethia in her borrowed wedding dress and Gabriel in his old gray suit—the best he had—stood at last in front of Nathaniel, he felt a sense of desolation so keen it was like pain.

As if she understood, Hannah put her arm through his. He smiled at her, but his lip trembled. The words of the wedding vow filled the room.

"You both mutually agree to be each other's companion, husband and wife..."

Silly of him. She had never really been his in any sense. Even when Gabe had fled and no one knew if he would ever find them again, she had ignored his advances. It was as though she were moving in harmony with some strange, set purpose in her own mind, some inner music. But she was still the embodiment of his youthful fantasies, the companion of his growing-up years.

Strange. He thought of their arrival in Quincy that morning, and how the women had clustered around Hannah and the baby Gabrielle.

"What a lovely child."

"She has dark hair like her father."

So many of them wanted to know about the child born during the exodus, and the delivery of her by Gabriel, that poor Bethia and the wedding took second place. Rusty noticed her consternation and felt sorry for her. As if that weren't bad enough, Gabe was soon surrounded by young women, still attractive in their makeshift clothes, who wanted to hear his side of the story.

He gladly accommodated them, pausing to greet the ones whom he'd known in Far West. When Corey entered the room with her unfortunate sister, Gabe clasped their hands and gave them smiles and attentive looks as he talked with them. Rusty shifted his feet, uncomfortable. What was wrong with Gabe? If it'd been him, he would've devoted all his attention to his bride.

When the brief ceremony was finished, people gathered around the new husband and wife. But the congratulations soon gave way to talk of the conference and the things that had happened so quickly.

"All them land purchases—a hundred and thirty-five acres south of Commerce," Calvin said.

Nathaniel gestured, trying to explain. "That's only the farm. The Hugh White farm. Then there's forty-seven acres more, and some sort of hotel."

"And that's just on one side of the river. Most of what they bought's on the Iowa side."

"I ask you, who's gonna pay for all that?" someone else asked.

Calvin shrugged. "Don't look at me."

The late afternoon light cast dark shadows in the room. Nat gathered his group together after the refreshments had disappeared. "It's time to be heading back. The animals need feeding at home. The ferry be leaving in another half-hour."

Half an hour to say good-bye to their friends and return Bethia's borrowed clothes. As they walked to the landing, Rusty thought Bethia looked pale and tired, on the verge of tears. She held onto Gabriel's arm as he led her through the throng of well-wishers.

"Well, doc. Looks like your days of freedom are over for sure."

"It happens to the best of us."

Gabriel looked strained and uncertain himself, as if dazed from what they'd just done. Rusty, keeping pace with them, felt a nameless sorrow, a wish that things could have gone better for them. Simply his loss, he thought; he'd get over it somehow. Folks survived all kinds of things. Hadn't Brother Hyrum just said that thousands of people had been driven from northern Missouri? The property loss alone he reckoned at $200,000.

Hannah acted subdued too. Tired, most like. Even the children were quiet. They boarded the ferry. When Nathaniel bent to put his hand on Bethia's shoulder, she did not smile back.

Hannah stood at the one window of her cabin. Late summer already. The morning light filtered through the thicket of trees and underbrush. As she watched, the wind caught the branches. Pools of light danced on the forest floor. Here she felt secluded, safe from everything except the marsh sickness. And thanks to Gabriel, she had managed to survive even that.

It had struck suddenly. A day of chills and fever, and then lying drenched in perspiration, too ill to move. Bethia had taken both Jody and the baby up to her own cabin, and by the grace of God, they had stayed healthy. But people were dying on both sides of the river; Sarah had told her.

"Why, the prophet himself, he took sick with it. Derned if he didn't git outa bed and start healing folks, right there in his own yard. He and the others went around laying hands on folks and praying. He even came over to Montrose, where a whole bunch of 'em were sick down in the old military barracks. And some of 'em got well."

Now she was well enough to have her children again. Gabrielle slept in the wooden cradle beside the bed. The child's dark lashes curved down over her cheeks, her lovely mouth open a little. She had the deep look of peace that sleeping children have. Hannah longed to take her out under the trees and let her sleep there, but Gabriel had forbidden it.

"Keep them inside as much as possible. We don't want them coming down with any fever."

So tired, Gabriel looked. Going about every day to the families stricken with the marsh miasma. He'd refused to take Bethia with him.

"You're best off staying home. I got enough sick folks to worry about."

Nat had taken Jody with him to do the chores. She could hear Nell barking, and the barks told her where they were. Over near the stable. Some trooper, Nell. If the crushed paw had healed, the dog herself was not aware of it. She followed Nat on three legs now, seldom letting him out of her sight.

Hannah drew the shutters in, to keep out the heat. She loved her cabin. Nat had whitewashed the walls, and made an extra room for the children. She bent briefly over Gabrielle, still asleep; the child's mouth moved in a dream.

Worried about Bethia. Couldn't Gabe see what was happening? No; he was too exhausted to notice. They had started well enough, to be sure. In fact, Hannah wasn't sure herself where the trouble lay. Maybe too many new things, all at once. The move to Montrose, the sudden isolation, the cabin all to herself. So different from the communal life in the Far West house. That was it—Bethia needed to be around people more. Weeks of being locked up with the care of two small children had been too much for her. Hannah sat down on the bed, wondering if she should speak to Gabe about it. If he didn't know anything was wrong, it was high time he did.

A noise on the path outside. Footsteps in the leaves. She opened the shutters. Gabriel himself stood at the door.

She hurried to open it before he could knock and wake the baby. Their eyes met; he smiled. She noticed in an instant that he looked less tired, even handsome in his boyish way, his tousled hair straggling over his forehead. Too busy to comb it, most like. She took his hand. "You're looking rested."

He pressed her fingers briefly. "I finally got a night's sleep. And you? *Comment ça va?*"

"I'm fit as ever. I can't believe I was so ill."

He crossed to the settle in front of the hearth and sat down. He had the old impish, mischievous expression she had remembered from their younger days. No wonder Bethia had loved him. She pulled out a chair beside the table. "There's soup in the pot. Want some?"

He moved his hand in a quick little gesture. "*Merci.* Maybe later." He glanced around at the cabin, then looked at her. "I came mainly to see how you were doing. And to warn you—don't try to do too much right off. Rest all you can."

"Does it come back?"

"It can. We need to be careful. I'm seeing a lot less of it now—this marsh sickness or whatever you want to call it. Old Charley says just to stay away from the river. But I reckon there's more to it than that. I think it's those swamplands. Something in there's not good for anybody."

Hannah smoothed her skirt. "Who'd ever imagine the things we've had to deal with?"

"Yes—and we're managing to overcome a great many of them. Like the frozen river—I didn't cross, but I hear a lot of folks just went right over on the ice. Emma and her three children. Now, that's courage. One child in her arms, the other two hanging onto her skirts. Going across, not knowing what was on the other side. When I get discouraged, I think of that."

She leaned forward. "Be you discouraged now?"

"No—things have calmed down some. I need to work on the cabin a little—repair some things. I'll get Eb to help."

"Maybe you need to spend more time at home."

He gave her a quick look, then shook his head. "I do what I can."

Now was the time. She drew a deep breath. "Gabriel, there's something I'd like to say."

He raised his eyebrows. "Say on."

"Well—" She paused. "It's about Bethia. I'm not sure you know it. She's—she's just not happy. I don't know if it's the loneliness, or what. Maybe she's bored. There's this—this discontent—something I can't explain."

He sat in silence for a moment. Then he nodded. "Blamed if I can figure it out. I've tried to give her everything I can. Sometimes it seems no matter what I do, it's not enough. And lots of times I'm too tired to make the effort. Maybe I'm not one to be married."

"It's not that. She loves you. I think she'd maybe do better in another place. With more people."

He gave a laugh. "Downtown Montrose? There's not a lot there. You can bet she doesn't care for Crazy Charley and the other folks I know."

She met his eyes. "Maybe if you referred to him as 'Mr. Charles Pearson, Esquire,' it might make a difference."

He raised his eyebrows. "Give him respectability? It's too late. Besides, he has a reputation to maintain—the best thief in three counties."

They both laughed softly. Hannah smoothed out a wrinkle in her apron. "Forgive me for suggesting it. You might need to find another sort of neighbor for your wife."

Gabriel sighed. "What you don't know—and I'm sure she doesn't—is that these little towns are full of folks like Charley. River rats, they call 'em. Fellers ready to take advantage of anyone they can. If they're smart, they c'n make a living doing it. Now, I figure it's better to make friends with 'em, and not try to fight 'em. 'Cause when the respectable folks have had enough of our strange ways and religion, maybe these very river rats'll come to our rescue." He nodded, as if thinking to himself. "Charley, now. I reckon he'd do anything for me if'n it came to that. I've earned his trust and his friendship."

Hannah started to speak. "It seems like—" At the same time Gabriel moved one hand in a nervous little gesture. "Do you reckon—" Then he stopped and waited for her.

"Seems like all the main settlin' is on t'other side of the river. Commerce. Joseph and all the other leaders be there. And the shop keepers, the business owners."

He smiled. "The rich folk?"

"No one's rich anymore, if they ever was. You know that. Everyone's startin' from nothin'. And yet they be building, making shops and cabins. Movin' their families in."

He frowned, his lips drawing together. "You're thinkin' I should get over there and make a place for her?"

"It might be one of the best things you can do. Bring her out of this state she's in. Her friends are all over there. Sarah and Calvin be thinking of buying land over there sometime soon. They're goin' across."

He gave her an abrupt look. "And what about you?"

She returned his gaze, puzzled. "I reckon I like it here. Nat's in a good situation—he likes the farm and the work. And Jean-Jacques needs him—you know he's gettin' worse." She gave a sigh. "Nat's talked some about going over and hiring out as a builder once things be settled here. But we'd keep living here." She smiled then. "We be safe here."

"I like it too—I have patients who depend on me. But Eb and I—we've always talked of a blacksmith shop. Maybe Rusty'd be interested too."

"Don't see why you couldn't do anything you wanted. Get a place on the other side, set up shop. Now's the time to start fresh. That's what folks are doin'. Your cabin here will always be waiting—you can come across and see patients whenever you choose. Twice a week, even. And Bethia—why, if we've guessed right, the move may be just what she needs."

The baby began to make little whimpering noises. Gabriel stood up. "*Eh bien*. Let's see what we can do. Seems that, first, like, I'll need a skiff. That's the thing about Charley—pardon me—Mr. Pearson,

Esquire. He can get you anything you need. And for a little extra, he'll most likely row it, too."

The baby started to cry. Hannah moved to pick her up. Gabriel nodded and walked toward the door. As he started down the path, Hannah saw that his head was bent, his black brows knitted together.

12

To Gabriel's surprise, the others had more enthusiasm for the plan than he would've imagined. Sarah's eyes brightened.

"I reckon we better git over there and get us some land before everyone else does."

"If we do it in time, we might get to see the apostles leave for England," Calvin said. "The missionaries and such. They be starting soon."

Eb shook his head. "Unless they're sneaky about it—the way the six of 'em snuck back into Far West last April and dedicated that temple site like they swore they would."

Rusty began to explain. "There was twenty others too. And if any of them Missourians had got wind of it, they woulda been killed for sure."

Nathaniel, still the head of the community, held up his hand. "Now, listen, everyone. I've been studyin' some. Here's what we'll do."

The plot they arranged to purchase lay near the river, on the flatlands. A path went off in a southerly direction, and just a short stroll led to the edge of a wetland area. Here cattails and rushes grew, and water birds of all descriptions perched on stumps and ends of logs.

"What a delightful place!" Bethia clasped her hands together.

"I'm glad you like it." Gabriel took her arm. "I reckon we can be happy here. Though it's a bit closer to the water than I'd hoped."

"Nonsense. It's beautiful."

The lot was big enough for two main structures and a garden. The first building, facing the road, would house a blacksmith shop and a room for Rusty and Eb. Bethia and Gabriel would live in two rooms behind the shop. Further back on the lot, they planned to build a log house for Calvin and Sarah. It would have a large fireplace for the main cooking area, and a room where Gabriel could see patients that chose to come to him.

Nathaniel rowed across with Pierre Dulac each day, and all of the men working together managed to put up most of the log house and the blacksmith shop building in two months. Then Nat and Pierre had to attend to the harvest for Jean-Jacques, now too weak to leave his cabin.

Gabriel, looking at the new structures rising between the road and the river, thought how they'd surmounted the obstacle of Bethia's health. She seemed content and happy, eager about each new thing. No longer bored or depressed.

To his dismay, the afternoon he moved their few belongings to their new quarters, she burst into the room.

"Why didn't you say? You might at least have warned me."

"About what?"

"Oh, you know. You know very well that Corey's family has the second house over."

The name sent a sudden shock through him. "Corey Langdon? I—I had no idea."

"You did. You chose it deliberately." Tears stood in her eyes.

He tried to collect his thoughts. "Really, Bethia, I—I wouldn't do such a thing. The rest of them wanted this site. I—"

She sniffed and fixed him with an accusing look. He shrugged. "I didn't plan it this way. However, I see no harm in having them as neighbors. Someone we know—is that so bad?"

She acted distant all through dinner, prepared in the big new kitchen by Sarah. Gabriel sighed and tried to eat. What was he in for now? Like as not, no one else knew. But Eb pressed his arm and gave him a questioning look.

"I'm all right," he replied. "We have to get busy and order what we need for the shop. I've made a list of things."

Thanks to Charley, Gabriel heard of a man in Carthage who was selling an anvil and other equipment. He and Eb borrowed the wagon and ox team from Nat and made the trip. With a down payment and the promise to pay the rest in three years, they brought back the anvil, hammer, tongs, bellows, and even a swage-block. They stood now, surveying the brick forge with the flue-chimney in place.

Eb gave a little cough. "I think we done right well."

Gabriel nodded, pleased that at least one thing was working out. "We'll unload and get things set up. Then I'll take the oxen to the stable and feed them—get them back across the river tomorrow. I reckon Nat'll be watching for them."

When word spread about Gabriel's medical training, his room in the log house had a steady stream of people with sore throats, bronchitis, asthma attacks, rheumatism and other ailments. Between his work as a doctor and his effort to teach Eb and Rusty what he knew about running a smithy, he felt more pressed for time than ever. But they were beginning to make enough money to support themselves. Gabriel tried to save a little, thinking of the trip they would eventually make to Virginia and the plantation where Eb's wife worked.

"That's the silliest thing I ever heard," Bethia said. "As if you're just going to go down there and find her."

"Stranger things have happened."

She sniffed. "Like as not, they'll steal Eb back, soon as he's in Virginia."

"How can they? He's a freedman, with papers to prove it. Besides, he'll be with us."

He was polite with Bethia, careful of his words, not wanting to upset her. But he was determined not to let her fears dictate his personal and professional life. He treated Corey and her family as he always had, and did not go out of his way to avoid her. She in turn acted friendly and pleasant, a good neighbor.

He missed Hannah and Nat, and tried to get across to see them at least twice a week. Sometimes he took Bethia with him, and after he'd attended to his patients, they talked of happenings on both sides of the river.

"Seems like you can't get away from the sounds of building," he said to Hannah. "A whole city's going up, right before our eyes."

"The same in Montrose," Hannah replied. "Folks movin' in. Nat goes out with the oxen about three times a week and does haulin'."

Once Gabriel made an unscheduled visit, alone. He found Nat in the stable. Gabriel leaned against the wall, breathing fast.

"Derned if I can figure it out. I've not been 'specially religious. But they say I'm called to be an elder."

Nat tramped toward him, pitchfork in hand. "Well, that's splendid. What's wrong with it?"

"I don't think I'm cut out for such a thing."

"Of course you are. The main thing an elder does is try to bring healing. And you do that already."

"I never figured I had that kind of strength. I mean, for spiritual things."

Nat put a hand on his shoulder. "I think you'll do fine. I reckon it's not us that decides such things."

Gabriel looked down, still uncertain. Nat leaned the pitchfork against the wall. "Why, you'll get to go on missionary journeys. See new places."

Gabriel met his eyes. "What about old places? Gallipolis? And Virginia."

"Why not? Wherever the Lord tells you to go."

Gabriel felt better. "I couldn't figure why they'd call me now, right at this time. Then I realized the local bishop was one of my patients. I treated him for something, and I reckon he got well."

Bethia seemed to care more about the ordination than he did. Then he realized that it boosted her standing in the neighborhood. *Eh bien,* he thought. Whatever helped.

The trouble was, Bethia had definite ideas about what a marriage relationship should be. She thought of the days in the Far West house when Gabriel had first expressed his interest in her. A gentle, steady series of romantic encounters, ended by the flight from Missouri.

What had gone so wrong? Now he came home exhausted, too tired to take her in his arms and talk with her. The bantering, the flattering words, all a thing of the past.

"Well, you be married now, you goose," Sarah said. "He chose you, didn't he? Look at him, working two jobs, even crossing the river to see sick folk. Now he's going to be an elder, and that's more work. And you wonder why he's tired? I reckon he's doing his best for you."

"I figured things would be different-like. That he'd spend more time at home."

Sarah snorted. "You need to think of marriage as a—a partnership. That's all it is, I reckon. He's workin' to feed you, and you're workin' to keep the home. Doesn't mean he's not interested, or likes you any less."

Bethia suppressed a sigh. "That's just it. He seems more interested in—in the government denying our petition for redress, than he is in me. He ignores most things I say. Or doesn't hear them—I don't know."

Sarah opened the door in the side of the fireplace and slid the pan of bread dough into it. "Well, I reckon everyone's upset about that petition. All the trouble to take it to Washington and have it denied. That's why they brought it before the conference—folks wanted to continue the appeal."

Bethia blinked, feeling depression settle over her. The same depression she'd felt when she'd thought there was no chance of Gabriel caring for her. Sarah sat down beside her.

"Aw, honey. He acts like a typical man to me. It'll be different when you have that first child. Then you'll be too busy to care what he's up to."

Another trouble—there was no child. Married almost a year, and no sign of a pregnancy. She began to cry, dabbing her eyes with her apron. She didn't want to mention this last to Sarah. Sarah wiped the bits of bread dough from her fingers.

"Just give it time. Time helps a heap of things. Let's set the table now. They'll be comin' in for some supper soon."

Bethia dried her eyes. Then there was the kidnapping incident. Like as not, that's all they'd talk about at supper.

A few miles above Quincy, a company of Missourians had crossed the river into Illinois and kidnapped four Mormon men. They had taken them back to Missouri to a place called Tully, where they imprisoned them in an old log cabin. After threats against their lives, the near hanging of one of them, and the beating of two others, they were let go.

Bethia was right; even before the first bite of food, Calvin was saying, "Even the gentiles is stirred up about it. Leastways on this side of the river."

Sarah said, "I don't see what good that mass meeting did. Just got folks more riled up."

Rusty reached for a biscuit. "They be sending a delegation to Governor Carlin. Them Missourians have got to know this can't be tolerated."

Beside her, Gabriel shook his head. "Why, even old Charley—you oughta hear him talk about the good Christian folk of Missouri. He says there's nothing worse than them chasin' us out, then comin' across to kidnap us now that we've gone."

Bethia put down her fork. "Crazy Charley?"

"Right. Even he can see injustice when it happens."

She felt anger rising within her. "I thought you weren't going to see him again."

"When did I ever say that? Just 'cause we've moved—when I go back across the river, he's usually right there."

"You know that old shack right by the wharf?" Eb said. "Folks think it's a boathouse. But it's where they live—him and Adriel."

"That Indian feller?" Sarah passed the potatoes. "Sounds like what Charley needs is a proper wife."

Gabriel began to laugh. "That's the last thing he needs. He sets a store by his freedom. Why, he even warned—uh, advised me to think twice before I got married."

Bethia could not contain her irritation. "And you—you actually listened to him?"

"I got married, didn't I? Here—have a biscuit."

Calvin wiped his mouth and put his napkin down. "The point is, we're not safe, even here. Why, even the river scum know it."

"Charley's not scum," Gabriel said. "He knows everything—and he might be more help than you think."

"I'm minded how the prophet said we should all stop stealing," Sarah said. "Seems to me that the river rats are the ones that are stealing. We're getting blamed for it."

Gabriel laughed again. "Well, like Joseph said. Our enemies looked out in the early morning and saw someone walking on the water, and they figured it was some Mormon going across to steal something."

Everyone laughed. Rusty, across from Bethia, looked down at his empty plate. When he raised his eyes, Bethia felt the full force of his gaze. She was thinking that maybe she'd married the wrong person—Rusty might have valued her more, paid more attention to her. He was handsome, to be sure, tall and broad-shouldered. His upper arms were muscular and powerful from work in the blacksmith shop. When he spoke, his voice was a deep baritone.

"D'you reckon there'll ever be a place where we can be in peace?"

"You mean like the Peaceable Kingdom?" Calvin asked. "The city on the hill?"

"Isn't that what we look for? What we seek to build?"

"I don't know, son," Calvin said. "Maybe this isn't the time for it yet."

"By thunder!" Gabriel stood up and threw his napkin on the table. "It's up to us, isn't it? We'll make this the time for it. We got to get busy and keep building."

Gabriel left the house with Eb close behind. Calvin stood up and nodded to Sarah, then retreated to the corner that served as his study.

"I reckon it's up to God," Rusty said, as if to himself. Bethia smiled at him, inviting him to stay and keep talking. He looked at her briefly, not smiling, and stood up to leave.

Gabriel was leaning up against the door post watching Eb shoe a horse for Jubal Langdon when he first heard of John C. Bennett.

"A doctor, you say?"

Jubal ran a hand through his shock of white hair. "Yep. High standing in his profession, according to the *Louisville Courier-Journal.*"

Gabriel felt a twinge of skepticism. "Is that a fact?"

"He be living over at Brother Joseph's house now, and folks say he's right smart. Knows everything about charters and militias and such like."

Eb picked up the horse's left front foot. "Tell him about the Invisible Baboons."

Jubal smiled. "That's 'Dragoons.' *The Invincible Dragoons.* Some group in Illinois."

With the tongs, Eb placed the shoe on the hoof. "What're dragoons anyway?"

Jubal tried to explain. "An armed force, like a militia."

"I be thinking they was a cross between dragons and baboons."

Gabriel was laughing now. "I like Invisible Baboons better."

Jubal said, "Well, he's still in charge of 'em. Brigadier general."

Gabriel shrugged. "I'm not impressed."

Jubal raised his eyebrows. "Well, I hope to tell you. Everyone else is." He winked at Gabriel. "'Specially the ladies."

Gabriel snorted. "Oh, hang the ladies. What do they know?"

"Well," Jubal said. "I reckon if I had his ways, I wouldn't have no trouble finding me a wife."

"You're having trouble?" Gabriel asked.

"The thing is, no one wants to take on a stepdaughter that's not right. And no one's much for courtin' Corey, either. Afeard they'd have to support her sister."

Gabriel couldn't believe it. "I'll tell you. If they'd let me have a second wife, I'd marry your Corey in a minute. And I'd take her sister too."

Rusty, wielding the bellows, gave a laugh. Gabriel and Jubal laughed too. Eb did not laugh. He shook his head and gestured toward the rooms where Gabriel and Bethia lived.

Gabriel drew in his breath. Had she heard? Then he shrugged. "Back to this Bennett. A brigadier general? Does that mean we have to have a militia?"

"It makes sense," Jubal said. "We need some means of defense, after all we been through. Even if it's just for show."

"Probably make a heap of folks busy," Eb said. "Keep 'em out of trouble."

"Tiens." Gabriel straightened up. "I reckon I'll pay this new doctor a little visit."

He walked down to the Smith house later in the afternoon and introduced himself to Dr. Bennett.

"Dr. Gabriel Romain. I heard about you, and thought I'd come down and meet you. Welcome you to the community, so to speak."

Bennett rose quickly from his chair, and Gabriel saw that the man was short in stature, just a few inches taller than himself. A fleeting impression...a thin face, dark-complected, and black eyes which appeared to dart everywhere. He had black hair flecked with gray, neatly combed in contrast to Gabriel's, which grew in waves and gave the impression of shagginess. He looked to be about the same age as the prophet, in his mid-thirties. Even though he shook Gabriel's hand and smiled, there seemed to be an air of superiority in the act, a disdain.

Gabriel smiled in return, uncomfortable, as Bennett spoke. "You haven't been a doctor long, from the looks of you. Where did you get your training?"

Gabriel told him. "From Dr. Henry Newton, in Mentor. That was before we left for Far West."

Bennett lifted his eyebrows. "Oh, yes. I presume you know that I founded the Illinois State Medical Society. I was privileged to teach midwifery, diseases of women and children, and, oh, yes—medical jurisprudence at Willoughby University."

Gabriel was feeling smaller by the moment. "I—I see. I didn't know that, sir."

"Tell me one thing," Bennett said. "With all your training, and your work here—why haven't you told these people to drain their swamp?"

"Swamp, sir?" He began to wish he hadn't been in such a rush to meet the man.

"That's where your miasm is coming from. Drain that area, and you wouldn't have all this sickness in the summer months."

Gabriel swallowed. "I've often thought so. But—we've just moved across from Montrose. We're still getting established here—"

"Well, no matter." Bennett smiled again. "I intend to tell them. In fact, I already have."

Charming, he was, to be sure. Disarming. But Gabriel felt uneasy, as if a warning bell was sounding in his mind. Something not quite right. He listened as Bennett went on.

"There're many other things I'd like to do here. Help the town get established. I see a need for certain forms of organization. Discipline. But we can't do everything at once." He spread his hands. *"Mais, c'est la vie."*

"Alors, vous parlez français?"

Bennett looked sharply at him. "You know French?"

"My first language—I was born in Gallipolis."

"Ah, the City of the French—yes. Well—" He looked uncomfortable. "I—uh—only speak a little French. *Un peu, seulement."*

Gabriel nodded, amused. "I see." After a few more exchanges, he took his leave. Later he walked down to the river with Eb and described the meeting.

"Now, why would he say something in French if he didn't speak the language?"

"It beats me. But they say that's what he does. He be saying things in French, German, other languages. Maybe to impress folks like me."

"I reckon that's it. He knows a little of everything, but only on the surface. So folks think he knows more than he does."

Eb gave a little cough. "Maybe so." They stood looking out over the expanse of water. Down to the southeast, clouds were massing; thunder rumbled. "Storm before long."

"Maybe it'll miss us. Hit Quincy instead."

As they turned to walk back, Eb said, "Brother Joseph must think he's a good man. He's been living in their house. If there was something wrong, don't you think he'd know it?"

"I reckon you're right."

They walked past the garden that Calvin had cultivated in their yard. Stalks of corn grew everywhere around the house and stable. By the time they reached the shop, the clouds had blotted out the setting sun.

13

JEALOUSY, GABRIEL THOUGHT. THAT'S all it was. Plain, simple jealousy. Forget that first meeting—a humiliating encounter. The man was now baptized, a member of the church. His brother in the faith.

Bennett's charming ways. Drawing patients away—mostly women. Ignore it. Pretend nothing was happening. He had enough patients anyway.

"No matter who leaves you," Jubal told him, "my family sure won't. Why, Corey—she thinks the sun rises in your direction."

Embarrassed. Surely Corey not wanting him to know such a thing. All the same, warmed, encouraged by their support.

Sitting with the others in the public square. Listening as Bennett spoke. No longer wincing as the man sprinkled his talk with foreign phrases. Joseph Smith doing the same thing. Everybody imitating John C. Bennett, his ways and mannerisms. The man of the hour.

But, *mon Dieu*—his accomplishments. Promoting the tomato, long considered poisonous, as a healthful food—actually getting people to eat it. Persuading them to begin draining the swampy area. Insisting that it would alleviate the sickness that struck every spring and summer. And in mid-December, the Charter of Nauvoo accepted and signed by Governor Carlin. A most liberal document, to take effect on February 1 of 1841. Provisions for the Nauvoo Legion, and a University of the City of Nauvoo, all due to the expert lobbying of Bennett.

"Sounds too good to be true," Nat said as they gathered to celebrate the birthday of little Gabrielle.

"She was really born November 21," Hannah explained to May, in whose house the gathering was taking place. "But this be the only time we could get everybody together."

"I can't believe she's two already." Gabriel took a seat on the settle, and Bethia sat beside him. Jody, five years old in October, ran over and buried his head in Bethia's lap.

"We should celebrate your birthday too," she told him.

"We did," Hannah said. "He had a ride in the skiff out to the island."

"And we should be celebratin' that new charter," Calvin said. "Whether you believe it or not, it's gonna happen."

They crowded around the two tables set together in May's front room to feast on roast turkey, corn bread stuffing, baked potatoes and yams.

"And tomatoes," Hannah said. "Put up last August, by a sister in Montrose. She gave me some—thanks to the influence of Dr. Bennett."

"Let's hear it for Dr. Bennett." Calvin raised his glass.

The others lifted their glasses too. Gabriel couldn't help groaning.

"What's the matter?" Bethia asked.

"Nothing. Nothing at all."

"A touch of Bennett-itis," Eb said, on his other side. "Nothing that a little cider can't cure."

Nathaniel finished carving the turkey and started to place pieces of meat on the plates stacked before him. As soon as each plate was filled, Hannah passed it down until everyone was served. Then she passed around the other dishes. Gabriel watched as Bethia put food on Jody's plate. For a fleeting moment he wondered that she didn't have a child of her own yet. An excellent mother she would be.

May carried a plate to Jean-Jacques, in his bed not far away. She sat beside the bed to feed him.

Sarah took a helping of stewed tomatoes. "I hear tell Dr. Bennett is an expert in the diseases of women. Midwifery and such like."

Bethia looked up, all attention. "Is that right?"

Gabriel sighed. "Actually, he considers himself an expert in just about everything."

Hannah laughed. "You don't like him much, do you?"

Rusty reached for the biscuits. "We all know how Gabe feels about Dr. Bennett."

Eb said, "He's been stealin' his patients, is why."

Gabriel spoke quickly. "Oh, he deserves a lot of credit for what he's done. I just get tired of hearing about it."

Everybody laughed except Nat, who looked at Gabriel and nodded. "I sense pride in the man. But I've not seen him that often."

Inside the house, the air was sweet with the scent of wood smoke and roast turkey, and the biscuits Hannah had baked. Gabriel felt a wave of contentment, thinking of the other times the little group had spent together. He turned to Bethia and smiled. But she did not smile back.

"Uh—pass the potatoes, will you, my dear?" he said quickly. She did so, still not smiling.

He split open the potato and put butter on it, puzzled. When the knock came at the door, Pierre got up to answer it. He closed the door and turned. "Gabriel. You're wanted."

Gabriel put down his napkin and went to the door. On the tiny porch outside, he found Adriel wrapped in a blanket.

"Charley's laid up. A fight with an Iroquois. One mean Injun. Knife wound. He sent me to see if you was here."

"Wait," Gabriel said. Back in the room, he faced the group, all silent for once. "May—do you have whiskey?"

Pierre stood up. "I have. I get some."

"If you have a needle and thread, I could use that too."

Pierre hurried back to the room he shared with Pentoga. They had moved into the main cabin to help May with Jean-Jacques. Gabriel was reaching for his coat when he felt Bethia's eyes on him. He glanced at her. She sent back such a look of utter disgust that it felt like a blow to the chest. What was it now? Because he was called out to treat someone, or because he'd asked for whiskey? Or something else—she hadn't conceived a child yet. Was that his fault too? He put his hand on the door handle and went to join Adriel. Pierre soon appeared with the articles Gabriel had requested.

"Go on back inside," Gabriel said to him. "I'll return as soon as possible."

On the way to their waterfront shack, he asked, "What was Charley fighting about?"

Adriel's voice was deep, a musical baritone. "Better you don't know."

"I see."

Once inside, he examined the wound, a gash in the thigh. "Charley, you're just plain lucky. Two inches more, and he'd have hit the artery."

Charley grunted, looking up at him. Gabriel gave the wound a liberal cleansing with the alcohol. "You hear me, Charley? Stay away from that Iroquois."

What to use for a bandage? No clean towels anywhere. Finally Gabriel tore pieces out of his own white shirt. As he bandaged Charley, he remembered—Bethia had made the shirt for him. He was in for it now. Then Charley spoke. "Thank you, son."

"I'm glad I was here."

"Something you should know. Your people be stealing—all up and down the river. They say everything was taken from them in Missouri. Now they take it back."

"I—I see."

"They say—some of them—that it's due them."

"Don't talk any more, Charley. Just try to rest."

"I thought you should know. It's not good—what they do. No good will come of it."

"*Eh bien.* I will—"

"Also." Charley went on. "Someone's spreading lies. Terrible lies. They say your leaders have more than one wife."

"Now, that's nonsense. Adriel, make him stop talking and rest."

Adriel stepped forward. "I'd listen to him if I was you."

"I'm listening. But that's just—just not true. If it were, I'd tell you."

Gabriel gave instructions about rest and a good diet. Then he turned to leave.

"How much we owe you?" Adriel asked.

"Why—nothing. Just make him rest."

"Then we're beholden to you."

Gabriel looked at him. "We are friends. Never forget that."

Adriel grunted. "Friends."

It was late when he returned to May's house. Hannah and Nat were busy straightening up.

"Lands sakes," Nat said. "Eb and Calvin took the rest of 'em back across the river already. They didn't want to drive that sleigh after dark."

"That's fine," Gabriel answered. "I'll just spend the night up in my old cabin. See Charley again in the morning."

Hannah looked at him. "I see you're gonna need a shirt, too."

"Used it for bandages." He sighed. "Bethia will be furious with me."

Hannah shook her head. "Let me study on it. I reckon Nat has an extra one."

"I'm in big trouble with her already. What can I do?"

Hannah patted his shoulder. "Like as not, you're doing just what you should. Keep in mind you can't please some folks."

"I sure can't please her."

"Well, then. Maybe she's someone that can't be pleased. Ever. And you have to try and live with it."

He told Nat about what Charley had said. Nat frowned as he listened, and his mouth worked at the corners.

"That's bad news. About the stealing. As for the multiple wives—we know that's not true. The stealing we'd better try and stop."

Having Charley for a patient proved to be both entertaining and informative. When Gabriel looked in on him the next morning, he didn't want to talk about his injury at all.

"Adriel wants to know why yer baptized for your dead relatives?"

Gabriel shook his head, momentarily puzzled. "Me? Oh—baptism for the dead. Joseph Smith said back in August that folks can be baptized for their family members—the ones that didn't have a chance to accept the gospel during their lives. So, some people are doing it. Hyrum Smith was baptized for their elder brother that died."

"A strange doctrine."

"I suppose. I haven't thought about it much. I don't reckon my father would want me to do it. Or my Catholic ancestors."

Charley grunted. "Adriel—the name means 'beaver.' He used to be known as Beaver. But fellers all started calling him 'Flat-tail.' So he went back to Adriel."

Gabriel thought that was a funny story and longed to share it with Bethia. Then he reconsidered—it would mean telling her that he'd actually treated Charley. What had gone wrong? He'd once considered compassion as one of her best qualities. Clearly he needed to talk with her.

She acted cool and distant when he returned. He waited until just before supper.

"Bethia—can you tell me what's wrong? I know you're upset. Is it me? Have I done or said something?"

She gave him a surprised look. "Well, no—I—" Then she swallowed. "I reckon you don't spend any time with me. You'd rather go off and treat some old Indian than stay with us. At a proper family gathering."

"But, dear. That Indian needed help bad."

"You got enough patients on this side of the river. You don't have to see people on the other side."

He nodded. "But they be the ones that really need me. There's plenty of doctors over here."

She sniffed. He spread his hands and shrugged. "I'll tell you what. If I tried to spend more time with you, would that help? I reckon we can take a little stroll after supper."

"In the cold?"

"Well—we can sit by the fire together and talk some. Or we can hitch up the sleigh and ride down to the place they're fixing up for the steamboat landing. No?"

She shook her head. He lifted a lock of her dark hair, and she pulled away. "I just want—I reckon I want to see you more often, is all."

"I'll try to arrange that. Spend less time in the shop. We've a new helper coming in, from the last group of English Saints. Name's Nigel." He pronounced it carefully, not used to the unusual sound of it. "Nigel Barrymore. An apprentice blacksmith from London."

She made no comment. He patted her shoulder. "That should give me a little more time."

She began to weep. "What I really want to know. Why don't we have a child by this time?"

He didn't feel surprised at the question. He'd wondered the same thing. He called on his medical training for the answer. "Sometimes it takes more time than we figure. I reckon with rest, and proper food—"

"You say that for everything!"

"Not—well, you'd be amazed how many times it helps."

She gave him the same look of disgust he'd seen back at the gathering. He shrugged. "Bethia, I know you want an easy answer. I wish there was one. I don't think anything's wrong with us. I reckon we haven't given it enough time, is all."

She looked down. "Even Hannah's expecting again."

"Is she, now? I didn't know." He sighed then. "I reckon we should wait, not get too upset about it." He searched for some hopeful comment. "Why—Emma, now. Sister Smith. I reckon she had to wait at least five years before she had a healthy child—one that lived. Now she has those handsome boys, and the girl they adopted. Like as not, we could adopt a child if we wanted. That's what folks do."

"That's not what I want."

Gabriel tried to smile, but he felt at a loss. "*Tiens.* Let's give it a little more time before we despair completely."

She lifted her head. "They say Dr. Bennett's an expert in women's ailments. Maybe I should go to him."

Gabriel waited before he spoke. Surely she knew how he felt about the man. "Go if you want. I reckon he'll tell you the same thing. Rest, relaxation, and good food." He sighed, not knowing what else to say. "Speaking of food, maybe we'd better go up to the kitchen before Rusty eats it all."

Gabe and Bethia. Twice he'd heard Bethia sobbing in her room. Something wrong. What, exactly? Rusty puzzled about it as he split logs for the forge and carried them to the wood box. At first he thought it was Gabe's fault—not spending enough time with her. But after watching Gabe for a while, he decided that Gabe was doing the best he could. Kind and courteous to her, never insulting her. Still she glared at him, acted impatient and provoked. Her words at May's house, when he'd left to attend the Indian: "I don't care if he ever comes back."

"I reckon I'm lucky I didn't marry her," Rusty told Eb. "Seems like he can't please her, no matter what."

"Marriage ain't supposed to be easy," Eb replied.

"Well, Nat and Hannah get along just fine. And my father and mother—why, they loved each other. And even my father and Sarah—they're a good pair."

"Maybe Gabe and Bethia jest need more time. I mean, to get used to the idea of being married and all."

Rusty shook his head. "I don't figure on getting married."

"I reckon you just made some woman very happy."

Rusty gathered up the last armful of logs and took them inside. Nigel, the new assistant, bent over the anvil, hammer in hand; they had left him in charge of the shop for the afternoon. Rusty nodded to him and tapped on the door to Gabe's apartment.

"Come on, Gabe. Time to go hear what John C. has to say. All the ladies will be there."

Gabe opened the door. "I'll be there in two shakes of a mule's tail. You start over—I'll see you at the store."

Once on the road, Eb spoke out of the corner of his mouth. "Hain't you got no sense at all? You want to make big trouble—sayin' that to him in front of her?"

"Was she there?"

"Well, I reckon. She usually is."

"Oh, come on. Even my father teases him about the women—about Corey Langdon makin' eyes at him."

Eb stopped suddenly. "Now, you listen to me. Corey's a good woman, with a lot to handle. A tough row to hoe, as folks say. And Gabe's never done anything out of line, with her or anyone else."

Rusty was puzzled. "I didn't say he had."

"Well, she's like to believe anything. Bethia, I mean. And there's enough rumors around without making things worse."

He looked at Eb. "What rumors?"

"You mean you don't know?"

"No. What are you talking about?"

Eb gave him a long, searching look. "If you don't know, then I guess you don't need to know."

Rusty wanted to hear more, but they had reached the store of William and Wilson Law on Water Street, where Bennett was preparing to speak. They made their way through the crowd and slipped inside.

From his position near the front door, Rusty had a good view of the crowd. He saw his father and Sarah up by the improvised speaker's stand, and Corey Langdon off to the right with two other young women. Where was her sister? Then he realized—Jubal himself was not there. He'd most likely stayed home with Casey that afternoon. Give Corey a chance to get out.

Rusty watched her with a mixture of pity and interest. With her strong face and alert eyes, she didn't look as if she needed sympathy. But that sister—a definite burden. He knew Corey liked Gabe, but he didn't know how much. Not that it mattered. Gabe was stuck now.

Strange feelings. No longer loving Bethia, he sensed the need for female companionship. He went over to visit Hannah at least once a week—not often enough, in his opinion. He'd thought of moving back across the river. But his father was here, and his friends Gabe and Eb. And he enjoyed the work in the smithy.

Gabe slipped in and joined them just as Bennett began to speak. Rusty watched the exaggerated mannerisms as Bennett strutted up and down. A little man, like a banty rooster. Rusty had heard somewhere that Bennett's favorite historical figure was Napoleon Bonaparte. Rusty felt indifferent toward Bennett, not liking or disliking him, although he found the foreign phrases and mannerisms pretentious. Amused at Gabriel's obvious antipathy toward him.

Trying to concentrate. Feeling sleepy in the warm room. He caught the words "...in relation to the municipal election." Bennett was introducing the gathering as the first of a series of public nominating meetings. Encouraging a diverse selection of candidates. Candidates being put in nomination for mayor, aldermen, city council, with only one candidate for each position.

Rusty was just beginning to think about supper. Hopefully, corn pudding and biscuits again. Out of the corner of his eye he saw Gabe smile and nod to Corey. Then Gabe slapped him on the arm.

"That's it. Let's get out of here."

"What?" He felt half-awake as he stumbled outside.

"He's gonna be mayor. There's no one running against him."

Eb ran to catch up with them. "He's just gettin' wound up in there."

Gabe stared straight ahead. "Wait'll ol' Nat hears about this. I have to look in on Charley anyway—see how he's doing. We'll go across tomorrow."

When they told Nat, he shook his head and smiled. "Give the man a chance. He's like to make a right proper leader. Hasn't he done good things for the city so far?"

On the way back to Nauvoo, Gabe talked about Jean-Jacques and his frustration at not being able to do anything for the man. "It's a fearful thing, this wasting disease. All we can do is try to make him comfortable."

"How long do you reckon he has?" Rusty asked.

"Hard to tell. Not very long." They knew that once Jean-Jacques died, the farm would belong to Nat, on condition that he take care of May till the end of her life. This he had sworn to do.

"You'd think it'd go to Pierre," Rusty said.

Gabe shrugged. "He hates farming. Always has."

"It's a nice farm," Eb remarked. "I reckon with a little help from Pierre, and Owen Crawford, he can keep it going."

Rusty gave a short laugh. "He's running it now, with no help from anybody."

After the elections, the conversations in the public house took a different turn. The Nauvoo Legion, which had been authorized by the city charter, became the main topic of discussion. Rusty, sipping his cider, heard the words swirling around him.

"Why call it a legion?" a young man asked.

The proprietor tried to explain. "It's what the Romans had. There's to be two cohorts—that's 'brigades' to you. One on horseback and one on foot. And they'll be mustering most every day on that flat place up on the hill."

An older man with a reddish beard gave a laugh. "If it's them same fellers that marched into Missouri to reclaim our lands, I reckon I'll take my chances on horseback."

The proprietor said, "You mean Zion's Camp? Yeah. I figure they'll all be in it."

Another man said, "We get brigadier generals too. One for each brigade. A first class militia. I reckon our enemies had better sit up and take notice."

The young man who had first spoken rose to his feet. "I hear tell Joseph Smith's just been proclaimed lieutenant general. There ain't been one of them since George Washington."

Someone else said, "And the new mayor's second in command. Major general. Can you beat that?"

The proprietor put another jug of cider on the counter. "He's gonna be one busy son-of-a-gun."

It had occurred to Rusty that if they were going to form a militia, there would have to be men to take part in it. But it seemed to hit Gabe with all the force of a disaster.

"*Mon Dieu!* Every male citizen of Nauvoo! Required to participate.

Required! If you miss a muster or a parade, you can be fined up to twenty-five dollars!"

"It says,'unless exempt by law,'" Eb said.

"What? You think Bennett's gonna let me off, just to practice medicine? Run a smithy? He doesn't even *like* me."

Rusty stepped over and put a hand on his shoulder. "It might be fun—to see how he does it. We might learn something. And with Nigel and Calvin, there's enough of us to keep the shop open."

"Are you out of your mind? They'll have to muster too."

"Look at it this way," Eb said. "We'll get to have uniforms, and the state'll give us arms. Leastways, that's what they said."

Gabe gestured wildly, his hair falling down into his eyes. "If you think I'm going to dress up and take orders from that—that manicured baboon—"

"I thought it was 'dragoon,'" Eb said laughing.

"*Ma foi!* Now I'm really annoyed."

Rusty and Gabe went across to the farm later that week. They took turns rowing the skiff Gabe had bought from Charley—twelve feet of splintery wood, patched with pine tar. Rusty liked being out on the water. The wind felt cool, fresh with the scent of spring. He squinted, dazzled by the sun dancing on the waves in little points of light.

"Watch out," Gabe said. "You want to run into the island?"

Rusty changed course. Finally they pulled up at Charley's dock. Adriel walked out to meet them.

"Charley's fine now. He's over at the public house."

"Bon." Gabe threw the mooring line over the piling. "I'll look in on him before we leave."

Adriel spoke out of the side of his mouth. "You been baptized for yer dead relatives yet?"

"Not me. Too busy taking care of the live ones."

They left Adriel and walked the four miles to the farm. They found Nat in the barn with the oxen. He scratched his chin, where the beard was growing. "Just in time to help with the planting."

Nat paused in his preparations as they told him about the militia and all the plans for it. He stroked his beard as he listened.

"Well, now, boys. I heard most of that talk. Folks in Montrose be fixing to join it too."

Gabe raised his eyebrows. "You're actually gonna do it without a fuss?"

Nat looked at them. "Not me. You know I don't hold with military doings."

"But—but they'll fine you. If you miss a muster or a parade—"

Nat laughed. "You're forgetting. I'm not a citizen of Nauvoo--don't intend to be. I don't have to do any of that. But I'll come and watch the maneuvers."

"That's it!" Gabe gestured excitedly. "I'm moving back over here! Back to that cabin—which I didn't want to leave in the first place."

"Don't be hasty," Rusty said. "Think of the shop, and—and Bethia."

"Isn't she doing some better?" Nat rested the pitchfork against the wall. "With all her friends there, and the things ladies do? Quilting and such like?"

"Oh—I reckon so." Gabe's voice grew calmer. "It's hard to tell, seems like."

"No doubt, it would upset her something fierce to move her back," Rusty said.

"Now." Nat gave a little cough. "About the militia. I reckon most every town in Illinois has one. Some are good, some not so good. The important thing is what they do with it, not the fact that it's there. Are they going to frighten our enemies with it? Stir up the Gentiles? There's plenty of folks against us as it is. Already there's an anti-Mormon party—Thomas Sharp and some other folks from down around Warsaw."

"How'd you know that?" Rusty asked.

"Charley. Gabriel's friend. He's a right smart feller—knows everything. He gets around."

Gabe gave a laugh. "You can say that again."

Nat went on. "And I don't know what you done for him. But he thinks the world of you."

"Just patched him up, is all."

"Hold up a minute." Nat put a hand against the side of the stall. "Before you leave, I just wanted to say—be careful. Both of you. Don't be so outspoken about the militia. Remember, if the prophet Joseph approves of it, like as not it's a good thing. If I was you, I'd probably just go and enjoy it. I don't think they're going to be fighting anyone."

Nat's words seem to have a soothing effect on Gabe. He nodded as they turned to leave. "One more thing to take up time, I reckon."

After that, he stopped his complaining and merely acted resigned. When Rusty's father made the offer of the horses, Gabe's disposition improved even more.

"Boys," Calvin said. "I have my eye on a new team—two young black mares. They'll pull the carriage, and be good for riding too. I'm giving you Jeb and Jenny, and what you do with 'em's none of my business."

Gabe said to Rusty and Eb that evening, "He's saying we can sell 'em if we want, and buy Jess out of slavery."

"In the meantime, let's ride 'em in the Legion," Rusty said. "We won't have to be foot soldiers."

They decided that Gabe, being the shortest, should have the bay mare Jenny. Eb rode Freedom, and Rusty took Jeb, the large gelding.

"And soon we'll have uniforms," Rusty reminded them. "Hannah said she'd make us some. French ones—with epaulets."

14

Just before sunrise. In the dim light, Nathaniel stood pouring grain out for the oxen. He patted the lead ox on the side of the neck, feeling the coarse fur beneath his fingers. The animal put his ears back and continued chewing.

Nathaniel took the pitchfork and fetched them fresh hay. Moving around the stable, he felt a sense of contentment, pride in this bit of land which was to be his, affection for the beasts which he fed and cared for. From outside, chickens clucked, a rooster crowed. He heard cattle lowing from a distance.

Suddenly a boom shook the stable. He tensed. The oxen raised their heads. Nell, outside the door, gave a short bark.

Thunder? No—too short. Most storms moved from the west. This sound had come from the east, across the river. He put the pitchfork in its place and stood wondering. Another boom.

Then he remembered. They had said it would happen. The cannon, signaling the dawn of that particular day. Feeling foolish, chuckling at his uneasiness, he picked up the dog. He felt her warm body against his chest as he carried her to the stable. She strained to lick his face. He patted her and shut her in the stable so she wouldn't follow him. "Stay, girl."

She whined and then was silent. He followed the trail up to his cabin.

"Be you ready?" he called to Hannah.

She hurried out of the cabin with the two children, all three of them dressed in their Sunday best. Hannah and Gaby wore matching dresses of light blue. Each child clutched a piece of bread smeared with butter and honey. Hannah carried a basket of diapers, and small white towels in case of any accidents with the bread or honey.

"Let's hurry." Nathaniel picked up Gaby and carried her down the path. He loved the feel of the baby girl in his arms, the tiny, honey-smeared hands moving up around his neck. Hannah followed, holding Jody by the hand. Owen Crawford and Pierre Dulac joined them just as they reached the ferry landing.

"A good day for it," Owen remarked. He planned to return later that day to feed the animals, so that Nathaniel and his family could stay overnight in Nauvoo.

As they hurried up the ramp, Nathaniel took Jody's hand. The early morning light shimmered on the water. "How many boats do you see?" he asked the child.

Jody gazed with astonishment, wide-eyed. Three other ferries were making their way up from the south, and when their own boat rounded the island, they saw another coming down from the north.

"I never saw so many." Hannah reached for Gaby, and Nathaniel handed her over. "Look, honey," Hannah told her. "There're little boats, too. Skiffs and canoes."

Nathaniel drew a deep breath. The air had the scent of fresh water mingled with fish and the faint tinge of smoke. Who would have thought it? The eleventh annual conference of the church, and the laying of a cornerstone for another temple. Maybe this one they would see to completion.

Owen spat over the rail. "Not too warm yet."

"Right cool for April," Nathaniel replied. "Be warmer on land."

Owen went on. "I reckon there be thousands of people. Look—you can see the tents and wagons set up on that flat place. And there's wagons still comin' in."

"They been pulling in all week." Nathaniel lifted Jody up. "See where all the people are camped?"

"Horses," Jody said.

"Oh, you'll see horses. Just wait till we get to the parade ground."

As Jody stared, open-mouthed, Nathaniel thought how it must look to the boy. First the expanse of blue water, dotted with darker wind-dapples. Then the boats full of people, the colorful pastel dresses of the women, the noise, the laughter, the excited voices. At the dock, Nathaniel took Gaby and passed her to Owen. Then he helped Hannah off the boat. Owen handed him the children in turn. In the press he thought he saw Crazy Charley and Adriel. People called to each other; horses neighed.

They walked first to Calvin's house, where Sarah and Bethia joined them. The two women embraced Hannah and hugged the children. Sarah looked at Hannah. "You want to rest a spell?"

"No—I be fine. I can't wait to see Gabriel and them in their uniforms."

"Let's go, then." Nathaniel shuffled his feet. "We'll miss the start of things."

They walked on the road muddy from the rains, with the smell of horses everywhere. As they walked, other people joined them—Corey Langdon and her sister, and some women he didn't know. Just as they reached the parade ground, Hannah stumbled, then regained her footing. He reached to take her arm. He remembered how he meant to ask Bethia if she would come and help Hannah for a time, now that she was expecting again. Like as not, Gabriel could spare her for a few weeks. He thought briefly that maybe Corey would do as well, if Bethia refused.

They found places on the edge of the field, under an oak tree. From their position, they had a good view of the ground and the reviewing stand. He unbuttoned his coat, ready to remove it and spread it on the ground for Hannah if she got too tired. He leaned over to ask her if she was all right.

"Look!" she exclaimed before he could speak. "They be coming in!"

Artillery boomed. Horses and riders advanced from the far side of the field, moving in rows of eight abreast. In front rode a little man on a bay horse.

"That's Bennett," Nathaniel whispered to Hannah.

"What a magnificent uniform!"

He wore tight buff trousers, a double-breasted blue tailcoat with twin rows of brass buttons, and a belt whose buckle gleamed in the light. He had high boots polished to a shine, and a shako with an ostrich plume on top.

"Any more of that gold braid, and he'll fall over," Nathaniel remarked.

"You have to admit—it looks dashing."

The rest of the horse brigade had varied uniforms, some with coats, some with only sashes to set off their Sunday best. Calvin, in the second rank, rode one of his new black mares. He wore a handsome brown coat made by Sarah. Jubal Langdon rode beside him, on a piebald mare. Just behind and to the left rode the three young men, Gabe, Eb and Rusty, all in the blue coats Hannah had fashioned for them. In contrast, their trousers looked shabby, their boots old and dusty.

"I'll have to finish their uniforms," Hannah said. "And they need proper hats."

Nathaniel gave a little laugh. "Shakos, with plumes?"

"Well, no. Something to keep the sun off."

"Looks pretty ragtag to me," Owen remarked.

"Just wait'll you see 'em drill," someone said. "They may not look like anything, but those maneuvers be as sharp as any militia in the state."

"What'll they be doin' next?" another man said. "Gettin' up an army?"

Like as not, it was those words that unsettled him. He glanced at Hannah, but she seemed not to have heard. She reached over to Bethia, who was holding Gaby, and straightened the child's lace collar. Maybe he was the only one feeling uneasy as Bennett began drilling the troops. On signal, they moved back and forth across the field, first single file, then two abreast. They all lined up facing the reviewing stand, then turned and crossed the field again. At a signal, they stopped as one man and drew up their weapons. Nathaniel wondered if they intended to fire, and if people in the crowd were safe from stray bullets.

"See that man?" Owen pointed. "Up there on the stand. The one on the end, with the long nose and slanting forehead?"

"What about him?" Nathaniel asked.

"That's Tom Sharp. Editor of the *Warsaw Signal*."

"The one that's been writing all the bad things about us?"

"The Mormon hater. Yeah."

What was he going to write next? That the Saints were well-drilled and battle-ready? Another salvo of artillery rang out, too loud. This time Gaby began to cry.

"Let me take her," Nathaniel said.

He held his baby girl close to him, feeling heartsick at all the pomp, the show of militancy. Then he heard the sound of trumpets. The band marched onto the parade ground. He watched, feeling Gaby's tear-drenched face against his own, as Lieutenant General Smith took the field on his magnificent black horse Charley. Following him, his staff, field officers and his personal bodyguard marched—twelve men in white uniforms with red sashes. A group of young women riding sidesaddle made up the rest of the retinue.

"If that isn't Eliza Snow!" Hannah exclaimed. "And Nancy Rigdon."

Another salvo of artillery went off, a salute to the commander. One of the ladies' horses shied and had to be brought back into line. "Them horses is skittish," Owen remarked.

Then Bennett was shouting something. Nathaniel's ears rang from the artillery noise; he strained to hear. Pierre Dulac moved over from the edge of the field.

"Bennett say the Legion is ready for review. What does that mean?"

"I think they be going to march past that platform," Nathaniel replied.

A carriage full of women in bright attire rolled onto the field. One of them presented a United States flag to the prophet, who promised that it would never be dishonored.

"That be a real silk flag," Owen said. "I heard them say."

As the cannon boomed, Smith and his company moved up and down the ranks to inspect the troops.

"Them's sixteen well-drilled companies," someone remarked behind them. "Think how many they'll have in a few years. Twenty thousand? Forty thousand?"

"All religious fanatics," someone else said. Nathaniel turned to see who had spoken. No one he could identify. He felt a sudden ache behind his eyes. The prophet took his place beside Thomas Sharp in the reviewing stand. Bennett was leading the entire Legion before them in review.

Maybe it was all right. His misgivings were needless. Like as not, Thomas Sharp wasn't thinking the same things he'd just heard. To be sure, it was a splendid spectacle, the smartness of the drills making up for the lack of proper uniforms. As the foot soldiers marched past, he caught sight of the new assistant blacksmith, Nigel Barrymore, whom he'd met once. An earnest young man in his late twenties, thin and round-shouldered, Nigel marched with a slight stoop. He had a long nose in proportion to his face, and deep wrinkles ran along the sides of his face from the outer edges of his eyes to the corners of his mouth. His mud-brown hair hung long on the back of his neck.

They lined up to march to the temple foundation. Lieutenant General Smith led the procession, followed in order by the brigadiers, aides-de-camp, the important visitors, the general staff and the band. Next came the foot troops, then the ladies and men. The horse troops brought up the rear. Nathaniel, still carrying Gaby, sighed as he marched with the crowd.

"What's wrong with Nat?" Sarah asked. "Indigestion again?"

Hannah's voice. "Oh, he just doesn't like a lot of military hoopla."

If the truth be known, he felt out of place in the city of the Saints. He longed to be back across the river, on his peaceful, orderly farm. He missed the animals already—Nell on her three legs, the chickens and barn cats, the two gentle oxen. But he pretended to give full attention to Sidney Rigdon, who spoke for an hour. Then a crane lowered the cornerstone into position.

"I hear tell it has the original manuscript of the Book of Mormon," Owen said.

"That's what they said," Sarah replied.

Nathaniel made no comment. He moved closer to Hannah as the prophet pronounced the benediction on the house of the Lord. "...that the saints may have a place to worship God, and the Son of Man have where to lay his head."

The next day, they watched as John C. Bennett was sustained as assistant president of the church, "until President Rigdon's health should be restored."

Bethia doesn't know how long she's been crying. Half the afternoon, it seems. She has no idea what time it is when Nigel knocks on her door.

"I say! Sister Bethia? Do you need help?"

She doesn't respond. No longer cares. She hears Nigel's voice in the shop. "Rusty? I say, is Gabriel about?"

"He went across the river early this morning."

"Well, there's trouble here. Run up and see if Sister Manning's at home."

"I'll try and fetch her."

Bethia makes an effort to stop. But the sobs keep coming from deep in her chest, convulsive spasms that shake her whole body. She buries her face in the pillow. *Lying on her marriage bed. What a joke.* As if she ever wants to see him again. *What she had heard that morning. The ultimate blow.*

Between sobs she tries to push the images away. But they keep coming back. First, Bennett's office, the little consulting room with its plush green chairs and oak desk, the top inlaid with leather. The wooden desk chair where he sat to listen to her. Then she is back, sitting stiffly in one of the plush chairs, her shawl falling back over her shoulders.

"...and—and that's the story. Married for over a year now. And no sign of a child." She feels timid and vulnerable, blurting out the secret which has haunted her for months. If he mentions rest and a good diet, she thinks she will just run out screaming.

He balances on the edge of his chair. His black eyes gleam; he smiles. "Well, actually, my dear, it may not be your fault. Possibly it's your husband who has something wrong."

She begins to feel better. What a concept. Maybe Gabriel is the one who needs the rest and the proper food. Then he is saying something else. It is a few seconds before she realizes that he is offering to take her husband's place, to supply the vigorous seed that is obviously lacking. She gasps. He raises his eyebrows and continues.

"Don't look so amazed that I should approach you in this way. You may not have heard, but our brother Joseph—yes, the prophet himself—is already setting the example by taking more than one wife. And he has said that such a liaison between a man and a woman—take, for instance, you and I—is no longer illicit. In fact, it has the approval of God."

She is afraid she will faint on the spot. *Control yourself,* she begs. As if that is not enough, he delivers the final blow.

"Now, I can see this idea is new to you. I'm sorry to have to tell you so abruptly. But, my dear—don't let it disturb you. The thing I speak of is happening all around you. Even your own husband. I hesitate to think how many wives he probably has already."

A pounding on the door. Sarah's voice. "Bethia? Bethia, open this door. Right this minute. Please. Let me come in."

Dazed, feeling numb. Bethia struggles to her feet. Amazing. She can still stand and walk like a normal person, can step toward the door. Bennett's parting words echo in her mind.

"You think about it. Even pray about it, if you want. Then come and see me again. Say, tomorrow. I'll be here all morning."

She unlocks the door, sniffing between sobs. Sarah pushes her way into the room. Bethia wonders how to tell her. *What if Calvin has other wives too?* A tightness, like a cramp, is spreading over her stomach and chest, even up into her throat. She cannot speak. She hurries back to the bed and collapses across it. Crying again.

Sarah, sitting beside her, strokes her back and makes soothing noises. Between sobs, Bethia blurts out half-sentences.

"Bennett...an appointment...this morning...wives...more than one wife. All of 'em doing it. Gabriel...even Uncle Calvin..."

Sarah's voice. "Gabriel? Calvin? Honey, they scarce got time for one wife. And they couldn't support 'em even if they had 'em."

Through her sobs, Bethia feels Sarah leave the bed. Footsteps. Sarah hurrying to the door, flinging it open.

"Nigel? Where's Gabe? Rusty, get in here."

Bethia hears Nigel's clipped, nasal voice. "Went across the river early this morning, he did. Took Eb with him. I say, is anything wrong?"

Rusty enters and Sarah closes the door. "First, get off those gloves and hang up that apron. You be goin' across to fetch Gabriel. Something mighty serious has happened, and I'm not sure what. Don't tell 'em—just bring 'em across. If you can find Nat, fetch him too."

A pause, then Rusty's heavy boots stamping on the floor. The door closes. Bethia hears him explaining something to Nigel; she can't make out the words.

"I don't want to see Gabriel," Bethia says, her voice rising.

"Not see your husband?"

"Not ever again."

Sarah sits on the bed. Bethia feels Sarah's hands on her head. Stroking her the way one would stroke a cat. "Sweet, he has to know. Whatever's happened, we can't keep it from him." She waits. After a while she says, "Why don't you tell me, and then we can make some sense of it?"

Slowly the words begin to tumble out. Sarah asks soft questions. "He said this when? After you told him you wanted a child?"

"I wanted to know why I couldn't have one. And he said—he said…" She repeats the words she can never forget.

"Now, wait a minute. He said 'everyone?' How could he possibly know?"

"I don't know. He just seemed to."

"Calvin, too. Now, that's ridiculous. Any second wife'd be dead afore she stepped across that threshold. Take it from me."

Bethia begins to relax. She even smiles as she brushes the tears from her cheek. Sarah looks at her. "As for Gabe. He's working his hind end off. Can't you see how tired he looks? When would he possibly have time for any such shenanigans?"

She tries to form the words. "He...Corey. He and Corey..."

"What's that, dear? Now, listen. You're absolutely sure the good mayor didn't touch you?"

"He—he put his hand on my shoulder. And—yes. He did examine me."

"That don't count. That be what he was supposed to do. Right? You went to him as a patient."

She nods.

"Although why you'd do that when you have a perfectly good doctor in yer own household, I can't figure."

"Gabriel doesn't know anything."

"Well, apparently, neither does Bennett. Although, I must say—"

"It—it was supposed to be a secret."

Sarah gives a short laugh. "Some secret. I reckon yer feeling some better. Come on up to the house, and you can rest while I set out the supper. T'aint much, to be sure. Some soup, and a bit of leftover ham."

Rusty arrived home after candlelight. By that time, Calvin had been alerted.

Rusty pulled off his jacket. "They be comin'. Gabe and Eb. Nat, too. I had to go across on the ferry on account of they had the skiff. But we all come back together. They be tyin' up the boat now."

Sarah set out another plate and put more apples in the fruit basket. Bethia tried to help, but her hands shook as she got down the extra mug.

Sarah looked at her. "Jest set down, honey, and rest some more. Soon we'll have things all straightened out, I reckon."

Bethia glanced down, her eyes filling with tears. "Gabriel's gonna kill 'em."

"Oh, nonsense. He has more sense than that."

"I just know it."

"Hush. Here they be."

The three burst into the room, Gabriel in the lead, with Eb and Nat just behind him. Gabriel hurried over to Bethia and put his hands on her shoulders. Remembering Bennett's touch, she flinched.

His voice was teasing, with an anxious undertone. "What's this about crying half the afternoon?"

"You'd best set down," Sarah said. "All of you. It's quite a tale."

Gabriel took the chair to the left of Bethia, keeping a hand on her shoulder. The rest gathered around the table. The candlelight set shadows dancing on their faces. Bethia looked down at the grooves in the pine table, embarrassed as Sarah told what she knew.

"And he said everyone was doing it. Right, Bethia? People you wouldn't even think of are mixed up in this business."

"That's news to me," Calvin said.

Nat gave a little cough and wiped his beard with a napkin. "It do sound like he's makin' excuses for himself. Tryin' to get her to believe him, so he can take advantage of her."

"If that don't beat all," Eb said.

Rusty nodded. "Could you pass the ham down here?"

Everyone glared at him briefly. Calvin sighed and passed the platter to him. "I don't feel 'specially hungry, myself."

Even in her shock and despair, Bethia felt the group hovering close around her, like a protective bower in a wind-swept field. The concern emanating from the little community filled her with unexpected hope—the terrible words she'd heard that morning seemed far away. Had she, in fact, imagined them? The words about Gabriel—she managed to sneak a sideways look at him.

He seemed angrier than she'd ever seen him, his face flushed, his mouth a grim line. A splotch of white was spreading around his mouth and nose.

"Gabriel?" she asked. He stood up, sending his chair flying backwards. He threw his napkin down and strode toward the door.

"Wait." Nat stood up too. "Where you going?"

"I'm gonna make Bennett wish he'd never been born."

"No!" Calvin and Nat cried with one voice. They rushed over to Gabriel, Eb racing just behind them. Eb braced himself against the door while Nat and Calvin took hold of Gabriel, one on each side. From what Bethia could see, he was struggling with both of them.

"Let me go!" He was twisting, panting. "*Mon Dieu!* Don't you see? I can't let him get away with this."

"I know," Calvin shouted. "Listen to us. There's a better way."

"Like conking him on the head and feeding him to the fishes. I thought of that, too."

Calvin was breathing heavily. Beads of perspiration stood out on his forehead. He backed away, shaking his head. Eb reached from behind and caught Gabriel around the neck. "You ain't goin' nowheres."

"Gabe." Nat was panting too. "Don't even think of jeopardizing your immortal soul in—in such a way. Just to punish him—it's not worth it."

Gabriel tried to straighten up. "Oh, I think it would be."

"Well, yer not gonna do it," Eb said. "Forget it right now."

"Come on back to the table." Calvin reached to pick up the fallen chair. "Just listen to us for half a minute."

Gabriel walked back and sat down. Eb followed him and stood waiting behind his chair. Calvin and Nat took their seats. Gabriel folded his arms and glared at them. "All right. You got half a minute."

Calvin glanced at Nat, then said, "First off, I reckon our friend Bennett has just made a disastrous move."

"Not *my* friend," Gabriel burst out.

"We know that. Now, this business about plural marriage is just plain nonsense. I think we should go and tell Joseph about it, soon as possible. If he doesn't know what's going on, he sure should."

"That sounds reasonable," Nat said. "Like as not, it's too late fer tonight. But if we go to his house just after first light, he'll hear us. Calvin and I will go, and Gabriel. He'll tell us what's right to do—I know it."

"What if he doesn't do anything?" Gabriel asked.

"Well, then you can go beat up the good doctor. But not till then. Agreed?"

"*Eh bien.* We'll do it. But it sounds like a waste of time to me."

Nat sighed. "A good thing yer not an impetuous person, Gabe."

"Maybe this is a time to learn some patience." Calvin looked at the soup, now cold. "How about some supper now? Will ye ask the blessing for us, Nat? God knows, we're in need of it tonight."

Nat's words seemed to bring a sense of peace to the gathering. Sarah got up to reheat the soup, and they ate their meal of bread and ham. They finished with the soup, which had beans and rice.

"A simple meal," Calvin said. "Good, nourishing food."

Bethia helped to clear the table. But the day's happenings haunted her; she felt a strange pain in the pit of her stomach as she wondered what the next day would bring.

"I'm sorry, Gabriel," she said on the way back to their rooms.

"Now, don't be sorry. Doesn't sound like your fault at all."

"I shouldn't have thought he could help."

"Well, it's done now. I should've paid more mind to you. I still think time is all we need." He put his hand on her arm, and this time she didn't move away.

15

Rusty and Eb were just opening the blacksmith shop when Calvin and Nat rapped on the door. Gabriel kissed Bethia and went out into the shop area. He'd thought the situation was serious enough to warrant his Sunday best, but he felt out of place already; Nat and Calvin had on their regular working clothes. Rusty had just started the fire. Nigel had not yet arrived.

"Come on, son," Nat said. They walked the short distance to the prophet's house without speaking. Their shoes made a crunching sound on the gravel. By the road's edge, droplets of dew, iridescent in the early light, quivered on the clumps of tall grass.

Distressed, numb from yesterday's news, Gabriel wondered that he could still notice the tracery of tree shadows on the walls, the mists rising from the river beyond the houses. Cattle lowed from far away, the sound made musical by the distance. Somewhere a dog barked, and a voice called out, rising in a question. No one answered. They went up the steps. Nat knocked at the door, and they were ushered inside by one of the young women who worked in Emma's kitchen.

"He be having breakfast. Yer welcome to go in."

The prophet was sitting at a table with his three older children and two other men, boarders at the residence. He stood up when he saw the visitors.

"Good morning, gentlemen. Just finishing. Would you care for anything to eat?"

Calvin shuffled his feet. "No, thank you. We came about something else." They knew that no one had much extra food to offer, not even the prophet.

"We need to speak with you privately," Nat said. "It's a delicate matter. We don't want anyone else to hear."

"Like, no Bennett." Gabriel's voice was louder than he'd intended.

Joseph looked at him and smiled briefly. Then he grew serious. A slightly puzzled expression crossed his face. "Brother Bennett isn't living with us just now. He's down the street at the Robinsons'."

Gabriel made a quick gesture. "Oh, in that case—"

"Come into my study." Joseph led the way. "We'll be undisturbed there."

Taller than any of them, Joseph had a commanding presence. His blue eyes had a strong, direct gaze, yet they did not look unkind. He indicated chairs for them, and sat down on the settle. "Now. What can I do for you?"

Nat drew in his breath to speak, but Gabriel beat him to it. "Hang it all. It's Bennett. Begging your pardon, sir. Major General John C. He's said things to my wife—made advances to her, if you will. Acted in a way that no doctor has a right to act. And most of all, no leader."

Joseph's smile had faded; he gave Gabriel a deep, searching look. "And you—"

"I'm ready to use him up, is what I am." He gestured, his hands in midair. "When I'm through with him, he'll wish he'd never laid eyes on her."

"Now, Gabe," Nat began. "Let's simmer down. Talk reasonable-like."

"I *am* reasonable."

"Beggin' your indulgence, sir," Calvin said. "He's overwrought, as you can see. It's on account of him bein' French and all—always ready to fly off the handle."

Gabriel was furious. "I am not."

Nat said, "'Course you be French—why deny it?"

"I meant that part about the handle."

"Now, sit back—stop waving your hands around. Let's just—"

Joseph was leaning forward. He looked as if he were trying not to smile. "Why don't you simply tell me what happened?"

Nat and Calvin spoke at the same time. "Well, yesterday—"

"Tuesday morning—"

"All right," Joseph said. "Nat, you go first."

Nat told what he knew of the situation; then Calvin spoke. Gabriel fidgeted—they were skimming over the most important parts. Finally Joseph looked at him.

"Brother Gabriel, do you have anything to add?"

"Well, sir. Aside from the fact that he used an innocent person's trust to take advantage of her, and told lies about all of us—I reckon I don't."

"That's right, Gabe." Nat looked at Calvin. "He be calming down a mite."

Gabriel gestured again. "But if no one does anything before nightfall, that man's gonna be catfish bait."

Calvin groaned. "Spoke too soon."

Joseph stood up and put his hand on the fireplace mantle. When he had their attention, he began to speak. "Now, let's not talk of catfish bait or any such thing. There's a way to handle this—this situation. Without resorting to violence." He paused. "You may wonder why I'm not more agitated, with all you told me. The truth is, I've heard it before. This is only one of several complaints—especially of his behavior toward women. So, let me inform you what's happening, as much as I can—but don't tell anyone else just now. Not even your families—'specially your wives. I know how women love to gossip.

"Now, then. Even as we speak, there're people looking into some aspects of his history. Hyrum in particular—I expect him back from Pennsylvania any day now. We don't wish to act too hastily, but certain facts are coming to light—and I think you may be assured that Brother Bennett will answer for his actions. We cannot take lightly these statements that promiscuity is condoned. It most certainly is not—and I hope you realize that."

"I was sure it wasn't," Nat said. "We wanted you to know what was happening, is all."

Joseph shook his head. "I'm fully aware of what he's been doing. He's a brilliant man, Dr. Bennett is, but, I'm sorry to say, less than stable. We accepted him because we thought his repentance was sincere."

"I'm satisfied." Calvin got to his feet. "We leave it in your hands."

Nat stood up. "What about you, Gabe?"

All eyes turned to him. He gestured as he pushed back his chair. "I reckon I can wait. I won't feed him to the fishes yet."

Joseph smiled. "I wouldn't, ever. Let us deal with him."

As they turned to leave, Joseph stopped them. "Brother Gabriel.

You're a new elder, aren't you? It might be a good time for you to go on your first mission—get your mind off things here."

"Mission, sir?" Gabriel hadn't given it much thought.

"That's a splendid idea," Nat said. "Go up into Michigan—get away from the heat."

Gabriel considered. "I reckon I'd go south—back to southern Ohio, where my family lives. And Virginy, just across the river. I—I'll study on it some."

"That's fine," Joseph said. "Get yourself ready. And let me know when you decide."

On the way back to the shop, Gabriel kicked little puffs of dust in the air. "How can I leave the shop to go off and preach?"

Calvin took off his hat and fanned himself. "Gettin' powerful hot. Now, son. You know Nigel and I can run that shop good as anyone. And with Eb and Rusty—"

"I was studyin' on taking them with me."

"Eb? Rusty? They ain't elders."

"We'd be goin' back to Eb's old territory. Time to get his wife. High time. And I need their help."

Calvin raised his eyebrows. "Eb I can see. But Rusty--"

Gabriel tried to summon his firmest preaching voice. "I have a plan, and I need Rusty too."

The two older men looked at each other, then nodded. Gabriel gestured as he spoke, animated now. "What about Bethia? I can't just leave her, after what's happened. And with Bennett after her—"

"We'll take care of her," Calvin said. "Don't doubt that for a moment."

Nat gave a little cough. "I'm hoping she'll come and help Hannah for awhile. Just a few weeks or so, maybe a month—help her over the hardest part of the pregnancy."

Gabriel shrugged. "You can ask her."

Nat said, "I'll ask before I leave. Then she can decide what to do."

If Gabriel had any doubts about his mission, they were dispelled a week later. He was leaning against the door jamb talking to Nigel when Eb nudged him. "We got company."

Gabriel straightened up and looked around. More customers? Two men on foot, walking up the gravel path. Dressed in black suits, as if about to conduct a preaching service. "We in trouble fer sure," Eb whispered.

"Whatever it is, I'll handle it." Gabriel stepped forward to greet them. "'Morning, gentlemen. Brother Packer, isn't it? And Brother Sneedley. How may I help you?"

Brother Packer, a short, red-faced man who had not missed many meals in his life, wiped the perspiration from his forehead. "It be mighty hot today."

"It's hotter'n hell in a bucket," exclaimed Brother Sneedley.

"Well, let's not go into the shop," Gabriel said. "You think it's hot here, wait'll you get in there with the forge."

"Well, now. Brother Romain." Packer gave a little cough. *Allergies and too much rich food, Gabriel thought.* "We've come on behalf of the committee that's raising funds for the temple. Now, you know it's gonna be quite an enterprise, with them plans and all. Bigger than Kirtland, they be saying."

Gabriel nodded, waiting for what was coming. Sneedley cleared his throat. A thin, lanky man, his face pale, with dark circles under his eyes. *Needs more sleep.* "Now, Brother Romain. We hear you be doing right well, with yer blacksmith shop and being a physician and all."

"I've got to pay my help." Gabriel wasn't sure how to tell them the shop was a communal endeavor.

"You seem to be succeeding." Sneedley went on. "I see folks lined up most every day outside yer place."

Gabriel shrugged. "We do good work."

"I reckon so. And that's why we expect a substantial contribution to the temple."

Packer nodded. "We're all expected to sacrifice. And if you have any amount saved—any at all—you know yer conscience be telling you to give it."

A vision flashed across his mind—the money he'd saved for Jess's freedom. At least three hundred and fifty dollars—he'd counted it last night. *How did they know?* Folding his arms, he looked off into space.

"Hmm. I'd have to study on it a mite. You see—" *Think fast, he begged himself.* "This—this blacksmith shop is owned by a number of people. There's myself, and Brother Manning—he's just up the hill there. Brother Nat has put a lot of work in it. And the rest of us is family—"

"We understand that." Packer took out his silk handkerchief and wiped his brow. "Still, we expect sacrifice and financial cooperation from everyone. 'Specially those who are blessed with profits."

"Tell you what," Gabriel said. "I reckon I need to talk with the others and figure out how much we can give."

"So, can't you do it now?"

Gabriel made a point of looking into the door of the shop. "Naw. They're not all here."

Packer stuffed the sodden handkerchief into his back pocket. He did not look happy. "Well, when shall we come back?"

Gabriel gazed off into space again. "*Eh bien.* How about—say, in a few days. Give us a week."

Packer and Sneedley looked at each other. Finally they both nodded. "A week, then. I hope you're prepared to be more than generous."

"We'll give what we can. Brother Packer, if I was you, I'd git outa that sun right quick and rest a spell."

Packer did not reply. Gabriel heard him puffing as they turned to walk back to the road.

"Well done," Eb said under his breath.

Gabriel waited till the money-seekers were out of sight. Then he began gesturing, doing an animated little dance on the doorstep. "We got less than a week to get outa here. Find Rusty. We'll start gathering provisions, feed for the horses and such. What we'll need for camping. We got to be as clever as Nat ever was. And twice as resourceful."

"Where you goin' now?"

"I'm off to see Dr. Weld. I reckon he'll take care of most of my patients."

It was just before noon when he knocked at Dr. Weld's front door. The woman who opened it, presumably Sister Weld, looked startled, her eyes wide. Gabriel spoke hurriedly.

"I'm so sorry, ma'am. I didn't mean to frighten you. I just wanted a word with the doctor."

She pushed back a lock of her graying hair. "Oh—Dr. Romain. It's all right. Most of the patients go around to the back."

He began to apologize again. She cut him off with a gesture. "It's no mind. Come on in. You see, we had kind of a scare two nights ago. Pounding on the door in the middle of the night. It's fine—you go on back. He's in his office, and there be no patients right now."

Wondering, Gabriel followed her down the hall to the office. She tapped at the door. "Dr. Romain to see you."

"Of course. Come in." Dr. Weld, a slender man of ordinary height, stood up from behind his desk. He looked to be in his early fifties, and had a pale face with thin, sensitive features. He had a shock of gray hair, neatly combed, and sparse gray eyebrows over hazel eyes. That particular day, the eyes had a tired, strained look, as if the man needed rest. They shook hands.

"I be going on a mission—leaving in a few days. Came to ask if you would watch over my patients for me. There's not very many, right now. Some older folk, a few women."

Dr. Weld nodded. "I'd be glad to. Let's go out on the porch where we can sit a spell. Care for some cider?"

"Don't mind if I do."

"Patient just brought me a fresh jug." Weld turned to his wife. "Dear, can you bring out the cider and two mugs? Thank you." He led Gabriel out to his back porch. Gabriel took a seat in the caned rocker, and Weld pulled up another chair beside him. Soon they were sipping cold cider. Weld gave a heavy sigh. "I vow. It's right good to relax a bit."

"It looks like you need some relaxing. Too many late nights?"

"Actually—one in particular. I reckon I haven't quite recovered."

Gabriel rested the mug on his knee. "Two nights ago?"

"Why, yes. She must have told you. Something very strange. I've never seen the like of it, and I've seen a great many things by this time. It started with this pounding on the front door. Loud pounding. Startled both of us wide awake."

"Expectant fathers can get right frantic."

Weld shot him a look. "This was no delivery. Well, my old lady lighted the lamp, and I rushed to get some clothes on. I flung open the door, and darned if it weren't George Robinson.

'Quick, Doctor!' he said—like a gasp. 'John C. Bennett has taken poison!'"

"Poison?" Gabriel clutched the mug. Some of the cider sloshed over and spilled on his knee.

"That's what he said. I grabbed my coat, my hat and bag. We climbed in the rig, and off we went. I asked how the accident had happened. 'Warn't no accident,' Robinson said. 'More like suicide.'

"Well, by this time I was fully awake. It seems that Robinson's wife had heard Bennett puking and moaning in his room. When she rushed in, he wouldn't tell her what he'd taken. He said he wanted to die. And all I could ask was 'Why?'

"Well, Robinson went on about how they discovered that he had a wife and children in Ohio—she'd gone to live with her father because of his affairs with other women. Now, according to Robinson, this had been known for a while. But Hyrum Smith had just returned from Pennsylvania with other news, and I hear tell he closeted himself with Joseph and Sidney for some time. Finally they called Bennett in. Sidney told Robinson he cried like a baby and said if the news got out, it would kill his aged mother. He begged for a second chance."

"What news?" Gabriel asked. "I mean, we've already got adultery, fornication, rumors about plural marriage—"

"He wouldn't tell. Anyway, we got to the house. That living room was full of people—William and Wilson Law, Judge Higbee, his sons Chauncey and Francis, Joseph's brothers Samuel and William. And Don Carlos too. I followed Robinson into Bennett's room. Sidney, Hyrum and Joseph were all there, at the foot of the bed. Sister Athalia—Robinson's wife—was trying to give him some water. The whole place stunk of vomit. I remember the words of that good woman: 'Thank goodness you're here, Dr. Weld.'

"So I checked the patient. Irregular pulse, not too strong. I asked what he'd taken. He refused to answer. I said that unless I knew the poison, I couldn't provide an antidote. He said he didn't want an antidote—he wanted to die. He asked for more water. 'I'm burning up inside.'

"So then Sidney Rigdon bellows in his oratorical voice, 'Well, Doctor—do something!'

"Well, I suspected arsenic poisoning. So I called for milk, and warm water for an enema. I administered ferric hydroxide, which I'd made up from a mixture of carbonate of soda and tincture of iron. I gave him morphine for the pains and spasms. Finally I told them, 'The main danger right now is exhaustion.'"

Gabriel couldn't believe what he was hearing. "Quite right," he managed to say.

"He was resting inside of an hour. The crisis was over. At one point he said, 'You should have let me die, Doctor.' It was then I noticed that his eyes were on Joseph, not me. Something was odd—well, the whole thing was very strange. I had this feeling that the entire incident was for Joseph's benefit—a dramatic way of demonstrating his repentance. I'm not even sure that poison had been a lethal dose."

"I reckon he would've known how much to take," Gabriel said slowly. "Him being a doctor and all."

"To make it look good without doing himself in. Well, that's the story. The next day he was up and about, a bit shaky, to be sure. But no mention of poisoning by anyone."

"I doubt you'll hear anything." Gabriel sipped the last of his cider. "And certainly not from the stand."

"Well, if I look tired, that's why."

Gabriel put the empty mug down on the tray. "I'm obliged to you for telling me. It makes some things clear. But it doesn't explain what Hyrum actually learned in Pennsylvania—what he told the others. It must have been damning, to get that reaction."

"I'm not sure we want to know. So, tell me about your patients."

Later Gabriel told Eb about his conversation with Dr. Weld.

"Ain't that something?" Eb exclaimed. "I hope you're not still fixin' to beat him up like you said."

"Not me. I figured he's suffered enough."

They spent the next few days preparing for the journey. In a large leather knapsack, borrowed from Nathaniel, Gabriel put a copy of the Book of Mormon, a pair of black broadcloth pants, and rain gear, together with a knife, hatchet and matches. Rusty would carry their cash in his saddlebags. "I'm not supposed to take purse or script," Gabriel said. "So I reckon you'll do it."

Eb planned to carry the few cooking utensils, apples, bacon, and bread with a hunk of cheese. They each carried a canteen of water, blankets for a bedroll, and oats wrapped in burlap sacks for the horses.

"Joseph know about the horses?" Eb asked.

"He didn't ask. But I reckon he'd approve if he knew what we were about."

"Sounds like you got everything," Calvin remarked. "Like as not, you be able to find most provisions on the way. Don't let them horses get too tired."

The day before their departure, Rusty and Gabriel took Bethia across to Montrose on the ferry. She was in one of her strange moods.

"I don't know how you're gonna be preaching and retrieving Eb's wife too. And taking care of horses."

"Well, don't fret about it," Gabriel told her. "If it can be done, we aim to do it."

They walked to the farm in silence. Once Gabriel asked if she were too warm.

"I be fine." She sounded annoyed. "But it's powerful hot."

"Be cooler in the woods," Rusty said. "Where the cabins are."

The men left Bethia at Nat's cabin and walked out to the barn to find Nat. Just as they reached the double doors, they heard Nat shouting at Jody.

"If I told you once I told you a hundred times. Stay away from the back end of that mule!"

Mule? They entered. A large, dark brown mule, his ears back, stood in the nearest stall.

"Name's Pete." Nat forked hay into the manger. "Got 'em at an auction, t'other side of Montrose. Trouble is, he's not the sweetest animal I ever met. Chased Owen all around the pasture this morning."

"Unpredictable, huh?" Rusty eyed the animal.

"Oh, he has an even temperament. Always unpleasant."

Gabriel began to laugh. "Kind of like Bethia."

Rusty laughed too, but Nat did not. He shook his head. "Must be hard, bein' a woman. Going through childbirth and all. Glad I don't have to do it."

"I reckon you're right," Gabriel said.

They ate a last meal with Hannah and the children. Nat gave them a final blessing. Then they said goodbye in the fading light. Gabriel kissed Bethia and embraced Hannah. Rusty hugged Hannah while Nat took Gabriel by the shoulders and gave him a long, earnest look.

"Good luck. And I don't mean just for the preaching."

16

Rusty couldn't believe it. On their way at last. After all the preparations for the journey, the frantic last-miinute details. And the delay. Just as they were ready to saddle up, Corey came running.

"Gabriel! My father—he's been coughing half the night."

Gabriel had followed her to her house while the others waited.

"Don't fret none," Eb told him. "Gabe won't stay longer than necessary."

"How do you know?"

"He's careful with Corey—doesn't want Bethia to be upset."

"But she's not even here."

Eb spoke slowly. "That's no matter. He don't want folks talking."

When Gabe returned, Rusty asked, "So how'd you get away so fast?"

Gabe looked at him. "I told him to rest, drink lots of water, and see Dr. Weld if he wasn't better tomorrow. And Corey'll see that he does it—you can be sure of that."

Now they trotted toward Carthage in the morning light. On either side stretched farmlands, cultivated fields, the stalks of corn waist-high. Roadside trees threw shadows across their path. There was a mistiness about everything; even though the sky was clear, they seemed to move in a cloud of haze.

"Heat's comin' on," Eb remarked.

At that moment Rusty felt comfortable, well-rested, excited about this particular adventure. Like a quest, it was. A rescue. Later, as the sun burned away the mist, he felt the heat on his back and neck. Tiring. Glad he didn't have to walk. Not wanting to complain—anxious to be a help, not a hindrance. They stopped to rest the horses. Rusty figured it was around noon.

"Time for lunch?" he asked hopefully.

Gabe glanced at him. "Not yet. We've a ways to go. I want to get beyond Carthage by nightfall."

Rusty sighed. Finally Gabe stopped in a sheltered grove. They hobbled the horses and turned them loose to graze. Then Eb opened his knapsack and pulled out bread and cheese, which Gabe sliced with his knife. They ate sitting under the trees. "Too bad we don't have us some cider," Eb said.

"Like as not, we can buy a jug when we go through town." Gabe cut up an apple. "These apples are old. Be good to have fresh ones again."

Eb chuckled. "You have to wait some for that."

Early dusk found them far from any town. "I reckon we camp out," Eb said.

Gabe nodded. "It's a warm enough night. We hardly need the blankets."

Gabe fed the horses while Eb and Rusty gathered wood for a fire. Later they sat around the fire eating bacon and fried apples. Rusty took a swig of the cider they'd bought. "Not bad." He passed it to Eb.

Eb drank and wiped his mouth on his sleeve. "Hope them towns is far enough away so that we don't get any surprise visits."

"Why?" Rusty asked. "Do they hate us all that much?"

"Well, you can't trust 'em." Eb waved a piece of bacon. "Ain't you heard what happened to the prophet, just payin' a social call on Governor Carlin? Went down to Quincy on business, I hear tell."

Gabe stretched his feet out. "And the governor treated him right fine, then sent the posse after him. They arrested him and turned him over to a constable and sheriff from—guess where? Missouri, of all places."

Rusty spoke quickly. "Well, 'course I remember. But you're forgettin' that What's-his-name—that judge—declared that the writ was dead. They had to let him go."

"Stephen A. Douglas." Eb took a bite of bacon. "Don't forget that name."

Gabe said, "I wonder if Carlin knows he just lost the support of every Mormon in the state."

Eb leaned forward. "Don't put yer feet in the fire, Gabe. You be hoppin' around, yelling in French. Wakin' all the snakes from here to the river."

Gabe drew his feet up. "I reckon you notice I didn't stop to preach in Carthage."

Eb grunted. "Too close to home. Like as not, they seed enough of the likes of us."

They slept around what was left of the fire, using their blankets to ward off mosquitoes.

Gabe did preach in a little settlement some miles east of Springfield. Rusty, curious as to how you went about such a thing, followed Gabe into the general store. Most of the town seemed to be gathered there, men in work clothes sitting around chewing tobacco. Gabe held up his hand and gave his brief announcement. "There'll be preaching tonight, if I can find a place to do it."

"Yer a preacher, son?" An old man spat a quid of tobacco across the room.

"Yes, and I can entertain you all. I have a message worth hearing."

"What do you say, Slim?" The man addressed the storekeeper. "How 'bout lettin' 'em have yer big room upstairs?"

And so it was arranged. "Easy enough," Rusty said to Gabe.

"Nat says it's fine till you start asking at churches. A lot of 'em refuse when they know you're Mormon. But then you find maybe one—"

"One's all you need."

Rusty counted twenty-eight people gathered in the upstairs room about two hours before candlelight—mostly men, a few women and children. He caught some of the comments.

"Why, that one feller don't look old enough to be allowed out by hisself."

"He's just short, is all. Look, they got a black man with 'em."

"I hope this ain't one of them all-fired abolitionist meetings."

Soon Gabe stood up, and all eyes turned to him. He introduced himself and talked about his growing up in Gallipolis, and how he had come upon a copy of the Book of Mormon. Rusty noted his friendly, easy way of speaking, not dynamic, like Nathaniel, but gentle, interspersed with humor and little comic asides. He read to them from the preface of the book:

" '...that they may know the covenants of the Lord, that they are not cast off forever; and also to the convincing of the Jew and Gentile that Jesus is the Christ, the Eternal God, manifesting himself unto all nations...'"

He told a bit of the story of the book, how it had come forth, and then went on to tell them that the true church of Christ had now been restored upon the earth. The whole presentation took about forty minutes. Gabe punctuated it with his usual gestures and animated facial expressions. On the whole, Rusty found it entertaining and interesting, even though he was beginning to think about supper and where he was going to find it.

Then Eb stood up and proclaimed himself a free man, loosed not only from slavery but freed by the knowledge of Jesus Christ and the love of the people he had found in the Church of Christ. Well-spoken. Rusty thought how he would have to bear his own testimony at the next meeting; he was glad he had some time to think about it.

Gabe answered questions from the audience. They asked him to preach again the next day, and he consented. One of the men offered to give them lodging for the night. They accepted.

The next day Rusty gave a short talk about how he and his sister Hannah had first heard the gospel preached in Allegheny County. What attracted them most was the concept of Zion, a city or gathering of people where God's will would be truly done upon the earth. "And the Lord called his people Zion, because there were no poor among them."

They managed to preach their way across Illinois and into Indiana. By the time they reached Indianapolis, Rusty found himself giving full-length discourses without any difficulty. All Gabe had to say was, "Rusty, we'll hear from you tonight," and he would prepare his thoughts as they rode eastward. He marveled at the way Gabe managed to vary his own sermons, with new ideas and new ways of presenting their message. The reception was unpredictable; sometimes they were invited to preach some more, and even to baptize. Other times they were ridiculed, even attacked with ranting and belligerent words. When they could find no place to speak, they moved on.

Once a man asked Rusty about the horses. "The last Mormons that went through these parts was on foot. And their shoes was about plumb wore out."

What to do? Reluctant to say they were to be used to buy someone out of slavery. Finally he looked at his questioner.

"I reckon we aim to be circuit riders, like the Methodists. And for that, you need horses."

Ohio. Rusty thought about the way they had come—the hardships, riding in rain as well as hot sun. A fascinating journey, never boring, for they didn't know what the evening might bring—a kind family to lodge them and a receptive audience, or doors shut against them and a campfire in the woods.

They reached the outskirts of Gallipolis in the late afternoon. It had just rained; the horses' hooves made sucking sounds in the mud.

"Just ahead. There's Dr. Beauchamps' house. And the blacksmith shop." Gabe spoke softly, his voice husky. They rode on. Rusty glanced at the buildings, many in need of repair. Nothing stood out as particularly different—an ordinary town, like most they had passed through. But Gabe's face had a look of wonder; his lower lip trembled, as if he were no longer sure of anything.

Rusty reined in his horse and followed behind Gabe. His thoughts wandered; he found himself musing about Gabe and Bethia. Did Gabe care that his marriage seemed to be more of a burden than a joy? Or was he unaware—too busy with his own work to know the difference? Gabe slowed his horse to a stop, then dismounted.

"We're here." He gestured at the two-story house of gray clapboard. It had stone steps and a front porch that stretched the length of the house and curved around one side. Gabe looped the horse's reins over the railing and tied them. The front door opened; Rusty watched as someone stepped out. A young woman, who looked to be the same age as himself.

Rusty blinked. Hardly more than a girl, but she caught his eye. Maybe it was her lack of height—short and slim, like Gabe, who looked younger than his twenty-four years. She stood at the top of the porch steps and stared, her mouth open a little. With her pale face, her gray eyes set far apart and open wide, her black hair cascading down around her shoulders, Rusty thought her the loveliest person he'd ever seen.

She gave a cry and flung herself down the steps. Gabe rushed to catch her and they embraced each other. There were exclamations in French, and then the girl was crying, weeping into Gabe's neck.

"I knew you'd come back! I always knew it!"

What secrets had Gabe been hiding? Here he'd left this charming girl and married Bethia. Rusty sensed the truth of the relationship a second before Gabe disengaged himself.

"Marie, these are my friends and traveling companions. Rusty Manning and Eb Wanfield. My sister, Marie-Françoise."

Rusty nodded to her as they dismounted. At that moment he felt incapable of speech. Her eyes flicked over them; then she turned back to Gabe. "So much to tell you. Oh, Gabriel. Our mother—*maman*—"

They embraced each other again. Rusty caught the words, "...died last April. We didn't know how to get word to you. Dr. Beauchamps said her heart just gave out. And she wouldn't do anything he said. You know how stubborn she was."

Still holding her, Gabe moved his head in a quick gesture. "Rusty, you and Eb see to the horses. Stable's in back."

Rusty took the reins of Jeb and Jenny and led them around the corner of the house. Eb followed with Freedom. Eb said something, but Rusty didn't hear. All thoughts of Gabe and his unfortunate marriage had vanished, along with any anticipation of supper. He moved in a daze, getting straw for the horses, removing the saddles and bridles. The last image of Marie filled his mind, the wide, gray eyes, the dark lashes matted with tears. Hair black like a raven's wing, the ringlets flowing over her shoulders. He stood holding a saddle blanket.

Eb prodded him. "I reckon you'd best keep the saddlebags with you. We don't dare trust no one."

Rusty shouldered the bags and followed Eb up to the house.

"Yes—we became Mormons when we reached northern Ohio. We went to work on a farm and joined up with the church. Now we be preaching some, but our real mission is to rescue Eb's wife. Swap our horses for her, if'n we have to."

Gabriel's voice seemed to echo in the dining area. They sat at the long table over the remains of supper, an excellent *coq au vin*. At the head of the table sat his brother Étienne, the oldest of the Romain children. Taller than Gabriel, he had put on weight over the years. His hair was gray at the temples, and he had wrinkles on his cheeks and forehead which Gabriel had not remembered.

Gabriel's older sisters Louise and Manon had both married and gone off to live in Kentucky, as Étienne informed him. The table seemed empty without them and their mother, but Marie, Gabriel's favorite, had remained. He gave silent thanks. Étienne lifted a chicken bone and pointed it at him.

"So you became a Mormon. Well and good. I don't know how long you figure on staying, but we'll have none of that preachin' around here. Not in this town, and certainly not in this house. *Comprends-tu*?"

Jolted, Gabriel choked on the last bit of chicken from his plate. Both Rusty and Eb were looking at him, dismay and uncertainty on their faces. Marie spoke quickly.

"Oh, Étienne, you know they're welcome to stay as long as they want. What's the matter with you?"

By this time Gabriel had recovered. He wiped his mouth on the linen napkin. "We have no intention of preaching here. As I said, our main purpose is to buy Eb's wife out of slavery. Once we have her, we'll head back to Illinois."

Étienne grunted and lifted the wine glass to his lips. Marie rose and began to clear the table. Gabriel caught Rusty's eyes following her as she moved from the table to the kitchen area. He looks smitten, Gabriel thought. Impossible. He's only known her a few hours. Maybe the French cooking has done things to his innards. Gabriel took a sip of wine.

"I think the best thing is for Eb and me to head out tomorrow—cross the river and find the plantation. See how the land lays. Rusty'll stay here with the horses. By the way, he's a fine blacksmith—you can use 'em down in the shop. Or he can do work around here."

Eb and Rusty both looked relieved. They lifted their wine glasses, filled with water at their request, and drank. Marie brought out a dish of baked apples covered with a crust of cinnamon and sugar. Rusty's face brightened as he saw it.

"You're a marvelous cook," he said as fervently as if he were preaching.

Marie laughed and set out a pitcher of cream. She began to spoon the apple mixture into smaller dishes. Étienne frowned.

"Suit yourself. I don't reckon I need any help in my shop. *Tiens.* We'll put you and Rusty up in the guest room. Your friend Eb can sleep out in the stable."

"*Pardon?*" Gabriel asked. "All right. If Eb sleeps in the stable, I reckon Rusty and I will just stay out there with him."

"Étienne—" Marie began. Étienne reached for the cream and poured it over his serving of apples. The rest waited as the cream was passed to them, then poured it on their dessert. Finally Étienne put down his spoon.

"Hang it all. Have it your way. All three of you in the guest room. But you'll have to sleep in the same bed."

"*Merci beaucoup,*" Gabriel said with exaggerated politeness.

The next morning they got up early. Marie prepared a breakfast of fried eggs, toast and coffee.

"Good coffee," Gabriel remarked.

"A long time since we had any," Rusty said. "Forgot how good it tasted."

"It's the sweet cream makes it special." Marie poured him another cup.

At the stable, they repacked the knapsacks. Gabriel had already stowed their cash in the bottom of his own. They packed enough provisions for three days. Gabriel looked at Rusty.

"The horses can use a good rest, I reckon. We'll be back soon as we can."

Marie came out to say goodbye. Étienne had left for his shop as soon as he'd finished breakfast. Gabriel hugged his sister.

"Take care of Rusty, now. Put him to work, and don't feed him too much. Rusty, look out for the horses. Like as not, we'll need to fetch one or two of 'em."

"Good luck," Marie whispered.

Gabriel and Eb set off toward the ferry landing. Eb said, "I feel bad about the horses. Havin' to git rid of 'em like that."

"They'll be well-treated. The worst of it is that we have to trade 'em for a living person. What does that say about our society?"

Once on Virginia soil, Gabriel looked at Eb. "Which way now?"

"We jest follow the river south, to the plantation. We can't miss it. It's between the Ohio and the river to the east."

They followed a wagon trace to the south, keeping the river on their right. They walked in the shadow of the thick woods. The air was sweet with the scent of balsam and crushed ferns.

"I sure do appreciate this," Eb said. "I'm never gonna forget it."

"Well, let's hope we can carry it through. This is all new to me."

"It'll be all right."

Gabriel had pondered about the best way to proceed. How did you deal with people who actually believed it was all right to own other human beings? "I reckon it might be a good idea for you to make contact with the slaves first."

"Well, of course. That's what I was planning."

"Can you do it without getting caught?"

Eb gave him a look of disgust. "What do you think? My people may be slaves, but they're not stupid. There be more ways to git around white folks than you ever figured."

"I would hope," Gabriel said.

They agreed that Gabriel would wait in the woods with the knapsacks and money while Eb approached the slave quarters. "If you aren't back in three hours, I'm comin' after you."

Eb put a hand on his shoulder. "You stay put. Just keep hidden. I'll be back right soon."

The footsteps died away. Gabriel sat down to wait, his back against a large ash tree. He knew he was hidden from the road; anyone who found him would have to come upon him suddenly. And he could hear their footsteps in the dried leaves well in time to be warned.

He had no call to be worried. Eb had assured him that his people, escaped slaves or not, had ways of keeping hidden in the woods and contacting each other. Still, things could go awry. Eb might yet need to be rescued. Gabriel put a hand on his only weapon, the knife which he had transferred from his knapsack to his belt.

The scent of the deep woods, of balsam and damp earth, made him feel lazy; he began to relax. He thought briefly of Bethia, hoping she had found a measure of peace with Hannah and her family. He wondered again what was wrong with her, and why he couldn't fix it. Such a change, in a few short years. And here his sister Marie hadn't changed at all. Older, to be sure. Prettier than he'd remembered. But she had the same liveliness, the concern for him.

Corey. Trying not to think of her. But her strong, resolute face filled his mind. Not only did he admire her; he knew she cared for him. Unsettling at first, the fact had become part of his life. He wondered if the time would come when he would have to take some action. Make a choice, for instance, and cause more pain. He hoped such a thing was a ways off.

Then he sat straight up. Why hadn't he thought of it before? Most likely Jess had given up on Eb. After all, it had been nine years. She had a second husband by this time, and Eb at that very moment was walking into that situation. He buried his face in his hands. *Why had they waited so long?* But what else could they have done? No money saved, nothing to bargain with. He sighed and rubbed his eyes.

Tiens. A noise. The sound of a footstep, then another. A steady crunching in the dry leaves. He sprang to his feet and picked up the knapsacks. Waiting.

The return of her favorite brother. That's what it took to make her realize how restless she'd felt. Not bored, exactly. A certain feeling of being trapped. Missing her mother and older sisters. Stuck with keeping house for Étienne. Not the easiest person to please.

In fact, she had to admit it. She didn't like him all that much. Her own brother. And the prospect of getting away from him, of being married to someone else in the town, grew dimmer each year. Most of the French families had already left for greener pastures.

Now, here was Gabriel again. After years of what appeared to be an exciting, interesting life. Come to rescue someone from slavery. He'd spent his early years leading people to freedom. Could he possibly lead her, too?

But even more significant, here was Rusty. Tall and broad-shouldered, muscular, more handsome than anyone she knew. A blacksmith like her father and older brother. He even looked French, with wide apart eyes and a direct, intent gaze. She found herself drawn to him, liking him more than she cared to admit. *Best to be careful.* If he had an inner spirit to match his looks, it would be luck of such magnitude that she didn't dare hope.

Now she stood looking at him, her arms folded, her fingers rubbing her upper arms. Gabriel and Eb had left to catch the ferry. He gave her a shy smile, as if unsure what to say to her.

"Be you cold, Miss Marie? I hope I may call you that."

"*Mais oui.* Just Marie will be fine."

"It's a mite chilly this morning. Why don't you go inside while I take care of the horses? Then I'll come in and—and do any work you'd like me to do."

She made a swift decision. "I'm all right. I'll stay out here with you."

She watched as he gave each horse a measure of oats. Before he bent to fork some hay, he looked at her. "I'm mighty sorry about your mother, Marie. I lost mine a long time ago, before my sister and I joined the church. It was powerful hard, when she died—my mother, that is."

She found that all she had to do to keep him talking was to ask him questions. Before he had finished with the horses, she had learned all about his family (Huguenots—Étienne would have a fit crosswise if he knew) and how he and Hannah had traveled to northern Ohio and then out to Missouri in a search for the land of promise.

"How did you meet Gabriel? And where does Eb fit in?"

He told her how Gabriel had rescued Eb from the river and how the whole group of men had met in Zion's Camp, the expedition to help the people in Missouri who had been driven from their homes. As they left the stable, Marie had the strange feeling that she knew them all—bearded Nathaniel and his wife Hannah, the little ones, Rusty's father Calvin and his second wife.

"How many wives do Mormons get to have?"

He laughed. "All the fellers I know just have one. There's lots of rumors about us, I reckon. But that one's not true."

"And what about you?"

"Me? I don't have any. Leastwise, not yet."

"So you just plan to have one?"

He looked at her. "If'n I'm lucky."

"So, is Gabriel married?"

A shadow crossed his face, a look of sorrow and hesitation. She wondered about it later. He quickly said, "He be married to Bethia. Sarah's niece."

"Is she pretty? Would I like her?"

"I reckon so. She's nice enough."

"Strange he didn't tell me."

"Like as not, he didn't get around to it. He has a lot on his mind, Gabriel does. First off, he's a doctor, with a bunch of folks to look after. Then he's an elder—a minister. And a blacksmith. The whole family helps run the smithy. At least the ones on the Nauvoo side of the river."

"A doctor, you say? *C'est vrai*?"

He told her how Gabriel got his medical training in Mentor before they all had to leave Ohio.

She climbed the wooden steps to the back porch. "I can see now why he didn't have time to write us any letters."

"He hoped he'd be settled first. And I reckon it never happened."

As she opened the back door, Rusty held back. "I see your woodpile needs some attention. If you tell me where the ax is, I'll split you some wood."

He worked most of the morning splitting logs. One of the neighbors stopped by with a chicken, payment for some work in the blacksmith shop. Marie set to work and prepared a dinner of *poulet roti* and baked potatoes, with fresh greens from the garden. When Étienne came home for the late midday meal, he demanded, "Why did you go and kill another chicken, just for the three of us?"

"Mr. Bouvier brought it by, as payment. Freshly killed. I thought it best to prepare it right away."

Étienne grunted and took his place at the table. Marie tried to suppress her impatience. Tired of having to explain every little thing.

"Excellent dinner," Rusty said to her during the meal. She noticed he had no lack of appetite. A heady feeling, to have someone appreciate what she had cooked. She tried to think when Etienne had ever complimented her in such a way. If he had, she couldn't remember.

The next day, she went out to watch as Rusty split the last of the logs.

"I think you're working too hard."

He straightened up. "I reckon I'm used to it. At home, they make me work—that is, there's a lot to be done." He paused. "And—Marie. For you I'd work my whole life long."

Their eyes met. "Would you, now?

"You can depend on it." He gave a shrug. "It can't hurt to ask. Would you come north with us, back to Illinois?"

She caught her breath. Afraid of waiting too long, she spoke hurriedly. "I reckon I will." Not wanting to seem too eager. "I'm ready for adventure. Some excitement."

Rusty laughed. "Well, that we can offer you."

He put down the ax. She removed her apron and they went for a stroll in the town. She showed him some of the older houses.

"These were all French families. Most of them are gone now."

"Gabriel told me." He took her hand. They came to the little church, built of dark logs, and the house where the priest lived.

"Rusty, you should know. I'm Catholic. I can't suddenly become a Mormon."

"Of course you can't. And it sure doesn't matter to me."

"What would I do in Nauvoo?"

"Well, I reckon you'd go to Mass, same as you do here. You see, it's not generally known, but the city is open when it comes to religion. There's other churches—most of the major denominations are in there. A lot of the population's Mormon, to be sure. But folks are free to worship where they choose."

They turned to walk back toward home. She drew a deep breath, feeling relief and apprehension rushing over her at the same time. "I'm trying to think of the best way to tell Étienne. I know he'll oppose it any way he can."

"Then don't tell him. Leave a letter where he'll find it later, and just come with us. That's what Hannah and I did when we left Allegheny County."

"I don't know—"

"Wait'll Gabe gets back. He'll know what to do. I reckon he's led enough people to safety. And he may have an escaped slave with him—he'll have to be doubly careful."

"What do you mean?"

He gestured with his free hand. "Well, if they refuse to sell her for what we've got—three horses and some cash—I figure Gabe and Eb will just take her. Steal her. Then she'll be a fugitive, and they'll have to get away fast. If they're caught, we're all in trouble." He gave her an intent look. "So you should prepare now—decide what you want to take with you. And I hope it's not very much."

She gave a nervous little laugh, but it sounded hollow. "It sounds like you live an—an interesting and exciting life."

He looked amused. "I reckon it's the times that be that way, more than us. But if you consider being chased out of one's home, from one place to the next, never knowing what we'll find—why, yes. I guess it be exciting. Maybe not the kind of excitement you want."

Afraid she'd offended him, she wondered how to make things right. They walked past the woodpile and up the steps to the back door. As they entered, he drew her close to him and kissed her on the lips. She had to stand on tiptoe to put her arms around his neck. They stood hugging each other. He had the scent of wood smoke about him, and fresh-cut logs. A strong, comforting smell. He kissed her again.

"Marie. *Je t'aime.*"

She pulled away and he followed her into the kitchen area. She took his hand. "This calls for a celebration. How about a glass of wine?"

"I'll have water," he said. "I'm not used to wine, and I might do something really dumb. Like asking you to marry me."

"You might do that anyway. And I might say yes."

He smiled. "I'd like to think you just did."

"Oh, Rusty, I feel so happy! I feel like—like dancing. Do you know this song? It's been in my head all morning.

Sur le pont d'Avignon
On y danse, on y danse."

"I know it!" He clapped his hands. "My mother sang it to us when I was little." They both sang.

"Sur le pont d'Avignon
On y danse, tous en ronde."

He grasped both her hands and they began to dance.

"Les jeunes filles font comme ci..."

She laughed to think of it. Two people who knew France only through the memories of their parents, dancing to a children's song from the fifteenth century.

"Oh, Marie. You'll wear me out." He stopped, then took her in his arms and kissed her again.

A noise. A sharp tap over by the back door. They turned to look.

Étienne stood in the doorway, breathing hard, his face red. She had never seen him look so angry. All gayety fled; she felt rooted to the ground.

"*Eh bien.* Why don't you keep dancing?" He spun his fingers in a circular motion. "Don't let me stop you."

They drew apart, too startled to speak. He walked toward them. "Now, then. I see you've done more than split wood."

"Étienne—" she began.

"*Tais-toi!* Go to your room! I see I may have to lock you up."

Love gave her courage. "I'm not going anywhere. If you want me to explain—"

"Nothing needs explaining. It's all quite clear. Sir, if you aren't out of my house in two minutes, I'm fetching my shotgun."

Rusty stepped forward. Marie saw that he towered over Étienne by a good six inches. "There's no need for that. I'll go out in the stable, if you wish. But I have no weapon. No desire to fight you." He paused. "Your sister and I—we be engaged. She's agreed to be my wife."

Étienne's eyes narrowed to little slits. "She's not marrying any Mormon. Even a French one. And that's final."

Rusty gestured. "Maybe if you knew about us—what we believe, and how we live—you'd look on us different, like. We be farmers and working folks, just like you."

"Be quiet. I won't run you off the property the way I should. But yer stayin' out with the horses. Only comin' in for meals. This afternoon yer gonna work repairing that shed. I'll be here to see that you do. And tomorrow, yer going to the shop with me."

"I'll be glad to do that, sir." Rusty looked relieved; he took a step toward her.

"And yer gonna keep away from her. No touching, no dancing. Else I'll have to lock her in her room."

"That's not necessary," Rusty said. "You have my word." He strode past Étienne to the door. As he opened it, he turned and looked at her. Their eyes met. He smiled briefly and gave her a broad wink.

She tried not to react in any way—Étienne was watching her. Rusty stepped outside and closed the door.

She waited, then managed to walk into the pantry as if nothing had happened. "Well, let's get some dinner on the table."

17

"WHAT DO YOU MEAN, she's not there?" Gabriel let the knapsacks fall to the ground.

Eb stood breathing hard, his face glistening with perspiration. "Like I said. She be gone. Run off." He gasped for breath; his chest heaved. Alarmed, Gabriel grasped him by the arm.

"Let's—let's sit down a spell. Here—out of the sun."

They sat side by side in a mound of dry leaves. Gabriel waited before he spoke. "Now. Tell me what happened."

Eb's lower lip trembled. He didn't look at Gabriel. "Well, first off, I went to our cabin, at the end of the row. A woman was there, name of Cinda. Our good friend. She told me Jess went off about a year ago, aimin' to find me."

"Damnation! I knew we shoulda got here earlier."

Eb looked at him. "Don't you see? She's free. They never found her."

"Did they look?"

"Well, I reckon. They always do."

Gabriel made a quick gesture. "Well, how do we get to her?"

"Blamed if I know. But here's the news—there's a child."

"A child?"

"A girl. Eight years old. Jess had her eight months after I left. Name Kenturah. They call her Turah."

"You saw her?"

"No—she was up at the big house."

"Now—wait a minute. Jess didn't take her?"

"No. She couldn't. But she told Cinda she aimed to get her. Somehow, some day, she'd come back for her."

Gabriel leaned back against a tree, then sat upright. "*Ma foi!* That's it."

"What's what?"

"If we take the girl with us, then when Jess returns, Cinda and them will tell her we're in Nauvoo."

Eb blinked. "That's the thing. Cinda told me Jess might never come back."

"All the more reason for us to take Turah."

"Cinda say the girl's not much use. All she does is sing little songs and make up stories. Draws pictures in the sand. She say they be fixin' to sell her south."

"We'd better get moving, then. I'm gonna make an offer for her. Maybe they won't want as much, seeing she's so young. Now—how do I find the master?"

"It's the mistress you want to see. My old master's daughter-in-law. She takes care of the slaves, sews their clothes and such-like. Jest go to the big house and ask."

"You'd best stay here. Rest—you need it." Gabriel hoisted the knapsack to his back. In a matter of minutes he was climbing the steps of the large white house. Emboldened by his new plan, he swung the door-knocker. One of the house servants, a man about Eb's age, opened the door.

"I'd like to see your mistress, please. I have business with her."

Before he could gather his thoughts, he found himself in a small room with books and an ornate white-and-gold desk. A woman a bit older than Hannah sat at the desk. She wore a rose-patterned pink frock, more elaborate than anything he'd seen in Nauvoo. She looked up at him. She had silvery-gray hair and stern blue eyes set close together.

"Excuse me, ma'am," he said. "I'm Dr. Gabriel Romain, from Illinois, and I'd like to make an offer for your girl Kenturah. She's just a child, not worth too much, as I understand. I'm ready to give you cash for her this very day."

The lady sat back in her chair. Her thin, pale brows drew together. "Why would you want Kenturah? She's absolutely worthless. As you say."

"I'm acting on behalf of her father, a freedman. He wishes to reunite his family."

She shot him a suspicious look. "Her mother ran off some months ago. I don't suppose you know anything about that?"

He gestured with both hands. "I have no idea where she is. I've never laid eyes on her. If she were here, I'd offer to buy her as well."

She sat looking out into space for a moment. Then she nodded. "The child hasn't been much use since her mother left. And to tell the truth, she wasn't much help before. Always daydreaming, her head somewhere else."

"I still want her," Gabriel said. "I'll give you—well, how about a hundred?"

"Make it a hundred and fifty. Most girls are worth a bit more, you understand."

"Oh, I reckon." Gabriel began to wonder how long he could keep up the sham of bargaining for a human being. *Patience*, he told himself.

She tapped her fingers on the desk top. "But it'll save me the bother of selling her further south. All right. I accept your offer. On one condition."

"What's that?"

"You're a doctor, you say? I need some medical advice."

"Of course." He felt on solid ground again.

In the course of listening to her symptoms and examining her, Gabriel found she had a mass in her right side. Some sort of growth.

"It seems to get some bigger every week. But I don't feel a lot of pain."

Doomed. His sense of compassion made him forget for a moment about her being a slave-owner. He gave suggestions for diet and rest. "And a bit of wine if you should feel discomfort."

She seemed to accept his words. "The other doctor said there was nothing wrong. At least you say there's something."

"There be many things we can't heal. We just don't have the knowledge yet. I'm sorry."

Finally she called the house servant. "Ben, go find Turah and bring her here."

Gabriel had just a few moments to think what to say to the child, who knew nothing about him and what had just happened. When Ben appeared leading her by the hand, Gabriel felt something turn over in his chest. The eyes staring up at him were Eb's eyes; her expression reminded him of the time when he'd pulled Eb from the river.

"Is there a place where—where I could talk with her alone?"

"Well, you're going to take her with you," the mistress said. "She's yours now. She probably wouldn't understand you anyway." She clapped her hands once. "Turah. Listen carefully. You've just been sold to this gentleman. He's a doctor, from Illinois. Now, you go with him and don't be any trouble. You understand?"

Gabriel tried not to wince at the words. The girl did not react in any way. Gabriel got down on one knee and looked at her. "Don't be afraid, Turah. I'm going to take you to your papa. He's waiting to see you."

Turah stood motionless, her eyes wide. *Scared half to death.* The mistress pushed back her chair and rose to her feet. "I tried to warn you. She's just slow and stupid. I still don't know why you'd want her."

Gabriel tried to sound as gentle as he could. "Come on, Turah." He held out his hand.

"A good whipping might get her attention," the mistress said. At that the girl stepped forward. She took Gabriel's hand and let him lead her toward the door.

"Good day, Mrs. Wanfield." He walked slowly out of the study and across the large parlor to the front door. He wanted to hurry, to get away from there, but he didn't want to frighten the child even more. Ben escorted them to the entrance.

"'Bye, Turah." Ben waited as they went down the steps. She turned her head.

"'Bye, Ben." Her voice sounded soft and musical, with a mournful quality. Relief rushed over Gabriel like the late afternoon breeze; she could speak after all. He gave her hand a tiny squeeze.

"Honey, we're going to find your papa. Then we'll go see Cinda and say goodbye to her."

She spoke again. "My momma. Is momma there too?"

"No. She's not. I wish she were. But maybe we'll see her someday. When she comes back here, Cinda will tell her where to find us."

Probably too much for her to understand. I didn't say it simply enough. But Turah seemed content. The corners of her lips turned up in a half-smile as they entered the woods.

Eb stood still as they moved toward him. His face had an expression of shock and disbelief. A natural reaction, Gabriel thought. He'd only known he was a father since just before noon. Gabriel suddenly realized they'd forgotten all about the noonday meal. Time to remedy that. He led Turah a few steps more.

"Turah, this is your father. Eb—"

To Gabriel's surprise, Eb flung himself on his knees. "I know it! Bless me, I wouldn't doubt it for a minute! You be my own child! The spitting image of your mama." He held out his arms, his face wet with tears. "Come hug your pappy. I swear, I'll never forget this day!"

Then Eb was embracing his daughter, holding her while tears coursed down his cheeks. She put her small, slim arms around his neck and they hugged each other.

"My, you be thin. Don't they feed you?"

"I was thinkin' it was time to eat," Gabriel said.

After the snack of bread and apples, they went to see Cinda and tell her what had happened. Gabriel waited outside while Eb and Turah entered the tiny cabin at the end of the row. Finally Cinda herself walked out, a large-boned, broad-shouldered woman in a calico dress. She wiped her hands on her apron and eyed Gabriel.

"Eb tell me you buy this child."

"Uh—yes. She be free now." He felt uneasy, not sure if she approved or disapproved. Eb and Turah emerged from the building, the child clutching his hand. Then Cinda nodded.

"You a right good man. If'n Jess comes again, I'll tell her where you be."

He wanted to say that Eb had earned a good part of the money himself. Cinda spoke again, this time to Eb. "It be dark before you reach that river, and it's fixin' to rain. 'Member that old shed, 'bout a mile from here? Used to hold a mule, but there ain't no mule now. You go up there and take shelter for the night. I'll bring you some supper soon as it's dark."

Gabriel gestured. "We don't want to put you to trouble—"

"Hush," Eb said. "We'll take it."

Gabriel tried to explain as they walked through the woods to the shed. "I didn't want to take her food—like as not she doesn't get as much as she needs."

"From the looks of her, she be doin' fine," Eb said. "Besides, it's not hers. It comes from the big house."

They found the shed and set to work arranging a place to sleep in the hay which was left. "Best to do it while we can still see," Gabriel remarked.

By the time Cinda arrived with a pan of stew, Turah lay asleep, curled up on one side. Gabriel could only think how small and thin she looked. Eb covered her with his jacket.

"Poor lamb," Cinda said. "This the best thing could happen to her."

They sat on the hay looking out into the night. Gabriel and Eb ate stew, sharing a common spoon. There was a spatter of rain on the roof. Cinda got up to leave.

"Jest put the pan there when you done. I get it in the morning. If'n yer lucky, that roof won't leak too much."

Working most of the day. Hard work, hauling wood. Keeping the forge hot on a warm day. Thinking of Marie, and how Jacob had worked seven years for Rachel. If the older blacksmith approved of Rusty's efforts, he gave no sign.

Walking home now in the late afternoon. Stepping over puddles in the road. As they turned the corner, a large pig looked at them and trotted away.

"So," Étienne said. "From the looks of things, your friends have returned."

Rusty, his mind on the pig and what there would be for dinner, wondered how Étienne knew. The house looked no different. Then he saw the three sets of footprints in the mud. The middle set looked very small; Jess must be tiny. He started to climb the steps.

"Oh, no, you don't. Yer stayin' in the stable, like I said. And tomorrow, the whole lot of you are leaving. Without my sister, I might add."

Without a word, Rusty walked toward the stable. He looked in on each horse and stood patting Jeb, his own mount. Jeb nuzzled his sleeve.

"No apples for you today. Maybe tomorrow."

He wondered how long Gabe and Eb had been at the house. With luck, Marie had already told them everything. He sighed and began forking fresh hay into the feed bins. The shadows lengthened. Whatever was happening inside, Rusty knew he was ready for dinner. He was going through the knapsack trying to find an apple when he heard the footsteps outside.

Gabe walked in. Without a word he sat down beside Rusty on the hay bale. Rusty looked at him. Gabe met his eyes, his face stern. Rusty blinked, puzzled. Then Gabe burst out laughing.

"I can't leave you alone three days. And here you have my sister wanting to marry you, and my brother ready to blow you to the next world with his shotgun. How did you do it?"

Rusty searched for words. "I'm sorry. I—"

"Land's sakes, don't apologize. I couldn't be more pleased. I was aimin' to ask if she'd come north with us. She's some girl—I can't tell you how I've missed her."

"So—what do we do?"

"I'm studyin' on it. I came out to fetch you to dinner, by the way."

Rusty stood up. "That's good news. I take it you rescued Jess?"

"No. She's already escaped. We have her daughter, though. Eb's child—a little bit of a thing. We had to travel slow 'cause of her—slept in a haystack near the ferry landing last night." They reached the back steps. Gabe put a hand on his arm. "Let me do the talking tonight. Don't say much at all. And whatever happens, don't act surprised."

Wondering, Rusty followed him into the house. Étienne sat at his usual place. He glowered, his mouth tightening at the corners, as Rusty approached the table.

"Why don't you sit here?" Gabe pulled out the chair beside Marie's place. Marie carried a platter of ham from the kitchen area. Rusty sat down, not daring to look at her. When their eyes finally met, Gabe spoke again.

"Turah, honey, this is Rusty. One of my good friends. Rusty, meet Turah."

Rusty had never heard such gentleness in Gabe's voice before. He looked at the child, who sat next to her father. "Hello, Turah, I'm glad you're here safely."

"It took a while," Eb said. "She don't walk fast as we do."

"Well, she's gonna walk out of here in the morning," Étienne declared. "Before I go to work."

Marie passed the ham and scalloped potatoes. Gabe speared a piece of ham. "I was figuring on giving her a day of rest. She's had plenty of excitement, these past few days. I reckon we'll start in two days."

"You'll start tomorrow. And Marie will stay in her room till you leave. I'll see to that."

Gabe cut his ham as he spoke. "I s'pose she's to have no say in the matter."

"None at all."

Gabe paused, pointing his fork at Étienne. "And why not? She's old enough to know her own mind."

"She'll not be doing something she'll regret later. Running off with the Mormons, indeed!"

Rusty expected Gabe to make an angry reply. Instead, Gabe shrugged and started to eat. "This's pretty good. Let's have some more of those potatoes."

Étienne cut the fresh loaf of bread, and Marie passed the slices around on the bread board.

"Eat up, Turah," Eb said. "We got to fatten you up before winter. Or the wind'll plumb blow you away."

"One good thing, we still have our horses." Gabe took some more ham. "I was figuring the mistress'd want them for sure."

"And she didn't?" Rusty asked.

"I never offered them." Gabe wiped his mouth with the linen napkin. "A little more wine, and I'll consider this a meal."

"A right good dinner," Rusty said. Marie smiled as she poured wine into Gabe's glass. Gabe raised his glass to Étienne in a mock gesture of acknowledgment, and drank.

Étienne spoke slowly, as if reciting a litany. "No matter what you do, yer still leaving in the morning."

Rusty said nothing. Marie no longer smiled; she sat looking confused and troubled. Gabe stood up and threw his napkin down beside his plate. "Excuse me." He strode toward the back door.

"We have berries and cream for dessert." Marie pushed back her chair and walked into the kitchen. Eb leaned over and whispered something into his daughter's ear. Suddenly there was a crashing noise outside. They froze, looking at each other.

Rusty was the first to move. He threw open the door and found Gabe lying at the base of the steps. Eb, close behind, raced down the steps.

"Help." Gabe's voice was weak. Rusty looked at Eb.

"Get on the other side of 'em," Eb said. Together they lifted Gabe to his feet.

"Help me up the steps," Gabe said. "I can't seem to walk."

By this time Étienne was in the doorway, with Marie and Turah just behind him. "How much wine did you have? Can't even make it to the privy?"

Gabe gave a groan. "Get me inside."

They helped him to a rocker beside the fireplace. "Something for my foot," he said. "It feels like I've sprained my ankle again."

Marie brought a chair, and he propped his left foot on it. He removed his boot and felt all around the ankle. "Nothing broken." Then he lay back in the rocker, his breath coming in short gasps.

Rusty and Eb stayed by his side. Marie brought a pillow for his head.

"Thank you." He leaned his head back. Rusty wondered that no one thought to ask about the morning and how they were to travel. Étienne, seeing how solicitous they were in the care of his younger brother, began to look concerned himself. After a while Gabe spoke.

"I reckon I can't get up those stairs tonight. Marie, if you'll bring a blanket, I'll just rest by the fire."

"I'll look in on you from time to time," Eb said.

"I'll feel some better in the morning. But I reckon walking's out of the question."

Finally Eb took Turah up to the guest room. Rusty left for the stable under Étienne's watchful eye. Étienne and Marie were preparing to retire upstairs as Rusty closed the door.

He settled himself for another night in the straw. Heartsick about Marie. How could he bear to say *adieu* to her forever as Étienne expected? Perhaps he wouldn't even have the chance for a last farewell. And how were they going to manage the trip home with Gabe injured?

Through the door of the stable, he saw that the house was now dark. The clean, fresh scent of the hay hung in the air, and the smell of the horses, as familiar as breathing. The sounds as they shifted their weight from one foot to the other, their sighings and snortings. He pulled some of the hay up over him. With all their troubles, at least they still had the horses.

Jeb woke him, nuzzling his shoulder. Morning. A light rain falling. Rusty brushed the straw out of his hair. As he fed the horses, he wondered if this was the day he'd get shot for daring to love Marie. He arranged the bridles and saddles on the sides of the stalls. Everything in order. When he walked up to the house for breakfast, the trees and buildings looked misty in the rain.

Gabe made a great show of helplessness as Rusty and Eb helped him to the privy. Once outside, he seemed to walk with a sturdier step. As they helped him back up the steps, he became dead weight in their arms.

"You just rest, now," Eb said. "Anything to be done, we do it."

"I've fixed extra pancakes." Marie began setting the table. "That should give him strength."

Étienne took his place at the table. The others gathered around, except for Gabe who stayed in the rocker with his foot elevated. Marie carried a plate to him. She sat beside him as he cut up the pancakes. After a moment she got up, walked into the kitchen and brought out a coffee pot and cups. She poured coffee into the cups.

"Well, Étienne. Are you going to send your injured brother out into the rain?"

He made a face. "I reckon not. But—well, hang it all. Are they gonna just *live* here for the next six months?"

"Not that long." Gabe gestured with his fork. "I have enough money. Don't worry none about feeding us. I can pay for anything we eat."

Étienne seemed to relax then; he shrugged. Gabe went on. "I'll give Marie some money this morning, and she can go buy what we need."

Étienne gave a deep sigh. "All right, then. I'll be going off to the shop. And I'll take your red-haired friend with me."

"Oh, leave him here," Gabe said. "Just for a few days. I really need him."

Étienne frowned, then nodded. "Well, I reckon no one's going anywheres."

Rusty was about to suggest that Eb go to the shop instead. He opened his mouth to speak. Gabe silenced him with a look. Rusty realized then—Étienne had no idea that Eb knew his way around a smithy. Étienne threw his napkin on the table and stood up.

"I'll be off, then." He looked at Marie. "I reckon you got your work cut out for you. Takin' care of an invalid."

Marie began stacking dishes. "I'll be fine. We'll do up the dishes first. Turah will help me, won't you, dear?"

They were carrying dishes to the sink as Étienne walked out the back door. Gabe waited until the dishes were washed and put away. Then he spoke in a low voice.

"Turah, I want you to watch at that window. Let us know if you see him coming back. Rusty, you get the horses ready to go. Eb, fetch the saddle bags from upstairs. Marie, you pack up what you need. And pack food for us—ham, cheese, bread. Apples."

Rusty looked at him. "But—"

Gabe leapt to his feet. "Where are my boots? The first thing I'm gonna do is hide that shotgun out in the barn."

Rusty started to laugh. "You be fine. You—you warn't hurt at all."

"I've been healed. Another miracle. Well, don't just stand there. Saddle up those horses."

In a short time they had things packed. "Two more blankets," Gabe said. "He'll never miss them. Here—roll them this way."

Marie took off her apron. "Let me just go up and change my dress."

"Well, be quick about it. Decide what you'd rather have—a good-looking dress or us getting out of here before he comes back."

"Do you reckon he'll come after us?" Rusty asked.

"Not unless he buys a new gun. It'll take him at least a week to find the old one."

At last they were ready. Rusty led the horses out. Gabe held Jeb while Rusty mounted, then hoisted Marie up behind him. "Whatever happens, just hang on to Rusty."

Eb held Turah in front of him as he sat astride Freedom. Gabe mounted Jenny and took the lead. "We're going out a different way. We're taking a trail not many know about—it's what folks use when they escape to freedom. Follow me—and don't do anything to attract attention."

Rusty followed close behind. "Rain's almost stopped."

"One good thing. But it's like to be wet where we're going."

They left the town and guided the horses into the woods. Hard to make out a trail with the dense forest all around and the leaves dripping. But Gabe seemed to know where he was going. After a while Rusty became accustomed to following so closely; he felt Marie's arms around his waist. He pressed her hand.

"You all right, my dear?"

"I've never been better."

"I'd like to think the way wouldn't be so hard. But travelin's not easy."

"I can cope," she said. "Whatever happens, we be together now."

His mind filled with a joy so intense he felt like singing. But he kept silent. All he could do was squeeze her fingers. To find this charming girl, in less than a week's time. Here he'd given up ever being married. How had he deserved such luck?

The path led through swampy places, wetlands where the horses had to wade. Then they began to climb; the horses' hooves hit the damp soil in a gentle rhythm. The trail widened to a wagon trace, and Rusty rode side by side with Gabe. In another few miles, they left the rain. The trees still dripped around them. It was mid-afternoon before they finally felt dry.

Gabe found a dry spot to camp for the night. "I'd find us an inn, but I reckon this is safer right now."

After a supper of ham, cheese, and bread, they made blanket beds on the two tarpaulins Gabe had packed. "Like as not, it's done raining. If it starts again, we'll pull the tarps over us."

"No stars tonight," Eb said to Turah. "All clouded over."

Rusty wondered if everyone felt as weary as he did. They settled into their blankets, and soon the darkness closed around them.

18

MID-SEPTEMBER. HARVEST IN FULL swing. Already fresh squash and tomatoes, and corn just picked. Bethia stands in the Dulac house, looking at the bounty piled on the sideboard. A roar of laughter from the table reminds her. She must see about setting out plates for the company.

Not company, really. Family. Just returned that very afternoon from Ohio. Apparently augmented by two. At the table, Gabriel sits gesturing as he describes the journey home. "There I was holding all three horses, and Rusty decides to slip and fall in the creek—"

"That warn't a decision! That bank was slippery as ice!"

Nathaniel sits smiling at the head of the table, and Owen stands leaning against the door. Hannah, not well that day, rests in a chair by the fireplace. May is in the bedroom with Jean-Jacques, who is helpless now with his wasting disease. Pierre and Pentoga have just carried a tray to him with soup and bread.

Rusty and Marie sit apart from the group, over on the settle. They look at each other; Rusty smiles. Bethia feels a sharp pang of jealousy. She could've had Rusty at any point; he is the one she should've married. Too late now. Here is Marie, lively and petite, her hair black as Gabriel's, giving a first impression of exotic, animated beauty.

And she, Bethia, is expected to produce supper for them. At least Eb and his newfound child have stayed on the Illinois side of the river. "Turah was very tired," Gabriel explained. "We thought it best that she get a good rest." Bethia sighs and wonders where to begin.

"Let me help you." Marie is standing beside her. "Let's see—what do we have?"

Bethia manages a civil reply. "There's bean soup in the kettle."

"Oh, splendid. And I see lovely tomatoes. Those will be fine. And Sarah gave us some ham when we stopped at Nauvoo."

Bethia sees that Marie's traveling dress is worn and frayed, and her hair is in disarray.

"You must have come away with nothing."

Marie begins rinsing tomatoes and cutting them. "I had no choice. My older brother was ready to shoot Rusty on sight. We left soon as we could."

They carry dishes and food to the table. Rusty walks over to help them. Bethia can't remember seeing him do that before. The others gather around. Gabriel has not moved from his place, to the left of Nat. "And that snake! 'Member when Eb found it in his bedroll?"

Rusty laughs. "That was just a little ol' black snake. To hear Eb take on, you'd think it was a python."

As they banter, Bethia has the feeling that everything they did was exciting, even rollicking, in a way no real journey could possibly be. And all she's done for two months is take care of children.

"Do any preaching?" Nat asks.

Gabriel looks uncomfortable. "Of course. Mainly on the way out. Coming home, we tried to be careful. Didn't want to attract a lot of attention. We did preach some in Indiana, and eastern Illinois."

"I just wondered, is all. We been hearing about falls in the river, and snakes in bedrolls."

"And two rescues," Gabriel says. "Don't forget them."

Bethia thinks briefly of how Gabriel introduced Marie to them.

"This be my little sister. Marie-Françoise. And we might as well tell you right off—she and Rusty be betrothed. They came all this way on the back of a horse, and they're still speaking to each other." This was followed by laughter. He went on to introduce the others to Marie. And in all the joking, he has not said one word in private to her, his wife.

Hannah sits at the foot of the table, paler than usual. Nat rises and fetches Gaby from the next room. He holds her on his lap and feeds her bits of ham. "By the way, Gabe. Your friend Charley's been askin' for you."

"Charley? Not ill, I hope."

"Not him. Strong as a horse. He says he wants to talk about some doings across the river."

Gabe takes a spoonful of soup. "This is good. What's happening across the river? I mean, that we should know about."

Nat makes them stop for a blessing on the food. "And bless the hands that have prepared it. Amen."

Bethia takes her seat beside Gabriel. *They've actually asked a blessing on me. When does it start working?* Nat puts a slice of ham on his plate.

"Well, let's see. Sit up, Jody—don't play with your food. Some of the apostles came back from England. And Joseph's arranged for them to be his assistants in business matters—in other words, to take care of land sales and such."

"I reckon that takes a burden off him," Gabriel says.

"Yes. Seems like he can't even turn around without folks criticizing him. Apparently there's some land they bought in the center of the city, only it ain't been paid for yet. Mr. Galland was s'posed to exchange it for lands in the east, 'cept it seems he's gone off somewheres with a bunch of the church's money. They be lookin' for 'em now."

"Slow down a bit." Gabriel speaks with his mouth full. "What happened?"

"Why, Galland was supposed to pay the interest on the property. Hyrum and him went to New York to do it, but Hyrum got ill. They haven't seen Galland since. Stop that, Jody. And they're talking about a debt of six thousand dollars."

Gabriel shakes his head. "And they expect us to pay that after all we been through?"

Owen says, "Then there's our friend Tom Sharp. He hates us so much that he's calling anyone who's not openly against us a 'Jack Mormon.'"

Gabriel laughs. "'Jack Mormon?' What'll he think of next?" He turns to Bethia. "Well, my dear. Are you—"

"Dr. Gabriel." May is standing in the bedroom doorway. "Can you come see my husband? He be having trouble breathing."

"Of course." Gabriel pushes back his chair. "I should look in on Charley too, long as I'm here."

Bethia begins to clear the table. Rusty and Marie finish the job for her, and then, despite her protests, they do up the dishes. "You go sit down," Rusty tells her. "Don't fret yourself none. You've done enough work for a while."

She should be grateful. Instead she feels annoyed, irritated by their energy and high spirits. Gabriel walks out of the bedroom, no longer smiling. She hears his words.

"Just make him as comfortable as possible. I'll see if I can find a sedative."

"Whiskey?" Pierre asks.

"Sure, if you have some. See if that helps." He walks over to the table. "I'm going over to see if Charley's around."

Bethia sounds more belligerent than she intended. "I don't see why you have to have anything to do with him. Just a no-account scoundrel."

Gabriel raises his eyebrows. "He's a friend. He may turn out to be more use than you think."

"Wait. Gabriel." Hannah's voice is weak. "Don't—don't leave yet."

"What is it?"

"Something's wrong. I've felt strange all day. The child—there's been no moving for three days. And, now—Oh!" She bends over the table, clutching her midsection.

"She sure didn't eat much," Rusty says.

She cries out again. Nat hurries to her side. He hands Gaby to Marie.

"Let's get her up to her cabin," Gabriel says. "In her own bed."

"I'll carry her." Nat lifts Hannah in his arms and carries her to the door. Rusty already has it open. Gabriel touches Bethia on the shoulder.

"Are you ready to assist me again?" he asks in a low voice. "What you see this time may not have a happy outcome. Be prepared for anything."

In the months to come, Bethia remembered looking back on that night as a turning point in her own life. Obsessed with wanting a child, she'd had little experience with what happens when things go terribly wrong. Gabriel took charge.

"Light those lamps, Rusty. It may be a long night. Nat, bring hot water, and soap. And all the clean towels you can find."

"That should keep 'em busy," he said in an undertone. He propped Hannah's head up with pillows. She gave a sharp cry and lay back, panting.

"Don't leave me." A tear trickled down her cheek. Gabriel sat by the bed and patted her hand. When he spoke, his voice was gentle.

"It's all right. We're here. And no one's leaving you alone."

She looked at him, her eyes wide. "I'm going to lose this one. Aren't I?"

"It doesn't sound promising. If it hasn't moved for three days—"

She nodded. He pressed her hand. "We'll see what we can do."

As the pains progressed into a regular rhythm, Bethia could not recall seeing so much blood. She tried to think—were the other births like this? The twins at Far West? Maybe her memory was faulty. Hannah's cries grew weaker. At last she turned her head to the side and slept.

Bethia looked at the baby, a tiny girl, stillborn. Gabriel wrapped it in a towel.

"Bid Nat and Rusty come in."

They walked in and stood, lines of weariness on their faces. Nat accepted the news in silence, then took Gabriel's place beside Hannah. "I reckon you done all you could."

"She's not out of danger," Gabriel said. "I'll be watchin' her most of the night."

Nat's lips tightened in a thin line. "I'll stay with you."

"If you wish."

"So will I," Rusty said.

"No." Gabriel poured fresh water into the basin. "You go on down to the barn, in that room with Owen. Get some rest. Bethia, I'm going to send you back to your cabin—get as much sleep as you can. You may be needed in the morning. Now, where's Marie?"

"They're ahead of you on that one," Nat said. "They all figured you wouldn't be going across the river tonight. Marie took the children up to Calvin's old cabin, and she and Pentoga made up the beds."

"I reckon we'll be here a few days. I want to make sure Hannah's all right before we leave."

Bethia left and made her way to the cabin in the dark. Once in bed, she curled up under the blankets, feeling chilled even though the night was not cold. She shivered, and her eyes filled with tears. The image of the tiny baby girl, perfect in all its detail, rose before her. How could a loving God allow such things to happen? Wiping her eyes, Bethia decided that God was either unspeakably cruel or he just didn't care.

She lay staring out into the darkness. She wished with all her heart that she could have been the mother of that girl, and that it had lived. Hannah had two already; why couldn't she, Bethia, have at least one? Even though she now knew the risks, she still wanted it more than anything else. And one way or another, she'd see that it happened.

She spent a restless night, and when Gabriel finally came to bed, she wanted to talk. "The baby," she began. "How—"

"Nat's fixing to make a coffin soon as it's light. We'll bury it up in the woods, with a special service."

She knew all about special services. Hannah's baby in Kirtland, her uncle Jake, the twin in Far West, Owen's wife Polly somewhere in eastern Missouri. The way strewn with graves. She began to weep then. "You don't even care."

"Bethia, for heaven's sake. I'm dead on my feet. I'm sorry about the baby—we don't know why these things happen. My main concern is for Hannah—she's resting well. Looks a little less pale. She needs our comfort and help, more than anything."

She sniffed. "You care more for her than you do me. Here she's borne four babies, and I can't have any."

"Bethia, honey. I really need to sleep. I do care a great deal about Hannah right now. I aim to see she comes through in good health. As for children—*Eh bien*. You know something? There's a real live child in Nauvoo. A lovely little girl. She needs your help. Desperately."

She stopped weeping. "Who's that?"

"Turah. Eb's child. She has no momma, at least right now. She needs to be taught to read and write. She likes to draw pictures in the mud, with a stick. I'm gonna see that she has paper, and colors—paints. And sing—she loves to sing. You can teach her songs. We even had her singing in French, when we made camp t'other side of Springfield." He yawned.

Intriguing. But daunting. A girl-child rescued from slavery, needing a complete education. "How does one begin with such a thing?"

But Gabriel didn't answer. He slept.

Gabriel slammed the door as he left. Hard.

He'd gone back to his cabin to pick up his jacket, which he'd forgotten when he stopped at the Dulac house for some breakfast. He'd looked in on Hannah and Jean-Jacques. Both resting comfortably. Nat was out in the workshop building a coffin, and Rusty was staying beside Hannah. Just time enough to go look up Charley.

But when he reached his cabin, there was Bethia. He'd assumed she was somewhere else—maybe with the children. As he grabbed his jacket, she confronted him.

"I know where you're going. And I think it's a disgrace. Meeting with that reprobate."

He made no reply. Shrugging, he slung his jacket over his shoulder.

"Just a minute. You aren't even listening to me. I'm gonna have my say, and say it now."

Still tired from last night. Annoyed beyond endurance. "Bethia, I'm dad-blamed tired of your telling me who I can see and who I can't. Excuse my language. Shouldn't speak to this person. Shouldn't spend time with that one. It's—it's like walking on eggs with you. I can't live this way. I personally don't care anymore." He was breathing fast. "I intend to see anyone I want, whenever I want. And if you don't like it, it's just too bad."

She began to cry then. He stepped forward to take her in his arms, but she spoke first. "I see the way of it. You don't even care how I feel. I reckon if I was Corey Langdon, you'd listen to me. Oh, yes. You'd listen well enough then."

He stopped, puzzled. How much did she know about his feelings for Corey? Had he been that obvious? He opened the door.

Her voice rose. "I'll tell you one thing. If you go down and see that Charley now, I'll—I'll never speak to you again."

He gave a harsh laugh. Even as he spoke, he sensed he was lashing out against someone who was defenseless. "Do you promise? I mean, can I count on that?"

She uttered a loud cry. That was when he slammed the door.

Now he walked on the sunlit path toward town, his head whirling with what had happened. What should he have done? What was he supposed to do now? Go back and say he'd never speak to Charley or Corey again?

He sighed. According to her, everything he'd ever done was wrong. Best not to take her too seriously. It was one of those clear mornings when the light and shadows stood out in sharp contrast. He walked in and out of the dark tree-shadows on the road. Like his life. In and out of shadows. By the time he reached the outskirts of Montrose, he felt better.

He found Charley in the public house and brewery near the waterfront. Charley held his glass aloft in salute as Gabriel walked toward his table.

"Thought I might find you here." Gabriel pulled out the chair across from him.

Charley gave Gabriel an intent look. "What's the matter?"

"Not enough sleep, I reckon. I had to deliver a baby last night. The Givens' child—stillborn."

"Sorry to hear that. The Givens' are right good folks. But that can't be all. You look like you lost yer best friend."

Gabriel shrugged. "A little argument with the wife, is all."

"See? Didn't I tell you? I reckon I tried to warn you." Charley raised his eyebrows and set his glass down on the table.

"That you did. What're you drinking?"

Charley called to the proprietor. "Bring another glass of yer best brew." He leaned over toward Gabriel. "This's better than the beer they got across the river."

"I reckon I can use it," Gabriel said.

"So—the little woman's givin' you trouble." Charley finished what was left in his glass.

"Hang it all," Gabriel said. "Nat and Hannah get along well enough. My own mother and father treated each other decent-like. And the Dulacs—Pierre and Pentoga, and Pierre's parents. They love each other."

"Give me a refill," Charley said as the proprietor set a full glass in front of Gabriel. "Now—the Dulacs. They both married Ojibwe women."

"I reckon that's right."

Charley tightened his lips and nodded. "Tell you what. If you want an Ojibwe girl, they be easy to find."

Gabriel shook his head and laughed. "What are you saying? I don't need another woman. I'm having enough trouble with the one I got."

"What I'm saying is, maybe you should do what yer prophet's doing. I reckon he be marryin' another wife every two weeks."

Gabriel took a sip and put his glass down. "I wouldn't be payin' attention to rumors."

"Well, some think it's rumor, and others think it's downright fact. But whether they be rumors or not, the whole city's like to come down around our heads. It's what I wanted to warn you about. Them Illinois folks are mighty disturbed—they think the Mormons are all gonna vote in a bloc. Upset the precious balance of power that's been set up."

"I see." Gabriel took another sip. "If'n that be true, I can't say I blame them."

"I like you and Nathaniel, and I know how you been driven from pillar to post. I hate to see it happen again."

Gabriel looked at the shiny table top. His eyes traced the pattern of the wood. "You reckon they be fixin' to chase us all out?"

"Well, not right away. If this plural marriage business becomes public, I don't think there'd be any restraining them."

Gabriel took a long drink. Then he smiled. "Now, how do you know so much about plural marriage?"

"I had a feller explain it to me. You see, when yer apostles started comin' back from England, the story is that Joseph took 'em for walks in the woods and told 'em about it. It's the restoration of all things, like in the Old Testament. What Abraham and David did."

"I believe polygamy is specifically condemned in the Book of Mormon," Gabriel said. "But if they're gonna bring back everything that was in the Bible, I hope they're not gonna start stoning people for adultery. Or for the wrong use of the name of God."

"This feller said it would take care of widows and orphans. And do away with houses of prostitution."

"Well, I reckon," Gabriel said. "Get everybody married. Who was this feller?"

"I—uh—forget his name. John something."

"Well, don't believe everything you hear."

They drank in silence, each looking out into the room. Finally Charley gave a little cough. "I figured you should know these things, is all. So, what happened on your mission?"

Gabriel told him about his sister Marie, and how he and Eb had managed to find Eb's child and buy her freedom. "But Jess had already escaped. Where she is now, no one knows."

Charley nodded. "Well, knowing you, I didn't figure you'd spend all yer time preachin'. And I see—Wait a minute. What did you say her name was? Your friend's wife?"

"Jess."

"Is she—I mean, is she a large woman?"

"I have no idea. I've never seen her. Judging from her child, I'd say she's not very big. Maybe about my height."

"There was a smallish black woman—if my memory serves me—workin' as a cook in a hotel down south of Saint Louis. Place called Wood River. And I think I heard them call her 'Jess.' Now, don't get excited. I may be mistaken. And she might be long gone by this time. But Adriel and I be makin' a trip downriver in a few days. This feller in Saint Louis owes us some money. Let me do some investigatin'. Don't get yer hopes up."

"These days, my hopes are never up."

Charley's dark brows drew together. "I mean, don't tell yer friend just yet. His name's Eb?"

"Short for Ebenezer. Last name be Wanfield. That's the name of the old master, what set him free."

"Wanfield. Eb Wanfield."

"Why would she end up in Wood River?"

"Simple. You just git on a river boat in Ohio, and you could end up anywheres along here. And don't think it's that hard to git on a boat without payin'. I done it lots of times. You let on yer somebody's servant or slave. Works every time." Charley fished a plug of tobacco out of his pocket.

Gabe raised his glass and drank. A shadow fell over them. "I reckon—" He looked up. Rusty stood at the end of the table.

Gabe smiled. "Caught in the act. Charley, this's my friend Rusty. About to become my brother-in-law. Sit down, and I'll buy you a drink."

Rusty frowned. "Believe me, I'd sure like that. But I've come to fetch you."

Gabriel paused. A sudden fear gripped him. "What's wrong? Hannah?"

"Hannah's fine. It's Jean-Jacques. He died peaceful-like—-he just stopped breathing. Like he went to sleep. Nat's workin' on a larger coffin now."

Gabriel got to his feet. "Don't know what a doctor can do for him now. But I'd best get back to the family."

"My condolences." Charley set his glass down and stood up. "Dulac was a good, honest feller. Hard-working."

They stood a moment, Charley nodding, his mouth a grim line. "I'd be pleased if we could come pay our respects. Adriel and myself."

"You do that," Rusty said. "Service probably be later this afternoon. Around four, most like."

They turned, and Gabriel followed Rusty out into the bright sunlight.

Bethia stood on a little knoll at the edge of the woods, her shawl wrapped around her. She held Jody by the hand. Marie, beside her, cradled Gaby in her arms. Nathaniel had placed a chair for Hannah, and finally she came walking down from her cabin, supported on either side by Gabriel and Nathaniel. She sank down in the chair.

Standing a little apart were Pierre and Pentoga, with May and the old priest, Father Ambroise, a short, ruddy-faced man who had officiated at both the Dulac marriages. Owen stood nearby with the two dogs, Nell and Whisky. The coffins, one long, the other small, lay on the ground beside the freshly-dug graves.

Just as Nathaniel, Rusty and Gabriel took their places with Father Ambroise, five men and two women from the town appeared. They carried dishes of food wrapped in thin towels. At the same time, Charley and Adriel stepped out of the woods and stood silent, their heads bowed. Bethia tried not to look startled. Nathaniel began the service.

It was not long. After Nat gave the opening remarks, he read the familiar words of hope from the Gospel of John:

"If ye love me, keep my commandments. And I will pray the Father, and he shall give you another Comforter, that he may abide with you forever; even the Spirit of truth...because I live, ye shall live also."

Gabriel spoke briefly, a moving, compassionate account of both lives, the man who had lived a long time and the tiny girl who had never drawn breath. The priest said some words about the integrity of the Dulac family, and committed the bodies to the earth. Then Rusty gave a closing prayer.

His prayer was simple, as solid as the earth itself, with a humble eloquence that seemed a part of the fields and woodlands, as natural as the fading light and the wind from the river. Bethia saw Marie looking at him open-mouthed, as if astonished that he could do more than tell jokes. Everyone waited a few moments in silence. Then Rusty and Nathaniel lowered the coffins into place, and the work of burial began.

19

GABRIEL REACHED DOWN TO run his fingers over the floor of wide pine planking. He touched the walls, feeling the boards smooth under his palms. A little whitewash on those walls, and the whole room would be full of light. His own office and study—he could hardly believe it. He stood at the window looking out at the log house where Calvin and Sarah lived. Soon Rusty and Marie would live there too, in the room where he'd once seen patients.

Beyond the house he could see the river, its surface shimmering with points of light. The opposite shore glowed with autumn colors, rich oranges, yellows and browns. His eye fell on the maple tree by Calvin's front door, its leaves redder than he'd ever noticed. As if the tree itself burned with an inner fire.

"What are you thinking?" Bethia stood beside him. She'd long since given up on not speaking to him.

He slipped an arm around her. "Oh, just how beautiful the fall is. And how handy to have this extra room. Once they got to working, I reckon Eb and Calvin did right well."

"You helped too—don't forget that."

"All I did was advise them—tell them what I wanted."

The office, behind the shop area, served as an addition to the two rooms he and Bethia already had. He could enter it from their keeping room, or come in from the outside.

She gave a little sniff. "I was hopin' we could use it for a nursery."

He paused, wondering how to answer. "I reckon that'll come later."

"I don't see why you had to have that outside door."

"Why? Well, so my patients don't have to come through the shop or the living area." He thought of the shelves Calvin was building, of oak and mahogany. And the desk which had been promised. It would fit under the window.

"It would've been all right with me."

"To have sick folks traipsin' through your sitting room? I reckon not." Most important, his patients deserved privacy from her prying eyes.

They had worked to enlarge Eb's living space, at the other end of the building. There was even a little side room for Turah, her own place. The sounds of the smithy drifted to them, the hammer striking metal. Out in the shop, Eb said something to Nigel, who laughed. Bethia spoke again.

"It just seems wasteful, is all. Another door when we didn't need it."

Gabriel gave a sigh. "Trust me. I'll use it wisely." *Change the subject.* "So, how're the wedding plans?"

"How would I know? You think they tell me anything? All I heard is, Sarah's making over a dress for Marie. And Hannah talks about baking little cakes. It's hard to do anything with the river in the way."

Marie and Rusty had stayed on the Iowa side, Rusty to help Nat and Owen with the harvest, and Marie to care for the children while Hannah recuperated. May had decided to go live with Pierre and Pentoga for a while, in their cabin closer to Montrose.

"You move into the big house," she'd told Nathaniel. "It be yours now. And there be more room for the young'uns."

"We'll keep that one room for you," Nat had told her.

"*Eh bien*," Gabriel said to Bethia. "I reckon all we need now's the wedding."

"Some wedding. There across the river, with no people but us watchin'. And not even a proper Latter Day Saint wedding. She wants to have that priest marry them—what's his name? Father Ambrose."

Gabriel laughed then. "It'll be all right. They'll be just as married as anybody. After all, it's how my parents got married, and the Dulacs. And don't worry about the Mormon marriage vow—that'll be part of it. Nat's going to do it."

"And they're not even gonna live there. They'll be here, with Calvin and Sarah."

"I surely hope so. We need Rusty in the shop. And I've missed Marie something fierce. They'll most likely stay across the river for a little while, in one of those empty cabins."

"And what a waste that was. Three cabins up there, sitting empty. Hidden up there in the woods, where no one in their right mind would want to live."

He wondered how to get her out of his office. "Shouldn't you be teaching Turah? I'm gonna start whitewashing these walls."

She left, and Gabriel went to fetch the whitewash and brushes. Calvin came in to help. "I needed a break from all that carpentry."

Soon they were spreading layers of white on the boards. Gabriel glanced out at the river. "Steamboat comin' in."

"Second one today. River traffic's pickin' up. We're lucky. These be prosperous times."

Gabriel remembered what Charley had said about the city coming down around their heads. "Some folks think it's not gonna last."

Calvin grunted. "Well, 'course it will. Just look at all we got. Two sawmills, a foundry, a tool factory. A steam flour mill. Why, dozens of shops. Not to mention the schools and bridges. And paved streets. Now, how many river towns got paved streets?"

"Nat says the harvest is good this year."

"I reckon! Why, you saw all the corn when you got back from your mission."

True. The people of the town had planted corn everywhere it could possibly grow. All the houses and buildings awash in a sea of corn. Calvin went on. "And I hear the cooperative farm on the edge of town did right fine. All them fellers without their own land, workin' their tails off."

Gabriel could hear Bethia and Turah in the next room. He smeared a strip of white under the window. He saw Eb heading up to the house—lunch time already? "That new hotel's comin' right along. Keepin' lots of folks busy."

"And the temple. You hear they're gonna dedicate that baptismal font in November? That big tub on the backs of the oxen? Then they'll be using it. Why, it won't be long till that whole building's finished."

"I reckon." People were leaving the steamboat landing and walking up toward the town in little groups.

Calvin said, "And as for entertainment—why, even ol' Tom Sharp himself should be glad. We got music, banquets, dancing and singing, parades, ball games—I tell you, something most every week."

There was a knocking at the shop door. Nigel would answer it. Gabriel dipped his brush. "To say nothing of the boat rides."

The knocking continued. He heard Nigel's voice, then Bethia's, reproving, complaining.

"Just a minute." Gabriel placed his brush across the paint can and hurried into the sitting room. Turah sat huddled at the table, a book open before her. He smiled briefly at her and walked out into the shop area.

Bethia stood at the door, apparently trying to close it. Gabriel heard the last of her words. "I told you, he's not here. And we don't want the likes of you coming around here again."

The door slammed before he could reach it. When he looked at her, she said, "I've already taken care of it. Go back and finish painting."

He pushed her aside and flung open the door. Charley stood there, a puzzled expression on his face. Without looking back, Gabriel stepped outside. "I'll be blamed. Charley—it's good to see you."

They shook hands. Charley was wearing respectable clothes for once, pants of black broadcloth and a jacket. Gabriel felt uneasy, not knowing fully what Bethia had said. "Forget about anything you just heard. You're welcome anytime."

"I figured that. She just said you wasn't here, is all."

It struck him that Charley, dressed as he was, had just got off the steamboat. Then he noticed the two other people waiting about ten feet away. He recognized Adriel, also dressed for a journey. Beside him stood a young woman in a faded calico dress. She was slender, not very tall, with dark skin and high cheekbones. Gabriel was thinking she had the loveliest eyes he'd ever seen. Then he drew in his breath. *Was it possible?* He found it hard to speak.

"Ma'am—you—be you Jess?"

At the same time Bethia started shouting behind him. "Get back! No! Don't go out there!"

Turah rushed past him and flung herself into the woman's arms. "Momma! Oh, momma!"

Jess held Turah and swayed back and forth. Gabriel looked back into the shop. Ignoring Bethia, he yelled, "Nigel! Go fetch Eb. Wherever he is, tell him to get out here!"

By the time Nigel returned with Eb and Sarah, both Turah and her mother were weeping. Eb gathered the two of them in his arms and raised his head, tears streaming down his cheeks. "The Lord be praised! This family be together at last!"

Calvin hurried out of the shop, a paintbrush in his hand. "If this don't beat all."

"A miracle," Eb said. "A dad-burned miracle."

After a moment, Charley shifted his feet. "Well, I reckon we'll be on our way. Just wanted to bring her by and make sure she was the right woman."

Eb wiped his eyes. "The rightest woman that ever was."

Sarah stepped forward. "Wait a minute. Charley, Adriel. You can't leave. This calls for a celebration. Come on up to the house, all of you. You too, Nigel. We got plenty to eat—fresh corn and tomatoes. Ham, too."

Sarah began to usher everyone up to the house. Gabriel said, "Nigel, I reckon we're closing the shop for the rest of the day." He hurried to cover the paint cans and put the brushes to soak. When he had finished, everyone had gone except Bethia. He looked at her.

"Aren't you going up to the house? Sarah could probably use your help."

"I—I have a headache. I think I'll stay here."

He made no reply. He didn't mean to slam the door behind him. It closed with a hard, wooden thunk, louder than he'd intended.

When Bethia finally appeared, halfway through the meal, Gabriel knew he was in trouble. Corey had come over to see what the excitement was about, and Sarah had invited her to stay. She'd taken the empty place beside Gabriel. They were listening as Jess finished her story.

"I waited a whiles in the woods. Waited all night on the Ohio shore. And when that steamboat pulled up next morning, I got on it."

Sarah pushed back her chair and indicated that Bethia should sit there. Then she fetched a stool from the kitchen. She brought Bethia a plate of food and set it before her. Bethia looked at it. "I'm—not really too hungry."

"Better eat, honey." Sarah put a fresh napkin beside the plate. "Lots of work comin' up, with that wedding happenin' any day now."

"But, Momma," Turah said. "Wasn't you feared of them paterollers?"

"I wasn't afraid of nothing. I just pretended like I belonged there, on that boat. I had a little bundle of things I said was for my mistress. And no one bothered me."

"That's what I figured." Charley took another ear of corn. "That's what I told Gabriel, way back in September."

Bethia gave a little intake of breath, then glowered at him. Everyone else looked briefly in his direction. He smiled and raised the glass of cider.

"How come y'all became Mormons?" Jess asked.

Eb began. "Well, Gabe found me in the river with my busted arm, and—Hang it all, Gabe. You tell it. You talk better'n I do."

So Gabriel found himself telling about their journey from one safe house to the next, how they'd walked north on trails known only to Indians and escaped slaves. Finally they'd reached the outskirts of Kirtland, in northern Ohio. As he spoke in his animated way, his fingers shaping the air with gestures, he sensed Corey leaning closer to him. For her benefit, and his rapt audience, he began to exaggerate.

"So here Eb could hardly move, and this feller Owen Crawford found us and took us in. Put us to work on his farm."

"'Course I could move," Eb told Jess. "It warn't that bad."

"I'll be blowed," Charley said. "So that's how it happened."

Bethia looked uncomfortable, on the point of tears. *What was her trouble? Trying to turn Charley away.* Gabriel decided he didn't care anymore. He began talking in an undertone to Corey, something about Owen's good-sized farm in Ohio. "I swear, with stalks up to here. I never seen such corn."

"So, how many wives does y'all have?" Jess asked.

Calvin laughed. "Question Number One."

"Honey, I only got you," Eb said.

Gabriel drank some more cider and set his glass down. "I don't know how these rumors get started. It says in our scriptures we should only have one."

Eb gestured. "And—and porcupines we should have none."

Gabriel choked on his cider and began to laugh. Corey laughed with him. Calvin was struggling to keep a straight face. "That be 'concubines,' I reckon."

Eb shrugged. "Concubines, porcupines. I don't want any truck with none of 'em."

Jess said, "Don't worry, dear. I'll keep the porcupines away."

Charley and Adriel left soon afterward. "See you back across the river," Charley said to Gabriel.

"I reckon. Come to my sister's wedding—it be right soon. Whenever they give the word."

Charley nodded. "If there be anything to eat, we'll be there."

By the time Gabriel had finished explaining to Corey that it would be a Catholic wedding, conducted by a priest, most people had left.

"I think that's fascinating," Corey said.

"Well, come over to it if you want. There won't be many folks there. But you know Rusty, and you'll have to meet Marie."

"C'mon, Gabe." Calvin pushed back his chair. "Let's go finish that room."

As he stood up, he saw that Bethia had left her plate of food untouched.

Rusty, with his habit of observing people and trying to understand them, still couldn't make head nor tail of it. The wedding had gone according to plan; he was officially married to the girl of his choice. And he felt happier than he could have imagined. What, then, was wrong with Bethia?

She'd acted cold to Marie, even rude, before and after the ceremony. Strange, seeing that Marie was her own husband's sister. Instead it was Corey who had befriended Marie—Corey and Eb's wife Jess. When he'd commented on it to Gabe, Gabe had said something about Bethia being fragile and that they had to look out for her.

Fragile? She looked strong enough to him. Toting wood along with the best of them, and cooking, washing, hanging clothes. Not sick with marsh fever or those other ailments that laid folks low. He thought of Don Carlos, the prophet's brother, and Robert B. Thompson, felled by the marsh sickness in September. Strong men, both of them. And Bethia had survived to this point without any sign of the disease.

After some time together in the most secluded cabin, he had brought Marie across to Nauvoo. The first snow was falling when they settled into their room in the big house. His father and Sarah welcomed them like doting parents, and Marie went to work cooking, and making clothes to replace what she'd left in Ohio.

Now, Rusty thought. Now Bethia would offer the needed friendship and help, and they would become good friends. Again it was Corey and Jess who stepped in, mainly Corey since Jess was a newcomer too. They made a pretty threesome on the city streets. If Bethia noticed, she said nothing.

"I'll never understand women," he said as he worked in the shop.

"I don't even understand men," Nigel replied. "The Masons, now. With all their secret signs and such. Who in their right mind would want to be one?"

"I dunno—heaps of folks. The prophet, and Hyrum, and a bunch of them. They all be meeting over in the new store, in that upper part."

"That's some store. I never saw so much stuff for sale. They say thirteen wagons carried it all up from Warsaw, after it'd been ordered from St. Louis. Sugar and molasses, salt, coffee and tea enough to kill a horse. Glass, and such-like. And now it's got the Masons, too."

Rusty picked up the hammer. "Like as not, they'll meet there till they find another place."

"I wonder what they do in there, anyway? All that secret stuff."

Rusty took the tongs and set a piece of hot metal on the anvil. "I reckon you have to be a Mason to find out."

Bethia opened the door to her rooms so that the heat from the forge would warm the whole building faster. "A cold morning," she remarked.

"Yer welcome to stay in here," Rusty said. "Get yourself really warm."

"No, thank you." She picked up a wicker basket full of clothes and walked toward the front door.

"Like some help with that?" he asked. "Looks right heavy."

She flashed him an annoyed look. "I can manage."

Later, when Nigel had left, Gabe came in from his study and sat by the fireplace. He rubbed his hands together. Rusty put down the hammer.

"Gabe, you told me Bethia was fragile. Yet she be carryin' loads that'd make a strong man flinch. And she won't accept help."

Gabe paused, as if thinking. When he spoke, he sounded hesitant. "I think I was speaking more of her mind, her spirit. Something's not what it should be, and I only know I can't help her. Maybe the persecutions did it—having to up and flee in the middle of winter. Or because she wants a child—I don't know. I reckon it's something none of us can fix."

"So it's her mind. Not her body."

Gabe sighed. "That's one way of saying it."

"And there's nothing we can do."

"We can try to protect her—make things easier for her. Look after her, the way Corey looks out for Casey. I don't know what else to do."

Rusty waited a moment. "I'm sorry."

Gabe nodded. They looked at the sparks from the dying fire. Then Gabe stood up. "Reckon I'll get us some more wood."

As winter gave way to spring, the work on the huge temple increased. Calvin lent his carriage and team of black mares to the enterprise, and the women made clothing, notably socks and mittens, for the workers. Calvin even took in one of the laborers, a gruff, grim-faced man called Davis. Rusty and Eb tried to give a tenth of their time to the construction, along with Nigel and Calvin. Between them, they managed to keep the smithy open and running.

Gabe, busy with his medical practice, gave money instead of time. Being short, he declared that others were far better at building than he was.

"That's the worst excuse I ever heard," Calvin said. "I could say the same thing 'cause I'm old."

"Well, just think of all the glory you'll get," Gabe retorted. "Me, I no longer care that much."

They talked of other things, the rafts of lumber that were coming down the river from the 'pineries' in Wisconsin. Gabe raised his eyebrows. "You can't tell me that's all going for the temple."

"Actually, it's not," Calvin said. "Some's for the Nauvoo House. And the rest? You might ask your friend Charley; he knows more than he lets on."

Rusty couldn't believe it. "Folks be stealing lumber?"

"Ol' Charley could steal anything," Gabe said.

Rusty began to hear rumors of special prayer circles in the upper part of the store, where strange doctrines were discussed. The group of Masons now had a charter for a Masonic Lodge. And the women talked of their new organization, the Relief Society.

"From what Bethia says, they aim to root out evil and bring respectability to this town," Gabe remarked as they worked.

"God knows it could use some," Nigel said.

"What evil?" Rusty pulled on the gloves and picked up the hammer. "I mean, what do they consider evil?"

"Oh, things like plural marriage, I reckon," Calvin said. "If there's any around, they aim to find it."

The door to Gabe's living quarters flew open. Bethia stood in the doorway, breathing fast.

"Gabriel. Sister Corey is waiting to see you." Her tone was cold enough to freeze salt water.

"Ah, Sister Corey." Gabe straightened up. "Casey most likely has the stomach ache again. Tell her I'll be right there."

He walked out the front door and started around to his private entrance.

20

WHEN GABRIEL PUSHED OPEN the outside door to his office, he found Corey sitting on the edge of the chair reserved for patients. She looked at him with startled eyes. A wadded handkerchief lay in her lap. *Weeping?*

He glanced around. "Casey not here?"

She wiped her eyes. "She's home with my father. I—I didn't come about Casey, doctor."

"I see." He closed the door and pulled his desk chair closer to her.

"It's not father, either. Oh, doctor—Forgive me. It's me. Something so strange has happened—and there's no one else to tell. I can't tell my father—he wouldn't believe me. And all the others are women. I'm not sure they'd believe it either. I—" She began to sniff, and held the handkerchief to her face.

He sat down, summoning his gentlest voice. "I'll believe you, Corey. You know that."

She fixed her intent eyes on him. Her face lit up with the straightforward, purposeful look that he admired. "All right—I'll begin with last night. Some man I didn't know came to our house and told me someone had a message for me. Or wanted to speak with me—I forgot just how he put it. I was to go over to the brick store—alone—around ten o'clock this morning."

"All right. And did you?"

"When I got there, someone told me to go upstairs. Two men were up there, and one—well, he was one of the highest persons in the church leadership. I was somewhat surprised. They asked me to sit down, and I did so. Then the lesser one started speaking.

"He said the time had come when men of high reputation in the sight of God could take extra wives—he called them 'celestial' wives—as in the days of Abraham. Since the goal was the restoration of all things, this was only another step toward the ideal way of life."

"I've heard that one before," Gabriel said.

"So then the high official began to speak. I was too astonished to do more than listen. He said he'd had his eye on me for some time, that God had given me to him, and that if I would participate with him in a special ceremony, not only myself but my whole family would enjoy an exalted status in the next world."

Gabriel was so intent on her words that he had to force himself to make what he thought was a comforting response. "Oh, no. Oh, Corey."

"And that's not all. When I finally made some protest, I was told that since I now knew about the doctrine, I would be condemned forever if I did not comply."

"Well, that doesn't sound like any religion I ever heard about."

Corey shook her head, then stood up. Her handkerchief fell to the floor. "They made me promise not to tell anyone."

"I should think they would," he said. "Shame on them."

"I—I'm supposed to think it over, and—and pray about it. Oh, Gabriel. What do I do?" Her lower lip trembled.

He stood up quickly. He put an arm about her and held her. She sobbed, leaning against him. Holding her close to him, he felt his mind whirling with unexpected emotions. Love and admiration for her, sorrow at all she had endured, shock and outrage at what she had heard that day. It made him want to weep as well. Instead, he whispered into her hair.

"Corey, my dear. You must be the brave person I've always known you to be. You must be especially strong now. Let me tell you why."

As he drew back to look at her, her eyes gazed up at him. *Full of trust.* He felt overcome. *Steady,* he told himself.

"First, let's think it through. I've always regarded Nathaniel as our leader, spiritual and in other ways too. He's not here, but I'm an elder now. So I'm going to tell you what I reckon he'd say.

"In the first place, it's against the law. And second, according to all I've read and studied, God just doesn't work that way. To 'condemn' someone because they refuse to comply with something—that's nonsense. So, whatever this is, it can't be of God. It's that simple. I don't care who your high official is. It's not Bennett, is it?"

She shook her head.

He gave a little cough. "I didn't think so. He uses a different technique. Now, what we have to do is be strong and steadfast, and true to the teachings we first learned. Believe me, this isn't one of them."

She nodded. "Oh, I know."

He grasped her by her shoulders. "Now, what we're going to do—"

A noise. The door to his living quarters flew open. Bethia stood there, her eyes wide, her hand to her mouth as if she were stifling a scream. He kept his hands on Corey's shoulders. *What to do?* Quick as thought, he resumed his professional manner. Not moving back, which would denote guilt, he looked at Bethia.

"Yes. What is it?"

Bethia began to blubber. "Buh—buh—Sis—Sister Simpson be waiting to see you. She's—"

"Very well. Just have her wait in there. I'll call her in when I'm ready."

Bethia swallowed. "Buh—she be—"

He crossed to the door. "Well, feed her some tea or something. I'll be finished in a few moments." He pushed her out into the other room and closed the door. "I knew I should've had a lock put on. *Eh bien*—first thing tomorrow."

Corey met his eyes. "Are you in trouble now?"

"No more than usual. Believe me—she'll survive. Now—as for you. My advice is to go on about your business. Don't go off alone—stay with people, if you can. If anyone invites you to a secret meeting, decline. And if they demand an answer, just tell them you're not interested. If there's any trouble, or threats to you, we can get you and Casey across the river to a safe place."

"Should I tell my father?"

He considered, then nodded. "I believe I would. Let me know what he says."

She stepped toward the door. "Oh, Brother Gabriel. Thank you so much for your words. You've always been such a help to me."

Should he hug her? He patted her on the shoulder instead. "Whatever happens, Corey, you've got a true friend here. We'll get through it somehow."

After she left, he sat staring at his white walls. *The rumor was true. It wasn't just Bennett. The thing they'd joked about was really happening. Even the members of his little community, his family group, were threatened by it. What did they do now?*

Nathaniel. Somehow he had to get over and see Nathaniel alone. It sounded preposterous. Would Nat believe him? He had to take that risk.

He opened the door to his quarters. "Ah, Sister Simpson. I'm so sorry to keep you waiting. Do come in."

She bustled in, a portly, middle-aged lady with grayish-white hair piled on her head. She made a clucking sound, like a well-fed chicken. He glanced at the keeping room.

"What happened to my wife?"

"She be in the bedroom. And if I heard right, I think she be a 'cryin'."

"Oh. Well, all right. Come have a seat."

"Do you want to see to her? I can wait a few more minutes."

He sighed. "No. I'll take care of her later." As he closed the door, he heard a new sound on the roof. A gentle rain was falling.

Marie had attended mass that morning. As she returned, stepping over puddles, she saw lilies-of-the-valley growing by a cedar stump. She picked a bouquet of them. Sarah had given her a white alabaster vase.

"Here. I don't want this. I don't even know where it came from."

If she put the flowers in the vase, with water, it would be a pretty gift for Bethia. High time she made friends with her sister-in-law. She would take it over that afternoon.

She walked down from the big house carrying the little vase of flowers. She intended to go around to the front of the shop and enter their living quarters that way. But then she saw that Gabriel's office door was ajar. She knocked, then pushed it open. No one there.

The door to the keeping room was open halfway. She raised her hand to knock. Then she heard the voices. First, a high-pitched murmuring, as if someone were speaking through tears. Turah, maybe? She couldn't make out the words. Then she heard Gabriel.

"Bethia, I assure you. *Mon Dieu!* How often must I repeat it? I'm innocent of everything you say."

Again the murmuring, louder now, and Gabriel answering.

"She's not any such thing! She's no one's spiritual wife. And certainly not mine."

The murmuring became blubbering, insistent, demanding. Again Gabriel replied.

"Of course I can't tell you what she said. It was in the strictest confidence."

Wondering, Marie listened for the words. She could only understand Gabriel.

"All right. Don't believe me. I don't care. But I'm not about to tell you what she said."

More blubbering. This time Gabriel's voice was no longer gentle. "Tell the Relief Society! Listen, Bethia. If you blow this up in your mind and made a big thing of it, you're going to make trouble for everyone. Do you want that?"

More sounds from Bethia. Gabriel gave a long, drawn-out sigh. "I can only tell you—if you do, you're not going to come out the winner. Trust me this time. I'm innocent, and so is Corey. We did nothing wrong. If you go making up stories, creating a scandal, it will not go well with you. It's not in your best interest. Do you understand?"

More blubbering, with sobs. Gabriel spoke again. "I'm not threatening you. I'm telling you. Oh, what's the use? I give up. I can't argue with you anymore. But remember what I said."

A door slammed somewhere. Then, before she could move back, Gabriel swung open the door. His face looked pale, his eyes as tired as if he'd missed a night's sleep. He glanced at her in surprise, then smiled. "Ah—Marie."

"Oh, Gabriel. I—I'm so sorry. I didn't mean to eavesdrop. I—well, I brought over this little bouquet for Bethia. Sort of a gift."

"It's right pretty." He took it from her.

"I don't reckon she'd want it right now. But the flowers don't last too long."

He set it on the desk. "I'll try to see that she gets it. Look—it brightens up the office already."

"Then maybe you should keep it. You need it more than she does."

"Oh, Marie." He took her in his arms and hugged her. "It's so good to have you close by."

She wondered what else she could say. "I'm so sorry for the trouble you're having. I had no idea."

He smiled and shrugged. "I think Trouble is my middle name. But this is nothing new. You have to be a jump ahead of her, and she caught me off-guard. I should've had a lock on this inner door."

"You need a rest. Come up to the house, and I'll brew up some tea."

"I need something stronger than tea," he said. "But, yes—I'll come."

Just when Gabriel thought he had enough time to go over and see Nathaniel, the thing happened with Bennett. He figured the trouble had probably started long before, but it came to a head on May 7, the day of the annual Nauvoo Legion parade and celebration.

The whole affair was billed as a 'Programma Militaire,' to be followed by a 'Repast Militaire' for all the participants and visiting dignitaries at the prophet's house. Gabriel remembered the usual wagons and carriages clattering into the city, the ferries bringing people from all up and down the river, the hundreds of tents pitched just outside town. Hannah and the children ferried across with Owen Crawford.

"Nat stayed behind. Pete the mule took sick last night, and Nat didn't want to leave him."

After the exercises by the Legion, the dinner and a speech by Joseph Smith, a grand sham battle had been planned. Major General Bennett was to lead one cohort, and Lieutenant General Smith was to command the other. At the last minute, Joseph refused to take his position, and retired to the background with his personal guard.

"What's happening?" Rusty asked out of the side of his mouth.

"Danged if I know," Calvin replied. "Looks like Wilson Law's gonna lead us. And What's-his-name. Brother Rich."

"Look smart," Gabriel said. "Get ready to move."

When it was over, Calvin learned from someone that Joseph had feared an attack on his life.

"He had a premonition-like. And he would've been out there all alone. A good chance for someone to pick 'em off."

Relations between Joseph and Bennett went downhill from that point. Ten days later, Bennett tried to apologize. Gabriel heard that he agreed to sign an affidavit denying that Joseph had ever taught him any doctrine contrary to the laws of God and man. Rumors ran rampant: Bennett had practiced abortion in addition to midwifery, had been expelled from a Masonic Lodge in Ohio for 'rascally conduct,' had approached young men in the Legion with intentions considered worse than plural marriage. Finally, Joseph Smith made public an edict of excommunication, which Bennett claimed to be an illegal act. "Folks signed it that weren't even there."

Shortly after, in late June, Bennett left town. Calvin brought the news to the blacksmith shop.

"Hyrum said Bennett's last words were about swearing to drink the blood of his enemies."

"If that don't beat all," Eb said. "I'd rather have whiskey any day."

Gabriel sighed. "He's up to no good, that's certain. But maybe we're rid of him for awhile."

Bennett had resigned as mayor of Nauvoo, due to 'circumstances of a personal nature.' In a special session of the City Council, before an audience of citizens, Joseph was elected acting mayor with Hyrum as his vice-mayor.

"I reckon that settles that," Calvin remarked as he stacked a load of wood.

But a few days later, more news came in.

"Danged if someone didn't shoot ol' Governor Boggs," Eb declared. "Over in Missouri. The 'extermination' man."

"He's not even governor anymore," Gabriel said.

"They took a shot at 'em anyway."

"They kill 'em?"

"Naw," Eb said. "Poor aim. But the thing is, they think it was one of us done it. After what they did to us."

"Well." Gabriel shrugged. "I wasn't there. And neither was anybody else."

"They think Porter Rockwell was. And they're thinkin' Joseph might have sent him to do it."

Gabriel snorted. "I don't see how they can prove such a thing."

Then Bennett came out with a series of letters in the *Sangamo Journal.* In the writings, Bennett accused Joseph of forcing him to sign the statement proclaiming the prophet's virtue, of making proposals of marriage to a number of women—whose names he published, of lascivious behavior under a cloak of religion, and of instituting hierarchies of women prostitutes. The townspeople talked of nothing else.

They tried to make light of it in the blacksmith shop. "Tarnation," Calvin said. "How'd he have time to do all that?"

"Land's sakes," someone said. "That *Sangamo Journal* wouldn't even exist if it weren't for all them letters."

But the damage was done. Every time Gabriel walked out in the town, he found someone else packing up and getting ready to leave.

"I don't want no part of this," one man told him. "My family and me, we've had enough. This's the last straw."

One day, on the way back to the shop, Gabriel met Jubal Langdon. Jubal had a large leather knapsack over one shoulder. Gabriel looked at him.

"Don't tell me you're fixin' to pull out too."

"Me? Where would I go? This is my home. These are my people. Most folks I know don't have any truck with those doin's."

Gabriel smiled. "Maybe most of those doin's don't exist."

"Well, hanged if I know where they are. Women prostitutes?"

He wondered if Corey had told him about the offer of marriage. Not wanting to ask, he said, "And how're your daughters?"

Jubal's eyes narrowed. "I scarcely ever see them, 'cept at meals. I tell you, if some rich man would take them off my hands, I'd be beholden. Where's this plural marriage when you need it?"

Gabriel refrained from laughing. "Brother Jubal. Whatever happens, don't make Corey do anything she doesn't want to do."

"She won't. She's stubborn, like her mother. She won't do anything less'n she's a mind to."

"I'm right glad to hear that." They parted.

Rusty was trying to explain Illinois politics to Marie and the Wanfields.

"See, there's these two groups—the Whigs and the Democrats. Now the Democrats have been around a while, but the folks that didn't hold with Andy Jackson formed a new party—the Whigs. A lot of important folks—manufacturers and merchants and such—got together and tried to defeat the Democratic candidate back in 1836. But they didn't win. People elected Van Buren, who was Jackson's choice."

Calvin said, "The one who wouldn't help us get our lands back in Missouri."

"The very one. I hear the prophet can't even mention his name without gettin' riled up."

Eb nodded. "Who can blame him?"

Rusty waved his hands. "Anyway, both parties have been thinkin' to get the Mormon vote. When the Whigs won and Harrison became president, he only lasted a month. And Tyler didn't do any of the things folks thought he would. So everybody started to favor the Democrats again. When Joseph said he didn't prefer one party above the other, the Whigs got mad as hornets."

Calvin pounded the table. "What he said was, the Democratic candidates had served the Mormons and the Mormons would serve them."

"Well, that was enough to really set 'em off," Rusty said. "They accused him of commanding his followers how to vote."

Gabriel stood in the doorway listening. "It's not just that. They're afraid of the Legion, and its military strength. They think we're gonna take over the whole state and then the country. *Mon Dieu! Us!*."

"Anyway," Rusty said. "The Whigs have picked a candidate for governor who's out to do us in. Use us up, as they say. This Joe Duncan wants to recall the public arms that the Nauvoo Legion was issued. He even says he'll repeal our city charters. And so a lot of newspapers are backing him, using the lies Bennett has told."

"So what about Ford?" Eb asked.

Rusty shrugged. "The Democratic candidate? He sounds like a good man—he's supposed to be well-grounded in the law. Educated and all."

"I don't reckon he has a snowball's chance in hell," Calvin declared.

"Well, you never can tell," Gabriel said. "I know who I'm voting for."

Eb shook his head. "D'you think if this Duncan feller wins, we'll all have to leave Nauvoo?"

A noise from the kitchen, a skillet banging on wood. "Oh, you men!" Sarah was shouting. "All you can talk about is politics, and having to leave. I'm sick of it! Just sick!"

"I ain't too fond of it myself," Rusty said. "I've left too many places."

Gabriel gestured, shaping the air with his hands. "You want to hear something funny? Joseph went and bought a new horse. He named him 'Joe Duncan' so he could say he was 'riding the governor.'"

Calvin said, "The thing is, if Ford wins, they'll say the Mormons did it. Seems like we can't win."

"Will you stop that?" Sarah shouted. "If yer gonna talk politics, go somewheres else."

Gabriel straightened up. "I'm going down to the shop. Y'all can come if you want."

"I'd better warn Bethia," Sarah said. "She's about to get an earful."

One good thing about the Bennett trouble was that it kept the Relief Society ladies from even considering Gabriel's relations with Corey. Anything else paled in comparison.

During the course of the summer, the church leaders sent out elders to contradict the things Bennett was saying. Calvin joined them briefly; he and Nathaniel walked to neighboring towns to defend the prophet. Gabriel stayed in the shop and kept busy with his business and medical practice. But he knew it was a hard time for the church and the city. He lay awake wondering if everything was really falling apart around them. If so, what would they do? Where would they go next?

Ford won the election, but he claimed it was without Mormon help. Nevertheless, he had almost unanimous support in Nauvoo.

As if Bennett had not done enough damage, he found one more way to harass and injure Joseph. After declaring in print that Joseph had instigated the shooting of ex-governor Boggs, he went over to Missouri carrying affidavits to that effect from various people and presented them to the new governor of Missouri, Thomas Reynolds. Boggs managed to swear out an affidavit against Joseph. The state of Missouri issued an extradition order, and Illinois governor Carlin, serving out his term until Ford could take over, signed an order for Joseph's arrest and surrender to an agent from Missouri.

"I'll be derned," Rusty declared. "Two sheriffs went and arrested both Joseph and Porter Rockwell."

"Didn't you hear the rest?" Gabriel told him. "They took 'em before the Nauvoo Municipal Court, and both of 'em were released on writs of habeas corpus."

"But them sheriff fellers'll just come back again."

Gabriel laughed then. "Let's see if they can find 'em."

By the time Carlin sent the sheriffs back to Nauvoo, Rockwell had escaped to Philadelphia and Joseph had simply disappeared.

"What did I tell you?" Gabriel said.

They later learned that Carlin had offered a reward of two hundred dollars for the arrest of either fugitive. Governor Reynolds offered three hundred for each of them, and some said the reward was as high as thirteen hundred.

Calvin shook his head. "With rewards like that, they'll find 'em for sure."

Gabriel shrugged. "I wouldn't bet on it."

Joseph remained in hiding until December, appearing in one place and then another, but never seen by those who sought to capture him. At different times he was rumored to be across the river, in locations close to Nathaniel and his hidden cabins. Gabriel wondered if Nat were harboring the prophet. It sounded like something he would do. Gabriel kept silent, fearful that if he discussed it with anyone, the wrong person might overhear and betray both the Mormon leader and the ones who sheltered him.

21

NATHANIEL HAD JUST FINISHED sawing a new shutter for one of the barn windows. He blew the sawdust from the top edge. Then he looked up and saw Gabe walking down from the house. Alone. Nathaniel wondered briefly where the others were.

Gabe tramped into the barn, shaking snow from his boots. He had snow on his shoulders and in his hair. Nathaniel leaned the shutter up against the wall.

"What'd you do—try to walk across the river?"

"It's not froze yet. I rowed over in the skiff."

Nathaniel stared. "In this weather? With Bethia and Marie? Even Rusty has more sense."

"Oh, no. I—I came alone."

Nathaniel gave a nod. "Well, I can't say I'm not glad to see you. You're just in time to help me hang this shutter."

"*Très bien*. Let's do it."

They walked around to the outside. Nathaniel made Gabe carry the small ladder. Nathaniel had the shutter, the hammer, nails and straps for the hinges. Gabe leaned the ladder up against the building and they set to work. "It goes better with help," Nathaniel said.

"So where's Owen?"

Nathaniel laid the piece of wood on the ground and pounded in the leather straps which would serve as hinges. Then he positioned the stick that would prop the shutter open and fastened it with a leather hinge. "He's feelin' poorly. Not as spry as he used to be. You might look in on him, seein' that you're here."

"*Mais oui*. I'll do that." Gabe shook the snow out of his hair. "I figured the Prophet Joseph was hiding out somewheres around here."

"Oh, you did, did you? Well, even if he was, you wouldn't hear it from me."

"I'm not askin' to know. I just figured, is all."

Nathaniel straightened up. In the daylight, Gabe's face looked strained, paler than usual, with lines around the eyes that made him appear tired. Not physically tired; he seemed robust enough. As if he carried some secret trouble. Nathaniel cleared his throat.

"I reckon you know the prophet's on his way to Springfield. Now that Ford's your governor, there's a chance to clear up this Boggs mess."

"I heard that him and a bunch of others was heading over there. Folks be waiting to hear what happens."

"Well, we all be hopin' for the best. Here. Hold this right there."

Gabe held the shutter in place. Nathaniel climbed a few rungs of the ladder and fastened the hinges at the top of the window.

"More light for Pete?" Gabe asked.

"Shelter from the cold, more like."

"How's that mule doing? I heard he took sick just before the big military celebration."

Nathaniel gave a cough. "He be fine now. Ornery as ever. I was the one, didn't particularly care about that military business. Never could see the use of it. Still don't."

Gabe frowned. "Is that the only thing you see wrong in the church?"

Nathaniel's mind was working. *How could he get Gabe to say what was bothering him? Bethia? The church?* "I see the militarism, yes. I'm not sure we needed to go that way. I also see a troubling materialism. Folks wanting the newest clothes, the best carriages, new things for their houses. Brick houses instead of wood. *Things*."

Gabe nodded, his brows drawing together. "I reckon you're right."

"Now, then." Nathaniel climbed down from the ladder. "What great crisis of faith are we going through now?"

"Uh—*pardon*?"

He looked at Gabe. "Well, you didn't row over here alone just to help me hang a shutter. So what is it?"

They carried the ladder and tools back into the barn. Gabe sat on a hay bale while Nathaniel opened and closed the window. Satisfied, he left it and turned to look at Gabe. "Come on. What's on your mind?"

If he expected some deep philosophical turmoil, he didn't get it. Gabe began speaking, gesturing, and in a matter of moments Nathaniel had the story. Someone in a high position had apparently approached Corey Langdon, of all people, with the idea of becoming a plural wife. When Gabe finished the brief tale, he gave Nathaniel a look of perplexed misery. Nathaniel tried to keep from smiling.

"Is that all?"

"Isn't it enough?"

"Well, don't you see, lad? It's all Bennett. This Bennett affair has influenced numbers of people—got their imaginations working overtime. Seeing things where there's nothing to be seen."

Gabe stood up. "But this—this was before Bennett ever defected. Before that sham battle."

"So? He be working his mischief long before he was excommunicated. Do you think I haven't read those letters? Pure poison."

Gabe shoved his hands in his jacket pockets. "This wasn't Bennett."

"So who was it? Did she say?"

"No. I—I was afraid to ask. I don't know—maybe Hyrum. Or Brigham. But, whoever it was, it was sanctioned by the highest leadership." Gabe was breathing fast.

Nathaniel felt a surge of sympathy. How could someone as intelligent as Gabriel be hoodwinked so easily? "Now, sit down, son. Your face is turning red. Are you trying to tell me that the prophet himself approved such a thing?"

"I reckon that's it. You've got it." Gabe sat back down on the bale.

"You're actually going to take the word of some silly young woman over a prophet of God?"

Gabe made a furious gesture. "She's not silly. She's—"

"I know. She's your patient. And you're willing to believe her implicitly. Without checking her story in any way."

Gabe swallowed. "I—she just seemed so sincere. I had no reason to doubt her. In fact, I was alarmed for her. For her safety. And these rumors about plural marriage—-they've been floating around the city for months now."

Nathaniel paused. "Well, we all know about the goings-on in that city. Any place where there's enough people, something's bound to happen. Like Willard Richards and Nancy Marinda Hyde. Taking up residence together in the printing office after the church bought it from Ebenezer Robinson. You think the prophet sanctioned that? Absolutely not. Like as not, he couldn't stop it."

"But—but Corey—"

Nathaniel stopped him with a glance. "If I didn't know, I'd think you were sweet on her yourself."

To his surprise, Gabe gave him a stricken, sick look, then buried his face in his hands. "Hang it all. I love her. I should've married her. I'm like to give up everything and run away with her. Her and Casey."

"So, now we have it." Nathaniel sat down beside him. *What to say to him now? God forbid he should leave the community.* "I know you've had your troubles with Bethia. I reckon no human relationship is perfect. But the thing is—she's so fragile, as you've said. Not strong. If you left her like that, it might destroy her completely."

"I know." Gabe gave a groan. "That's why I haven't done it."

"And to leave us—to leave your sister Marie, now that you've found her. To leave Hannah and Eb and the others. You'd regret it. You think you'll be happy. But you can't build happiness on the misery of others. I reckon it just doesn't work."

Gabe sighed. "So what do I do?"

Nathaniel tried to speak sternly. "Be a man. You know where your responsibility lies. Remember your priesthood, and your marriage covenant. You made a vow before God." In a gentler voice, he said, "Just don't see her. As a patient, maybe. But try to keep away from her as much as possible."

Gabe looked up. "That might work. It's only when I'm with her that I feel this—this tremendous affinity."

Nathaniel stirred the ground with his foot. "I reckon I only really loved one woman. And I still love her. So I can't put myself in your shoes. But all this advice I be giving you—I reckon it's what I'd do."

"It's good advice." Gabe sniffed and rubbed his nose on his sleeve. "I do appreciate it."

"Let's go up to the house now. Hannah's had barley soup simmering on the fire all morning. That'll warm you up, and you'll feel some better."

"I reckon." They both stood up. "Then I'll see if I can help Owen."

"I'm sure you can. And I'll pray with you before you row back across." Nathaniel put his hand on Gabe's shoulder, and they started up to the house together.

Gabriel felt devastated. Not only had Nat refused to believe him—in a moment of weakness, he had blurted out his feelings for Corey and what he was tempted to do. Of all the stupid things. He might just as well have told the prophet himself.

If he expected sympathy, he didn't get it. Rowing back across the river, he vowed to be a stronger person, to discharge his duties with responsibility. That was what adults did, in spite of inner feelings. *Be a man.* Nat's voice echoed in his ears, along with the rising wind. Safe ashore, he tied up the skiff and tramped home.

"Well, where have you been?" Bethia demanded.

"I went across to see Nat. A few words of counsel from one wiser than I."

"You went across in this weather? Are you out of your mind?"

"Not completely. But I may get there yet."

She gave him one of her odd, pitying looks and turned away. He went to change into dry clothes.

All that winter he kept busy, either in the shop or with his patients. He even took on more patients, ones Bennett had abandoned. He tried to give as much attention and care to his work as he could. He treated Bethia with deference, trying not to roil the waters. When they became roiled anyway, he simply backed away. And no one, not even Marie or Eb, suspected he had any feelings other than those of toil and responsibility.

In early January, Joseph appeared before Judge Pope of Springfield. The judge found fault with the affidavit from Missouri, saying that if Joseph had committed a crime in Illinois, he would be subject to the laws of that state and not Missouri. Also, Boggs had not stated the facts of the case, but only expressed his opinion that Joseph was guilty. Since Joseph had affidavits to prove he was in Illinois at the time of the shooting, the judge ordered that the charges be dismissed.

Jubilant, Joseph and his party rode home through the winter cold to a long celebration, with a special Jubilee Song composed by Wilson Law and Willard Richards. They sang it with feeling in honor of the triumphal day.

The next week, they had an even bigger celebration, a party which included dinner for seventy people, the singing of the Jubilee Song, and another song written by the poet Eliza R. Snow. It was the fifteenth wedding anniversary for Emma and Joseph.

The winter was so cold that the river froze solid for four months. The cold kept everybody preoccupied, intent on staying warm. Gabriel for the most part avoided Corey and tried to keep her out of his thoughts. But toward spring, he found that he felt better if he called on her family from time to time. He stopped in to see how Casey was doing, and how Jubal's health was. She looked at him gravely and assured him that all was well.

After these brief encounters, he walked with a spring in his step, feeling exhilarated, even lightheaded. One day, toward the end of May, he went up to the main house in search of a pencil and found Marie alone.

She was sitting at the table, her chin propped in one hand.

He smiled. "I know where Rusty and Calvin are—down in the shop. But where's Sarah?"

"She's out visiting. I think she went to see Corey."

"Ah." The name sent a little jolt through him. "Nothing wrong, I hope."

Marie looked at him, her eyebrows raised. "Just neighborly visiting, I reckon. Did you hear about the steamboat?"

"The 'Maid of Iowa'? Looks like Joseph becomes the half-owner in another week."

"It seems strange—a church in the steamboat business."

"Might make it cheaper to get across the river." He sat down next to her. "And how're you doing? It seems we haven't had a chance to talk in a coon's age."

She gave him a searching look. "And whose fault is that? I never saw anyone for piling on the work."

"*C'est vrai*. Maybe I can relax a bit now."

In the silence that followed, he sensed they were both thinking of the same thing. In an incident last week, Bethia had accused him at the family table of having plural wives. Tired beyond belief, he'd made no defense. Sarah had escorted Bethia back to her living quarters and sat with her until she'd calmed down.

Marie spoke now. "I'm surprised you didn't say anything when Bethia accused you."

"I'm just plain tired. Whatever I said, it would make no difference. I've about given up."

"In what way?"

"Oh, I reckon—tired of repeating things to her again and again. As if I could afford more than one of her."

She nodded. "Most wives aren't like that."

He laughed then. "I would hope not."

In a softer voice, she said, "You deserve better, Gabriel."

He thought of Nat's words. "Well, nothing's perfect, I reckon."

"This doesn't even come close."

He said nothing. She went on. "There's someone I know who'd make you a perfect wife."

"Who? Corey? Listen, Marie. I don't care how perfect she is. I'm married, and there's nothing I can do about it. I chose it, and at the time it seemed like the thing to do. Bethia wasn't always this way. And at times, it seems like the fog lifts, and she's a reasonable person."

Marie patted his hand. "You asked me how things are going. Rusty is truly a wonderful companion. I could not have chosen better."

He took her hand in his. "I'm most happy to hear that."

"I want you to have the same kind of happiness."

He gave a little cough. "I don't think that's possible, right now. And it's partly my fault. I don't have the strength to deal with it—all her moods. I get exhausted—my spirit, not my body."

She drew closer to him. "I've always been one to follow my heart."

He laughed. "My heart says to run away. Get up and flee."

"Then do it. I'd be with you. Rusty and I—we'd go wherever you do."

He smiled. "I doubt that. And here you are, a good Catholic, suggesting such a thing. That's what Bennett did. Left a wife and children because he didn't want them anymore. No." He pressed her hand. "Life is a series of trials, as I'm sure you know. And this is mine. Oh, Marie. Help me to do the right thing. Not just for me. For all of us."

She sat for a moment in silence. Then she got up from her chair and threw her arms around his neck. "I'm with you, Gabriel. Whatever you decide."

His voice had a teasing quality, but he was deeply touched. "I'm blessed to have such a sister. Makes it almost worth-while." He stood up.

"Oh, Gabriel." They hugged each other. "I wish things were different for you."

"Well—let's make the best of what there is. I'd better get back to the shop, or someone'll think you're one of my plural wives."

Laughing, wiping away tears, Marie sat down again. Gabriel pocketed a pencil from the table and walked toward the door.

Sunday, June 25. Rusty stands beside Gabe and Eb with the other men; there is a lull in the Sunday service.

Suddenly Hyrum appears, a tall, agitated figure. A murmur rises from the assembly. He calls for silence. Then the news. His brother the prophet has been kidnapped. A gasp comes from the crowd. Then the murmur of voices drowns out all other sounds.

Hyrum holds up his hand. He calls for volunteers, riders to go out and find Joseph, and make sure his rights are protected.

Rusty looks at Gabe and Eb. All three surge forward, making their way with countless others to the Masonic Hall, as Hyrum has requested. But there is not enough room in the building, so they reassemble on the green. Hyrum divides them into search parties. Seventy-five are to go with Captain Dan Jones on the 'Maid of Iowa' and search boats on the river as far as Peoria, to make sure the prophet is not a prisoner on one of them.

Another group, approximately one hundred and seventy-five men, are to ride out that night. Under the command of General Wilson Law and William, his brother, they are to divide into squads and take different routes in search of the prophet. Rusty, Gabe, and Eb are selected to ride in the first group, under Wilson Law.

They alert Marie and Jess, then saddle their horses. "Tell Bethia for me," Gabe says to Marie. "I haven't time to explain it all afternoon."

Soon they are on the road with the others, riding frantically, trying to keep going. Rusty has no need to spur on his horse; the big gelding has plenty of spirit and energy. Eb and Gabe have no trouble with their horses. But other men are whipping their mounts, urging them to hurry. One man even forces whiskey down his horse's throat, in order to keep moving.

"No need for that," Gabe says in a low voice.

Rusty is not about to abuse his horse. As they ride, bits of the story echo around them.

"Brother Joseph took his family and went up to Dixon to visit her sister," one bearded man says. "Seems Emma's not been well, and he thought t'would do her good."

Another rider says, "Some good! To have her husband arrested on them Missouri charges again."

"It's Bennett's doing. I'll wager that!" a voice shouts behind them.

The bearded man speaks again. "Anyway, Hyrum got a message from a judge in Springfield. Governor Ford had been obliged—get that, now—*obliged* to issue another writ against Joseph. A requisition from our friends in Missouri."

"Those blasted pukes," someone says.

Another voice says, "I'll be hanged if it's not a regular summer event. They might as well schedule it in, every dad-blamed year."

The bearded man finishes his story. "So Hyrum sent two fellers—Stephen Markham and someone else—to ride like all hell was after 'em and warn Joseph. Only they got there too late."

Rusty and the others learn later that the Missouri officers disguised themselves as Mormon elders and, under that pretext, arrested Joseph at his sister-in-law's home. While they were holding him captive at a tavern in Dixon, an agitated crowd of onlookers finally managed to get lawyers in to see him. The two lawyers sent for the master in chancery. They also sent for Cyrus Walker, an Illinois lawyer who was campaigning in the vicinity for election to Congress.

Cyrus Walker agreed to help, in return for the Mormon vote. Having no choice, Joseph promised it to him. Markham later reported Walker's delight. "I am now sure of my election, as Joseph Smith has promised me his vote."

Joseph sent Markham back to Nauvoo by steamer to ask for Hyrum's help. Meanwhile, Emma and her children returned to Nauvoo by themselves.

The two Missouri officers were reprimanded by the master in chancery and released under a writ of habeas corpus. They took Joseph toward Ottawa, as far as Pawpaw Grove, where they learned that the Ottawa judge, before whom they were supposed to appear, was out of town. They then planned to travel to Quincy, about two hundred and sixty miles, to appear before Judge Stephen A. Douglas.

By the time the first group of riders from Nauvoo finally found Joseph, the party consisted of the prophet, his lawyers and friends, the officers from Missouri, and a number of citizens from the area who were curious about how things were going to turn out. When Joseph saw the Nauvoo riders approaching, he wept. "I'm not going to Missouri this time! These are my boys!"

Rusty's group, commanded by Wilson Law, reach the party two days later. The Law brothers halt their horses and jump to the ground. They both embrace the prophet with exclamations of joy. Amid the stamping and neighing of horses and cheers from the men, Joseph climbs back into his hired stagecoach. About that time, someone declares that Nauvoo and not Quincy is the nearest town where a writ of habeas corpus can be heard.

At that news, general rejoicing prevails. Only the arresting officers look uncomfortable. Joseph sends word ahead to the city, and the party, augmented now by the new riders from Nauvoo, continues.

A strange procession it is. First the stagecoach, with Joseph, his lawyers, and the officers who have taken him prisoner, themselves prisoners of the state of Illinois. Then the friends and curious onlookers, all surrounded by the riders from Nauvoo, so that none of the principal parties can escape.

In the rest before the final leg of the journey, Rusty and the others decorate their horses' bridles with flowers from the prairie.

"Might as well enter in a spirit of celebration," Gabe says.

As they approach the city, they are met by another procession.

"Listen!" Gabe holds up his hand. "Music!"

The band is playing. Emma and Hyrum are both on horseback, followed by a train of carriages and riders. In front is Lorin Walker, leading Joseph's favorite horse, Old Charley. Joseph mounts Charley, and with Emma by his side and the band playing 'Hail, Columbia,' he leads the triumphant parade into the city.

The guns and cannons sound; the streets are full of cheering people who follow the procession to the prophet's house. Out of the corner of his eye, Rusty sees that Gabe is wiping away tears. Rusty smiles. Aloof, practical Dr. Romain, overcome by the moment.

The crowd does not disperse until Joseph promises to speak to them later that day. At around one o'clock, fifty of the prophet's friends sit down to a dinner served by Emma. The two officers sit at the head of the table.

Later, Calvin remarks that Joseph treated the officers far better than he himself had been treated. After the Nauvoo court had heard a half-day of testimony, it discharged Joseph because of a lack of substance in the arrest warrant.

But the affair is not over. Calvin tells what he has heard.

"Some folks be sayin' that the Nauvoo court had no power to set aside the authority of the state of Illinois."

"We still in trouble?" Eb asks.

"Well, the prophet is safe, for now. But people in the other towns aren't happy about it. And the governor—he's mad at everybody. Us, the lawyers, and Cyrus Walker."

"What I want to know," Gabe says. "How's the prophet gonna make good his promise to Walker? He can't deliver the whole Mormon vote."

"I s'pose he could, if he asked the people." Calvin says. "Folks'd do anything for him. But then the whole state'd be upset."

Gabe nods. "And rightly so."

In view of the events which happened later, Rusty liked to remember the glad entry into the city, and the rejoicing which followed. In retrospect, he could not think of an occasion when the prophet was more loved, the people more secure and happy, and the city more beautiful. In memory of that day, he kept the garlands of wildflowers entwined around Jeb's bridle until they had all disintegrated.

22

"I'LL VOW, THERE'S MORE trouble than a hog caught in a bramble bush." Calvin pounded his fist on the table.

"What is it now?" Sarah called from the kitchen. "Maybe I shouldn't ask."

Rusty raised his voice. "Well, you heard about the two puke officers running off to the governor and demanding he send the state militia to arrest Joseph."

"But he didn't do it," Calvin declared. "At least, not yet. I reckon he's holding off everything till after the elections."

"That's why we sent Backenstos off to Springfield," Gabe said. "So he could see the lay of the land, and maybe figure out how the Democrats were gonna treat us if they stayed in power."

"But this Hoge thing is just ridiculous," Calvin said. "Even William Law says so. Backenstos hasn't even got back yet. And Hyrum went and promised Joseph Hoge the Mormon vote, 'cause he has an eye on a seat in the state legislature. Law called it 'pure politics.' And here Joseph's promised the vote to the Whig candidate. Cyrus Walker."

"We're gonna have both sides mad at us," Gabe said.

Eb pushed back his chair. "And when that militia comes, they'll drive us out for sure."

"Now, that's enough!" Sarah made a clatter in the kitchen. "You men! Can't even discuss politics without talkin' about being driven out! I'm sick of it! Do you hear?"

"I reckon we better go somewhere's else," Rusty said.

"All the same." Gabe stood up. "It'll be interesting to see how the leadership gets out of this one."

The people now believed that Hyrum had received a revelation: the Mormons must support Hoge. Sunday, the day before the elections, Joseph spoke to the assembled crowd, telling them that if Hyrum had received a revelation, it was most certainly true. As for himself, Joseph declared he would vote for Cyrus Walker.

"A neat trick," Gabe said. "Hope it works."

Hoge won the election by a small majority. The Whigs blamed the Mormons for the loss of the election. Other people blamed them for being able to swing elections, and bitter resentment festered on both sides.

Rusty sat in the public house with Nigel, hunched over mugs of cold cider.

"Sure has been hot," someone said. "Never saw a hotter July. And dry. Where's the rain?"

"And August ain't much better," Rusty muttered, to no one in particular. He and Nigel raised their mugs and both took hearty swallows.

"That's bloomin' good." Nigel rubbed his shirt sleeve across his mouth.

"Perks you right up," Rusty replied.

The door opened behind them. Rusty turned to see. The man who entered looked familiar, but Rusty couldn't place him. One of their customers, most like. Or maybe a patient of Gabriel's. The man carried his coat, as if he'd just come from some official meeting.

"I need a stiff one," he said to the proprietor.

"Sorry. All we got is cider, beer and wine. The city ordinance don't allow no hard stuff."

"I know. How 'bout a beer?"

The proprietor poured it from a spigot on a wooden keg. The man took a seat at the table next to Rusty and Nigel. "Man alive—if you knew what I just heard."

"What?" The others drew closer.

"I'm not supposed to tell. Oh, what the blasted heck. Everyone's gonna know about it anyway."

"What?" they sang out in chorus.

"They just had a meeting—the Stake High Council. We was all

over in Hyrum Smith's office, only Joseph wasn't there 'cause he was feeling poorly. I was in there 'cause my uncle had told me to meet him there. And someone asked, sort of innocent-like, if there was any truth to the rumors of plural marriage. 'Cause folks had heard so much about it, doncha see? So Hyrum got up and went across the street. He came back with this document, which he claimed was a revelation. Said his brother had written it down last month, and someone had burned the first copy—I forget just who. So they made another one.

"Well, Hyrum started to read this thing to the High Council. Now, it began nicely enough—lots of high-flown language. Then it talks about the 'new and everlasting covenant.' Toward the end you get the part about a man being able to have as many wives, or 'virgins,' as he wants, because if they are given to him by God, he cannot commit adultery."

There was a shocked silence. Rusty looked at Nigel, who raised his eyebrows. Then a voice from behind them gasped, "Well, I'll be hornswoggled!"

"I don't believe it," someone else said. "What do they drink at those High Council meetings?"

"And that ain't all," the news-bearer said. "Hyrum declared that if they rejected it, they would be damned, or words to that effect. Then—you shoulda heard 'em—that council just fell apart. Three really came out against it. There was—let's see—William Marks, the president of the High Council, no less. Then, Austin Cowles and Leonard Soby. Those three raised such a ruckus that the whole council divided into polygamous and anti-polygamous groups."

"Well, can you beat that?" someone said.

The murmur of voices grew louder.

"What happens now?"

"What's gonna happen when them gentile newspapers get ahold of it?"

"What I want to know is—when do I get my share of virgins?"

Shaken, Rusty finished his cider. He nudged Nigel. "What do you think? This is—this is not what I've been taught."

Nigel put his cider mug down. They stood up and made their way out of the building. Nigel knitted his brows together. "I have to think that things change. Concepts change. If the Prophet Joseph said it, how can we reject it?"

"Well, I reckon we have to use our own minds. Our intelligence. You know the scripture—First 'you must study it out in your mind: then you must ask me if it be right.' 'Me' being the Lord, not the prophet."

Nigel frowned again. "You're saying the prophet might be wrong?"

"I think he's wrong on this. He, or whoever concocted that document."

Nigel paused. "I'm not sure—"

"If they presented it to the whole church, it wouldn't be accepted."

"But—-but if we reject it, we're damned. Don't you see? There isn't a choice."

Rusty shrugged, impatient. "Well, maybe there should be."

Nigel entered the front of the shop and reached for his apron.

"'Bout time you got back," Eb said.

Rusty walked around in back and found Gabe relaxing between patients.

"Come sit a moment." Gabe indicated his office chair. "Been out for a drink, I hear. What'd you have? You look like you seen a ghost."

Rusty related all that he'd heard. Gabe sat blinking, his hands clasped with his fingers moving up and down. As Rusty finished, he saw that Gabe's lips were deathly white.

"So what do you think?" Rusty asked.

"I think some mighty strange things are afoot."

Rusty spread his hands in a little helpless gesture. "What do we do?"

"Why—nothing. I reckon the less we get into it, the better. We'll just keep on with the shop, and whatever else we're doing. Let me study some on it. I don't know what else we can do."

"But—"

"And do me a favor. Don't tell Bethia what you've heard. She already thinks I have half a dozen wives. Although, how I can possibly support them hasn't entered her head."

Rusty nodded. "I'm sorry.

"I'm sorry for us all. Charley says when our enemies find out, we're done for."

"Do we make plans to leave?"

Gabe waited before he spoke. "I reckon we'll stay put and see what happens. But it sounds like the secret's already out."

"Shouldn't we let Nat know?"

Gabe sighed. "I already tried. He didn't believe me."

"He didn't?"

"No. I'll wait till he hears from someone else. Won't be long, I reckon."

Rusty sat feeling depressed and baffled. Gabe tapped him on the knee. "Don't fret none. Maybe things'll change. We're safe, for the moment. Let's just wait. And don't tell any of the women yet. All we need is Sarah having fits."

End of August. Intermittent rain all morning. Gabriel stood at the window of his sitting room, looking out beyond the big house to the gray river misty in the rain. Ferry just landing. He looked over and smiled at Bethia who sat mending a shirt. Their eyes met; she did not smile back.

Still angry with him. He'd gone out to the public house earlier with Eb to get the news, and stayed a little too long. No news to report. Just the old business about Dr. Robert Foster, a Mormon, who'd ridden to Carthage to be sworn in as the new school commissioner. He'd been met by a group of armed men angry over the election results and what they considered to be Joseph's defiance of the law in the recent kidnapping. Dr. Foster was able to take his oath of office, but their enemies were now holding anti-Mormon rallies.

"Derned if they want to keep us all out of office," someone had said.

"They say they want to destroy Joseph Smith's political strength," the proprietor remarked.

"Seems like they want to destroy us all."

Gabriel sighed as the memory of their voices echoed in his mind. Then he saw a familiar group walking up from the ferry landing.

"I'll be busted! It's Nat and Hannah, and the children! Come over in the rain. Wait—he's carrying something."

He rushed out the door and met them as they reached the big house. Bethia followed. Nat's bundle proved to be a ham and two dressed chickens. "It's time for us all to get together. And what better way then over food?"

Sarah and Hannah set to work in the kitchen, and in the late afternoon the little group of friends gathered around the table. Gabriel looked with approval at the ham and chicken, corn, beans, fresh tomatoes and peppers, and crusty bread. But he felt puzzled, too. This was not like Nathaniel. Had he heard something, maybe about the document on polygamy? All through the meal, Gabriel wondered.

He looked across at Eb and Jess as they put choice bits of food on Turah's plate. Marie sat next to Jess, with Rusty on her left. Nat was explaining the Ojibwë method of planting corn.

"All done by the women. They put a kernel in the hole. Then around that they plant the beans and then the squash, all in a circle. And derned if it doesn't keep the pests away."

"That's right smart," Calvin said.

At last, when the children had been ushered off to play, Nat folded his napkin.

"I reckon there be some strange things happening—ideas that people say are new doctrines. And frankly, they leave me at a loss. I'm hopin' some of it's just speculation."

Here it comes, Gabriel thought. He leaned forward, one elbow on the table. Calvin gave a little cough. "You mean, like baptism for dead family members?"

"No. That's nothing new. I'm more concerned about this—-this plurality of gods."

Gabriel said, "I suppose you mean like the Trinity? The Father, Son, and Holy Ghost being separate entities?"

Nat ran the napkin through his fingers. "That bothers me—yes. I always figured they were all one. Three aspects of one Supreme Being."

"But Joseph saw two personages." Calvin gestured with his knife. "In his initial vision."

"So?" Nat shrugged. "Why can't God take any form he wants? I'm talking about God the Father now. And, as far as the Holy Ghost—"

Calvin moved his hands along the edge of the table. "Seems to me like they fade in and out. Sometimes it's one, sometimes it's three. Or two."

Then Marie began to laugh. They all looked at her. She took a sip of water. "Oh, excuse me. I'm just a woman, and not even a Mormon. But you're trying to figure out the Trinity. And it's not possible." She looked at Gabriel. "Tell them. Don't you remember the story about Saint Augustine?"

He did, and he told it the best he could. "Augustine was walking on the beach—it was a kind of vision, and he was meditating on this very subject. He came upon a small boy who had dug a hole, and was trying to fill it with sea water. Augustine asked him what he was doing, and the child replied, "It would be easier for me to put the whole ocean into this hole, then it would be for you to understand the Trinity.'"

Silence. Then Calvin nodded. "Well, I reckon it's one of the mysteries they talk about."

Nat said, "And this talk of a God above our one God, and everyone getting to be a god over his own world, and populating that world—"

Calvin's thick, gray brows drew together. "You mean, that our God was once like us? And someday we'll be in charge of a world of our own?"

"Exactly." Nat wiped his mouth with the folded napkin. "All speculation. And nothing to do with our original teachings."

"Just a minute." Rusty paused in his food consumption. "Where are you getting all these notions?"

"Why, from bits and pieces of sermons, and what other people have said. And Gabe's friend Charley keeps me informed."

"Charley knows more than you think," Gabe said. "He gets around to a lot of places."

Nat went on. "And I don't reckon he's half the scoundrel that he wants folks to think he is. Why, when he brought me word of that plural marriage document—"

Gabriel felt Bethia stiffen beside him. "What document?"

"Oh, that one," Sarah said. "About the virgins."

Nat stopped to explain, for Bethia's benefit. "There's apparently been some sort of document sanctioning plural marriage. Now, I'm not sure the prophet wrote it. Parts of it don't sound like him—being condemned if you don't comply with it, for instance. But he obviously approved it or it wouldn't have been read to the High Council."

"Why didn't I know about it?" Bethia asked.

Gabriel patted her shoulder. "We figured you had enough on your mind."

She sat glaring at them. "You mean, you all knew, and no one told me?"

"*Eh bien,*" Gabriel said. "It happened just a short while ago. Word's still getting around."

Calvin gestured with his knife. "In fact, I think it was supposed to be kept secret. So not many people know about it yet."

Bethia threw her fork down beside her plate. "Well, that explains everything. Gabriel's already practicing it—has been, for some time."

Nathaniel slammed his fist on the table. "Listen, Bethia. We don't need any such accusations here. He's not doing it, and has never done so. The ones that are involved are not that many—mainly from this special group that Charley says is meeting over above the store. That may change when they finish the temple. In fact—that's what I want to talk about.

"All this is contrary to everything we've been taught. Now—I wouldn't be in a hurry to attack it—let's see where they go with it. It might be that the men in leadership positions will change their views and make some statement. Clarify things a little. But in the meantime, I would urge caution. No sudden moves. Stay where you are; keep on with your business."

Eb looked up. "What if one of these mobs comes after us? Like the folks mad about the elections."

Nat tightened his lips together, then spoke. "Well, I'm staying put. No one's driving me out this time. As far as folks are concerned, it's still the old Dulac place. That's another thing I wanted to tell you. I'm not running anymore. I just don't have it in me. My family, and Owen—we're staying, no matter where the others go."

"What if they come to your place with guns and torches?" Eb asked. "Burn your cabins, like they done before?"

"They have to find them first," Nat replied. "I reckon you wonder why I hid 'em so careful-like. One more thing. Any trouble over here, you just come across the river. We can hide all of you. Keep the skiff handy. And Charley has another—he'll row you across if you need it."

It was late. As they were leaving to go to their various sleeping places, Nat walked over to Gabriel. Hannah was already bedding the children down in the guest room. Nat put his hand on Gabriel's shoulder. "I owe you an apology. And your friend Corey, too."

Gabriel nodded and clasped Nat's other hand. "She's all right—no new proposals."

"And Jubal? Is he well?"

Gabriel was able to tell him that all the Langdon family was in good health. "I just saw them three days ago."

"I fret about them," Nat said. "These be strange times, and I fear some of us be weaker than others."

Gabriel took a deep breath, aware of Bethia listening intently by his side. "If we have to flee to Iowa, I'll try to bring them, too."

"Well, we won't worry none about that yet. But trouble's a'coming—it don't take a prophet to figure that out."

Calvin gave a short laugh. "You be listening to Charley too much."

Nat gathered the ones that were left and offered a prayer commending them to God's care, and exhorting them to remember the pure and simple teachings of the gospel.

As they walked back to their rooms, Bethia sniffed. "Well. There's a lot you didn't see fit to tell me."

Gabriel searched for what to say to her. "I'm trying to protect you, is all. And I'll continue to do that. As for what I hear, I'm not always sure what's true and what isn't."

"And what's all this about Corey?"

He sighed. "I guess I can tell it now. She had a proposal of marriage from someone who already had a wife. Like what happened between you and Bennett—she was shocked. I reckon she's over it now—she knows what to do."

She was silent, and in the dim light he could see that she was biting her lip. "Oh, Gabriel. What are we going to do?"

"Well, right now, we're going to bed. Let's not worry about troubles that aren't even here yet. We'd best enjoy what's given to us, while we can. And maybe nothing bad will happen."

Bethia had cried most of the morning. She cried at the slightest excuse, it seemed. Crying now because Gabriel had gone to the public house to meet Charley and Adriel.

"They said they'd come over this morning, and they'll have news. They're better than the *Nauvoo Neighbor.*"

But mainly she cried because of an underlying discontent. She was not happy, and she felt she should be. She thought of all that the city offered, the festivities, music and dancing. Three bands it had—a brass band, the Nauvoo Legion Band, and a quadrille band with stringed instruments. Didn't they enjoy quilting parties, cornhusking parties, trips on the riverboats with band music, where they danced by moonlight? And the suppers after the quilting parties, where the men joined them for dancing, singing, and games that lasted till midnight?

Among the most popular events were cotillion parties, held as benefits for missionaries or families in need. Many of these took place at the Mansion House, the handsome two-story house which Joseph had built for his family. In fact, they had just added a two-story wing to the back, with a kitchen and dining room on the ground floor and ten bedrooms above.

Bethia thought of the celebration, the sign *'Nauvoo Mansion'* raised by the family, and the great party on the opening day. She remembered the house itself decked with flags and bunting, the new red carpet from St. Louis, marble-topped tables and a glittering chandelier. Outside, they'd built a stable big enough for seventy-five horses.

She and Gabriel had attended, along with two hundred others. The dinner, prepared all day, consisted of prairie chickens, wild turkey, hot breads, mashed rutabagas, pumpkin pie, and cider. Rusty was beside himself with delight, but Gabriel said, "As far as I'm concerned, they could do without the rutabagas."

There was Joseph in his best clothes and Emma in a new dress, greeting the guests as if they had not a care in the world. Maybe this talk of enemies in the neighboring towns was all just nonsense.

Suddenly she knew what would make her happy. A new house! A house of her own, where she could preside over dinners. Maybe she could have quilting parties, and even cotillions. And maybe—just maybe—the gayety and excitement would make up for the cradle which was still empty. Of course that cradle had not been built yet, but she knew Calvin or Nat could fashion one in a very short time.

She greeted Gabriel with the idea when he returned. He looked at her, his black brows drawing together, then sat down in their rocker.

"Let's think a moment. You want a house?"

"Yes. With a proper kitchen and a dining room. Like the Mansion House."

He gave a short laugh. "So that's it. Bethia, we couldn't afford a house like that in a million years."

"No. Nothing that big. Just a—a house of our own."

He nodded, staring off into space. "Well, I can see where living behind a blacksmith shop isn't the lap of luxury. How about—well, we could move in with Calvin and Sarah, and Rusty and Marie could come down here. Then I could still have my office here."

"No. You don't understand. I want our own house. Then we can have parties."

He made a grimace, his mouth a tight line. "I'm sure we could have parties in Calvin's house. As it is, there seems to be a gathering every week. Not to mention all the other events around town."

She gestured, insistent. "I want a place of my own."

He said gently, "There's always those cabins across the river. We could move into one of them, and be safe if the troubles came again."

"There're no troubles coming. I want to stay in Nauvoo."

He blinked and gave a sigh. "I hear you. Well, maybe we could see about renting a house. A lot of folks have left, but there's always more flocking in. Let me see what I can find."

"Why can't we build one?"

"Well—most of the lots are taken around here. We'd have to go up on the hill, or down the river a piece. Are you sure you want to move that far away from our friends and family?"

She felt the fog of indecision creeping over her. She tried to sound determined. "I only know I want a house where I can prepare meals and—and have quilting parties and such-like."

Gabriel sat lost in thought. Then he nodded. "Very well. If that will make you happy, I'll see what I can do. But it sounds like a lot of extra work that you don't have here."

She made no reply. Finally he got up and walked into his office. He closed the door, but she could still hear him shuffling papers and opening the desk drawers. If he thought he could conceal anything from her, he was mistaken.

Something moved outside the window. Calvin was walking down from the big house, a newspaper in his hand. She heard him knocking at the office door and Gabriel opening it.

Calvin's voice: "There's an editorial in the *Times and Seasons* you oughta see. By the prophet himself. He wants us to elect the man who will obtain justice for us, and he promises to find that man."

Bethia yawned. Politics again. She leaned her head back in the upholstered chair and began to plan her new house.

A tall, black-haired young man was the first with the news. "I'll be dad-blamed! Derned if Joseph Smith isn't running for the Presidency!"

"Of the United States? You must be daft!" the proprietor said. "Where'd you hear that?"

"It's all over town by this time. Willard Richards moved it, and the apostles all voted—unanimously, by the way—to propose a ticket with Joseph at the head."

"Did he accept?" the proprietor asked.

"'Course he did. He said they'd have to send every man who could speak in public out to campaign for him. He actually said, 'There is oratory enough in the Church to carry me into the presidential chair the first slide.'"

"If that ain't something," someone else said.

"He also said we've had Whig and Democratic Presidents long enough; we need a President of the United States."

Rusty gulped his cider with the words whirling around him. He hurried to tell the others in the blacksmith shop. Calvin and the rest thought he'd had too much cider.

A week later he took Calvin and Gabe with him to the public house. By this time, a pamphlet had been completed and mailed out to at least two hundred leaders of the country: *Views of the Power and Policy of the Government of the United States.*

"He wants to revoke imprisonment for debt," the proprietor said.

"He's gonna turn prisons into seminaries of higher learning," a grizzled old man said.

"He wants to put felons to work on roads and such-like. Public projects," someone else remarked.

"I like this," the proprietor said. "He's gonna economize in national and state governments to lower taxes."

Calvin listened, then told Rusty and Gabe, "That slave business'll never pass. To petition slave states to abolish slavery by 1850, and reimburse slaveholders from the sale of public lands."

"Why not?" Gabe asked. "I'll drink to that."

"But it's not economically feasible. Those southern states are based on a slave economy. I'm not saying it's right, mind you."

Someone else said, "I like the idea of a national bank, with branches in each state."

"That idea's already been vetoed twice by President Tyler," the proprietor said.

As they left the public house, Calvin said, "All these proposals be good. But I can't think he's looking to win. The most it can do is get the Whigs and Democrats off our backs. And possibly get some support for our losses in Missouri."

Sidney Rigdon agreed to serve with him on the ticket, and moved to Pennsylvania to establish residency there. All that spring, the elders went out and campaigned, preaching the gospel and expounding Joseph's views. Rusty went out with his father Calvin to outlying towns in western Illinois. Gabe and Eb headed for Iowa, where they joined Nathaniel and Owen Crawford. They tried to leave at least two men at any one time to manage the blacksmith shop.

"It's Nigel's turn to go out next week," Calvin said.

As they were preparing to leave on one of their journeys, Bethia ran out weeping and stood in front of Gabe.

"Buh—buh—what about the house you promised me?"

"House?" Gabe blinked. "Oh. Well, let's get this election over with first. If Joseph wins, you can have as many houses as you want."

"I just want one."

"Well—I'm looking into it."

"House?" Calvin asked as they walked away.

"She wants a house. A house of her own, where she can have parties."

"Oh. Knowing her, I'd drag my feet on that one, if'n I was you."

"That's what I'm doing. The thing is, I've made some inquiries about building. You either get the land and lumber from the Law brothers at a cheaper rate, or you go through the Church and pay more. The first way, you incur the wrath of the leadership—they've already told the brethren not to work for Foster and Law. The second way, you get fleeced."

"Another reason why I wouldn't do anything right now," Calvin said. "From what I'm hearing, the Law brothers are in a heap of trouble with the Church. I wouldn't like to be in their shoes."

Rusty, walking on the other side of his father, wondered briefly which would do them in first—the outside troubles or the internal dissent.

23

On the whole, Gabriel liked William Law. Law, a convert to the Church, had come down from Canada with his brother Wilson and was considered well-to-do, having invested in land, farming, building, and industry. For the last two years, William had served as Joseph's counselor in the Presidency, along with Sidney Rigdon.

Displeased with the prophet's control of real estate and threats to excommunicate anyone who bought land without his approval, Law upheld the opinion that work on the Nauvoo House and the temple should take second place until all the townspeople had decent housing. With Dr. Robert Foster, Law began to buy lumber from the Wisconsin pineries, intended for church buildings, and to use it for business properties and housing.

Joseph, expecting persecution from all sides, appointed forty city policeman to patrol Nauvoo night and day. They were to maintain the peace, but also to protect him from his enemies. Anyone who opposed official Church policies began to express a decided uneasiness.

"Did you hear?" Calvin said. "Someone built a fire on the river bank, down by William Marks' house. He figured sure those police were trying to intimidate him, and he requested they be questioned before a session of the City Council."

"I hear Leonard Soby was scared, too," Rusty said. "Someone came right out and told him he was considered one of Joseph's enemies."

"That's a shame," Calvin replied. "These be strange times. All the more reason for us to steer clear of any trouble."

Gabriel wasn't sure about the steering clear. He didn't like the notion of a police state. It didn't take much figuring to realize that the so-called 'enemies'—Leonard Soby, William Law, Francis Higbee, William Marks and others—had been dead set against any concept of polygamy.

From Gabriel's visits to the public house, he picked up the sense that Law considered Joseph a fallen prophet, but not a false one. The final blow for Law was his belief that Joseph had made overtures to Jane, his wife.

"It's getting interesting," Gabriel told Calvin. "I hear Law's demanded that Joseph either confess and repent before the High Council, or have his behavior exposed to the world."

"Just keep out of it," Calvin said. "It'll all be forgotten next week."

The next they heard, the group of dissenters had found each other and were meeting together. On March 24, Joseph spoke to the townspeople and declared that a conspiracy existed against him. He named the Law brothers, Robert D. Foster, and Chauncey Higbee. In April, members of the High Council met and excommunicated Foster, along with Wilson, William, and Jane Law, for 'unchristianlike conduct.'

"Their names be published in the *Times and Seasons*," Calvin declared. "But I reckon they're not leaving town. They got too much business interests here."

A few days later, Rusty and Eb came home with the news. "They're settin' up a whole new church," Rusty declared. "Foster and the Laws and them. William Law's gonna be at the head of it."

"They've gone and ordered a press," Eb said. "They're gonna publish a new paper. They be calling it—what was it?"

"The *Nauvoo Expositor*," Rusty said.

The press arrived by steamer from St. Louis. The new owners hauled it through the city and set it up, without any interference from the citizens. Meanwhile, William Law was released as Joseph's counselor, Robert Foster lost his office as surgeon general of the Nauvoo Legion, and Wilson Law was suspended as major general of the Legion. Complaint was made against both Law brothers in the Masonic Lodge.

William Law persuaded the grand jury in Carthage to indict Joseph for adultery and polygamy. Foster charged him with false swearing. But when Joseph rode to Carthage for trial, the case was deferred until the next meeting of the circuit court.

"I'll be derned," Calvin said. "The *Nauvoo Neighbor* has come out with all sorts of bad things against the Higbee brothers. Charges from the old Bennett times."

On June 7, the long-awaited issue of the *Nauvoo Expositor* saw the light of day. Calvin came running with it to Gabriel's office.

"Look! It talks about the control of land in and around the city. They accuse Joseph of violating the rights of the Nauvoo Charter. And they don't have anything good to say about his political ambitions."

"Let me see," Gabriel said.

"No—wait. Here's the part about his 'moral imperfections.' That can only mean polygamy. Yes—they talk about this girl being taught the principles of plural marriage by the prophet himself. But that's just a story. Made-up. Oh, here. Austin Cowles, William Law and Jane all claim to have seen the revelation about the virgins. Ten virgins! They can have up to that many."

"I gotta see that." Gabriel snatched the paper away from him.

"Well, blazes. Don't tear it. I have to show that part to Sarah."

It didn't take long for news of the first issue to spread all over town.

"You got yours yet?" the tanner called from the door of his shop.

"I'm going up there now," the proprietor of the grog shop answered.

"Better hurry. They still got some copies left."

The City Council held a meeting that Saturday. Gabriel hurried over in the windy, overcast morning with Calvin, Rusty, and Eb. "I reckon if we're lucky, we can get seats in the back," Eb said.

Gabriel was amazed at how many had come. Families of the councilmen, business owners, wives, anyone who could crowd inside. Gabriel found Corey, alone without her sister or father, and went to stand beside her.

"I left Casey with a neighbor," she said.

He nodded. "It's really something, isn't it? It says a lot about the power of the press."

"Or the power of the people. Everyone wants to find out what's gonna happen. Those who know the real story, and the outsiders."

In the session, which carried over into Monday, Joseph denied the *Expositor* charges and declared the publication of libel not authorized by the Constitution. According to members of the council, the publishers stood accused of seduction, theft, pandering, and counterfeiting. As for the revelation on polygamy, it did exist, Hyrum stated, but it concerned happenings in former times, the days of Abraham, Isaac and Jacob.

"That's a neat way out of it," Gabriel muttered.

The paper was declared a nuisance, and since that amounted to disturbing the peace, the council directed the mayor to have the nuisance removed. Joseph gave orders to the marshal, who was to be aided by Nauvoo Legion troops.

Gabriel and his friends managed to slip out the door before the rush of the crowd.

"It's late," Corey said. "I have to get home."

He gave a little wave of his hand. "Whatever happens, I'll tell you."

She left. Calvin leaned close to Gabriel. "I don't reckon he had a choice. Running for President and all."

Gabriel shrugged. "I don't see why he couldn't just let 'em have their newspaper. And their church. It sure didn't bother me. I mean, the *Warsaw Signal* has printed worse."

"I don't know. I'd say he has a low tolerance for opposition."

They joined the crowd of people who followed the police and the Legion members. They left the lower town and marched along Mulholland Street past the temple. One of his patients nudged Gabriel. "How come yer not up there marching with the Legion?"

"No one asked us," he replied. "Thank God I'm not. I don't think they need everyone for this—this enterprise."

"Besides, we're cavalry," Calvin said.

The sun was setting as they reached the store. The men in the grocery across the street gathered in the doorway to watch. Gabriel caught a glimpse of the rebel group exiting the store and locking the front door.

"By heaven," Calvin said. "This crowd's filling the whole street."

"Be quiet," Gabriel hissed. The city marshal stepped forward and read the order in a loud voice.

"'You are here commanded to destroy the printing press from whence issues the *Nauvoo Expositor*, and pi the type of said printing establishment in the street...'"

The marshall asked one of the rebels for a key to the store. The man refused. Two policemen came forward, sledges in their hands. Then

Francis Higbee stepped out from the group of dissenters. He looked directly at Joseph.

"Just a minute. If you lay hands on that press, you will date your downfall from this hour!"

The policemen pushed the young man aside and mounted the steps. The store's guard, known to everybody as Big John, rushed in front of the policemen and started swinging at them.

"Derned if he didn't fell them both!" Calvin said. The crowd moved in front of them. Gabriel, short as he was, tried to stand on tiptoe. He had to rely on Calvin for what happened next.

"Another policeman's rushing up. Big John's got him. Oh, wait. The prophet himself's getting into it."

The crowd noises increased. "What's happening?" Gabriel asked.

"I think Joseph took care of Big John. He's staggering around, looking dazed. Porter Rockwell and them others are gettin' that door open."

There was the noise of splintering wood. The crowd parted, and Gabriel was able to see the printing press smashing into the street. The overturned type cases followed, then copies of the *Expositor* and other loose papers. Someone dumped cleaning fluid over the pile and lit a sulfur match. The fire blazed up. Boys from the crowd rushed over and began picking up pieces of type.

"I'd say it's over," Gabriel remarked.

"There's another fire in the shop," Calvin said. "Look there! And that rebel group—they've all disappeared. I don't see a one of them."

"Lost in the crowd, most like," Gabriel said.

Calvin went on. "If I was one of them, I'd leave too."

"Let's go home," Rusty said. "It's way past supper time."

Marie's hands trembled as she set the table for the noon meal. Sarah, stirring the soup, glanced over at her.

"Land's sake, child. Don't look so frightened. We been through worse than this."

"But—the dissenting group. I told you what someone said when I went to Mass this morning. They've left the city. Completely left. The Laws got their families on a steamboat, on their way up to Burlington."

"And good riddance, if you ask me. Stirrin' up trouble—that's all they did. Of all the things we didn't need—"

Marie put the last dish on the table. "You don't think they had cause for grievance?"

"If they'd been tending to their business, doing what they shoulda done, they wouldn't a had time to make such mischief, I reckon."

The door burst open. Calvin and Rusty hurried in, followed by Gabriel. Calvin waved a folded newspaper.

"The *Warsaw Signal.* Wait'll you hear this." He moved the dishes aside and spread it out on the table. Rusty met Marie halfway around the table and embraced her while Sarah shouted about them wiping their feet.

"Raining all morning! And the three of you tracking in mud!"

For a moment Marie felt reassured by the normalcy of it all—Sarah yelling, Rusty hugging her. Then Calvin began to read.

"Robert Foster has a letter about—let's see—'the unparalleled outrage perpetrated upon our rights and interests by the ruthless, lawless, ruffian bands of Mormon mobocrats—'"

"That's us," Gabriel interjected.

"'...at the dictum of that unprincipled wretch Jo Smith—'"

"You get the impression they don't like him much, either," Gabriel remarked.

"Quiet. Here's Thomas Sharp: 'Citizens arise, one and all!...We have no time for comment, every man will make his own. Let it be made with powder and ball!'"

"That don't sound good." Eb shook his head.

Marie felt herself trembling. Rusty pressed her close to him. "Don't worry," he said in a low voice. "You wanted excitement—-remember? But we're well protected here."

Sarah's mouth formed a grim line. "Well. What happens now?"

"Nothing." Gabriel shrugged. "We eat. Tom Sharp's been spoutin' off for years. It's what sells papers."

They took their places at the table. Eb came in with Jess and Turah, and Bethia finally joined them. Marie sensed a guardedness, a constraint, as if everyone were afraid to speak of what might lie ahead.

Calvin asked the blessing on the food, then took a mouthful.

"Good soup." He folded up the paper and put it under his chair. Marie tried not to look troubled. Rusty pressed her hand.

"Eat, my dear. And let us do the worryin'."

Rusty loved something even more than his sister Hannah and food, and that was Marie. To see his treasured new wife so upset made him wonder if they were indeed as safe as he'd thought.

To be sure, they had the Legion, five thousand strong. What the Gentile press called 'a Mormon army.' But word came in of mass meetings at Warsaw and Carthage, none of them with friendly intent. He'd heard that Joseph had written careful letters to the governor relating the events leading to the destruction of the press. One letter even put the Nauvoo Legion at the service of the governor.

Joseph and seventeen others were charged at Carthage with instigating a riot in destroying the *Nauvoo Expositor*. When the sheriff came to arrest them, Joseph refused to surrender. Instead, he secured a writ from the Nauvoo Court. Joseph, Hyrum, William W. Phelps, John Taylor, and some others were tried and acquitted before Daniel H. Wells, a non-Mormon judge in Nauvoo. The sheriff returned to Carthage without any prisoners.

Then all hell broke loose, as his father described it. There was talk of some seven hundred citizens rallying in Carthage in great excitement. The *Warsaw Signal* reported three thousand men enlisting in Rushville, and hundreds more taking up arms in McDonough County, Keokuk and Green Plains. People demanded that Governor Ford send out the state militia. Citizens threatened to take up arms and march on Nauvoo if the governor did not act.

"What do you think?" Rusty asked Gabe.

"I reckon we wait, and see what old Tom Ford decides to do. If you figure you be in any danger, just take Marie and get across the river. Go now, if you've a mind to. That river's rising. Any more rain and we'll have more water than we know what to do with."

"We'll stay," Rusty said. "For now."

On June 18, his father scratched on their bedroom door. "Get dressed, quick as you can. Don't alarm the women. The Legion's been called out."

They hurried down to get Gabe and Eb. Nigel was just starting up the fire.

"Leave it," Calvin said. "We've been called up. The city's under martial law."

The troops began assembling near the Mansion House. Joseph appeared before them in full military uniform and addressed them from the foundation of a building under construction. Rusty wasn't sure how long he spoke, but it seemed like more than an hour.

"It is thought by some that our enemies would be satisfied with my destruction; but I tell you that as soon as they have shed my blood they will thirst for the blood of every man in whose heart dwells a single spark of the spirit of the fullness of the Gospel...we are innocent of the charges which are heralded forth through the public prints against us by our enemies..."

Rusty, with the others, vowed to stand by him to the death and sustain the laws of the country, and protect the people from mob violence.

"That were quite a speech," Eb said on the way home.

"It may be the last one you'll hear for some time," Calvin replied. "Things being all confused like they are."

Rusty got the word that afternoon—he and Eb were to help dig trenches and pitch tents at the eastern edge of the town, where they would make camp. He bid a tearful good-bye to Marie, and Eb met him at the front of the shop. Shouldering shovels, they walked up the road.

"I can't make it out," Rusty said as they dug. "We're supposed to dig this entrenchment, and manufacture artillery. But then he says no gun will be fired by us during this trouble."

"Blamed if I know." Eb spoke out of the corner of his mouth. "Don't just stand there. Keep digging."

"And the messengers. They've gone out asking for volunteers. I hear they've asked the apostles in the east to all come home, with arms. I mean, like Brigham Young—he's in Boston. Heber C. Kimball and Orson Pratt—they're in Washington now. And William Smith and Parley Pratt—they're all to return at once."

Eb sighed. "Now, are you gonna make me dig this thing all by myself? Start workin'."

"Bethia, honey. Listen. They're digging trenches so you won't have to worry. This city's well protected. We got the Legion, the police force—the charter that guarantees our rights. Joseph thought of everything. This won't be anything like Far West. It just can't happen."

Bethia made no move. She sat in the wooden chair, listless, her face without expression. Alarmed, Gabriel waved his hand in front of her eyes. She blinked, then drew back. He continued.

"Best thing we can do is go on with our everyday living. I'll keep seeing patients, I reckon, even if the shop closes for a time. But it'll open again. Folks always need a blacksmith."

She made no reply. Gabriel said, "Now, I hear there's a quilting bee this afternoon, over at Corey's. I reckon they won't have music and dancing afterward—well, they might. But it's a chance to get out and do something normal-like. You and Marie."

She spoke then. "I don't want to."

"Sarah and Jess—they'll most likely go, too. It'll be good for you."

"No."

After a while Gabriel tired of it and went into his study. He looked at his desk. Nothing of interest—old newspapers. A copy of the *Warsaw Signal,* with one of the infamous 'Buckeye' poems. His eye flicked over the verse.

BUCKEYE'S LAMENTATION FOR
WANT OF MORE WIVES

I once thought I had knowledge great,
But now I find 'tis small;
I once thought I'd Religion, too
But now I find I've none at all—
For I have but ONE LONE WIFE,
And can obtain no more;
And the doctrine is, I can't be saved,
Unless I've HALF A SCORE!

Other than the statement, *'This Buckeye child lives in Nauvoo/ And some there are, who know how true/ A friend he ever was to you, in days that's past,'* there was no clue to the poet's identity. Everyone had speculated. *William Law? Francis Higbee? Or someone completely unsuspected?*

Gabriel sighed. At the same time he thought of what he'd heard in the blacksmith shop. Someone had heard William Marks say that Joseph had come to him declaring that unless it could be abolished, polygamy would destroy the church. Joseph reportedly said that what he thought would be a benefit to humankind had proven otherwise. According to Marks, Joseph had pronounced it a 'cursed doctrine, and that there must be every exertion made to put it down.'

Gabriel buried his face in his hands. So what was the truth? Was Joseph completely innocent? God knows, he had never promulgated it in public, and had indeed spoken against it on the occasions Gabriel had witnessed.

His advice to live as normally as possible broke down with the events of the next few days. As far as he could determine from the bits and pieces he heard, Governor Ford had refused to help Joseph, insisting that his actions were wrong in destroying the press, and that unless he appeared in Carthage to answer charges, the city of Nauvoo would be under threat of attack and possible destruction by irate citizens. Nevertheless, even though the governor considered Joseph to be in the wrong, he would be afforded protection.

"Now, that just don't make sense," one of their customers proclaimed.

Then Gabriel heard that Joseph and Hyrum had escaped across the river, now in flood stage. Leaderless, people started to panic. Hundreds had already left the city, including most of the merchants on the hill. Gabriel began to make plans to get his group of friends and workers across to Iowa. He was wondering how to get word to Crazy Charley, when the news came.

Fearing an attack on the city, Hyrum and Joseph had returned and were preparing to give themselves up. That very day they were riding toward Carthage in a company of sixteen others—city council members charged with riot—and a number of friends. It was a beautiful, sunny morning. Around noon, the party returned to Nauvoo in company with Captain Dunn and a militia of the Union Dragoons, whom they had met four miles outside Nauvoo. The order from Governor Ford, countersigned by Joseph, called for the confiscation of all state arms held by the Nauvoo Legion.

"That about does it," Calvin said. "I reckon that's the end of the Legion, as far as the Governor is concerned."

"That ain't fair," someone else said. "We only mustered in self-defense, we did. And all the other militia got to keep their arms."

But another order, this one from Joseph, commanded that all personal arms be secretly stored in another location, to be ready if needed.

It was six in the evening before Joseph and his party started back to Carthage. Captain Dunn and his militia followed soon afterward, bearing the weapons from the Nauvoo Legion.

"Well," Calvin said. "There goes both our leaders and our arms."

"The leaders'll be back, I reckon," Eb said. "And soon."

Three days later, the governor himself favored the citizens of Nauvoo with a visit. Standing close to Calvin, Gabriel heard the governor's words.

"A great crime has been committed by destroying the *Expositor* press and placing the city under martial law, and a severe atonement must be made...Depend upon it, a little more misbehavior from the citizens, and the torch, which is already lighted, will be applied, and the city may be reduced to ashes, and extermination would inevitably follow, and it gives me great pain to think that there is danger of so many innocent women and children being exterminated. If anything of a serious character should befall the lives or property of the persons who are prosecuting your leaders, you will be held responsible."

"That's the most insulting speech I ever heard," Calvin remarked.

They learned later that Ford had disbanded his accompanying troops before he reached Nauvoo, for fear they would find some pretext to start a battle if he kept them with him. Instead of having their commanders march them home, he set them loose in the fields. Some went home; others headed back to Carthage.

A clatter of hooves. Horses neighing, shouts in the late evening. Cries of anguish. Something wrong. Terribly wrong. Gabriel stepped out through his office door and met Calvin coming down from the house. Calvin gave him a quick, stricken look. Together they hurried out to the main road.

The horseman had galloped at breakneck speed from Carthage to bring the dreadful news. Hyrum and Joseph both slain, assassinated by troops while under protection in the Carthage jail. Calvin grasped Gabriel's shoulder as they heard; for a moment Gabriel feared the older man would faint.

"I feared they'd kill 'em," Calvin finally managed to say.

"What did you expect?" someone else said. "They're worse than Missouri pukes."

"So much for the governor's protection," another man said.

Eb came out to join them, and finally Sarah, Marie, and Rusty walked down and stood with the crowd in front of the Mansion House. It was as if they derived strength from each other, just standing there massed together, tears streaming down their faces. Finally they began to disperse.

As they reached the blacksmith shop, Calvin drew his little group in a circle and offered prayer commending them all to the Almighty in their shock and sorrow. They embraced each other, then left for their living quarters.

"I reckon I'll not tell Bethia just yet," Gabriel said. "She's like to cry all night."

Calvin patted his shoulder. "I reckon we all will. Do what you think best. But don't let her hear it from someone else."

"I'll tell her at first light."

When Bethia did hear, she set up such a crying spell that Gabriel finally had to send for Sarah. "I can't deal with her any more."

Sarah wiped her hands on her apron and went in to sit with Bethia. Even with the door closed, he could still hear, "Buh—buh—buh—"

He sighed and walked around to the front of the shop. No Nigel. He made sure the "Closed" sign was on the door. Then, as he started to walk back around, he saw Corey hurrying toward him. Her thick lashes were matted with tears, her hair hanging down one side in a partial braid, as if she'd just awakened.

"Oh, Gabriel," she murmured. He took her in his arms and they stood for a moment. "I just heard. What on earth happens now?"

"Well, I reckon they'll bring the bodies here. There'll be a funeral and a burial."

"No. I mean, what happens to us?"

"I—I don't rightly know." People were gathering in front of the Mansion House. "Look. Someone's reading something."

They walked over to hear what it was. A letter, addressed to Mrs. Emma Smith and Major-General Dunham of the Nauvoo Legion. Written from Carthage by Willard Richards. The prophet and his brother lay dead, and John Taylor wounded. The people of Nauvoo were told not to rush out of the city, to stay at home and be prepared for an attack from Missouri mobbers. The governor had promised to render every assistance possible and had sent orders for troops.

"Well, ain't that a laugh," someone said.

The crowd hushed him. The reader of the letter concluded with a phrase from the opening paragraph: "My brethren, be still, and know that God reigns."

Gabriel and Corey walked back toward the blacksmith shop. "I reckon it'll be a spell before they bring Joseph and Hyrum home." he said.

"I reckon so."

He pressed her hand as they parted. He met Sarah just stepping out of his living quarters.

"Bethia's settled down a mite. I tried to get her to sleep some. Seems like she'll be all right for a while."

"I sure do thank you. I have to get word across to Nat."

Sarah looked at him. "You think he doesn't know by this time? Like as not, we'll see them all later on today. I'd best get the house ready."

Gabriel wondered at her getting ready for guests when they were supposed to be preparing for Missouri raiders. But of course—she hadn't heard the letter. He shook his head and went to find Calvin.

24

Impossible. To describe the tremendous love and devotion the people had for their prophet and leader, and what a void he left in their lives. As if a great tree had been suddenly wrenched out of the earth, leaving a gaping hole in a forest of saplings. Gabriel, sitting at his desk just after noon, his neglected journal before him, knew he could not attempt it.

He sighed and laid down his pen. In the next room, Bethia was making weepy noises. Time to comfort her. Although what to say to her, in his own grief, he could not imagine.

A knock. He turned, startled. A patient, on this day? He rose, but before he could reach the door, someone pushed it open. Nathaniel tramped into the room. His face was pale, his eyes red with weeping, the tears even now trickling into his beard. Gabriel hurried to embrace him.

"When did you hear?"

"This morning. Two hours ago, I reckon. Your friend Charley—" Nat's voice broke and he could no longer speak. Gabriel held him tight and patted his back.

"Hannah come with you?"

"They're all here. Up at the house. Owen, too."

"Who's taking care of the farm?"

"Pierre and Pentoga. They'll see the animals get fed." Nat fished a handkerchief from his pocket and blew his nose.

Bethia walked into the room then, and Nat held out his arms to embrace her. She no longer cried hysterically, but her face looked strange. Without animation. Her mouth drooped listlessly.

"Let's go up to the house," Gabriel said.

Sarah had enough presence of mind to feed the children, and set out some bread and cheese for the others. "Eat. We got to keep our strength up."

Rusty moved in on the food, but even he could not manage to eat very much. Marie stood by, and Gabriel knew she was trying to be as helpful as she could. Bless her, he thought.

Noises in the street. A low murmur of voices. The little group filed out slowly to join the crowd in front of the Mansion House. Nat and Hannah walked first, Nat carrying Gaby in his arms. Hannah held Jody by the hand. Marie and Rusty walked hand in hand, then Eb with one arm around Jess and the other around Turah. Gabriel tried to take Bethia's hand, but she jerked it away. Last came Calvin and Sarah, with Owen Crawford.

Others joined them—Corey with her sister and father. Then Charley and Adriel slipped in beside them. Charley made his way up beside Gabriel and patted his shoulder. The crowd began to move up toward Mulholland Street and the unfinished temple. They joined a larger crowd already assembled, with more people pouring in from the farms outside town.

Gabriel wasn't sure at what point the moaning began. He knew that it was called keening and originated from the new converts from Ireland and Wales. It grew in intensity until it seemed to fill the whole space. Others not from the British Isles listened in wonder, then added their own voices.

At last they saw the two wagons approaching over the open fields. Eight mounted militiamen rode beside them, one at each wagon wheel. A lone horseman, Willard Richards, rode behind. The crowd, thousands by this time, walked out across the prairie to meet the wagons. Samuel Smith, the prophet's younger brother, was driving the first team. He looked pale and weary, sick with grief. The keening lament increased, drowning out all other sounds. The crowd surrounded the wagons and escorted them back to town, through the streets to the Mansion House.

Willard Richards, overweight to begin with, appeared exhausted. He dismounted and signaled that he wished to speak. The crowd grew still, waiting to hear the words of one who had witnessed the event.

He advised them to keep the peace, and added that he had pledged his honor and his life for their good conduct. He reminded them that

Brother Taylor lay seriously wounded in Carthage, too ill to be moved. He urged them to trust to the law to deal with the assassins, and to God to avenge the wrongs. Sorrowing, the people agreed as one to leave vengeance in the hands of God.

The people were asked to go home until morning, while the bodies were prepared for burial. Gabriel thought of Joseph's wife Emma, expecting another child in addition to the four she had. He gave a silent prayer that if God took care of anyone, he would take special care of them.

At eight o'clock the next morning, the doors opened. People began moving through the Mansion House dining room in a slow procession. Gabriel passed through around noon with his family and friends. Both Joseph and Hyrum lay in coffins lined with white cambric and covered with black velvet studded with brass. A glass lid with brass hinges lay over each face.

Joseph looked normal enough, but Hyrum, shot in the head, appeared disfigured and swollen. Gabriel smelled the tar, vinegar and sugar mixture which simmered on the stove to disguise the odor of death. His eyes met those of Dr. Richmond, the physician who had helped prepare the bodies for burial. The man looked resigned and unhappy; he apparently had to stay there most of the day. Gabriel gave him a faint, sympathetic smile and received a slight nod in return.

They left the building. "Wasn't that buh—buh—beautiful?" Bethia exclaimed.

Gabriel had thought it was horrible. He said nothing, and they gathered in the big house where Sarah had set out plates and mugs. Bethia said again how beautiful she'd thought everything was.

"So." Nathaniel sat down at the table with Gaby on his knee. He leaned forward on one elbow. "The burning question is: Who's going to lead the church now?"

"Why, Sidney Rigdon, I reckon." Calvin stood with his hands on the back of his chair.

"But he's not well," Gabriel said. "Old age has got the better of him."

Sarah sniffed. "Besides, he's in Pennsylvania. He's not even here."

Gabriel looked at her. "*Mais oui*. And you know why. He thought he was running for vice president."

Calvin said, "Well, then. How about William Marks? Now, he'd make a tolerable leader. He's opposed to plural marriage and all that foolishness."

"But he's only a local leader." Rusty snatched up a stray bit of cheese as Sarah set out bread, cheese and ham. "President of the High Council."

Then Eb spoke. "Wasn't you there when Joseph put his son Young Joseph on the stand? He said it loud and clear. 'There is my successor when I depart.'"

Calvin thought a moment. "I reckon he's said that to a few others. I recall, back in Kirtland, he told David Whitmer the same thing."

"Well, the Whitmers are long gone," Nat said. "And Young Joseph be only twelve years old. The church would have to be held in trust for him. Sidney could do that. Or Brother Marks."

Rusty began to laugh. "Aren't you glad Bennett's not still around?"

"Brigham Young," Calvin said. "I reckon he's the logical choice. President of the Twelve Apostles and all."

Nat reached for a piece of ham. "Well, whoever it is, I hope they get rid of this plurality of gods idea. And the talk of plural marriage."

Calvin bowed his head. "We'd better say the blessing quick, before Rusty eats it all." He blessed the food and began slicing bread. "Most of our trouble comes from gathering together in a large group. When we left Missouri, it was Brigham that started the gathering business again."

"Now, wait," Gabriel said. "We're supposed to build the city of God. A just society, or however you want to think of it. And you can't do it sitting around by yourself."

Calvin pointed the bread knife at him. "Well it sure gets folks upset. A big block of people all crowded together. Swinging elections, gettin' up an army. And I don't know what all."

Nat ran his fingers through his beard. "Now, William Marks—"

Sarah slammed down her plate. "Oh, you men! What's the matter with you? The prophet isn't even buried yet. And you going on about his successor. I never heard the like!"

"She's right." Rusty spoke with his mouth full. "Whatever happens, it won't be us that decides it. Could you pass the ham down here?"

Calvin nodded. "I reckon we'll have to wait till all the apostles and such get back into town. And Brother Rigdon."

Gabriel thought back to that conversation several times in the months that followed. It seemed to embody the feelings of others whom he encountered.

When Rigdon and the apostles returned, a meeting took place in the open air which decided the issue. Brother Sidney tried to present his claims to church leadership in the morning. But his voice was weak, and the wind was against him.

In the afternoon, Sidney tried again. But Brigham Young spoke from the back, with a voice like thunder. Numerous people swore they heard the voice of Joseph, that the mantle of Joseph had fallen upon Brigham. A show of hands came from the thousands gathered. Brigham and the rest of the Twelve were sustained as the church leaders.

"I reckon that settles it," Calvin said.

The shops, reopened now, continued their business. The blacksmith shop stayed open late into the evenings, to make up the work that people needed done. And construction of the temple took precedence over everything else.

Nigel had been keeping company with an English lady. "We aim to be married in the temple, when it's ready. Sealed to each other for time and eternity. Then we'll receive our endowments."

If there was anything Gabriel didn't need, it was to be sealed to Bethia for eternity. To Nigel he said, "Amen, brother. I hope it all works out for you."

"Oh, it will. God has assured it."

Gabriel couldn't remember just when the adherents of James J. Strang appeared on the streets of Nauvoo, preaching a simpler brand of Mormonism.

"I hear he be of Huguenot descent, like us," Rusty said.

Calvin snorted. "Well, don't let that influence you none."

"He doesn't hold with plural marriage or any of that endowment foolishness."

"Careful what you say," Calvin said. "Brigham has already called him a wicked apostate."

Strang, newly converted, claimed to have a letter from Joseph Smith. It authorized him not only to take charge of a group of Saints up in Voree, Wisconsin, but to assume leadership of the whole church.

That fall, the 'wolf hunts' began, and the anti-Mormon newspapers, led by the tireless Tom Sharp, strove to increase hatred of the Mormons.

It became obvious to Gabriel and the rest, that the murderers of Joseph and Hyrum would not be brought to justice.

"The blasted cowards," Calvin declared. "You can't prosecute the whole lot of 'em."

In January of 1845 came the repeal of the Nauvoo charter. Now the city was left without legal government, and no means of dealing with lawlessness. Brigham, under advice from Governor Ford, incorporated part of Nauvoo as a town, but a town could only cover one square mile and had no court, only a justice of the peace. With one town incorporated, Brigham adapted the church government to civil use. He assigned bishops and deacons to maintain peace in each ward.

The Nauvoo Legion, now illegal, was still used in maintaining order. Most important, work went forward on the temple. The walls went up and were topped by thirty capitals, each composed of five huge carved stones. The largest weighed more than two tons. These were raised in place with cranes and ropes.

On Saturday, May 24, a large multitude gathered for the laying of the final capstone on the southeast corner of the building. Then the band played and the people shouted the Hosanna shout three times.

"It ain't even finished yet," Calvin told Gabriel. "And here they are, a whoopin' and a hollerin'."

"You got to admit, it's pretty impressive," Gabriel answered.

Nigel gave a little cough. "And, like Brother Brigham said. If God will sustain us till it's all built, then we can get our endowments."

On September 9, some time after the ones charged in the Smiths' murders had been declared 'not guilty,' the citizens of Green Plains and Lima met in a schoolhouse. They intended to discuss how they could get rid of the 'Morley Settlement,' a little group of Mormons on the prairie some twenty-five miles south of Nauvoo. Someone fired a shot into the schoolhouse. The next day the mob began burning Mormon houses, barns, and crops. The depredations continued for a week. The mob of three hundred men managed to burn one hundred and seventy-five houses and farms, and drove out the whole population.

"Blamed if it ain't happening again," Calvin said.

"Let's think what to do," Rusty said. "Shall we ask Nat?"

"He's not going anywhere," Gabriel reminded them. "Didn't you hear him say? Let me study on it some."

Having proclaimed himself leader, Gabriel wondered what to do.

The best thing was to wait. If worse came to worse, they could all go across the river.

Then the announcement. Ford decided that peace would only prevail if the Mormons all left. He sent a contingent of four men to persuade Brigham Young. Finally Brigham agreed. The Mormon leaders and a thousand families would leave Illinois in the spring, and then, if means allowed, the whole church would follow. If the Mormons failed to keep their promise, 'violent means will be resorted to, to compel your removal.'

"That does it," Calvin said. "Time to leave."

"No." Gabriel tried to sound firm. "Wait."

Preparations began for the mass departure. Where were they headed? All they knew is that it was somewhere to the west, across Iowa, maybe even as far as the Rocky Mountains. Far enough so they could live undisturbed.

Most of the shops would now manufacture wagons, or items for the journey. People began trying to sell property. The construction of the temple continued at a furious pace. Gabriel gathered from bits of conversation that they all intended to receive their endowments before the final exodus.

Whatever happened, Nauvoo, as they had known it, was doomed. They had six months to get out. Gabriel finished his journal entry, closed the book, and stood up. Time for a decision.

He walked up to eat the evening meal with his family group. They talked of the usual things—Rusty eating too much, Marie trying to sew a quilt by herself.

"You need help," Sarah said. "And a friend with a quilting frame."

Gabriel, looking around the group, knew that he would have to talk with each one of the men. Eb and Rusty would support him, he knew. But he needed Calvin with him as well. It was clearly time to tell Nat.

The morning dawned fresh and clear. He left the blacksmith shop in the hands of Rusty and Nigel, and walked down to the river. As he was untying the skiff, he heard a voice behind him.

"You can't go across all by yourself."

He stopped. Eb came up beside him.

"I reckon I could," Gabriel replied. "If'n I had to."

"Well, you don't. Get in, and I'll push us off."

A comfort, to have Eb with him. As Eb rowed, Gabriel thought again of his decision. Was it the right one? It had occurred to him that if he followed the main group out to the west, he might be able to have Corey as his second wife. Then they could both take care of Casey and Bethia. But was it the right course?

They tied up at the wharf near Charley's place and walked out to the farm. Eb looked downcast, as if worried for himself and his family. Gabriel tried to cheer him up.

"Don't look so troubled. We been in these straits before."

"That's why I'm worried."

"We came through before."

"I didn't have a wife then, with a girl-child."

"Come to think of it, I was single, too."

They tried the house first. "He's in the barn," Hannah told them.

They found Nat harnessing up the mule. "We be fixin' to haul off some rocks."

Gabriel rushed forward, gesturing in his eagerness. "Well, don't haul 'em off just yet. We got something to tell you."

Nat looked at him. "You mean, about the agreement to leave Illinois? I already know. And stay away from Pete's back end, there. He's like to kick you so hard, you won't need to worry about anything ever again."

Gabriel stepped around to the animal's head. Pete laid his ears back.

"Watch out." Nat looked amused. "He'll bite you if he can." He tied the reins to the hitching post. "All right, now. Come over here. And don't get kicked."

Nat put a hand on the split rail fence. "So, what's on your minds? Don't tell me yer figurin' on going west."

"We got to do something," Eb said.

"Some folks are stayin' put." Nat squinted in the sunlight. "Like me. I told you I was tired of running."

"I'm not going west," Gabriel said.

"That's good. Like I said, not everyone's fixin' to leave. You can come here if things get bad. But I reckon nowhere's really safe."

Gabriel nodded. "I feel better, movin' on."

Nat's mouth tightened. "So, where you going? Off by yourselves?"

"North. North to Wisconsin. Voree, to be exact."

"Ah." Nat paused, and his dark eyebrows drew together. "Brother Strang's followers hit some fertile ground."

Eb was staring, open-mouthed. Gabriel began to make his case. "They be preaching the early gospel, like we first knew it. And there's something about him—he may not be able to take Joseph's place. But everything he does sounds prophetic. He seems to know what he's doing."

Nat smiled. "Sounding and acting be one thing. Being a true prophet is another."

Gabriel shrugged. "Well, that's my decision. And I think it's a good one."

Out of the corner of his eye, he saw Eb nodding in agreement. One family was with him, at least. He went on. "And Wisconsin—it's not that far. But, the Rocky Mountains. Or Oregon—wherever they be going. The hardships on that journey—my heart aches for them just thinkin' about it. As a physician, that is."

Nat nodded. "It's a far piece. They'll have to help each other."

Eb spoke then. "For Wisconsin, you jest get everybody on a steamboat and get up there. Take the river as close as it'll get you. Then pay someone to haul you the rest of the way."

Gabriel gestured. "If'n we can get Rusty and Calvin to go with us, we'll take most of the tools and machinery from the shop. Set up a smithy there."

"Folks always need blacksmiths," Eb said.

Nat nodded again. "Well—good luck. I reckon you could do worse. And if things fall apart up there, like as not you can always come back here. All this persecution—I reckon it'll blow over by then."

Gabriel gave a sigh. "Sometimes I wonder—what's it all for? Look at all the cities we've tried to build."

"Kirtland," Eb said. "Independence, and Far West. And now Nauvoo."

Gabriel gestured, talking with his hands. "We keep seeking. Always seeking. Seeking the Kingdom of God. The place where there will be justice and—and peace. Where no one shall hurt nor destroy. And it's never there."

Nat waited a few moments before he spoke. "Blamed if I know. The only thing I can figure is—maybe we be a better people, for all the seeking."

Gabriel said, "You reckon we'll ever get it right?"

Nat's mouth worked, the way it did when he was thinking. "We're told that—that someday it'll happen. And I reckon it will. We may not live to see it."

"Maybe Voree," Eb said.

Nat sighed and nodded. "Maybe so. Let's have a word of prayer before you go back across. Pete'll wait. He's so ornery he doesn't care what we do."

Gabriel shrugged, amused. "Why don't you sell him to the folks heading west?"

"I was hopin' you'd take him to Voree."

As Gabriel rowed back across the river, Eb spoke from the stern. "I reckon you set my mind at ease. I been worried about Jess bein' a runaway and all. Afraid someone'd nab her and take her back to Virginy. Up north in Wisconsin, I reckon she'd be safer, like."

"It's like to be mighty wild up there. Beautiful—that's what the folks in the pineries say. 'Cept for the winters. And, yes. I reckon Jess would be safe."

As it turned out, Rusty and Marie were eager to follow him on his northern venture. Calvin had to think about it. Finally he said, "Hang it all, I can't let my son leave without me. Hannah's safe with Nat. And Wisconsin's not that far. But, Rusty—he's my youngest."

Bethia put up a fuss. "Why can't we go west with all the others?"

"Well, first," Gabriel said, "I reckon it's more of a journey than anyone's figured. And I don't hold with some of the things they're teaching. I think it's best to go north."

Jubal Langdon, even though Gabriel urged him to go north with them, elected to follow Brigham Young. His family decided to travel together with Nigel and his new bride.

"*Eh bien*," Gabriel said. "We'll see that you have the best wagon we can put together. And oxen. We got to get you some oxen."

When they went across the river for a final reunion with Nat and Hannah, Gabriel got a surprise. Charley greeted him at the dock. "Hear you be goin' up to Wisconsin."

"Right. New fields are calling."

"Woods and rivers, more like," Charley said. "Lakes so big you can't even see across 'em. That's *voyageur* country."

"That's where we're headed."

"Well, don't think you can go there without us."

"What?" Gabriel wondered if he'd heard aright.

"Me and Adriel. We're joinin' up with you, if you'll have us. Someone's got to keep you out of trouble."

"But—"

"Truth is, with most of you gone, it's gonna be fairly boring around here. Nothing to steal, for one thing."

"Well—of course. Come along. We'd be pleased to have you. But—you're not exactly Mormons. Of course, neither is my sister."

Adriel stood up from inspecting his fishing boat and walked toward them. "Who says we're not Mormons?"

"Nat baptized the both of us yesterday," Charley said laughing. "And confirmed us in the evening."

Later Gabriel got the true story from Nat. "Charley says he never saw anything like it—the way we cared for each other. Said Joseph Smith was one of the finest men he'd ever known. Said we were the first folks to treat him and Adriel like real human beings. Even said he was ready to repent of any wrongdoing—said he was too old for stealing anyway. So when they both asked for baptism, I went ahead."

Gabriel could only whistle and say, "I'll be dad-burned."

In the early morning, long before they were to board the steamboat, Gabriel walked down to the Nauvoo side of the river. Mists were still rising from the water-surface. In the places where the mist had cleared off, he could see the island and opposite shore, so close he felt he could almost step across.

Someone moved behind him and a little to the right; he turned. Corey stood, looking out to the west. She met his glance and walked toward him. "I came to say good-bye."

His heart lurched in his chest. "That's right good of you. I—I was hoping I would see you once more."

They stood shoulder to shoulder. She said, "I reckon it's a good day to travel."

"I reckon so."

He wondered what else to say to her. As he gazed at the lovely stretch of water, a sense of the immeasurable beauty and the limitless possibilities of life flooded over him like a wave. *Now was the time. Ask her to run away with you. Take Casey, begin again in some far-off place.*

Turning to meet her eyes. Knowing it wouldn't work. To leave the group which looked to him to lead them north, to abandon faith, family, his belief in community—it would take a kind of strength he didn't think he could summon. Besides, he was a leader now. And domestic happiness didn't necessarily go with the position.

"Corey—I'll not forget you. It's been a—well, a joy to know you. To know there's someone like you in the world."

She said nothing. He went on. "I—I wish things could have been different for us. I've often wished that. But life seems to be full of trials, and I reckon we just have to do the best we know how. That's what I tried to do."

"I understand." She touched his arm. "We have our responsibilities. Casey is mine. And sometimes I worry about my father."

"Nigel's strong. He'll give you plenty of help. As for me—I reckon I have to be strong for everyone else. The little group that depends on me."

"You'll do fine."

It was time to part. He pressed her hand. "Whatever you do, have a good life."

"You, too. I'll not forget. In all my prayers, I'll remember you."

They turned and walked back together. Looking at her brave, determined expression, he felt reassured that he had given her no cause to mourn, no false promises. He had done nothing to make his family ashamed of him. He had not even declared his love for her, but the words seemed to hang unspoken in the still air.

"Good-bye, now," he said. *Adieu, my own true love.* He walked up to the house, where his family group was waiting, and closed the door behind him.

On an early evening in the autumn of 1846, Nat stood on the shore near Montrose. He carried a sack of flour over his shoulder.

His son Jody, eleven years old, walked up beside him. Tall like his father, the boy had hands and feet too large in proportion to his body, and a shock of red hair. "What do you see, Father?"

"A skiff. With a lone rower in it. Looks like a young man. Comin' across from Illinois. He doesn't look to be armed. I reckon it's safe to go down and see who 'tis."

Nat set his sack against a tree trunk. They walked over to the rickety pier. The young man rowed close enough to throw Nat the line. Nat looped it around the nearest post.

"I thank you," the young man said.

"You've had yourself quite a row. Come from Nauvoo?"

The man looked too thin, his face pale, as if he weren't in the best of health. Not enough time in the open air, most like. The man gave a cough before he spoke.

"Yes. I—that is, I had to travel by land to get around the rapids. Water low, and all that. So I hired me a carriage. And when I came over the last hill, I saw this lovely sight—the city just glittering in the morning sun. I saw this amazing edifice—"

"The temple?"

"Yes. That spire—radiant with white and gold. I wanted to see the city up close. So I rented a skiff and rowed over to the main wharf."

"I see," Nat said.

"But there was no one there. No one greeted me. No one moved. I went into empty workshops, smithies. Beautifully cared-for houses, well-tended yards, all lying empty. I went into gardens, drank from wells. No one stopped me. It's like they all just up and left."

Nat sighed. "I reckon they did."

"Orchards and fields—there's all this bounty, and no one's harvested it. Grain lying ungathered, rotting on the ground. I—well, finally I did see some people. There were armed men around the temple—sort of a scruffy lot. When they heard I was a stranger, they showed me some of the building. Lots of refuse, cruses of liquor, broken drinking vessels—now I don't reckon the Mormons left those."

"I reckon not," Nat said. "Most of the Mormons be gone. If you go over to the flatlands here—" He waved his hand to the northwest. "—you can see what's left. The very poor. The sickest ones, the elderly, who almost didn't make it out in time."

"But—what'll happen to them?"

Nat looked at him, wondering how much to tell him. "Oh—the usual thing. Some will die, some will give birth. Most others'll just shiver all night in little tents, try to keep warm. In time, the folks who've gone ahead will send wagons back for them."

"Oh." The young man's face was a picture of misery. "How can such things be?"

Nat shrugged. "Blamed if I know."

The young man swallowed. "I'm Thomas Kane, by the way. Colonel Thomas Kane. I first heard of the Mormons last spring—I was a clerk in my father's office. In Philadelphia."

They shook hands. Nat introduced himself and Jody. "Well, it's a strange, sad history. There're a few of us who stayed. We keep very quiet. Others have gone off—some to Texas, some to Wisconsin. Pennsylvania—that's Sidney Rigdon's group. Most of 'em headed out west."

"Can't anything be done to help them?"

Nat scratched his beard. "I've taken in some of 'em. Got three cabins full of folks. I've spent most of the past year building and repairing wagons. Gave away my two oxen—there was a family that needed 'em more than me."

"You *gave away* your oxen?"

"I got a mule that's mighty strong. He helps with plowin' and haulin'. Figured I didn't need the oxen. Not as much as the folks goin' west."

Kane shook his head. "I think I'll go take a look at those people. The ones still waiting. Where did you say—"

"Just over that rise, there. You can't miss 'em."

The young man started to climb the slight hill. Jody plucked at his father's sleeve. "Why does he want to see them, Father? They make me want to cry."

"Derned if I know. Who knows? Maybe if the right person sees it, some good'll come of it."

Nat walked over to pick up the sack of flour. Then he turned for one last look at the temple with the fading light on it. The city seemed to glow in the twilight, as if it were alive with voices and human activity, like the old days. How deceptive is distance. He felt a burning behind his eyes, and when he looked away, his cheeks were moist.

"Let's go, son. Your mother be wondering where we are with her flour. And it's time to feed old Pete and the rest of the critters."

About the Author

Elaine Stienon grew up in Detroit, Michigan, and attended the University of Michigan, where she majored in English and American literature. In her senior year she won a Hopwood award—a prize in creative writing—for a collection of short stories.

Since that time, she has had stories published in literary magazines such as *Phoenix, South*, the *Cimarron Review*, the Ball State University *Forum*, and the *Bear River Review. The Way to the Shining City* is her fifth published novel.

She has had a life-long interest in history, especially the history of the early Mormons and the difficulties they experienced on the American frontier. She lives in Ann Arbor, Michigan, where she devotes her time to writing.

The watercolor featured on the cover was painted by Joyce Thumm, who lives in Independence, Missouri.